HOZARK'S REVENGE

SPACE ASSASSINS 5

SCOTT BARON

Print Edition ISBN 978-1-945996-40-5

"It is often said that before you die your life passes before your eyes.
It is in fact true. It's called living."

– Terry Pratchett

CHAPTER ONE

The wet smack of a blood-dampened fist echoed off the cool stone walls. It was not the first blow to be cast on this day, nor would it be the last. The young woman hadn't planned on being beaten today, but then, sometimes things just don't go according to plan. And her plan was to find Visla Maktan.

Visla Zinna Maktan was a difficult man to track down. Not just because he was one of the more powerful magic users in the combined systems, which afforded anyone a higher degree of security, but also because of *another* rather unique status.

Visla Maktan was a member of the Council of Twenty, a galactic, power-hungry group that had strong-armed their way into controlling most of the known systems over the centuries.

Given the sometimes truly heinous acts the Council carried out in their quest for more power and control of the inhabited systems not yet under their yoke, it was only natural that they would take security a bit more seriously than most. Scores of disgruntled people whose entire worlds had been forcibly placed under Council control, or who had witnessed their families enslaved or worse, would have great interest in causing the Twenty harm.

But getting close enough to so much as lay a finger on one of the Council's inner staff or guards was daunting enough of a challenge. To actually reach one of the Council themselves? It was only in those rarest instances of foolish overconfidence that an individual Council member had been reached. And even then, they were so powerful that the threat was neutralized with the greatest of ease.

Recently, however, one of their own had not only placed himself in a precarious position, he had actually fallen in the process, his light snuffed out by a Ghalian assassin, and in front of his own men, no less.

Word had spread like magic fire through the ranks, and the Council had reacted as one might expect of those whose braggadocio was often greater than their common sense.

They had quietly doubled, or even tripled, their personal security details, while publicly downplaying the entire incident, stating the death of Visla Ravik had been no more than a fluke, and entirely of his own doing. That it had been a Ghalian assassin at whose hands--and fangs--he had fallen, was not mentioned at all.

It was this unfortunate shift in security protocol that had snagged several infiltrators and spies, most of them actually under the employ of the other members of the Council. While they may have worked together as a unified body in public, the backstabbing and scrabbling for power behind the scenes was just as Machiavellian as found in any fiefdom or feudal world.

But one spy was unlike the others who had been unexpectedly found out. One inoffensive and utterly benign woman of robust stature and sweet demeanor had been caught during a surprise sweep of Visla Maktan's staff. She was a relatively recent hire, her orange skin and warm, yellow eyes only adding to her cheerful appearance.

She had been working in one of the kitchens on one of the

many worlds upon which Visla Maktan had a residence, helping keep things tidy, preparing staff meals, and procuring supplies from vendors.

The visla hadn't been to that world in ages, and there was no telling if or when he would be dropping in. His comings and goings had always been unannounced, but after the fall of Visla Ravik, they were even more so.

And so it was that this spy passed the time, ingratiating herself to the other staff, building trust and establishing herself as an integral cog in the estate's internal workings. This could have gone on for some time. The best of spies often spent years on assignment, worming their way into places so slowly that none ever once suspected they could be anything but what they appeared.

Now, however, the sweet kitchen worker all had known as Zanna was beaten and chained in a dungeon, a guard keeping eyes on her at all times. That is, when she wasn't being tortured by her captors.

It had been a particularly specialized bit of casting that had pierced her magic during an unannounced sweep of the property's grounds, and the Wampeh's magical disguise had fallen in the process.

"Ghalian!" the caster leading the sweep called out when Zanna's orange coloring abruptly shifted back to her natural pale skin and black hair--much to the surprise of her fellow staffers.

The guards who had been accompanying the caster quickly surrounded her, all of them training their blades and konuses on the intruder, ready to slay her if she so much as moved a muscle. Ghalian assassins were not to be trifled with, and it was only their relative distance from the target that had allowed them to survive as long as they had. Or so they believed.

Zanna, however, was not an assassin. Her skills lay in her

considerable gift for subterfuge and infiltration, not in fighting off hordes of armed guards. But escape was something spies were also trained in, and Ghalian were known to vanish into seemingly thin air from their cells when captured, leaving a great many confused guards to pay for their failure in their duties.

This was different, however. A visla had recently been killed, and any spy was treated with a great deal more concern than in previous years. And a Ghalian? None wanted to face the wrath of their employer if one such as this escaped on their watch.

"I will come quietly," Zanna said, slowly raising her empty hands over her head.

The guards led her to the estate's dungeon, keeping their distance and having called in reinforcements. Nearly two dozen now stood ready should she move to flee, though within the constricting environs of the subterranean corridor, to try would be utter folly.

The time for escape would present itself, but this was definitely not it. To make such an attempt would mean certain death, and that was not what she had in mind. Not one bit.

This particular estate was one of Visla Maktan's smaller retreats, and as such, its dungeon facilities were quite small and lacking the myriad devices often used in prying the truth from prisoners that the larger facilities possessed. But once the head of the visla's personal guard heard of this intruder, a specialist would be dispatched, and they would bring with them the full weight of the Council of Twenty.

In the meantime, however, the locals would do what they could, crude as their methods may be. To pry any information out of a Ghalian would be a massive coup in their favor.

"Who hired you, Assassin?" the captain of the guard asked.

Zanna merely spat the blood from her mouth and smiled at him and shrugged. It was about all she could manage from her position, chained to an interrogation chair.

"You can make this easy, or you can make it hard," the man continued. "We have ways--"

"Of making me talk?" the captive said with a chuckle. "I believe I have heard this speech once or twice before. I know how this works, Captain."

"Then you know I can make things very, very unpleasant for you."

"Indeed. But you should also know that I truly know nothing. I was simply hired to keep an eye on things around here, nothing more."

"Liar. Why would a Ghalian do this sort of job?"

"We are not all about killing, you know. Information is an important bit of trade, after all. Your visla knows a thing or two about that, I'm sure. In fact, all of the Council have retained our services on many occasions."

The captain's face remained impassive, but inside, he shuddered. The thought of these disguised killers silently lurking among the staff of other estates was terrifying.

"I don't believe you," he finally replied. "But we have ways of--"

"Yes, yes. Let's just get on with it then, shall we?" she said with a resigned sigh.

Zanna had been tortured before, and it was not pleasant in the least. But she had been well trained, and the Ghalian spy was more than prepared for whatever her captors had in store. And until the visla's personal guard arrived, she would be treated with kid gloves.

Or so she had thought.

The caster who had been leading the search strode into the chamber and glared at the restrained woman. She could feel the relatively substantial power he possessed. An emmik, no doubt. Not as strong as a visla, but if possible, it would be nice to feed on him before making her escape.

But that would require placing herself at a bit too much risk for her liking. Unless the opportunity presented itself, getting far away as quickly as possible would be the order of the day.

"Who hired you?" the emmik asked as he turned his back to her and unlatched a small case on the nearby low table.

"You know I cannot reveal that," she replied. "But you likely also already know it is probably one of the other Council members. Such a suspicious group, always digging into one another's affairs."

The emmik turned back around, and Zanna felt a sudden surge of fear in her body. On his wrist was a slaap, and a considerably powerful one at that. The magically charged tool was stronger than a konus, and entirely martial in function. Only a fool would attempt to use a slaap for torture spells. The results could be catastrophic.

Or they could be effective at prying out even the most stubborn of secrets, though often at the cost of limbs and permanent damage to the subject. The wicked smile on the emmik's face told her he was well aware of that fact.

"Now, we have a few days before the visla's man arrives to interrogate you. But I intend to get answers from you long before then."

The emmik flexed his power, melding it with the magic stored within the slaap, then uttered the smallest of torture spells.

"*Koxora malecti*," he said, testing out the device.

Zanna writhed in pain, unable to contain herself.

It was unlike a Ghalian. Their training typically allowed them to go to a safe place within themselves in these instances. But this emmik, greedy for recognition and advancement, was pushing the envelope, seemingly unaware of exactly how much damage he was truly doing. It was always a risk when the inexperienced did the torturing. But usually they were not in possession of a tool of this degree of power.

The captive slumped in her seat, drawing in rapid breaths as she regained her bearings. She hadn't cried out at least, of that she was proud. But this interrogation was going to be far worse than she had anticipated. And it just might kill her before she could make her escape.

CHAPTER TWO

"Now, are you more in the spirit of cooperation?" the interrogator asked with a cool confidence in his voice.

Zanna was drenched in sweat, her long dark hair plastered to her skin. Her eyes were bloodshot from the strain. Her lips chapped and cracked from the dehydration of the overwhelmingly powerful and damaging torture she had been subjected to.

And it had only been a single day.

She knew at this rate there was no way she would be able to withstand the barrage. Her carefully honed Ghalian mind might finally snap, and her many secrets would be theirs for the taking--provided they didn't kill her in the process.

It was not what she had hoped for by any stretch, but one option presented itself to her, and given the circumstances she found herself in, Zanna could think of no other alternatives.

She drew upon what little energy she had left and raised her head to look her torturer in the eye. The emmik had done a fine job, she had to admit, and she had used up nearly all of the power stored away within herself in the process. Only the smallest bit remained. An emergency reserve Ghalian spies were trained to sequester and preserve at all costs.

"You wish to know who hired me?" she said as her vision focused on the emmik. "To uncover the secrets of the Ghalian?"

"You know I do. And, from what I have already shown you, I think you are now quite aware that it is only a matter of time before I succeed."

"Oh, you believe that, do you?" she replied, her composure returning slightly during this intermission in her torment.

"We already know you are Ghalian, and you are obviously very well trained. But I can spare you this pain. Believe me, if you think this is bad, just imagine what Visla Maktan's personal inquisitor will do to you."

She had a few ideas, and amazingly, they were better options than what this man was currently engaging in. The *professionals* would subject her to many types of torture, to be sure, but nothing near as permanently damaging as what this inexperienced fool had done to her.

In his zealous haste, he had crossed a line, using incompatible forms of magic for what should be delicate and precise work. And with the visla's men arriving in but a day, he was more than willing to continue. This was his one opportunity to show his worth and climb that ladder within the organization. Hell, he might even be promoted to the visla's personal retinue if he pulled this off.

Zanna had read the man, of course. Not using any magic, but simply relying on her skills of observation, as she'd done for countless years in her trade. This was a power grab, and no matter what she said, the man was blinded by visions of elevation in status and the better life that would accompany it. There was simply no way to deter him with talk.

"You really think this is going to end well for you, don't you?" she said as she slowly pulled her last stores of magic together, coalescing the power in a small bundle of potential waiting to be unleashed.

"Oh, it *will*," the man replied, confident in his complete domination of his prisoner. "You will tell me what I wish to know, or break in the process. I can see it in your eyes, you know what I say is true."

Zanna shrugged. "Your technique, while extremely crude, is, admittedly, quite potent," she noted. "And given enough time, I have little doubt that you would indeed gain from me the information you seek."

"As I said––"

"*But*," she continued, "you did not take one very crucial thing into consideration."

"And what is that?" he asked, cocky as ever, but with a slight uncertainty creeping into his voice.

Zanna did not reply to him. She just stared, holding his gaze for several uncomfortable seconds. Finally, she flashed a little smile and spoke her final word.

"*Moragalis*."

The lone utterance had barely passed her lips when her body suddenly thrashed once, then went still. The smile, however, remained on her lifeless lips.

"What? But, how could she?" the emmik blurted as he raced to her side, quickly reciting every healing spell he could think of.

None of them took hold, however, and his prisoner remained quite dead. She had killed herself rather than give up her secrets, and he was about to be in a world of shit for it. He might even learn some of Visla Maktan's interrogator's finest tricks, but not from the position of a bystander. It was the worst-case scenario he had not even thought to imagine.

He spent a good several minutes pacing the chamber, unsure what, if anything, he could do to at least lessen the punishment he would receive for overstepping his orders. A prize prisoner was dead, and on his watch. Under his direct supervision, no less, and as a result of his actions. And there was nothing he could do about that.

What he did not know was that the visla's head of security had seen this before. Not for quite a long time, mind you, but in his earlier years he had witnessed a captured Ghalian perform the same thing. Utter the spell that not only stopped their heart, but ruptured it irreversibly, killing them in an instant. No one would be reviving them to pull out any information no matter how powerful they were.

It had shocked him at the time. For one, he'd been certain the prisoner had no magic left within them. He very quickly learned that some Ghalian possessed the skill to spread tiny bits of magic in their bodies, locked away for years and years until all but forgotten. Reserved for this one, final option.

He also learned that Ghalian did not fear death. Those who dealt in it their whole lives--even the spies belonging to that secretive order--accepted it as something that might come for them at any time. And that was part of the reason for their myriad successes in the field of assassination and intrigue.

The Ghalian approached any conflict with the mindset that they were already dead and had nothing to lose. Of course, that did not prevent them from doing all in their power to survive every encounter, but the fear of death was something not to be found within them.

The emmik straightened his tunic and took a deep breath, then strode from the chamber.

"I have retrieved a name," he said victoriously.

"Well done, sir!" the guard outside the chamber congratulated him. "Shall I move the prisoner to the regular cells?"

"There will be no need. She perished in her foolish efforts to resist my power."

"Sir?" the guard asked, suddenly very uneasy.

“Place the body in the cold room. We shall hand her over to the visla’s man when he arrives.”

“But what of––”

“I will relay the information to him and him alone. See that he is sent to my chambers upon his arrival.”

With that the emmik strode off with the air of a perfectly confident man, leaving the guard to put the dead spy on ice. Once back in his chambers, however, he would have to work fast. He had a plan, and it was not without risk, but knowing the subterfuge and backstabbing within the Council, he thought it could work.

There were twenty members. Well, nineteen, now that Visla Ravik was dead. He just had to choose one. Not Ravik’s brother, though. He was too busy attempting to take his seat on the Council, invoking the claim of familial ascendance, as was his right, but he was nowhere near as powerful as his brother had been, and more than one power user of significant strength was vying for the seat.

With all of that jockeying for more influence, spinning a tale about the spy giving up another Council member’s name just as she perished would be a convincing lie both hard to prove and relatively easy to believe. Much was afoot within the Council, and shifting tides led to many unusual things, least of which was subterfuge by fellow Council members.

All of the other members of the Twenty would be on higher alert now, of course. Once word of a Ghalian in their midst reached them, it would only be natural. They were already on edge after Ravik’s death, and this would serve to ramp up that paranoia even further.

The emmik had no idea what his lie would do in the long run, but for now it should buy him some time. And, perhaps, a minor increase in status. And as the visla would not directly accuse another of the Twenty of spying or attempted assassination, his lie would go uncontradicted. He just hoped it stayed that way.

In the meantime, word of the capture and killing of the Ghalian quickly leaked out to the spies and agents spread throughout the Council's many ranks. Most were mere agents, doing a job. But a few were fellow Ghalian, and they had just lost one of their own. Something that not only made them rapidly secure additional informants in case a similar sweep was coming to their particular estate, but also an act that inspired them to redouble their efforts.

One of their sisters had fallen, and they would take her sacrifice to heart.

CHAPTER THREE

The small knife flew through the air in a gleaming blur, striking the target fairly close to center. From the distance it had been thrown, the accuracy was relatively impressive. More importantly, it had embedded deep in the wood. The throw, had it been aimed at a living thing, would have very likely been fatal.

"Better," Hozark said with an approving nod. "You have greatly improved your distribution of force, young Jinnik."

"Thanks, Hozark," Happizano replied as he trotted over to retrieve his blade from the target.

"Yeah, not bad, kid," Laskar added.

The copilot had taken to watching the boy's lessons on occasion, though he also tended to let out an unimpressed sigh from time to time. Laskar, though only a minorly powered caster, was also something of a proficient knife thrower they had discovered.

It had been something of a revelation to his traveling companions when he first revealed the skill. But talent springs up in unusual ways from time to time, and it seemed he was actually fairly proficient in that one area of power use.

The direction of one's internal magic to help guide a thrown knife to its target was not exactly what anyone would call a secret technique. In fact, it was about as widely known as one could imagine such a trick would be. But the ability to actually do it with any degree of accuracy, now *that* was something to take note of.

Many could push their projectiles forward with magic, but most were casting the spells with the mere hope that they might strike their intended target. But Hap was different in that regard. He possessed the Jinnik bloodline, and with it, a rapidly growing magical potential that might even exceed his father one day.

For now, however, he was still a novice, taking his first steps in the ways of magical and manual combat, and his knife-throwing skills showed the diligence of his practice.

He had been on a circuitous tour of the training houses of some of the greatest masters in the galaxy, learning what he could from the esteemed experts, each of whom knew and respected his Ghalian protector.

Hozark, while trained as a Ghalian, had spent much time studying the methods of every school he could over the years, always adding more to his seemingly endless repository of martial techniques. Most from his order did so. It was what made them so difficult to defend against. The Ghalian possessed an almost encyclopedic knowledge, enabling them to counter and defeat nearly any enemy, regardless of style.

And now Happizano was dipping his toes into the welcome waters of that world. Not as an aspiring assassin, but as an eager learner, hungry to feed this newfound passion. Hozark was only too happy to oblige. For after Master Corann and Master Prombatz had imparted their last lesson to Happizano, Hozark knew he could not take the boy to other Ghalian training houses.

Yes, Hozark was one of the Five, and as such he could take Hap anywhere he wanted, but the boy was still being sought by the Council, and bringing him to any of the secret Ghalian facilities could potentially put the secret locations at risk and open them up to a conflict he greatly wished them to avoid.

And so they traveled, he and Demelza introducing Happizano to new sights and ways of thinking as they visited training house after training house. The boy was seemingly constantly practicing under the watchful tutelage of Master Hozark and the other instructors he met, with little time for rest or play. But he'd found something better than play.

To everyone's surprise, Hap found that he actually truly enjoyed this sort of thing, as was clear in his progress. It showed in his improved attitude as well. They had all been grateful for that.

Life aboard the mothership could be trying at the best of times when the boy acted up. But they were now down two of their number, and tensions were a little high.

Laskar had taken over piloting duties while Uzabud scoured the systems with his pirate friends in search of Henni. It was not status quo, aboard the vessel, but Bud had made it clear he would not be swayed.

She'd been kidnapped, snatched in battle, and right from under his nose. It was something Bud had taken personally, and *very* seriously. So seriously that he called in more than a few favors to set his tracking and rescue mission in motion, hitching a ride with Lalaynia aboard his former captain's rather formidable pirate ship, leaving Laskar in charge of his own craft while he was gone.

He had set off hoping to find word of her sooner than later, but they all knew it would be a difficult task. Even Dohria, the greatest of Ghalian spies, had been unable to dig up so much as a whisper of the odd girl's present location.

"There was talk of a strange jump," she had relayed, surprising them all with an unannounced visit as the group discussed their next steps. "Not anything about their final destination, mind you, but it seems a very unusual sort of magic jumped Visla Maktan's ship far from its intended destination."

"We saw it jump," Bud grumbled.

"Indeed," Hozark agreed.

"Yes. But what you did not see was that it was none of the visla's Drooks who had cast that spell. Apparently––and this is only rumor at this point––a young woman was dragged aboard as a captive. And it was in a fit of panic that her power flared, engulfing the entire craft and jumping it to parts unknown."

Laskar's eyes widened with surprise, but Bud just nodded grimly when he heard the news as he pondered his next moves.

"Hey, Laskar?" he finally said, turning to his copilot. "How do you feel about taking over the ship for a while?"

"Wait, what do you mean, take over the ship?"

"I mean, I'm going after her."

"Well, I'm coming with, obviously."

Bud shook his head. "No, you aren't. I need you to stay with Hozark and Demelza. Fly them and the kid wherever it is they need to go. We've still got an obligation to help him find his father."

"It can wait."

"No, we can't put Hozark in a bind like that. Regardless, this is something I just have to do. So, will you help them out? Get 'em where they need to go?"

"Thank you for your concern, my friend, but if Laskar truly wishes to accompany you, we shall find other means of transport," Hozark said.

Laskar hesitated, unsure. It was a big deal being promoted to captain, albeit a temporary position, but he was clearly conflicted about leaving his friend to fend for himself. Of course, the man would be in the company of some of the most dangerous space pirates in forty systems, so that did weigh in his advantage.

"All right," Laskar finally said. "I'll do it. But where are we going to be going anyway? We don't know where to even start looking for Hap's father."

"True," Hozark replied. "But there have been more reports of instances involving weapons powered by Visla Jinnik's magic, is that not correct, Dohria?"

"It is, Master Hozark," the spy replied.

"So? It doesn't mean we'll find him."

"But his trail is yet warm. We only just missed him on Gravalis. Had we arrived perhaps a half-day earlier, we would have had a better path laid out for us. Why, we might even have caught Visla Maktan in the act as he drained power from the poor visla."

Laskar shrugged, unconvinced. "Sure, it sounds good. But they were long gone by the time we got there."

"Yes, that is rather disconcerting."

"How so?"

"It seemed obvious from the hasty departure that they somehow got wind of their impending visitors."

"You mean there's a mole in the network?" Laskar asked, shocked that it could even be a possibility in the tight-knit group.

"Highly unlikely," the master assassin replied. "It could have been any of a number of things that prompted our prey into flight. In tenuous, covert situations such as theirs, it often does not take much to spook people into a hasty evacuation. Signs of which we clearly saw."

"Yeah, but they also have the resources at hand to pack up an entire secret operation and skip out on a moment's notice," Bud pointed out. "That points to a very well-funded group."

"That it does," Hozark replied, then looked warmly at his friend. "Be safe, Uzabud. I would very much like it if you returned to us in one piece."

With that, it was decided. Bud quickly packed his go bag full of weapons of particular violence, then took the fastest of the small craft mounted to his mothership's hull and departed for his rendezvous with Lalaynia.

It was only at dinner that night, after his day's training had ended, that Happizano noticed yet another member of their party was absent. He had been so intently focused on the foot-trapping and tripping techniques the grizzled old mercenary who ran this particular training house was showing him, he hadn't even noticed the departure of Bud's little ship.

"He just left?"

"Yes, young Jinnik. But do not concern yourself. Eat. You will need the energy for tomorrow's lessons," Hozark said.

"But he didn't even say goodbye."

"You were in the middle of some rather intense training," Demelza pointed out. "He did not wish to disturb you. But do not worry, he will be with Lalaynia, and she will undoubtedly take very good care of him. Her people are looking high and low for Henni, and the Ghalian network is seeking her as well. I know it is not what you wish to hear, but at least know that all eyes are searching."

Hap's posture slumped slightly, but he shrugged it off and kept eating. Nothing, it seemed, could diminish his appetite for long.

"I just hope he gets back soon."

"As do we all," Hozark said, wondering how his friend would fare in his quest. "As do we all."

CHAPTER FOUR

A wet thwack sounded out in the dim alleyway, a fine spray of blood Rorschaching onto the wall.

"I think he may have broken something that time," Saramin said.

"Perhaps," Lalaynia agreed as they stood guard while Bud had "words" with a Tslavar mercenary wearing the attire of the Council's unmarked goon squad.

Stripped of his konus, his hands bound to the wall behind him by strong magic, the Tslavar was helpless against Bud's pummeling. But the green-skinned man was keeping his mouth shut. It was admirable, in a way. Most mercenaries were terrible at keeping secrets. This one, it seemed, was made of sterner stuff than his comrades. Or he just knew he would face worse if he spilled the beans.

"I'm gonna ask you again," Bud growled as he paced back and forth in front of the man.

"And I'm gonna tell you the same thing," the captive shot back. "I don't know *nothing* about any starry-eyed girl."

Thwack.

The Tslavar's head rebounded against the wall behind him.

"Ooh, a double-negative," Lalaynia noted with a quiet chuckle.

"Yeah. And he definitely broke something that time," Saramin said.

The wiry boy was only a teenager, but he had matured a great deal since he and Bud had flown together, his thin body filling out with hard-earned muscle after years of back-breaking work. And under Lalaynia's tutelage, he had developed into quite a fine pirate, far more than just a cog in the machine. In fact, at the rate he was going, Bud could easily see him commanding his own ship one day.

Also counting in the boy's favor was his utter calm in the face of violence. Bud was doing what needed to be done, and that was all there was to it. Sure, he noted the damage being inflicted upon the Tslavar mercenary, but it was more academic than any true concern.

The Tslavar winced a bit at Bud's next blow, the impact on what was clearly a fractured cheek finally making a dent in his stoicism.

"You ready to talk *now*? Because I can do this all day."

"I'm telling you, I don't know about this violet-haired bitch you keep asking about."

Thunk.

Bud's fist sank deep into the man's stomach. Had he not already vomited up the remains of his last meal in the earlier stages of Bud's interrogation, he certainly would have now. But all the mercenary could do was retch and gag as he tried to regain his breath.

"Uzabud, a word, please," Lalaynia said quietly.

Bud stepped back from the trapped man and wiped the blood from his knuckles on a rag. "Keep an eye on him, Saramin," he said, then walked to where Lalaynia was waiting. "Yeah?"

"I know you've got a vested interest in this, Bud, but it really looks like this guy doesn't have anything to give us."

"He's one of them, Laynia. He's wearing their kit."

"Sure, Bud, but it's a big galaxy, and not every hired merc is going to be privy to the internal goings-on of the Council, let alone the details of highly confidential kidnappings."

"But--"

"Look, I like Henni. The girl has some fire in her, no doubt, along with a healthy dose of crazy, which, I must admit, I find rather endearing."

"Why doesn't that surprise me?" Bud joked.

"Why, whatever are you trying to say, Bud?" she replied with a sly grin.

Bud ignored her wisecrack. "*Anyway*, Laynia, the word in the network is something unusual happened out in the black nearest this system. Something that left a magical residue an awful lot like a Zomoki jump might. One of particularly sizable magnitude."

"I know, Bud. I'm the one who found you that intel, remember?"

"Yeah, I know. And I appreciate it. And you know as well as I do that this is our best lead so far."

"Sure it is. But just because they *possibly* jumped into the area *near* this system does not mean they came into it. For all we know, they could have just fired up their Drookonus and moved on to another place, without anyone here being the wiser."

"And that's what I'm finding out."

"If you don't kill the guy first."

Hearing those words from the lips of the Valkyrie-like pirate brought a chuckle to Bud's lips.

"Why, Lalaynia, are you getting soft on me?"

She flashed an amused grin. "Bud, I'll gladly disembowel the bastard myself here and now with a smile, but that still won't get us any closer to finding Henni. We need to move on to other leads."

"But--"

Her face hardened slightly. "No, Bud. You have five more minutes, then I'm calling it."

"He knows something, I can feel it."

"Then you have five minutes to find out whatever that is." She studied him quietly a moment. "You seem pretty agitated. I wasn't going to ask, but is there something between you two?"

"Me and Henni? No, of course not."

"You're acting as though there is. And I wouldn't blame you. She's a feisty one, and a good laugh. Not every day you find a spirited woman like that."

"I'm telling you, Laynia, she's just part of my crew. I'm getting her back, just the same as I would for anyone taken under my watch."

Lalaynia glanced at the bloody rag in his hand and the pummeled mercenary secured to the wall and raised her brow with an amused grin. "Whatever you say, Bud. Now, come on. You've got five minutes, so do what you've got to do."

"And then what? We walk away?"

"Yes. Once we dispose of the body, that is."

Bud paused. "Damn, Laynia. You've still got it."

She chuckled. "Just because I know when to cut losses and move on does not mean I have developed a forgiving streak. That bastard's a Tslavar mercenary working for the Council of Twenty. If he wasn't important to you, I'd have killed him myself twenty minutes ago just for sport."

A grin spread across Uzabud's lips. "You know, I forgot how much I enjoyed flying with you, Captain."

"Why thank you, Bud. Now, if you'd please get on with it, our connections have been busy reaching out to their networks far and wide, and we have several other decent leads to follow up on. That is, unless you're planning on going back to your friends soon."

"You're stuck with me for now," Bud replied. "I'm not giving up until I have solid word on Henni. They took her. Right out from under me."

"*Under* you?" the pirate captain said with a laugh.

"Oh, shut up. You know what I mean," he shot back, mirth in his eyes. He turned back toward his captive. "All right, five minutes, you say? Let's see what I can get out of our friend here in that little time."

CHAPTER FIVE

The invisible barrier separating the only two guests occupying the entire cell area was quietly held in place by a rather impressive amount of magic. No ordinary prisoners would have warranted such a display of power, but then, these were not ordinary in the slightest.

"You are getting the hang of it," Visla Jinnik said to his young pupil. "I can sense the intent behind your spell pushing it to fruition. Keep trying."

For her part, the violet-haired young woman sharing the space was a bit less enthusiastic. But then, she had only just learned that she possessed *real* internal magic of her own. A most unusual variety at that. And, apparently, far more than anyone had dreamed to anticipate.

It had manifested from time to time over the years--a bit of force here, some escape assistance there--but never to the degree she had just cast so recently. Henni, it seemed, was of a race thought to be extinct. A people who possessed a type of magic akin to that of the massive, fire-breathing Zomoki.

Not the ones still flying around like rabid beasts, but the Old Ones. The dragon-like creatures of high intellect and great magical abilities. *Those* Zomoki could cast mighty spells, and they possessed the power to jump many systems in a single bound. It was a feat that all but the most skilled Drooks were unable to perform.

But Henni, like the Zomoki of old, also seemed to possess the ability to cast *silently*. It was something not even the most powerful visla could achieve, for the words to the spells were required to bring their intent to fruition. It was the nature of the thing. Magic simply could not take shape without the sounds intoned aloud.

Now, those truly skilled in the casting arts could do so *nearly* silently, the spells no more than a whisper, but they still had to be said aloud. Henni, it seemed, was not bound by that near universal rule.

The young woman sat cross-legged on the cell floor, a fine sheen of sweat on her brow from her efforts. But it was an internal struggle vexing her, not one of muscle over matter. The small chair she was focusing her attention on simply would not budge.

"I can't do it."

"Yes, you can," Jinnik said with utter confidence. "Relax into yourself. Don't force it."

"It's just not working."

"It *is*. You may not feel it, but trust me, I can sense your power trying to assert itself."

"How can you be so sure? There are plenty of people using magic in this place. Maybe it's just theirs bleeding over."

"I told you, Henni, your power is different. And I have to say, it's really most astonishing, and utterly unlike any I've experienced before."

"Then why isn't this working? It's just a simple pushing spell, but I can't make it work."

Jinnik grinned. "You keep calling it that, but what I have taught you is an extremely powerful offensive spell. Yes, you can simplify and call it a pushing spell if you like, but it is so much more than that. Only the strongest casters would even attempt this spell, and, yet, you, a novice, have almost made it work."

"But it just moves a chair."

"For now. Once you master your power, you will be able to blast holes in walls with it."

"You mean *if* I master it."

"Oh, I have faith in you, Henni. You're quite remarkable. Stubborn, yes, but remarkable. And that stubbornness might just be the thing you need to help you unlock your potential."

Henni shifted uncomfortably. Visla Jinnik could tell the young woman was uncomfortable with being praised in this way.

"Okay, I'll tell you what. You've got the words perfect for that one already, and all you really need is to focus and direct your internal intent. But let's shift to something else for a while."

"Like what?" she asked. "You want me to pull the chair instead of push it?"

Jinnik ignored her snark. He'd seen the same frustration in his own son from time to time, and was familiar with the ways to work past it.

"I am going to teach you another spell. An incredibly powerful one that I want you to practice every single day, first thing when you wake up and last thing before you go to sleep. If you do as I ask, it will eventually become second nature to you. Something you can cast without even thinking about it."

"Great, so I'll be attacking people in my sleep, then?" Henni asked. "Not exactly the best way to keep friends."

Jinnik laughed. "Oh, Henni. This is not an offensive spell. This one is strictly defensive. As my instructor once told me, 'There is no point in possessing a strong offense if you cannot mount a simple defense.' He was right, you know. It's a trap a great many casters fall into, focusing nearly all of their energies on learning how to fight but not how to defend."

"But if you land a strong enough spell, you win," Henni noted.

"Though not always," Jinnik countered. "And if you are dealt a strong counter spell, you will very quickly learn that no matter how powerful your offensive spells are, you cannot employ them if you are unconscious or dead."

"I don't know. It just seems unrealistic. I don't have any skill at this stuff."

Jinnik sighed. His son had been the same way during the earliest days of his instruction. And those were just the simplest of spells and cast while using a konus for assistance. But Henni's reaction brought those memories flooding back just the same.

Henni's eyes sparkled in the dim light of their cell. The frustration was surging within her, but this was a manifestation of her power she simply couldn't grasp. A different gift, however, made a sudden appearance.

Without warning, Visla Jinnik was an open book to her, and she saw what he was, as well as what he had been. Henni realized his formerly aloof persona was gone, a victim of his humbling imprisonment. She could sense many of his old attitudes, cast aside in recent times, as well as his immense power.

She could also read his great sadness.

He missed his boy terribly, and was willing to do anything to get him back. Unfortunately, that had already resulted in a great many deaths at the receiving end of his power, either directly, or indirectly.

"You'll see him again," she said. "Hap's a good kid, and I know he wants to see you too."

"What did you say?"

"Your kid. He's fine. And you need to stop beating yourself up about Maktan misusing your power. You thought they had your son. You didn't have a choice."

Jinnik's open book abruptly slammed shut so hard it made the young woman wince.

"Hey, what did you do?" Henni asked.

"Apologies," he replied. "It was an instinctive reaction. I did not know you were a reader."

"Well, yeah, but it doesn't always work. But how did you shut me out like that? I've never had that happen before."

"Some vislas possess the strength to block readers such as yourself, though it requires a bit of effort at first. I, however, have had a few instances in the past that called for me to shut myself off. It is something I can now do without really thinking about it."

"What kind of thing would make you close up like that? You're the most powerful visla I've ever met."

"Perhaps, but in negotiations, sometimes readers are surreptitiously inserted into the proceedings in an attempt to gain an upper hand."

"Oh, I get it," Henni said. "Kind of like cheating at gambling by having a friend give signals."

"In a sense, I suppose," he replied, the hard-sealed barrier around his mind slowly softening once more. "You know, your ability to do that so naturally makes me wonder if we should go with natural, instinctive lessons for the moment. What do you say we shift to the very first spells a child ever learns?"

"What, an illumination spell?"

"Precisely. So simple any child can do it, but here, without a konus, it would draw only upon your internal strength."

Henni hemmed and hawed a moment. "Well, I guess I can try."

"Excellent. Take your time. Build the spell inside yourself. Think the words and feel the intent, but do not speak them aloud. Imagine you have a konus to draw from, and then cast as if you fully expect the spell to work. As if you *know* it will."

"Okay, but I don't know if it'll do anything."

"We shall see soon enough," he replied.

Henni focused her energy on the space in front of her, calling up the spell every child learns in their earliest years. The illumination spell that lets them overcome the natural fear of the dark innate to nearly all species.

"Good, keep at it," Jinnik said as a faint glow began to form in front of Henni.

She felt a flush of adrenaline as she realized it was actually working, but instead of making her spell falter, the chemical surge strengthened her casting until a glowing ball of light hung in the air in front of her.

"Very good. Very good, indeed!" Jinnik said with a pleased grin.

Henni felt a burst of excitement at her progress. That, and an unusual surge in confidence led her to try something else. She shifted to a spell she learned many years later. A kindling spell.

The ball of light sputtered, then shifted shape, reforming into a ball of fire. Jinnik's eyes widened at her unexpected trick. Henni smiled wide, then cast the extinguishing modification, ending the spell.

"Henni, that was wonderful!" Visla Jinnik exclaimed. "Why, if you can do that, I would imagine that--"

He fell silent as the sound of footsteps echoed in the hallway, growing louder.

"Stay calm, Henni. I will be all right," Jinnik said.

But Henni's eyes were sparkling, and she was alarmed.

"They're not coming for you," she said. "They're coming for *me*."

CHAPTER SIX

"The little bitch bit me!" the Tslavar guard complained to his companion.

Henni glared up at him from the ground, a thin line of his blood on her lips, which were curled into a cruel grin despite the punch he had landed on her.

"Idiot, you can't hit her. The visla made it *very* clear, this one's not to be hurt. She's special."

"She's a pain in my ass," the bleeding guard griped.

"Oh, of that there's no doubt. But do you want the visla mad at you?"

The guard hesitated a moment in thought.

"That was a rhetorical question, idiot. And why would you even let her get that close to you without just activating the control collar? That's what the damn thing is there for."

"Well, yeah. But she *bit* me."

"I don't care if she booted you in the mivonks, you don't lay hands on the visla's pets. Now, come on. Niallik left clear instructions until she returns."

"I don't see why she doesn't just do it herself," the guard whined.

"Because she's the visla's favorite. And she's forgotten more about interrogation and torture than you and I have ever learned. So, come on already. Let's just get this done."

The guard looked at the small woman and cast the lightest restraint command to her collar. Henni's limbs locked up, but she found she could still move, albeit uncomfortably and with little grace.

"Behave, you hear?"

"Fuck you."

He increased the spell, adding pain to the mix. Henni resisted as best she could, but soon enough she cried out from the agonizing spell.

"Okay, okay!"

"Thought so," the guard said, releasing the spell. "Now, come along. You're going to use your power and do what the visla wants."

"How's that?" Henni asked as she was led to a low table with a few freshly forged konuses on them.

"Power these," the Tslavar reiterated. "That's all you have to do."

The devices were so hot that she could still smell the acrid tang of smoke coming off the metal. Somewhere very nearby was a smelting facility. Likely similar to the one she and the others had found abandoned on Gravalis. Right before the whole place nearly collapsed on their heads, that is.

"You want *me* to power *those*?"

"That's what I said."

"Sorry, but that's just not going to happen."

"Do what we tell you or—"

"Shut up, Makkis," the other guard cut him off. "Sorry for my friend there. He can get a bit carried away at times."

Henni gingerly touched her bruising cheek. "Gee, ya think?"

"Well, you did bite him," he replied with a friendly laugh.

"But seriously, all you have to do here is just power these up. Even just a little bit will suffice. Anything is a good start."

"Still not happening," she said. "Nice try, though."

"Come now. We don't ask much."

"Listen, I don't even know *how* to do what you're asking. But honestly, even if I did, there's no way I'd lift a finger to help the likes of you assholes."

The guard's good cop charade ended as quickly as it began. "Fine," he growled, a nasty grin forming on his lips. "You want to play it the hard way? We play it the hard way. But you should know, you're not the only one whose ass is on the line. If you don't do as you're told, your friends will suffer too."

"Oh, that's rich. Do you even know who my friends are? You want to talk about suffering? When they get their hands on you, you'll find out what real suffering is. The horrible things they'll do to you will make your head spin. That is, if they let you live that long. And if I don't get to you first."

The guard let out a deep laugh. "You don't frighten me, *girl*. You have no power over me."

Henni chuckled.

"What's so funny?" he asked, a bit unsettled by her utter lack of fear.

"*You* said I have power," she replied.

"Wait, what?"

"You said I have power, and you want to use it. But then you said I have no power. So, which is it?"

The exasperated guard sighed. "Just do as you're commanded."

"And use the power you just said I don't have? Wow, you keep contradicting yourself, you know that?" she said, turning to the guard she'd bitten earlier. "Your buddy here really sucks at this, you know that?"

"Are you *sure* I can't hit her?" the Tslavar guard reiterated.

"No, you cannot. But we *can* do this," his associate said as he cast a nasty stun spell.

Henni fell to the ground, barely conscious and utterly unable to move.

It was a ballsy move, using magic so near the freshly forged konuses. The slightest miscasting and it could have been a catastrophe. But in the heat of the moment he had forgotten Niallik's warnings.

"Help me with this annoying wench," he said.

"Help you what? You knocked her out."

"Help me put her in the chair."

"Oh."

The two men picked up Henni's immobile form and carefully secured her to the sturdy, magic-imbued chair that Visla Jinnik had become so familiar with as his power was stolen from him day after day.

It was a brutal process, and one that left him utterly drained. But as he was not charging the konuses of his own free will, it was the only way his captors could use his power.

Henni sat slumped in the chair, her arms and legs fastened in place. A small table was placed in front of her, likewise imbued with the same power-funneling magic the chair possessed. An uncharged konus was set on the table, warm and waiting. The Tslavar in charge flashed a cruel smile.

"Okay, let's get this show on the road."

Visla Jinnik woke from his fitful nap at the sound of gruff voices drawing near. He sat up in his dimly lit cell and watched the entry spell disengage. The two Tslavar guards strode in and roughly tossed Henni's unconscious body onto her cot.

"What did you do to her?" Jinnik demanded to know.

"Shut up," the now-bandaged Tslavar said with an annoyed snarl.

Jinnik clocked the newly dressed injury. From what he could tell, it seemed to be about the size of a bite. A bite from a rather small prisoner, in fact. Jinnik kept a straight face, but his amusement, and esteem for his cellmate, increased.

The guards took the man's silence for concern, likely not only for the girl, but for himself as well. He didn't dare raise too much of a fuss. Not while restrained in his control collar. And on top of that, they knew what a drain the chair was on him. In fact, if they weren't careful, it was quite possible they could drain him to the point of death.

The duo laughed maliciously at the formerly powerful man's silence and strode from the cell, locking the pair in once more, leaving them alone in the empty holding area. Jinnik studied the unconscious girl's face with concern.

Henni cracked an eye open.

"They gone?" she asked.

The visla found himself chuckling with relief. "So, you *were* paying attention to the defensive spell lesson."

She smiled and sat up. "Yeah, but it still hurt, though."

"Well, you did only just learn the basics. Well done, though."

"Thanks," she said, rubbing the bruise on her face. "But what's with that stupid chair thingy? I mean, damn. It's not comfortable, sure, but they were making such a big deal about it. Not like sitting in a hard chair is going to break anyone, am I right?"

He looked at her with surprise. "You did not feel your power being tapped? Being stolen from you?"

"Uh, no. Is that normal?"

"Anything but. Just like you, my most unusual friend."

"Huh," she replied with a shrug. "So, now what do we do?"

"Now?" he asked, rising to his feet and walking close to the magical partition between them. "Now we continue your training."

CHAPTER SEVEN

Laskar was a talented navigator, no doubt, and a skilled pilot as well. But he was not Bud, and the subtle difference in the casting that propelled the mothership was tangible to Hozark and the others.

For one, their liftoff had been quite rapid--as was also Bud's usual preference--but with Laskar at the helm, it lacked the extra dampening spells the pilot typically layered in place as second nature. Laskar, it seemed, was far more interested in getting them aloft and moving than their comfort.

Then there was their streaking through the atmosphere into the darkness of space. Normally, Bud would make the transition so smoothly his passengers wouldn't even know they'd passed the exosphere. But Laskar was more focused on the destination than the journey.

Of course, Laskar had piloted the ship plenty of times in their recent adventures, but as it was usually during one emergency or another, the rougher ride went unnoted. But now, as they flew at their leisure, it rather stood out.

Once in space, however, he was in his element, and their

flight transitioned to a far smoother one as he prepared them for their journey.

"We'll be there in just a few jumps," the copilot said from his perch in Bud's pilot seat. "Shouldn't take long at all."

"Thank you, Laskar," Hozark replied. "Please inform me when we are ready for the final jump to Arkoval."

"Will do."

Hozark nodded, then went to join Demelza and Hap in the galley. The youth was eating heartily, as a growing boy is wont to do, and was already well into his second helping when Hozark arrived.

"We shall be arriving at Arkoval in just a few jumps," he said, taking a seat with the others.

"What's this Arkoval place, anyway?" Hap asked. "Another training house?"

"In a manner of speaking, yes. I believe you will enjoy this one more than the others, however."

"Why's that, Hozark?"

"You shall see, young Jinnik," he replied with a little grin.

In a relatively short time, they would complete their jumps and land at their destination. Then the young trainee's fun would truly begin.

"Aargun!" Hap blurted with excitement as they exited the ship.

The blind, mute assassin smiled and held up his hand in greeting.

"The blind guy's here?" Laskar asked, a bit surprised. "And Prombatz too?"

The Wampeh master nodded to the group as he walked to greet them with his convalescing student.

"Yes. Master Prombatz settled here for a short while," Hozark replied. "The rays of this system's blue sun have a restorative effect on many, and as Aargun is nearly entirely healed, it was decided to bring him here for the final stage of his recovery."

Laskar looked closer at the blinded young man. It was true what Hozark said. While some things would never heal, the injured Wampeh looked about as healthy and robust as any. More so, even. He had obviously been training hard, and his frame had filled out from his somewhat gaunt figure when last they'd seen him.

Aargun was once more a solid, muscular man. A Wampeh Ghalian aspirant, though one whose final test had proven near-fatal and had left him mute and blinded for life.

"Master Hozark, it is good to have you with us. All of you," Prombatz said, then turned to Demelza and Laskar, giving each a little nod.

"Thanks," Laskar replied.

"It is a great pleasure to see you once more, Master Prombatz," Demelza said. "And I see Aargun is even farther along in his recovery."

They watched as Aargun squatted down to greet Hap, moving as though he was not blind at all. With a quick bit of sleight of hand, he flashed a small dagger, which then disappeared as abruptly as it had appeared.

"Cool! Can you teach me that?" Hap chirped.

Aargun nodded and rose to his full height, then motioned for Happizano to follow him.

"Hey, Hozark. I'm gonna go do some knife stuff with Aargun, okay?"

"Enjoy yourself, young Jinnik. I shall be interested to see what you learn when we return from our task. You go train and have fun, and we shall see you in a few days."

Hap grinned broadly and trotted off with Aargun.

"If you were not close, it would be difficult to note his handicap," Demelza noted as she watched the pair walk away.

"Indeed," Hozark agreed. "His recovery is truly impressive. You have done well in bringing him here, Prombatz."

"Oh, this was just a convenient and quiet world to complete his convalescence. But really, he was more or less mended before we arrived."

As Aargun walked, he did so without hesitation, avoiding people and obstacles as if he were a sighted man. And from the way he moved, it was clear it was not merely from knowing the layout of the city and where objects were located ahead of time. He was adjusting his path in real time without missing a step.

"He was rather distraught at the news of Henni's capture," Prombatz noted. "The way the two of them could communicate without words was quite a spirit-raising bond."

"The girl's a reader," Laskar noted with a shrug. "Just not a very consistent one."

"But she was with him," Demelza noted. "And if her power could be focused, perhaps she could learn to truly develop that gift one day."

"If we find her."

"Yes. If we find her."

Laskar turned to Prombatz. "Hey, what ever happened with his silent casting trick? Did you figure out how he does it?"

He was referring to a startling revelation that had been made when they'd last seen the Ghalian master and his pupil. It seemed that whatever had happened to Aargun in the course of his torture and experimentation, his captors had somehow unwittingly unlocked an ability that pretty much no one possessed. Not even the greatest vislas could do what Aargun could.

He could cast spells without uttering a word.

Of course, that was made a necessity when they cut his tongue out while he was Visla Maktan's prisoner, but even so, it should not have been possible. Yet Aargun had adapted, it seemed. Evolved into something new.

"His silent casting is progressing quite slowly," Prombatz replied. "He can still only produce the most basic of spells."

"Nevertheless, it is an amazing ability," Hozark said.

"Oh, indeed," Prombatz said. "But even if this talent does grow, it will still be quite some time before he is able to cast with any true power."

The two Ghalian masters had assumed Aargun's life within the order was forevermore to be that of an invalid. A crippled brother whom they would look after until his dying day. The young man would be part of their organization for life, but he would never be a Ghalian assassin again.

Aargun, however, appeared to have other thoughts on that subject, and as he healed and grew stronger, it was becoming quite clear that despite his lack of a tongue, or even eyes, his abilities were growing by the day. So much so that the two Ghalian masters were beginning to reconsider their earlier assessment.

"You know why we have come to you, Prombatz," Hozark said, switching back to the business at hand.

"Yes, I heard. A contract on Visla Maktan. No easy task, that one."

"It certainly is not. But we are up for the challenge," Hozark replied. "So, about my request. You will be able to watch Happizano while we are away?"

"Of course. Though I do wish I were traveling with you on this particular contract."

"If things do not go as we hope, you may yet get your opportunity."

"Then let us hope it does not come to that. It is quite the dangerous contract, this one."

"We are prepared," Demelza interjected. "And it is *personal.*"

Prombatz nodded. "Yes, I heard. Master Orkut. Such a terrible loss, one of his age, skill, and arcane knowledge. He was arguably the finest living bladesmith, though there had been more than one previous account of his death."

"His prior ruses had been successful, for the most part," Hozark replied. "But now, I am afraid, he is truly gone."

Prombatz looked at the faces of his fellow Ghalian. They were too well trained to show it, but each was certainly looking forward to ending Visla Maktan for what he had done.

The Ghalian master nodded once. "Happizano shall be safe with us while you perform your task," he said.

"Thank you, Prombatz. And should we fall in this effort, I request you carry on our task of searching out the boy's father. One of the Five must reunite them, if at all possible. Though he is quite difficult to locate."

Prombatz nodded. "I have heard that more weapons have turned up bearing Visla Jinnik's magic."

"Yes, they are still using the boy's father, and we will do all we can to bring them back together. But that issue shall have to wait for the time being. We have actionable intelligence as to the whereabouts of Visla Maktan."

"Then you had best get to it," Prombatz said. "This shall not be an easy contract to carry out. Good hunting, both of you."

"Thank you, Brother. We shall see you soon."

CHAPTER EIGHT

The bodies of the two Council guards were bundled up and disposed of before their blood had even begun to cool. The few droplets of that precious fluid that had spilled on the paving stones had also been magically cleansed, leaving the entire scene spotless and devoid of any sign of struggle.

The two assassins had become rather accustomed to working together, though it was not the Ghalian way. Nevertheless, Hozark and Demelza moved through the estate as a single unit, anticipating one another's moves and remaining utterly undetected.

As for the two dispatched guards, they had also gathered and hidden their personal effects during the hurried cleanup, making it seem as though the two slain men had simply completed their rounds and left. Suspicion would not be raised for at least a day, if not longer.

Hozark took point, leading the push through first the outer, then the inner perimeter of the building. Their intel had said there was a very good likelihood that Visla Zinna Maktan was secretly staying at this particular property. There was even an unmarked Council transport sitting in the landing area.

Unfortunately, after a thorough search, much of it under cover of both shimmer cloak and magical disguise, the two Ghalian assassins had reached the same conclusion.

"He is not present," Demelza noted after they swept the visla's personal suites.

"No, he is not," Hozark agreed. "Back to the ship at once."

He and Demelza made a silent, rapid exit from the estate grounds, quickly covering the distance between the property and the landing field, where Laskar sat anxiously at the controls, waiting for their return.

"It took you long enough," he said when they finally came aboard. "Is he dead?"

"He was not there," Hozark replied. "Get us airborne and away from this world."

"Where to?"

"We shall decide that once we are in another system," the master assassin replied.

Laskar noted the tension hanging around both Hozark and Demelza. Each of them had a personal stake in this. When Master Orkut had perished, it flipped a switch that the normally stoic killers rarely saw triggered.

But now they were acting not only on their contract, but also with the desire for a bit of payback. While it might make them perhaps a tiny bit reckless, it also made them even more dangerous than usual. And that was saying a lot.

"So, he'd already left?" Laskar asked once they'd exited their jump to a neighboring system.

"No," Hozark replied.

"But you said--"

"It would seem the visla had never been there in the first place," the assassin clarified. "This was a decoy. Not a trap, mind you, but a decoy."

"Wait, but why a decoy?"

"A bit of misinformation spread far and wide by the Council as a general preventative measure, it would appear."

Laskar hesitated. "Uh, that's not normal, is it?"

"No, it is not. But there is much upheaval within the Council's ranks with Visla Ravik's recent demise. It has created an opening in the Twenty, and as a result, there is undoubtedly a great deal of jockeying for his position."

"But I thought his brother was taking his place. It's right of ascendancy by blood."

"Normally, yes. But Ravik's brother is not as strong as Ravik was, and thus finds himself facing challengers. One of them, a Visla Netryk, would seem to be a particular threat."

"But that doesn't seem right. It's a familial claim."

"If blood is thicker than water, then power is thicker than blood. And Netryk is *strong*. Perhaps even stronger than Visla Ravik himself ever was. It would seem his brother has quite a fight in store, and there is no guarantee the weaker man will prevail merely because of his familial claim."

Laskar furrowed his brow with confusion. "But how does that affect Maktan?"

"*All* of the Twenty are on heightened alert after Ravik's death. It is an unstable time, and things have a way of spiraling out of hand in situations such as these. It is a wise move, and one I would take were I in their shoes."

Hozark took a small scroll and crossed off the estate on the planet they had just come from.

"How many more?" Laskar asked.

"There are a great many, I am afraid. Visla Maktan's family has been in power a very long time, and as a result, he possesses a significant number of properties, any one of which could be his current hiding place."

"Or none at all," Demelza noted. "He might be in another location entirely."

"True, though I believe the visla would stay at a facility he considers safe. And nothing feels safer than one he himself owns."

"Makes sense," Laskar said, sliding closer to get a better look at the rather lengthy list. "Mind if I take a peek?"

"Of course," Hozark replied, handing him the scroll.

"Wow, this guy owns a *lot* of properties."

"As I said."

"But you know, it seems like if your spy network is getting misinformation, then it's most likely they're aware people are probably looking at them."

"Which is logical," Hozark said. "Where are you going with this?"

"Well, it's a little off the cuff, but hear me out," Laskar said. "The thing is, it's far easier to let information selectively leak from a larger facility, right? Like, there will be more loose lips by the very nature of the place. But a guy like Maktan, he probably never really interacts with the regular staff, so it would be easy for a carefully placed rumor to be spread by one of his people."

"A normal tactic," Demelza noted.

"Right, obviously. But here's the thing. If you look at every property with a staff large enough to be reasonably manipulated like that, you can probably eliminate well over half of this list. And then if you take it a step further and assume they'll be trying to go somewhere with an exceptionally minimal staff, you can further reduce the list to only include those properties. I mean, just those two tweaks and you've cut the most likely locations to what? Five or ten?"

"Mark them, Laskar," Hozark requested.

"Sure," he said, marking a small x beside each of their best options.

Hozark took the modified list back from him and surveyed it a long moment. It was counter to what the spy network had been hearing through the rumor mill, but the copilot had made a good point.

"Of these, which do you feel are the most likely locations?" he asked.

"Me?"

"Yes, you."

"But I'm just a pilot. I'm not a spy. I don't know anything about—"

"You have a good sense for Council tactics, and an outsider's eyes can oftentimes prove quite valuable in revealing what so-called experts fail to see."

Laskar took the list and studied it a long moment. "Well, if you really want my opinion, I would think one of these three would be the best bet. I mean, all of the ones I marked have good potential, but from what your list says, these three also have walled-in landing areas within the compound, as well as a smaller residence detached from the main property. Seems like the perfect place to hole up while keeping the main building seemingly empty."

"Yet having the benefit of those facilities nearby for creature comforts, should they be required," Demelza mused. "An unusual appraisal of the situation, but I like it. Master Hozark? What are your thoughts?

Hozark nodded approvingly. "You have a knack for this, Laskar," he said. "I shall reach out to the Ghalian network and have them redirect their efforts to these three properties in particular. It will take our operatives a day or two to make contact, but we should have an idea if your hunch is correct soon enough. You have done well."

Laskar nearly blushed at the praise. "Well, I don't know about that," he replied. "Let's just hope I was actually right."

Hozark nodded. "We shall soon find out. For the moment, however, we shall await their report with Master Prombatz."

CHAPTER NINE

Prombatz was only slightly surprised to see Hozark and the others return so soon. Had their intel been accurate, it made perfect sense that they would have completed their contract and ended Maktan as quickly as possible.

But it seemed that was *not* the case, and from what Hozark had informed him, it could be some time before they acquired the actual location of their target. Laskar's contribution to the search, however, had impressed the master Ghalian. Hozark's flying companion possessed a bit more strategic insight than one would have assumed, given his usual demeanor.

Being promoted to captain, even if but temporarily, seemed to agree with the man, and he settled into the role with a fair bit of relish. Uzabud would be back with them soon enough, but for now, Laskar was in charge of the mothership, and he was enjoying the boost in status.

"How strong were the defenses?" Prombatz asked as he and Hozark strolled the grounds.

"Fair, but not particularly difficult," he replied. "Demelza and I made quick work of the only pair of sentries that would be an issue. The rest of the estate, while well-protected, was not at all a challenge to move through."

"Shimmer cloaks?"

"Yes, as well as a few cast disguises. All rather standard efforts, but with a non-productive outcome."

"All of that just for show, then?" Prombatz mused. "It would seem your assessment of the Council's countermeasures is correct, then. Diversionary tactics intended to draw out would-be assailants while hiding the true location of the remaining nineteen members. This could make things a bit more difficult."

"Indeed. However, Laskar's insights were quite logical. I have hopes one of the targets he suggested will prove to be as he posits they might."

"Ah, yes. He does seem to have stepped up his game since taking charge of Uzabud's ship during his absence. I must wonder if perhaps he would be better served captaining his own craft, rather than flying second-in-command aboard another's."

"Perhaps when this is all resolved," Hozark said. "He is proving his worth, that is for certain. But tell me, has Happizano made progress in these past few days?"

"He and Aargun do appear to enjoy one another's company, and teaching the boy does raise both of their spirits, though I must admit, I believe your violet-haired friend's ability to communicate with him is a treat Aargun sorely misses."

"If I know Uzabud, he is doing everything in his power to ensure Henni's safe return."

"May he be successful in his endeavor," Prombatz quietly said.

Having lost Aargun to the Council's agents in an ambush that had been meant for him had left the Ghalian master with a lingering drive for at least a modicum of revenge. It was not normally the Ghalian way, but, much as the killing of Master Orkut had affected Hozark and Demelza, what had been done to Aargun had made things personal for Prombatz.

Death, injury, torture, all were normal risks of their profession. But what the aspiring assassin had suffered crossed a line. They were trying to do something with the Ghalian. Experiments had been conducted. And with the recent rescue of a feral young Ghalian amidst a crashed ship of enslaved Ootaki and Drooks, they finally had a good idea what.

Maktan had been attempting to steal the Ghalian ability to take another's power. He had failed with Aargun, but the discovery of a feral youth who possessed the gift among the powered captives being experimented upon showed that this was no one-off attempt. The visla was trying to find a way to make that power his own. Anything to make himself even more dangerous than he already was.

"How is the boy?" Hozark asked, referring to the malnourished, wild young Wampeh. "Corann should have had him placed with the healers by now."

"Yes, he has been nourished and cleaned up from his ordeal, but he does not speak any dialect our translation spells can identify, which is making these early stages of rehabilitation a bit difficult."

"Odd. The spell should work for all languages," Hozark mused.

"Yes, most odd. But I wonder if it might be possible he is *truly* feral. That he never learned a real language for the spell to translate."

It was a novel idea, and it did make sense, for one could not translate grunts and growls that had no defined meaning. But that would put the boy on the same linguistic level as an animal. If that were the case, Corann's people would have their work cut out for them.

"Whatever the issue, I am sure every effort is being made to help him adapt to his new life," Hozark said. "Our people will do all they can in that regard. The boy clearly possesses the gift, and he is strong at that."

"Yes, but without communication, and at his age, no less, it shall be difficult to train him in the ways of the order. To bring him into the fold."

Hozark nodded, pondering the unusual scenario. "Time, Brother Prombatz. It is something we are fortunate to possess in abundance, for it seems our new ward's recovery and subsequent training shall require a lot of it."

The following afternoon, the group assembled out in an open dining area beside the building Prombatz had been calling home. The air was warm and clear, and the food plentiful and good, having been sourced from nearby farm stands.

Happizano was in a fantastic mood, happily showing off the moves he had been practicing while the others were away. Hozark and Demelza were quite pleased with his surprising progress.

"Well done, young Jinnik. You have put in much effort, I can see."

"Thanks, Hozark. Aargun and Prombatz have been really great."

"Not bad, I've gotta admit," Laskar added.

For the copilot to admit anyone had done anything well was a bit of a surprise given his usual cocky attitude. It seemed that taking on the pilot's mantle had helped mellow him in more ways than one.

"Master Hozark?" a servant said.

"Yes?"

"A visitor requests you," she said, pointing to a stocky, deep red-colored man with three-fingered hands, a thick beard of bristling, wire-like hair, and plate-like ridges of hardened tissue that gave his shoulders the look of a linebacker.

"If you will excuse me a moment," he said to the others.

Hozark walked to the visitor, who gave a slight bow before

engaging in their discussion. It took only a few minutes, then the man turned and left.

"What was that all about?" Laskar asked.

"Dohria has informed me that Visla Maktan *is* almost certainly at one of the targets you helped identify, Laskar. Well done."

The copilot looked confused. "Hang on a minute. Dohria sent that guy to pass on the message? I thought she always did it herself, like all of your spies."

"Oh, that *was* Dohria," Hozark clarified.

"*That?* But that was a totally different person. And gender. And species, even."

"Yes. A most impressive feat, even among our kind. And now you can see why she is by far our top operative."

Laskar let out a whistle. "Holy shit, that's amazing. I mean, I'm not like Henni or you guys, but I usually can sense magic on someone, but she gave off almost nothing."

Prombatz nodded. "She is known for using a great many conventional methods of disguise along with her magic, though she is uniquely talented in masking her spells as well. It is an incredibly rare gift, and one that allows her to perform her job all the better."

"Indeed. And now her efforts have given us Maktan's *real* location. And, again, thank you, Laskar, for helping narrow the search," Hozark said.

"No problem, I'm glad to help. But which one was it?"

"Visla Maktan is quietly hiding at his estate on Trazzip."

"Trazzip? That was the smallest of the ones on the list."

"Yes, though it is still a somewhat palatial estate. However, Dohria informs me the main building appears to be entirely buttoned-up and unoccupied, and only a modest cruiser is parked in the courtyard landing site."

"A ruse?" Demelza asked.

"Indeed. No one expects a visla, let alone one of the Twenty, to be at any location, even one as small as this, without making a fuss. There is normally a rather large retinue attending the Twenty, and very overt security forces scrutinizing any who come close. It is what makes them so difficult to eliminate, even on the incredibly rare occasion of there being a Ghalian contract on them."

"So he's there unguarded?" Laskar asked.

"Oh, he is most certainly guarded," Hozark replied. "Just in a manner that is not readily seen. We shall have our work cut out for us, drawing close and landing a killing blow before he is able to focus his considerable power against us."

"And if he senses you coming before you're close enough?" Laskar asked.

Hozark paused a long moment. "Let us ensure that does not happen," he finally replied. "For I intend for only one person to fall in the completion of this contract, no matter how difficult it may be. And his name is Zinna Maktan."

CHAPTER TEN

The intel had been checked and double-checked, the network of spies and informants quietly verifying many individual snippets of a far larger picture. Only a very select few agents, such as Dohria, knew the full scope of what was being sought out. And everything had checked out. This was definitely what they sought.

"Slowly, and from afar," Hozark instructed their pilot. "With the utmost caution. We shall have but one chance at this."

Laskar nodded and continued his work plotting their course to the quiet little world of Trazzip. It resided in a lightly populated system with but four planets orbiting its warm yellow sun. There was little in the way of trade or resources to speak of, but for a quiet little retreat, the world served its purpose quite well.

It seemed about as simple a final jump as any might make, but the pilot knew full well that any rapid approach or abrupt maneuver could very well trigger whatever hidden security measures Visla Maktan's guard had put in place.

Much of the additional magic sprinkled throughout the approach vector was fairly standard in form. Just a smattering of wards and warning spells, any of which could be triggered by the mere presence of a craft regardless of its intent in the system. But those were obviously placed for a reason.

Carefully hidden in the inky black were an additional layer of spells, cast in such a manner that all but the most skilled would miss their presence entirely. If some mercenary or ruffian attempted to avoid the only *mostly* hidden wards, they would steer themselves right into the *true* security measures. And the results would almost certainly be fatal. And that was the point.

The key to this somewhat difficult approach was to fly as if you hadn't a care in the world rather than taking evasive actions. To avoid the most obvious of spells, but to trip the more hidden ones as if taken by surprise. No real damage would be done, but the clumsy triggering of those initial smaller spells would make the ship appear to be precisely what it was not.

An innocent craft stumbling across a hidden defensive ward.

"Anything?" Hozark asked as Laskar maneuvered toward the glowing orb of Trazzip.

"Just a little turbulence," Laskar joked.

"We are in space, Laskar. There is no turbulence."

"Well, yeah," he replied with a chuckle. "But seriously, it's just a few trigger spells. Nothing major, though I did have to slightly alter course to make sure I hit a few more of them. Gotta put on a good show, after all."

"So long as we do not stray into the real defenses, we shall be fine. Good work."

"Thanks. So, where exactly do you want me to put the ship down? Not anywhere near the visla's estate, obviously, but it's not a really busy planet. Our options are kind of slim."

"Dohria mentioned this issue and offered an interesting solution."

"Oh?"

"There is a recreation facility on the far side of the world."

"I didn't see any mention of that in the notes."

"You wouldn't have. It is, how shall I put it? An establishment of a *unique* nature. One whose visitors typically do not wish to announce their true reasons for visiting."

Laskar sat quietly a long moment, seemingly confused by Hozark's circuitous description. "I don't get it."

Hozark sighed. It seemed his attempts at a genteel description had failed. His fellow Wampeh cracked a little grin.

"It is a whorehouse, Laskar," Demelza blurted. "Is that clear enough?"

The pilot's posture straightened, as did other parts of him, no doubt. "Well, why didn't you say so? You want me to, uh, really sell the deception?"

"If you wish," Hozark replied. "The facility does offer regular massage services, as well as a full spa. Amuse yourself as you wish for the first hour or so after we depart. But after that we shall require your return to the ship to monitor for our skree call in case of any emergency situation."

"Okay. But how are you going to get all the way to the estate without being noticed? Your ships were mounted to the hull when we started our approach. They'll notice if you detach now."

Hozark smiled. "Oh, dear Laskar. Demelza and I activated our craft-mounted shimmer cloaks before we made our final jump. To any observers, those two ships have never been in the system at all."

"Wait, I didn't know you did that. And aren't those incredibly costly to maintain through a jump?"

"Yes, they are quite a drain on magic if left engaged for a jump. However, as we are mounted to this far larger vessel, we simply tapped into the additional reserves to increase the spell's power and keep from draining our ships as we make the approach."

"Huh. That's pretty clever."

"Thank you. It is not our preferred method, but given the

circumstances, it seemed our best option. When you land, we shall disengage our docking spells and fly free, all within the far less magically draining confines of the planet's atmosphere."

It was a flaw shimmer cloaking possessed. The masking spells could hide a ship in space, but the power draw was massive, and the results were often lackluster and not worth the amount of magic expended.

Piggybacking as they had done provided an unusual work around for the situation at hand, using the bulk of the mothership to not only provide a more convenient surface to camouflage against, but also a secondary power source that allowed the ships to remain fully charged until they launched.

"See those?" Laskar asked, pointing out a smattering of cargo craft and small shuttles dotting the landscape.

"Yes," Hozark replied.

"Those are all Council ships. The visla has a whole shitload of backup hiding out around here, disguised as civilian craft."

"Yes, I am aware," the master assassin said. "But very astute of you to notice. Many would have taken those craft at face value. How did you discern their true nature?"

"The way they're parked," he replied. "Like, they're all supposed to be on the ground doing whatever, but each of those ships is still in launch configuration and ready to fly at a moment's notice. Civilians don't do that. But Council goons and mercenaries? Oh yeah, that's second nature."

Hozark let out a low chuckle. "Well done, Laskar. *Very* well done."

"So, what are you two going to do now?"

"Demelza and I shall fly to the visla's estate. From there we shall begin our infiltration. As the situation is fluid, we shall then devise our final plan once inside the compound walls."

"You gonna skewer him from behind?"

"I doubt I could draw my blade close to him without it being noticed. He is a visla, after all, and though the meek and relatively harmless façade may cause him to appear an easy target, given what we have learned of his actions so far, I have reason to believe with some certainty that is anything but the case."

"We shall be forced to adapt and modify on the ground," Demelza added. "Normally a trap would likely be enough. Plenty have walked right into our spells in the past, but with Visla Ravik dead and a power grab in motion, it seems very likely they will be on high alert. The other Council members are too opportunistic to let a chance to consolidate more power slip by."

"Demelza is correct, of course," Hozark noted. "Which means we shall be forced to perform a full infiltration on short notice."

"Wait, you're going to do the disguise thing and walk right in?" Laskar asked incredulously.

"Indeed. There is simply too much left to chance if we leave trap spells for the man. He might not trigger them, and we must be absolutely certain his fall is permanent."

Laskar nodded, but his countenance said he did not like this plan one bit. "But what if the guards––"

"Do not worry yourself about them," Hozark replied. "This is not your normal contract, nor is Maktan your average target. There shall be no mercy for his guards this time. Swift and decisive, that is how this must play out. And his guards shall fall with him."

"Isn't that a bit, uh, *different* from what you usually do?"

"Yes, but once Visla Maktan is gone, these guards would simply move along and be reassigned to another member of the Twenty. Only this time, they would have first-hand knowledge of our tactics, and that is something we simply cannot allow. That is a learning curve that we shall cut off before it begins. And now, Laskar, please, set us down and go about your act. Demelza and I have much to do. If all goes well, we shall return and dock with the ship and none will be the wiser."

"And if things don't go well?"

Hozark flashed a wry grin. "In that case, I just hope you are standing by your skree and are ready for a quick escape."

CHAPTER ELEVEN

To any observing, the tall man who exited the newest vessel to arrive at the "spa" facility on Trazzip was just like the others who frequented the establishment. The way he stretched languorously as he set foot on the landing area while taking in the sights, filling his lungs with fresh air and the faint aroma of perfume, was that of a man perfectly at home in a house of ill repute such as this.

And there was his smile, and that gleam in his eye as he made his way down the short pathway to the main entrance. This was a truly happy man, and once inside he would surely spend well and enjoy his stay.

While all eyes were on Laskar--both those of the staff as well as the handful of Visla Maktan's plainclothes guard--Hozark and Demelza were free to quietly separate their shimmer ships from the mothership. It took a little extra power and a bit of patience to make their departure utterly unnoted, but the two assassins were more than up to the challenge.

They settled into their pre-arranged flight pattern and began the long slog to the Maktan estate, leaving Laskar to do whatever he felt he needed to do to keep up the disguise. Neither really wanted to know the details of what that would entail.

The pair stayed relatively low due to the faint cloud cover that was present that day. Had they ascended much higher, their movements would have been plain for all to see despite the use of their shimmer cloaks. Clouds could be excellent cover when hovering stationary, but movement would quickly turn them from a misty protection to a liability.

The planet was small, and the craft fast, and in short order the two Ghalian arrived at the Maktan estate. Both had their senses on high alert as they reached out for the defensive spells certain to be hidden in the skies around the property.

Sure enough, it seemed multiple layers of wards and traps had been placed at varying altitudes, leaving only a pair of clear paths in and out of the property's airspace. The assassins could have pushed ahead, navigating the hidden passageway unnoted, but to do so would have also placed their ships within the defensive array, and if something went wrong, they would certainly not wish to have their craft within that perimeter when it locked down.

Instead, they each touched down outside the estate's grounds and defenses, tucking their shimmer ships into a small copse of trees, where they would be highly unlikely to be accidentally stumbled upon. Then, the two joined up for the approach on foot.

They ran most of the way, their muting spells muffling the sound of their footfall while their shimmer cloaks were left idle. They were going after a visla, and a rather powerful one at that. They needed to conserve every drop of magic they could.

Though both were well-fed on power and carried several konuses and slaaps in addition to their blades, using any of that precious magic was something to be avoided if at all possible.

The expenditure to keep their cloaks active as they ran could very well be the difference between success and failure should the assassination devolve into full-on magical combat.

The grounds within the estate's high walls was their destination. If intel had proven correct, and if the visla held to the habits of his daily routine despite the somewhat locked-down nature of this retreat, then he would be outside for his nightly post-dinner stroll any time now. The perfect time to end him, when he was not safely ensconced within the labyrinth of the property's corridors and chambers.

It seemed that Visla Zinna Maktan had long been in the habit of going for a post-meal stroll. It was a practice he had first taken up years earlier when he and his wife had first become a couple. Over the years, the two had continued the practice, and now, even as a widower, he still continued despite the now solitary nature of the walks.

He had not taken a new wife after her death, it seemed, nor had he had any lovers of any consequence. That was good. That meant he would almost certainly be on his own as he walked. There was a single child of their union, a son, but he was fully grown and had a life of his own far, far away. No one else would be caught up in the night's affairs.

This was between the assassins and Maktan. As it should be. If things got ugly, there would be no need to hold back for fear of the slaughter of innocent bystanders, as was the duo's preference. They were killers, but of a precise nature. Indiscriminate slaughter was not their stock-in-trade.

The Ghalian navigated their way through a moderate series of traps and pitfalls as they approached the compound wall. Neither had spoken a word the entire approach, nor would they until the task was completed, if possible.

With prey such as a visla on the Council of Twenty, every little edge they could give themselves counted.

Of course, unless the visla was specifically casting amplification spells to suss out potential intruders, they would be fine, but there was no sense tempting fate. Both had engaged their shimmer cloaks as soon as they'd come within visual range of the property, so aside from the visla himself, none in attendance should have the power to note their approach.

Many employed the use of shimmer cloaking, including some Council bodyguards, but none were as proficient as the Wampeh Ghalian. It was just one of the many things that had helped make them the greatest order of assassins in the galaxy.

Demelza stopped short when she sensed Hozark abruptly slow his approach just in front of her. A moment later her senses keyed in to what had caught his attention and frozen him like a statue despite his shimmer cloak.

There was a trace of magic in the air. A familiar scent of power. Not entirely what she'd sensed in the past, but rather an unguarded, unmasked bit that possessed that familiar feeling she'd encountered before. Maktan's power, but not being disguised and altered this time.

He was in a safe place, one of his homes, and this brief, unprotected glimpse at his true magical signature informed them both of two things. First, it was definitely Maktan's power they had encountered before. Even though it had been altered and disguised, blended and obscured, the bloodline's true nature could not be entirely erased.

Second, the man possessed as much power as they had feared. Perhaps even a bit more. It was no wonder Ravik had worked beneath him, even though both were vislas. Maktan, despite his passive, and frankly unimpressive, reputation within the Twenty, was *strong*. His public persona was one thing, but what he had done in secret was another.

Confident they had not been sensed, Hozark began moving once more, Demelza close behind. They still had to pierce the outer perimeter wall to enter the estate, but for two such as they, that should pose no significant problem. Once inside, however, things could get very interesting, very fast.

Both hoped that if that happened, the visla would fall quickly. From what they had just sensed, anything less could very possibly be more than they could handle, even with their efforts combined. In any case, they would find out soon enough.

CHAPTER TWELVE

Walls were funny things. People often took one look at an imposing stone beast of an obstacle in front of them and simply gave up, assuming the thing to be utterly insurmountable. But Hozark knew better.

Walls had many ways to pass them, be it over, under, around, or even through, and this was no different, though there was a fair amount of additional magical protection in this particular instance.

Intruders would most often seek to gain access at the most remote portion of a wall. It was for precisely that reason Hozark and Demelza quietly made their way to the exact opposite portion, opting for the well-lit and guarded entryway.

Multiple layers of traps and alarm spells had been placed at all of the nooks, crannies, and perceived weak spots in the defense, cast in a manner so as a lesser intruder might not have noticed them. These two, however, made quick note of the obstacles and shifted their course to the least expected of ingresses.

Knowing that the visla was here surreptitiously gave them an advantage. The main gates, though guarded, as they always were, had not received any overt addition to their fortifications. To do so would have drawn attention to them, and thus made it obvious the visla was on the grounds, the exact opposite of what was desired.

Therefore, what was normally considered the most difficult point of entry for uninvited guests was actually one of the easiest. Once you got past the sentries, that is. Fortunately, skilled use of a shimmer cloak could accomplish that with relative ease.

The gateway to the inner confines of the estate proper would take a bit more effort to navigate, but fortunately for the pair of assassins, the visla was in the habit of walking the gardens and pathways just within the outer wall. All they had to do was get to them.

Invisible to all, the cloaked duo crept past the sentries with the greatest of stealth, moving slowly, yet decisively, casting muting spells about themselves in addition to their shimmer spells.

Once inside the short tunnel through the wall, they split to opposite sides as they slid forward toward the beckoning opening to their destination. But they did not rush through. There would undoubtedly be additional guards, wards, and alarms placed all about now that they were inside the wall and out of sight of passersby.

Now it would be okay for the visla's guard to have a somewhat more overt presence, though they would still keep it as hidden as possible, lest the minimal staff still on hand take note and start gossiping.

Hozark and Demelza both did as their training dictated, feeling for the tendrils of magic that would undoubtedly be blocking their way. Sure enough, with patience and skill, each found the delicate web of magical alarms and trap spells woven over the tunnel's opening.

They could have disarmed them, but with the likelihood of

roving patrols coming across the deactivated spells before their work was finished, they instead used gentle force to push the triggers aside, allowing themselves a small gap through which they could pass undetected. Once on the other side, they simply let the magic slide back to its original place. It required a bit more magic than they wished to expend, but there was simply no other option.

Before they moved on, a faint marker was left on the key strands, which would allow them to readily attach to them for a reverse of the process in a hurry on their way out if needed. Ghalian were known not only for pulling off the most difficult of assassinations, but also for almost never being caught. This sort of precaution was one of the reasons why.

The sky was dimming, but there was still a fair amount of light as the sun lowered on the horizon. Long shadows had begun falling across the estate, and soon enough it would be dark. But the visla dined relatively early, and thus, his post-meal stroll would be done in the waning hours of the planet's long day.

The intel on the property had described the maze of pathways that wove through the gardens, and Hozark was pleased to note they had been almost entirely accurate. Of course, some small changes always occurred when groundskeepers replanted items or shifted a small crop from one area to another, but for the most part, it was as expected.

And that meant he and Demelza would be carefully creeping ahead while *avoiding* the pathways.

The trigger spells were expertly laid. Whoever had set them for the visla's protection was quite skilled and had a solid grounding in defensive tactics. Obviously, this head of security was more than a figurehead.

But shimmer cloaked as they were, the two Ghalian assassins could still move through the grounds relatively easily;

it just took more time, as they had to avoid the pathways. And as skilled shimmer users, when they held perfectly still, they were all but impossible to detect. In short order, they moved into what would be the most advantageous position from which to close the gap and strike when the visla appeared.

One shortcoming of the plan was that they did not know which path Maktan would take. And that same uncertainty was woven into the warding spells on the paths. As the man walked, however, his very presence would clear the path in front of him. A clever tactic, but one that would do him no good if his attacker was waiting patiently for his approach, rather than moving toward him on their own.

Hozark sensed magic around the area, but only a lone shimmer-cloaked guard was apparent to him. It was unusual, feeling those traces without contact, but he quickly put those concerns aside as the visla himself stepped out into the gardens for his walk.

The man was older, but not what one would call old. Late middle age, perhaps, but still in fine health from what he could see. Tall, with straight posture and a confident stride, the visla slowly began his walk, taking deep breaths of the evening air as his meal settled in his stomach.

It would only be a matter of time before he made his way to either Hozark or Demelza, and as utterly motionless as the pair were within their shimmer cloaks, he would not notice them at all unless he was actively seeking them out. And here, in the safety of his own estate, why would he even think to expend such power?

Hozark watched the man walk. *Unimpressive*, he thought to himself, a bit surprised at the man's countenance. He had expected something *more*. But Visla Zinna Maktan was something of a letdown. But then, many of the most devious of killers seemed quite different from their true natures.

Maktan took his time, deep in thought, it seemed, as he slowly made a circuit of the grounds. He had chosen a route that would not bring him to Hozark for a little while yet, but the assassin was quite familiar with waiting, and his patience was legendary.

"A message for the visla," an unexpected courier called out from the far end of the courtyard.

Hozark felt his stomach tense as the fool abruptly rushed onto the path, triggering multiple wards and alarm spells. The grounds burst into light, the defensive spells illuminating every square inch while the pathway became a defensively charged blockade, shielding the visla from all sides.

Less than a second later, Hozark realized why he had felt that extra bit of power in the air, as well as why the visla was still not using any of his power to pierce shimmer magic. Dozens of shimmer-cloaked security guards leapt into action, surrounding the visla, providing a living shield, and one bristling with weapons both conventional and magical.

In a matter of seconds, the protective detail rushed Maktan from the area rather than engage the courier, who was now lying stunned on the ground. It seemed an honest mistake, but these guards took no chances. Many ruses were made to seem as such, and Hozark could not help but admire their discipline as they bundled the visla off to the nondescript ship waiting in the nearby courtyard.

The craft did not wait for any entourage, but leapt into the sky the moment the visla was aboard, heading straight for space as guards encircled the downed courier while others fanned out to scour the grounds.

Hozark moved quickly for the exit, knowing Demelza was doing the same. The tunnel would be guarded as before, but perhaps a few additional sentries might have been summoned into position as well.

None of that mattered, though. With the spells triggered,

making an exit required far less finesse than their entry had necessitated. The wards pulled aside quickly, and the duo raced through the tunnel and out the far end just as the elongating shadows reached the wall. In no time they had melted into the oncoming night without a trace.

CHAPTER THIRTEEN

"You do realize what you interrupted, right?" Laskar grumbled, straightening his clothing as he climbed back aboard the parked mothership. "I mean, talk about timing."

Hozark and Demelza didn't even respond to Laskar's annoyance. He had been well aware of their time constraints when they undertook this mission, and he had no one but himself to blame if he'd taken too long to engage in whatever shenanigans he was up to when his skree blurted out the recall message.

"Stupid freaking dumb luck," he grumbled as he slid into the pilot's seat. "So, I assume we're out of here in a hurry?" he asked, dropping the fully charged Drookonus into its receptacle and bringing up the ship's power in an instant.

"No, we are not," Hozark said. "Hold back a moment."

"But I thought you said we'd have to run if the alarms tripped. Make a hasty escape. That sort of thing."

"And we would have. However, in this instance, we were not the parties responsible for the tripping of that alarm."

"What do you mean?"

"There was another present. One who foolishly stumbled right into the visla's defensive measures."

"Another assassin? What were they doing there?"

"No, not an assassin," Hozark corrected. "A mere courier who just happened to step in the wrong place at the wrong time."

Laskar looked confused.

"He triggered the alarms before we could reach Maktan," Demelza clarified. "The visla's guards swarmed the man and surrounded the visla before we could act."

"That fast? Wow," Laskar marveled. "How many were there? Couldn't you have just taken them out too?"

"There were dozens," Hozark replied.

"*Dozens*? Holy shit. Overkill, much?"

"I would not say so," the master assassin said. "They were merely being extra careful in their duties protecting the visla. Obviously, with Visla Ravik's demise and the turmoil within the Council, they were expecting something, even if they did not know what. I will say, however, that the additional layers of security went far beyond our initial intel on the property, and it seems he has a rather talented captain of the guard running his protection detail."

"Almost sounds like you admire the guy," Laskar joked.

"It was a very well-configured defensive strategy," Hozark replied. "And regardless of whether he or she is my adversary, I respect a tightly run ship."

Laskar snorted with both amusement and frustration. "You seem pretty okay with these guys putting the kibosh on your hit. I mean, the visla got away, and now he's going to be on high-alert for future attempts."

Hozark could see where Laskar was going with this and quickly cut him off before he worked himself up into a tizzy.

"Yes, it is an inconvenience, and yes, our efforts were stymied this evening. But it was all by happenstance, not a specific rebuttal of our tactics. In fact, that we were not detected even after the alarms had been triggered attests to the efficacy of our stealthy approach and camouflage."

"But he got away!"

"He did, but we now know which ship he was flying out on, and the Ghalian network will be keeping a very close eye on it from this point. He may employ decoy vessels again and swap out, and it may take some time to reacquire him at another suitable location, but it shall come to pass, sooner or later."

The pilot shifted in his seat, uncomfortable with the situation and antsy just sitting on the ground when they could be flying in pursuit, or escape, or pretty much anything other than waiting.

"So, we're just going to sit here?"

"For now. This craft has drawn no attention, partly thanks to your performance at this establishment, for which we both thank you. However, if it were to abruptly depart so shortly after Visla Maktan effected an emergency egress, some would take note, and if they happened to work for the visla or the Council, that would bode very poorly for us indeed."

Laskar realized they were right. It was frustrating, but they had no choice but to let the spies do their thing and keep an eye on Maktan's ship while the trio sat on this rock and did nothing. It was a fate he reluctantly resigned himself to.

"It's still weird, if you ask me," he said. "I mean, there's no reason he should have that many guards. Not for a plain old babysitting gig at his own estate. There was no reason for the old man to be so paranoid. Whatever's going on within the Council, Ravik was killed in *battle*, not in a stealthy assassination. So why all the extra men?"

Hozark nodded his agreement slowly. "It was a bit unusual, yes. However, it is clear that his security captain knows *something* unusual is afoot. Even if he cannot discern what exactly the threat is. And his use of shimmer-cloaked guards shows he is well-acquainted with unusual forms of warfare."

"They were shimmer-cloaked?" Laskar asked, the shock clear on his face. "You didn't think to mention that in the first place?"

"It was irrelevant, Laskar," Demelza said. "What is done is done, and we have had a temporary setback in our plan. That is all. And whether the visla has a dozen men guarding him or a hundred, we are Wampeh Ghalian, and we shall complete our contract, one way or another."

The look in her eye told him that while she was calm about the evening's failure, she was also still harboring quite a grudge for the murder of her mentor. Master Orkut may not have been a Ghalian, but he had clearly made an impression on her all the same.

"So, what now?" he finally asked after a long, frustrated sigh.

Hozark leaned back in his seat and kicked his feet up. "Now? Now we shall let the network do what they do best. They shall track his ship, keep tabs on his whereabouts, and as soon as he settles in a location suitable for our needs, we shall strike once more. And this time we will not miss."

"Uh, I meant what now as in, what do we do now that we're stuck here on this planet with nothing to do?"

Hozark let out a little chuckle. "My apologies, Laskar. Perhaps I was getting a little ahead of myself."

"Ya think?"

Hozark ignored the snark. The fellow was obviously out of his element, and the frustration was getting to him.

"In answer to your question, now we relax and focus our minds on the task ahead of us."

"But what about me? What can *I* do?"

"There is not much *to* do, I am afraid."

Laskar's shoulders slumped a moment, then slowly began to straighten until he was fully upright. "Hey, I was just thinking. If we're not going anywhere, how long do you think we'll be stuck down here?"

Hozark considered the question. "I would think another few hours should provide us enough time to fully establish our cover story and avoid scrutiny upon our departure."

Laskar grinned and rose to his feet and headed toward the door. "Well then," he said with a bright grin. "If you'll excuse me, I have some unfinished business to attend to. See you back here in a few hours."

With that he strode back to the house of ill-repute, determined to make the most of a bad situation.

"It is not going to be as easy as you told him," Demelza said when the ship was clear. "Our spies will likely not be able to keep track of that craft once it jumps."

"I know," Hozark replied. "But it seemed pointless to concern him with that detail. Now, come," he said, heading to the galley where they could better sit and discuss their failed attempt. "Let us go over what we learned of our dear Visla Maktan this evening."

CHAPTER FOURTEEN

The flight back from Trazzip was relatively quick, given the lack of need for a circuitous route to mask their flight path. Laskar had plotted only two misdirect jumps, and had done so in a far more pleasant mood than he had been in when the contract on Visla Maktan had failed to be completed.

That he made his return to the ship some hours later with his hair a bit ruffled and his cheeks a bit flushed told the waiting assassins all they needed to know. At least he had let off some steam--or whatever else--and his mood would be far more agreeable for it.

The two Ghalian were in decent spirits as well, though for other reasons. While they had failed at their attempt to end Visla Maktan once and for all, it had been through no error or fault on their part. It was simply bad luck, as was wont to happen on occasion.

Their intel had been accurate. That was important. And their ingress into the fortified estate had been successful. If not for the unexpected appearance of a hapless courier, they would likely have been able to complete their task.

The mishap had also almost certainly spared them a

significant amount of harm. With the dozens of hidden guards, each of them skilled in the use of their shimmer cloaks, it would have been a difficult escape even with their own camouflage in place and after having drunk deeply of the visla's power.

It had made sense for there to be a robust security presence lurking around the grounds, but this had been a bit much. Of course, a visla on the Council would have a solid defense strategy and guards close by.

In fact, the only reason Visla Ravik had fallen as easily as he had was due to the battle he had been caught in the midst of. Had his men not been dealing with hordes of combatants rushing them, they'd certainly have provided the man an additional line of defense. But Ravik was a powerful caster, ready for all comers, and cocky because of it.

But it had not been brute strength that overcame him, but rather, a clever bit of misdirection. Hozark's injuries had been feigned, or at least exaggerated, causing the man to discount him as a threat.

It had been the last mistake he would ever make.

"How has the boy behaved?" Hozark asked after they touched back down on Arkoval.

Master Prombatz nodded his greeting to his fellow Master and associates as they strode into his residence.

"He is doing quite well, actually."

"Where is he?" Laskar inquired. "It's unusually quiet for having the kid around."

"Training with Aargun," Prombatz replied. "We shall join them momentarily. But first, tell me, was the attempt a success?"

"I am afraid not, Brother," Hozark replied. "The intelligence was sound, and our ingress successful, but, as is known to happen, an unexpected variable was inserted themself into the mix."

Prombatz nodded knowingly. More than a few of his

contracts had suffered such events over his lengthy career. It simply came with the territory.

"I am sorry to hear it, Brother."

"It is the way of things," Hozark replied with a little shrug.

"Indeed. Well, come along. We shall join the others. I am sure your young friend will be happy to show you what he has learned in your absence."

The Ghalian master led his guests through the building to a small courtyard surrounded on all four sides by high walls. Muting spells shielded them from any outsider hearing the goings-on within. So far as anyone in the area knew, this was just another unremarkable building, like any other.

The truth, however, was a different matter. Most notably, it currently housed several of the deadliest killers in the galaxy.

"Hozark!" Hap blurted out when he saw his friends' arrival.

"Hello, Happizano," he replied.

Aargun turned slightly and nodded to the new arrivals. Had it not been for his lack of eyes, it would have seemed as though he was looking right at them. His other senses were picking up the slack for his missing eyes and had become even sharper, it seemed.

He was doing well. Recovered from his ordeal and well past merely recovering to a state of health, Aargun was thriving. And not just with the joy of training his young friend. He had also been gradually learning to cast stronger spells without the use of his tongue. They were still the most minor of things, utterly inconsequential for an assassin such as he, but the mere fact he could cast silently at all was a marvel.

"Hey, check this out!" Hap called out.

He turned to face a wooden target far across the courtyard and drew his small dagger from its sheath. The boy paused a moment, collecting his thoughts and focusing on his goal, then hurled the blade in one smooth motion.

The knife flew true, more or less, and sank deep into the

target. Hap had tapped into his magic to help guide it and add force to the throw, as he'd been shown. And, to his delight, the concept was finally sinking in and becoming second nature.

"Well done, young Jinnik," Hozark commended. "A most impressive throw, indeed."

Laskar, however, was not impressed. This was one thing he too had skill at, and he seized the opportunity to show off. His own knife flew across the open space, sinking into the target's center with a solid thunk.

"I don't see what the big deal is," he said with a cocky grin, then strode over to retrieve the two blades. He sheathed his own and handed Hap his smaller knife. "Don't get me wrong, you're getting better, but there's a long way to go."

"Always with the ego," Demelza sighed. "It is not a competition, Laskar. He is but a child, young enough to be your own. Of course you are more proficient. You are an adult with years of experience under your belt."

"She is correct, Laskar," Hozark noted. "And it is unbecoming a grown man to belittle the accomplishments of a hard-working youth."

"Yeah, yeah," Laskar grumbled, chided by not one but two Ghalian, his little show of skill downplayed. "Hey, Hozark," he said, rebounding from the ego hit. "I forgot to ask you earlier. Was your ex there? That Samara chick? It must have been tough, seeing her with Maktan, I bet."

If an emotional response had been what he had expected, Laskar was going to be disappointed. Hozark ignored the man's tone. He was impulsive and childish in his ways despite his years, evidenced by his defensive remark, but he was still a damn good pilot and part of their team, even if abrasive at times.

"She is not my ex," he replied casually. "And no, there was no sign of Samara there."

"She might have been cloaked too," the copilot noted.

"And I would have sensed her."

"But she's a Ghalian. A talented one at that, from what you say."

"One of the best, indeed. But I know her magic."

Laskar shrugged, his little dig not making so much as a dent in the assassin's stoic armor. "Weird, though. I mean, she's working for him. Your ex and the Council's big bad visla. You'd think she would have been there."

"Whatever task he has her performing, she was not present anywhere nearby, from what I could discern," Hozark replied calmly.

Prombatz and Demelza watched the exchange impassively, but both noted Laskar's attitude. It seemed that despite his bit of relaxation and respite in the ersatz spa facility, he was still a bit grumpy. And now, like a child, he was having a bit of a tantrum, though in his far more restrained manner. At least his age provided that modicum of maturity.

"Well, it's probably for the best that she wasn't there," the copilot continued. "No one wants to fight a crazed, vespus blade-wielding assassin lady, anyway. I mean, except you, I guess. It's like some kind of love-hate thing, isn't it?"

"Neither, dear Laskar," Hozark replied.

"Hozark," Prombatz interrupted, "there is a matter I would discuss with you, if you have a moment."

Hozark turned back to Laskar. "If you will excuse me, we can continue this later," he said, then walked off with his fellow member of the Five. "What is it you wish to discuss?" Hozark asked when they were clear of the courtyard and well on their way toward the building's kitchen.

"Oh, I merely thought you might enjoy a cool beverage after your long trip," Prombatz said with an amused grin. "Away from that rather abrasive man."

Hozark chuckled. "Thank you, Brother. I would be delighted."

. . .

Evening brought with it a sense of relaxed calm to the reunited group. Hap and Aargun had enjoyed Demelza's rather robust addition to their day's training exercises, and all three of them were famished by the time dinner rolled around.

Hozark and Prombatz had taken the opportunity to engage in a little private training of their own, the two master assassins working through forms in private.

While the vast majority of the time they performed for up-and-coming Ghalian students, this was one of those rare occasions allowing them the freedom to practice things in which only the upper echelons of the order had been trained.

Each Ghalian developed their own personal style as part of their evolution through the myriad fighting systems in which they spent their days and nights, but it was only at the highest levels of the order that two masters could really let their foot off the brakes and show their truest forms.

Occasionally, injury would occur, even among the best of them. It was only natural. But the vast majority of the time the combatants would emerge from their session with no more damage than a few scrapes and bruises, which a simple healing spell could easily repair. And a good meal only added to the recovery.

The group tucked into their meal with particular gusto, and conversation was held to a minimum by the food rapidly filling their face holes. Finally, after a rather satisfyingly light dessert of whipped fruit in a pastry shell, they all settled down for a casual bit of conversation over a post-dinner tea. They were in the midst of a lively discussion on the merits of single versus dual blade wielding in combat when there was a knock at the door.

Prombatz excused himself and returned a moment later with a young Ghalian dressed in clean, simple attire. On his hip rode a wide pouch. A courier.

"He has requested to speak with you, Demelza," Prombatz said.

"Thank you," she replied with a nod, then rose from her seat. "If you will all excuse me a moment."

Demelza led the young man from the room into one of the adjacent chambers and offered him a seat. He politely declined.

"You have been requested," he said simply.

"Oh? By whom?"

"Master Corann," he replied.

Demelza nodded once. It was all he needed to say.

"I shall depart at once. Do you head back that way?"

"This was my only task in this system."

"Then please tell Master Corann I shall see her shortly."

The messenger bowed slightly, then took his leave. Demelza walked back to join the others, her arrival interrupting the conversation that had begun again in earnest.

"Everything all right?" Happizano asked.

"Yes, everything is fine. I have to go see Corann," she said, her attention focused on Hozark. "I shall be departing at once."

"Fly safe, Sister," Hozark said. "And give Corann my greetings. I shall visit her soon."

"I shall inform her, of course."

Happizano hopped up from his seat and ran over to give her a farewell hug. She reciprocated, though a bit awkwardly.

"Come back soon!"

"I shall try, Happizano," she replied. "I hope to see you all soon."

With that, she bade her final farewells and headed out to her shimmer ship. A few minutes later, she was gone.

CHAPTER FIFTEEN

The flight to Corann's home was uneventful, and Demelza made good time, even in her small craft. Uzabud's mothership could handle far longer jumps, but there was no need for such a thing at the moment. The message had requested her presence, but it had not been one of urgency.

Demelza flew in casually and landed in plain sight, her shimmer cloaking not once engaged. To those near Corann's abode, this was a familiar face returning. Not an assassin, but merely Demelza, the kindly older woman's niece.

It was a convenient front, and one that let the Wampeh come and go without raising an eyebrow, for only the tiniest fraction of a fraction of their species even possessed the gift, and of those, it was yet again a tiny percentage who actually became Ghalian assassins.

"Demelza! Lovely to see you again so soon!" Corann said warmly as she strode out to greet her "niece" on her front porch.

She waved sweetly to her neighbors as she gave Demelza a big hug.

"So glad to see you too," Demelza gushed. "Let's go inside. We have so much to talk about!"

The pair stepped back in through the porch door and dropped the façade as soon as they were inside.

"Thank you for coming so quickly," Corann said.

"Of course, Master Corann. I departed as soon as I received the message."

"And Hozark? Prombatz?"

"They are well, and they send you their best wishes. As does Happizano."

"Ah, the boy. Is he still practicing his spells?"

"Yes. And knife work as well. He is actually becoming fairly proficient at throwing a blade."

"I am glad to hear that," Corann replied.

"And what of the young Wampeh? The feral?" Demelza asked.

Corann's look of calm faltered a fraction. "He is well enough, though he is still quite wild. I do not know if we will be able to rehabilitate him, truth be told. His life prior to Council capture seems to have been rough, and only worse once in their grasp."

"I am hopeful he can be brought around."

"As am I. But at least he now has a name. Jokka is what he is called, and he seems to at least tolerate the moniker."

"It is a good name," Demelza said.

"I think so." Corann then shifted gears. "I heard about the troubles you had with Visla Maktan during your attempted contract on Trazzip. That he had a rather robust shimmer-cloaked guard force."

"It is true, there were a great many of them, which was something of a surprise. And they were quite skilled in the use of their shimmers, no less."

"This could pose a problem, should the visla become accustomed to piercing shimmer magic as a course of habit. And if he is surrounded by shimmers on a regular basis, he very well may."

Demelza knew this could be a problematic possibility, but there was little they could do about it. Or so she thought.

"I have a task for you," Corann said after a moment's thought. "One that may very well tax your abilities to the extreme."

"I am a Wampeh Ghalian," Demelza replied. "What would you have me do?"

Corann smiled at the woman's confident response. "I wish for you to search out something. An item of great power of a most particular nature. And one that has not been seen for generations."

"I can have the others prepped and ready in--"

"No. You must do this task alone," Corann interrupted. "You and you alone have the insight to achieve what I am asking of you."

"But Master Hozark, he is one of the Five."

"And you are more qualified than he for this task."

Demelza was taken aback. She never dreamed to compare herself to the great leaders of her order, yet Corann, the leader of the Five, was telling her she possessed whatever it was that the others lacked. She could do what the Five could not.

"I do not understand, Master Corann."

"You shall soon enough," the older woman replied. "There is an object. An item of some sort, that provides the user with the ability to avoid detection when using magic, even if that magic is wearing a disguise. It is said that not even a powerful visla can pierce its protection without much preparation."

Demelza suddenly realized what it was she was being sent to find.

"The *Quommus*?" she asked. "But that's just a myth. A legend. It doesn't really exist. No one even knows what it's supposed to look like."

A little grin creased Corann's lips. "So we all believed," she replied. "But new information has come to light in the wake of the tragedy that befell Xymotz."

Demelza felt a slight twinge at the name of Master Orkut's now defunct world. The greatest living swordsmith had fallen at Maktan's hands, and somehow, this task related to that.

"How does that pertain to the Quommus?" she asked. "It has only been spoken of in tales around fires late at night. It was just a made-up device."

"Or so we thought," Corann corrected. "But it seems that Master Orkut had taken precautions in case of the event of his untimely demise--though he had already made himself *seem* dead to all. Or so he had thought."

"What do you mean?"

"He was privy to certain things only a select few of his lineage were granted access to. Arcane knowledge passed down over the generations."

"But now he is dead."

"Yes, we have lost a great man. But his legacy lives on in his son."

"He mentioned him from time to time. That he possessed his father's gifts. And that was why Master Orkut was in hiding on Xymotz. So his son would never have to worry about the Council the way his father had."

"That much is true," Corann said. "But his son was also versed in other things. Secrets only to be revealed should tragedy fall. And word of his father's true demise reached his ears, at which point a sealed message held in his possession was sent to me. One that had been drafted relatively recently, it would seem. After your stay with Orkut, in fact."

"Oh?"

"Yes. And it mentioned you by name."

Demelza was taken aback by the revelation. She'd been laboring for Master Orkut for some time, hoping to gain his favor to craft her a sword of her own from his legendary hands.

But he was dead. And yet she was mentioned in his final correspondence with the order.

"Do you recognize this?" Corann asked, showing a drawn symbol to Demelza.

"Yes. It is one of the arcane sigils Master Orkut had stamped into some of his tools and possessions. There were an entire series of them, though he never explained their meanings to me."

Corann smiled a satisfied grin. "You are familiar with them, then. Good. Very good."

"Why is this good?"

"Because, it would seem he knew more of the Quommus than he let on. And, in fact, he may have been one of the few living beings knowledgeable in the ways of those who originally crafted it."

"But he never said anything of this to me."

"Nor would he. But you have spent the most time with him in recent years of any who are still living. And for this reason, you very well may succeed where so many others have failed."

"You want me to seek out the Quommus?" Demelza asked. "It is akin to a Spontis hunt. An exercise in futility. Many have sought it over the centuries, but none have ever succeeded."

"Yet, with Maktan's abilities to sense magical disguises, and all of the additional guards protecting him, the Quommus is precisely the thing you need if you wish to get close to him."

Demelza pondered what was being asked of her a long moment. "I shall do as you ask, Master Corann, but I worry this shall be a futile endeavor."

"Perhaps," Corann replied. "But perhaps not," she said as she handed her a folded parchment. "Take this. It contains Orkut's final message. It is cryptic, but you knew the man better than most. Perhaps you will be able to make sense out of it."

Demelza knew better than to protest that she really barely knew the man at all. "Thank you, Corann. I shall do my best."

Demelza then took her leave, making a friendly, loud show of it for the neighbors as she boarded her ship, carrying a large basket of fresh-baked goods, as was Corann's habit. Those she would leave with Happizano and the others.

It would take but a moment to stop and inform them she would be away, and possibly for some time. Then she would begin her search in earnest. Whether it was a wild goose chase, she would find out soon enough.

CHAPTER SIXTEEN

Uzabud had long ago given up his pirating ways for the somewhat more relaxing lifestyle of a smuggler and ship-for-hire, though he did still specialize in the more adventurous of tasks and potentially dangerous of cargo.

But ever since Henni had been kidnapped right in front of him, blasted unconscious and hauled into a Council ship by Maktan and Ravik's forces, he had found himself traveling down the slippery slope toward his former self. Not the gregarious pirate who was quick with a song or a funny tale.

The *other* one. The one people didn't talk about.

That Uzabud had been thought long vanquished. But it seemed that in times of extreme duress, such as when a member of his crew was taken prisoner to have lord knows what sort of experiments performed upon her, that deeply buried bit of aggression came clawing his way back to the surface. And he was *pissed*.

"I said I don't know!" the bloody-faced man twice Bud's size said just before the angry pirate's fist smashed into his already broken nose yet again. "Please, I'll tell you whatever you want to know. Just stop hitting me!"

"I think you're lying to me," Bud growled, cocking his arm for another go.

"I swear, it wasn't my ship that took her!"

Bud paused, the konus on his wrist glowing faintly, but the charge lessening as he held back, to the relief of the man on the receiving end. Bud had been using an unusual technique in his "enhanced" questioning. One he'd learned from his travels with one of the deadliest assassins in the galaxy.

He was using his konus to amplify his punches, while simultaneously casting healing spells, allowing him to inflict maximum damage, and, thus, pain, while not actually killing the target of his rage.

If Hozark had seen him in action, he would have likely been quite impressed at the combined spells his friend was weaving within one another. For a layman to cast in this manner was highly unusual. But, then, this entire situation was unusual.

"You were bragging about your time with Visla Ravik. All the worlds you had helped subjugate. You were part of the group that attacked Inskip."

"No, I wasn't with them."

"Liar."

Bud's fist slammed into the man's face yet again. Interestingly, this entire exchange had been taking place in a rather crowded tavern. It was a rough and tumble sort of establishment, but nevertheless, the beating Bud was handing out was a bit much, even for this place.

The crowd was watching from a distance, the lot of them held at bay by a small band of particularly hardy pirates, led by a Valkyrie of a woman who towered over most of them. Lalaynia had never seen Bud in quite such a state, and that was saying something, given the years they'd flown together.

He had been a near indispensable part of her crew in the early days, and she would not have risen so quickly to the upper echelons of piracy without his capable hands piloting her ship.

Now she had moved on, flying a larger and far more deadly craft with a likewise larger and equally deadly crew. But she and Bud had come up in the pirating world together, and she felt she owed him something of a debt, though more out of friendship than actual obligation.

"You almost done?" she called out loudly across the tavern.

Bud seemed to remember where he was at the sound of her voice, and the enormous, yet blubbering man before him was clearly of no use.

"Yeah. We're done here," he said, releasing the man, who slumped to the floor. He then turned and stormed out the front door.

Lalaynia and her men stepped back from the group they'd been keeping from interfering. It was tense, but as none had actually been harmed in the process--aside from the poor fellow Bud had been interrogating--a relatively calm exit was made while the tavern's proprietor looked on.

"Sorry for the inconvenience," Lalaynia said as she tossed him a small pouch of coin. "For your trouble. And the mess."

Minutes later, they were all safely back aboard her ship and quickly rising from the planet's surface. As soon as they were clear of the atmosphere, her pilot jumped to a nearby system. One where Bud hadn't made quite such a mess. It was a far better place to reassess and adjust their plans.

Bud was sitting in the galley when the young pirate he'd known since his earliest days came looking for him.

"Bud? You okay?"

He looked up at the fresh-faced youth. The boy had filled out even more since he'd last seen him. Wiry. Strong. A sharp look in his eye. Some were made to follow, but young Saramin was clearly made of hardier stuff.

"What's up, kid?"

"Lalaynia asked that you come to her quarters," he relayed.

Bud knew he had gone a little bit overboard back there, so

this wasn't entirely unexpected. "Okay," he said, slowly rising to his feet. "Better get this over with sooner than later, I guess."

He walked the corridors, reflecting on the day's efforts and their disappointing lack of results. Before he knew it, he was at Lalaynia's door.

"Come," she said as the chime sounded.

"Hey, Laynia. Saramin said you wanted to see me. Look, I'm sorry I didn't get better intel from that--"

"Shut up and sit down," she said, gesturing to a nearby seat as she poured two tall glasses. "Let's have a drink, you and I."

"No thanks. I'm really not--"

"You don't understand," she said with a bit more force. With her *captain's* voice. "*Let's have a drink.*" It was not a request.

Bud accepted the glass and took a sip. He raised an eyebrow. This was the *good* stuff. Normally that meant a celebration, but he had a sneaking suspicion that was not the case today. She sat across from him and sipped her own drink, quietly staring at her friend a long while before finally speaking.

"We've known one another a long time, Bud."

"That we have."

"And we've been through a lot. More than most would believe."

"Some good times, those," he agreed with a bit of nostalgia.

"And in all of those years, I never once felt that I had to watch my back around you. Not once. But today? That shit you pulled?"

"Look, I know it was a bit extreme. But the guy--"

"Bud, you were reckless. It was a crowded location, unsecured, and potentially packed with that goon's friends. We were lucky only a few were there or it could have devolved into a real problem for all of us."

"But the guys are more than capable--"

"That's not the point," she cut him off. "There are ways to do these things, and that was not it. You going off the plan like that is unacceptable. You're better than this, and you know it." She stared hard into his eyes. "We're friends, Bud, and I want to help you, really I do. But I have a responsibility to my crew as well, and I won't jeopardize their lives for no reason. So get that cold, in-control edge back before you get yourself, and the rest of us, in a mess we can't just walk, talk, or buy our way out of. We clear?"

Bud knew she was right, and the realization of what he'd really done sank in. Her point was indeed clear. And it hurt that she'd actually had to say it. He was her friend and colleague, and it should never have needed voicing at all.

"Yeah, we're clear," he finally replied. "Shit, I'm sorry, Laynia. I fucked up."

"Yes, you did," she shot back, then downed the rest of her glass. "Keep your head on straight and we're all good. Now, drink up and get the hell out of my quarters. I need some shut-eye after all that nonsense."

Bud emptied his glass in a gulp and rose to his feet. "Captain," he said with a nod, then stepped out her door, heading for his own bunk. He had a lot of thinking to do. Or sleeping. Or both.

CHAPTER SEVENTEEN

The away team who had accompanied Bud and Lalaynia on his impromptu interrogation were all gathered in the pirate ship's spacious galley, a facility large enough to accommodate the main bulk of the crew at a single seating. Those who eat and bond together tend to fight harder together, and Lalaynia thought the modification was well worth the expense.

It was still too early for dinner, but Bud had something he needed to get off his chest. And in the process of making amends, he was cleaning out his personal supply locker as well.

"What's with the spread?" a stout turquoise-skinned man named Otsmund asked. His hands were up in a questioning gesture, but his pair of mid-torso tentacles were already grabbing delights from the assorted delicacies laid out in front of them.

"It's my way of saying I'm sorry," Bud replied. "Look, I really messed up yesterday, and it put you all at risk. It was stupid and selfish of me."

The pirates shifted a bit, uncomfortable with this unexpected show of open emotions. Bud really *had* changed in his years away.

"Hey, it's no big deal," Otsmund said, clapping him on the shoulder. "We're men of adventure. It was nothing we couldn't handle, right, fellas?"

A chorus of agreement rang out, though some of the mouths were muffled by the food they'd been unexpectedly presented. Bud had intended to use the crates of pricey goodies as bribes, but he had more than enough aboard to make up for his mistakes and still have a decent stash should the need arise.

The thing was, it *wasn't* all right. Not by a long shot, and they all knew it. But Bud had come through with an apology, and an impressive one by pirate standards. And with that, it was now water under the bridge.

Of course, had he *truly* screwed up, he'd have had to throw a proper feast far greater and far more expensive than this little nosh. Fortunately, he had not made a blunder of that magnitude in many, many years, and he had no desire to start now.

Lalaynia watched the entire exchange from the doorway, where she was casually leaning. She caught Bud's eye and gave a little nod of approval. All was well aboard her ship once more, and they were good. The pirate captain gestured for Bud to join her while the men stuffed their faces like kids on a sugar bender.

"Nicely said, Bud."

"Thanks, Laynia. And again, I really am sorry about yesterday."

Lalaynia nodded once but said nothing. Bud noted, however, that a faint smile was threatening to escape her lips.

"What's so funny? Lalaynia, what aren't you telling me?"

She let out a little chuckle and punched him in the shoulder. "Oh, Bud, how I've missed your antics."

"Uh, not exactly following you, here."

"Of course you aren't," she said, her grin broadening. "The thing is, while yes, I was upset with your shenanigans, your ridiculous little display in the tavern did actually manage to help your cause a bit."

"What are you talking about?"

"While you were so focused on the muscle, a rather nondescript fellow from a cargo ship that just happened to be loading up nearby slipped outside to make a skree call to his ship. It also just so happens that one of my inside men has been prepping to do a little hijack job on that particular ship––it was a rather tasty cargo, after all––but when he overheard their conversation, he reached out to me, and I put the plan on hold."

"What did he say?"

"Well now, *that* was quite interesting. Our little skree-calling friend alerted his captain that there was someone roughing up one of Ravik's former goons in town. Someone who was looking for *the girl*."

"*The girl*?" Bud asked. "He said it like that? Like he knew who we were looking for?"

"Now you're getting it."

"Wait, you knew this *yesterday*?"

"Yep."

"Then why the hell didn't you say something?"

"Because you were pissing me off, Bud. And with the way you were acting, all flying off the handle like that, I thought you deserved a night of shame to think on it."

Bud's temper flared a moment but was quickly quenched. She was right and he knew it. He'd messed up, and there was no one but himself to blame for it. But now? Now there was something to go on. Actionable intelligence. Lalaynia watched the gears turning in her friend's mind.

"Yes, Bud. I can see you wondering, so I'll spare you the suspense. My man on board their cargo ship is still embedded and is keeping tabs on them. The hijacking is on hold for the time being, so he'll just be riding along, playing his part and reporting in as he can."

"And what about Henni?"

Lalaynia rested her hand on his shoulder. "Bud, you have to

relax and go with this. For all we know the lead will turn out to be a dead end. There's just no way to tell. And for that reason we will be continuing on as we have been, following other leads and tracking down your violent little friend."

"Thanks, Lalaynia. I can't tell you how much this means to me."

"I think I understand. And don't you worry, if that ship winds up anywhere notable, our inside man will let us know as soon as he's able. But it's not one of Ravik or Maktan's craft that he's aboard, so for now it seems they're just a simple cargo ship making its rounds."

"Ravik's dead."

"Yes, I know that, Bud. But that doesn't mean all of the resources that were under his control have just suddenly evaporated into thin air. Those crews and vessels are slowly being absorbed by the other members of the Council. And his brother, of course, though I don't think that poor sap is going to manage to claim his familial seat the way things are going."

"Good. One less Council member from the Ravik bloodline would make the galaxy a better place," Bud grumbled.

"Come on, now. You know better than that. Sometimes the evil you know is far preferable to whatever might come next."

Much as he hated to admit it, he knew she was right.

"So, if that ship doesn't do anything interesting, will you still take them?" he asked.

Lalaynia paused for effect, giving Bud a long stare. "I'll wait, for your sake. But not too much longer. That score has been a long time coming, and it cost me a hefty amount of coin to set up. They'll still be visiting other systems and loading the ship for a little while longer if my intel is correct. But when it's full to the gills and ripe for picking, I'll have to move on it whether we have word of your friend or not. You understand how it is."

"I do," he replied. "Only a fool would let an opportunity like that pass."

Lalaynia smiled wide. "I knew you'd understand." She clapped his back with a grin. "Now, why don't you go socialize with the others. I'm sure it would do you as much good as it would them."

"I don't know, Laynia."

"I do. Stop your moping and get your ass over there. That's an order."

"An order? Are you suddenly my captain again and not my friend?"

"Who's to say I can't be both?" she shot back. "Now go eat, drink, and be merry. Don't make me force you."

Bud chuckled, resigned to his fate. "Okay, I'm going."

"Good. And don't worry, if I hear anything, you'll be the first to know. But breathe easy. Knowing your friend, I have a feeling she'll be just fine."

CHAPTER EIGHTEEN

Visla Dinarius Jinnik was still damp with sweat though he'd been lying on his low cot for a good half hour since being dumped back in his cell. He'd lain there for some time before sitting up to drink some water, at Henni's insistence, then flopping back down for a bit longer.

"Eat something," Henni said through the invisible divider separating them.

"In a minute. I just need to rest a bit longer."

"No, you need to eat something," she insisted. "*Now*. And don't give me any lip."

The visla, one of the most powerful magic users she had ever seen, was seemingly as weak as a child after yet another session at the hands of their captors. They were draining the man of his power, though not without some difficulty. One such as Jinnik would not give up his magic without a fight, no matter what tricks they might employ.

Additionally, now that he knew his son was safe and out of the hands of his captors, he had begun resisting their efforts even more. Weakened as he was, he could not fight them outright, nor could he let them on to the fact he'd learned the true status of his boy. That would be bad.

If they knew he was aware of their ruse, they would likely pull out all the stops and drain him to within an inch of his life, not only to take his power, but also to prevent him from rallying his strength to make an escape. Or worse, to take his revenge.

Even with their restraint, however, the process was taking a toll. Every time he was returned to his cell after a session in the draining chair, Visla Jinnik looked just a little bit weaker. As if his base level of power was taking longer to restore itself.

Henni looked at his ashy complexion as he forced himself upright to eat some of the food remaining on his tray from the morning. He did not look well at all.

"They'll kill you if they keep going like this. They're taking too much," she said.

Visla Jinnik flashed a tiny smile. "Perhaps. But I must resist. I cannot allow them to use my power to harm others any more than they already are."

"But the chair."

"Yes, they will take it from me by force, but I won't make it easy on them."

Henni fixed her sparkling, galactic eyes on him, a look of concern clear on her face. "If you fight them too hard, they just might kill you."

Jinnik sighed and chewed another bite of stale bread he'd saved from his earlier meal, then washed it down, a bit painfully. The last session had apparently taken more out of him than he cared to admit.

"Perhaps they will," he finally said, clearing his throat. "But I feel that it will not be an intentional act if they do. Not yet, at least. Whatever it is Visla Maktan has planned, he needs power, and a lot of it. And if he's still got his men powering his weapons from me, that means he does not yet possess another means to do so."

"But what if they find one?"

"They very well may, eventually. They think you could be such a source, but it seems their process does not work on your unusual magic, and if they are unable to tap into your gift, they will still need me. For now, anyway."

Visla Jinnik slowly rolled his shoulders, stretching out the aching muscles of his neck and back, then rose to his feet and walked to the chair he'd left sitting at the invisible partition between their cells. The magic was still holding strong, he could feel. Whoever had cast the spell was keeping it refreshed.

"Are you ready for some more practice?" he asked his violet-haired friend.

"Now? Aren't you tired?"

"I am not the one training," he replied. "So, what do you say we get to it?"

Henni reluctantly moved to her now-familiar training spot--a small patch of the floor in the middle of her cell--and took a seat on the smooth stone.

"Remember what you've been focusing on. Not only the words in your head, but the intent behind them. Push with your *will*, not the words alone."

Henni had been gradually expanding her reach with the powers contained in her diminutive frame, and Jinnik found himself thrilled at her progress. He had hoped to begin training his son in the finer points of harnessing his magic in the coming years now that he was finally old enough, but this hot-tempered young woman was proving to be a most rewarding pupil. And with his incarceration and enslavement, Visla Jinnik had found his ego deflated and his appreciation for the little things greatly enhanced.

It was far from ideal, but it did make him a much better teacher than he would have otherwise been. And hopefully he would apply those newfound skills in training Happizano; should he survive his imprisonment, that is.

Henni closed her eyes a moment to focus her inner strength. It was something the visla was trying to train out of her before it became a habit, for the simplest of things, such as closing one's eyes in battle, could lead to a rapid demise.

Her eyes snapped open just a moment later. She only required a brief moment to compose herself. It had been becoming easier and easier to tap into that magical state of mind now that Jinnik's tutelage had keyed her in to what she needed to focus on.

"Move the chair," Jinnik instructed.

Henni turned her attention to the chair in her cell. It was a clunky, solid item, no doubt made that way so angry prisoners could not hurl it at the guards when they came to retrieve them. Her eyes brightened in the dim light, the sparkling galaxies contained within glowing faintly.

With a concentrated effort, she cast her spell, thinking *push!* as she directed the magic at the chair. But rather than the chair moving, Henni found herself sliding backward across the cell on her rear. Not exactly what she had in mind.

"You are getting better," Jinnik noted. "Very impressive."

"I was supposed to move the chair, not the other way around," she groused.

"Yes, well, you do not weigh much, now do you?" he said with a chuckle.

"It's not my fault I'm small."

"I know. Forgive my mirth. But do not worry, we will work on the anchoring portion of your casting next. Normally it is not required so soon, but most do not show your strength and acuity so quickly. It may be the Zomoki-like power you possess. Or you may just be good at it, I really can't say."

Henni seemed a bit uncomfortable with his words, though she did a fairly decent job of keeping that to herself. Nevertheless, he was a man of both power and perception.

"Something is unsettling you, Henni. What is it?"

"To be honest, the Zomoki thing is kinda freaking me out a little. I mean, they're monsters."

"The Zomoki you see today, perhaps. But once, not all that long ago, there existed another kind of Zomoki. The Old Ones. Wise and powerful creatures with whom a few vislas even formed lasting bonds."

"But they're gone?"

"Yes. Dead, all of them. The last of them killed in the Council attack on Visla Balamar. But let us not focus on the negatives of the past, but, rather, on the positives of the present. You can cast as they could. Silently, without a single word spoken aloud. Do you have any idea how incredible that gift is?"

"Uh..."

"It is utterly incongruent with a woman such as yourself. It's what smells strange about you."

"Excuse me?"

"I'm sorry. I should clarify. I meant your magic. The smell of your magic. You see, some sense vibrations, others feel auras. You read people. Others, such as myself, can smell different flavors of magic."

"I never heard of that before," Henni said, curious what more he could tell her about herself.

"Oh, there are a great many gifts possessed by magic users. I will do my best to--" Jinnik abruptly fell silent. "They are approaching," he said, knowing full well that he was not who they were coming for. He had been drained far too recently. They were coming for Henni. "Be strong," he said as the guards entered the cell.

Henni held her tongue, simply rising to her feet, obstinate and fearless as she was ushered from the chamber.

CHAPTER NINETEEN

Henni's captors were leading her down the familiar corridor to the smelting facility where the dreaded *chair* was located. Visla Jinnik had been drained by the terrible device on such a regular basis they might as well have inscribed his name on it.

The young woman was not worried, however. They'd tried to use it on her on more than one occasion now, and they had achieved the exact same success rate.

Zero.

It amused her to no end.

"So, are you guys gonna get fired if you screw up again?" she said, egging on the guards. "Or maybe they'll just demote you to cleaning out the Bundabist pens."

Henni knew she was considered valuable to them, and as such she had quite a bit of leeway with her conduct. They couldn't harm her lest they reap the wrath of Visla Maktan, and none wanted to risk that. So, she talked as much trash as possible, poking and prodding them with the glee only immunity could grant her.

"With your horrible success rate you must be on your final warning by now, am I right?" she asked when the pair continued to ignore her. "I mean, the visla can't be happy with your constant failures. They really do pile up, don't they? I'd hate to be in your shoes when--"

"Enough!" the lead guard blurted, drawing his hand back to strike her.

"Don't do it," his comrade warned. "You know she'll be pissed if you rough her up."

"Yes, she will," Henni said with a nasty grin.

The guard turned to her, casting an equally cruel smile. "He wasn't talking about *you*," he growled.

For a brief moment, Henni was unnerved.

"What do you mean by that?"

"You'll see. Now keep moving!"

They shoved her along down the corridor and into the smelting chamber, but rather than strapping her into the chair that Visla Jinnik knew so well, they steered her across the chamber to where a gray-green-skinned woman sat reclining on a low seat. She was wearing a color-shifting, skin-tight suit that almost resembled fish scales, and she appeared to have gills on her stout neck just behind her ear nubs.

Her charcoal-gray hair had an oily sheen to it and was pulled back in a tight ponytail, leaving her broad forehead and black eyes exposed.

"Ah, there she is," the woman said in a coo that was both mellow yet also threatening.

This one was unlike the usual guards and weapons specialists, and her smile was warm and inviting. But the vibe Henni was getting was *not* good. There was something *dark* about her, and though she only sensed the briefest flash of it, Henni didn't like it one bit.

Like Corann, she realized, placing her finger on her discomfort. *This one's got that same feel.*

When she'd met the leader of the Wampeh Ghalian, Henni had instinctively read her and had sensed the thousands who had perished at the woman's hands. Her sweet, motherly exterior hid what was essentially a bloodthirsty monster capable of incredible carnage.

This woman was part of the visla's operation, so, despite her pleasant demeanor, given the company she was keeping and her presence in this facility, Henni reasoned she must be similar to Corann in that respect.

Henni reached out, willing herself to open up to the woman's true self. She'd been honing the skill with Jinnik's help, and though it was still entirely hit-and-miss, she was at least gaining the beginning of a degree of control. But with this woman it was nearly impossible to read her at all, save that initial flash.

"Oh, such a thorn in my colleagues' side," the woman said, slowly rising to her feet.

She was stocky in her build, solid, yet feminine in her movements. The skintight body suit she was wearing only seemed to accentuate her motions, while enhancing her frame. It was clear that she possessed a powerful musculature beneath that exterior.

She moved close and reached out, her long fingers gently caressing Henni's violet hair.

"Such lovely locks you have," the woman said.

Henni felt a strange tingling on her scalp.

"Hey, lay off, creep."

"Now, now. Don't be rude," the woman replied, then grabbed Henni by the head, her fingers pressing tightly against her head.

Henni shuddered as she felt the woman's magic probing her through the woman's fingertips. It was a horrible violation, and there was nothing she could do to stop it. Thankfully, a few short moments later, the woman let go.

"What the hell?" Henni blurted, confused and a little disoriented.

While her new torturer had been probing her with her dark power, Henni had been able to loop the connection back on the woman and had read her as well. For just the relatively short period her fingertips had been squeezing Henni's head, the young woman could read her like a book. And what she saw was horrifying.

This one was worse than the others. *Far* worse. A dark soul, indeed. And she had ill-intentions on her mind. She was not a reader in the sense that Henni was, that much was clear, but she did possess a somewhat similar gift.

"My, my. Aren't you an unusual one?" the woman purred. It was a horrifying sound.

"What's your problem, lady?" Henni shot back with a false bravado she was definitely not feeling.

"Problem? Why, there is no problem. At least, not now. You are a most interesting specimen, I must admit. Such a unique inner strength. And your resistance to our methodology? It's utterly unheard of. So much so that when I was informed of the strange problems my associates were having with you and our extraction chair, I couldn't help but wonder if you'd perhaps somehow come in contact with the Balamar waters."

"The Balamar *what*, now?"

"The rarest of the rare. Priceless. And something one like you would never have access to. But now I see what it is about you," the woman said with a smile that chilled Henni to the bone.

"Oh, you do, do you?" the young woman blustered.

"Indeed. It would seem you somehow possess a power not entirely unlike our ancient winged friends, though you spit sarcasm rather than fire. You also do not possess a scaled hide. With this Zomoki-like power, it is no wonder the chair will not work on you."

"Yeah, nice try with that," Henni said, enjoying her brief moment of superiority. Sadly, it was to be short lived.

"See what we mean, Boss? She's impossible," the nearest guard said.

"Yep, that's me. Henni the Impossible. And since your little chair-thingy won't work on me, you might as well cut your losses and just let me go now."

The woman leaned in close and smiled with a warmth that froze Henni to the core. "The chair might not work on you," she said, "but I think I have something that might."

Henni strained against her control collar, wishing ever so much to claw the woman's eyes out. But the magic held her back.

"Screw you, lady," she spat with venom.

"You may call me Niallik," the woman replied. "And I believe you will soon be changing your tune, whether you wish to or not." Niallik turned to the guards. "Please, bring her, if you would be so kind," she said, then strode casually from the chamber.

CHAPTER TWENTY

"Seriously?" Henni asked as she looked around the room. For a torture and power extraction chamber, it was not at all what she'd expected.

"You disapprove?" Niallik asked with a deceptively kind smile.

The violet-haired girl scanned the room for implements that might be used to torture her or otherwise force her to give up the power she was only now beginning to understand. But all she saw were a few seemingly random and quite unintimidating bits of apparatus that didn't appear to be made for torture at all, and a simple tub full of water.

It seemed as though she had gone from a potentially difficult situation into a rather easy one. Or so she thought.

"Over there," Niallik commanded.

The goons muscled Henni toward the tub of water the woman had gestured toward. From afar it had seemed innocuous, but as she neared, Henni could feel a malevolent tug from the water itself. There was power in it. Magic, and the bad kind at that.

A look of fear flashed across Henni's face, and she pushed back fiercely.

"I'm not jumping in no Balamar bath!" she blurted, windmilling her arms in a futile attempt at escape.

Niallik merely laughed. "Oh, my sweet, ignorant child. You think those are Balamar waters?" she said as she glanced at the guards, who seemed to find the proposition as amusing as she did. "Why, just a few drops of those waters are priceless. And an entire tub of it? Why, you could buy entire worlds with that amount of wealth. Systems, even."

"So, that's not those Balamar waters, then?"

"No," Niallik replied. "But I do think you will find this quite interesting nonetheless."

She nodded to the tub, and the goons pushed Henni forward. The young woman fought with all her strength, but the two men simply lifted her up off of her feet while Niallik engaged her control collar. The magic paralyzed her while the woman stripped her of her clothes.

Henni was turning red with fury, held aloft, nude, by her captors.

"Now, now. No need to be shy," Niallik cooed. "No one means you any harm. Not in *that* way, anyway."

She nodded to the guards, whereupon the two men dumped her into the tub, lowering her into a reclining position. The control collar's power quickly began to fade, but rather than fight to get out of the tub and flee, Henni found herself actually feeling quite good.

The water was warm, and it tingled ever so pleasantly on her skin. In just a moment she began wondering why she had been struggling to avoid the tub in the first place. This was comforting. This was good.

"Yes, that's it. Very good. You see? This isn't so bad at all, is it?"

Henni was doing her best to think up a snarky comeback,

but she was simply too relaxed to bother, drifting off into a comfortable nap, embraced by the tub's magical waters as they gently leeched out the tiniest trace of her power.

The young woman's inert frame was light, and with her finally not thrashing and struggling and being an all-around pain in the ass, the guards were able to maneuver her slumbering mass back into her cell with ease.

Visla Jinnik, drained as he was, watched from his cot, pretending to be asleep in hopes of picking up any carelessly spilled tidbits of information. The two men were relatively tight-lipped, however, and said nothing of any importance.

They had just dumped Henni onto her cot then turned and headed out, leaving her to recover.

"Henni, are you awake?" Jinnik quietly asked when they were gone.

She lay still, unresponsive.

"Henni, they're gone. You can speak now."

Still nothing.

Visla Jinnik reached out with his slowly recovering power, probing the girl's state even through the magical partition between them. It would cost him a bit of energy casting this particular type of spell, but he had developed a fondness for this young woman, and was actually concerned for her wellbeing.

Fortunately, it appeared that while she was soundly asleep, she had not been harmed in whatever process it was that had rendered her so. There were still some faint traces of magic lingering on her, but it was unlike any the visla had ever encountered. It was not good, though, whatever it was. Of that he was certain.

It would be some time before she would wake from her slumber, it seemed, and until then, he would not be getting any answers from his young friend.

. . .

Niallik was quietly sipping a steaming mug of herbal tea when the two guards returned to the draining chamber. The woman looked utterly at ease. Pleased, even, as she studied the small vial of glistening liquid in her fingers.

"She is back in her cell?"

"Yeah. Sleepin' like a baby," the nearest man replied.

"Wonderful," Niallik said with a contented grin. "That wasn't so difficult, was it?"

"Nah, not really," the man admitted. "And if you can do that, maybe we can finally get rid of that Jinnik fella. He's a real pain in our arses, if you know what I mean. Always fighting back and whatnot. He's not making any of this easy."

"Nor would I expect him to," Niallik said. "But no, we cannot be rid of the visla just yet. He may still be of use to us."

"But you were able to take the girl's power. So why do we need him anymore?"

"Because, my thick-skulled friend, the girl is an incredibly difficult and unusual subject."

"You can say that again."

"And normal extraction techniques have no effect on her, as you know. But my specialized method does seem to prove that it can, in fact, be done," she said, holding the tiny vial up to the light.

The swirling liquid inside gleamed as it flowed. The sparkle was akin to the light in Henni's galactic eyes.

Niallik watched it with fascination, then let out a little sigh. "It is, however, an extremely slow process, and at the end of such a great effort, all I was able to refine from all of that work was this. An entire tub's worth of expenditure, as well as a very difficult bit of casting, and all I could condense from it was this small amount. And after such a prolonged extraction session, no less. That is simply not acceptable. Not yet, anyway."

"Well, at least you got something from her. It's more than we'd been able to do."

"Precisely. But it is not enough. Not for our employer's needs. So, you see, we will not be ending the visla just yet. Not while he can still power our weapons. But we do have a promising new option on our plate. Now I just need to figure out how best to utilize her before Maktan and his lapdog lose patience."

CHAPTER TWENTY-ONE

Samara stood calmly in the emmik's receiving area, utterly unimpressed by the show of power and connections displayed prominently throughout.

Yes, he had been working closely with the now deceased Visla Ravik. And yes, he was also a vital henchman for Visla Maktan. But the emmik himself was only moderately powerful on his own, and while dealing with an assassin of her caliber, despite her being under his command, his attempts at intimidation were simply laughable.

That didn't stop him from trying, though, and her lack of reaction only served to irritate him further.

"It is not your place to question, Samara. You are merely a tool, and one being wielded at the visla's express command," the emmik stated. "No thinking. No back talk. You are not meant to think. You are meant to act. A tool to be wielded without question."

She knew he was correct, of course. He had been the Council overseer during the assault that had landed them the young violet-haired woman, and they had butted heads about it at the time. Taking young women prisoner was distasteful to Samara, though hers was not to question but to obey. But for a Ghalian assassin, taking a subservient role was not exactly an easy ask.

"This is not right," she said, repeating the same argument she'd been making ever since they snatched up the unusual young woman. "The girl is an innocent."

"Says the assassin," the emmik laughed.

"Even assassins have a code," she replied. "And the Ghalian abide by them."

"Good thing you're no longer a Ghalian, then," he shot back, knowing the barb would land but she would not dare strike him down. Not unless she wanted to face the fallout that would bring down upon her.

Samara ignored the comment, denying him the satisfaction of a reaction. "I may no longer be with the order, but that does not change my sense of honor," she replied, maintaining her composure. "And kidnapping and enslaving an innocent is abhorrent. Preying on those weaker than you for mere profit is a coward's game."

"You care to tell Visla Maktan that? He ordered this one's capture *personally*. But if you believe you know better than he, I can call him, you know. Send an urgent skree to him. Maybe he'll come visit us personally to have that discussion with you face-to-face."

Samara had dealt with Visla Maktan on a few occasions, and she knew better than to keep baiting his lackey, so she bit her tongue and let it pass.

"Smart girl," the emmik said with obvious relish. "Visla Ravik may have given you some leeway with that lip of yours, but he's dead now, and rest assured, Maktan will not be so generous."

The stocky woman they had brought in to work her special talents on their newest prisoner entered the room with an air of satisfied confidence. Like Samara, she had no fear of the emmik, only a toned-down air of obligation. But unlike the Wampeh, she had no compunction about experimenting on anyone. Not the visla, not the girl, no one.

"What is it, Niallik? You'd better have something for me," the emmik grumbled.

"Oh, I do," she said with barely suppressed glee. "The girl definitely has power. Precisely how much I can't judge. Not yet, anyway. And it is a *very* unusual type of magic."

"She made an entire ship jump several systems when she panicked, Niallik. Believe me, we all know she has unusual power."

"Well, yes, obviously. But your people have been unable to do anything about it so far."

"Again, we know. Get to the point, woman."

Niallik kept a neutral expression, but Samara knew full well the woman wanted nothing more than to plant her fist in the man's face. It was a feeling she was quite familiar with.

Niallik took a breath. This was work, and she was being paid, and quite well at that, so she let it go, as she'd done on far too many occasions for her liking--but to the great benefit of her personal wealth.

"Yes, of course," she said with a warm smile. "I'll just get to it, then. The girl is in possession of a type of magic I've only heard rumor of, and only a few times in my career at that. One thought to be a wives' tale. But it would seem she is the real thing."

"Which means?"

"She contains a variety of magic akin to that of the Zomoki of old, though somewhat different in its presentation. As you know, the visla has been utterly unable to tap the power from the Zomoki he's captured thus far. And like those, and the several Wampeh he's drained as well, this one *seemed* to be impossible to draw from as well."

Samara's look of outrage showed through her calm visage, despite her best efforts.

Niallik smiled warmly, enjoying twisting that knife a little.

"Oh, you didn't know about that?" she asked. "Visla Maktan has attempted this process of a few of your fellow Wampeh. Those who possess your unique gift. I think there may have even been a Ghalian involved."

Samara held back, but her every cell wanted to rip the woman's throat out with her fangs, consequences be damned. Instead, she stood quietly. A Ghalian did not give in to emotions, and she was still one, in spirit if not name.

"So what of this one?" the emmik asked. "She's been nothing but a pain in the ass since we captured her. Can we use her power, or is this just another waste of time and resources?"

"Oh, most definitely. But harvesting it will be a challenge," Niallik replied, holding up the small vial of iridescent liquid.

The emmik's eyes widened. "You did it?" he asked, excited by what this meant.

"I did."

"Excellent. Then we can finally eliminate that fool Jinnik. Drain him completely and ramp up production. The visla will be pleased to hear that—"

"You should have let me finish," she interrupted. "You may not kill the visla. He is the best source you have at the moment."

"But you said—"

"I said I was successful with the girl, but that harvesting her magic will be quite a challenge. This tiny vial, potent as it may be, was the result of an entire session, and its extraction required a great deal more effort than anticipated."

"So use more, then. Squeeze it all out of her!"

Niallik shook her head. "You don't understand. Either you wait patiently for me to perfect the process, or the girl dies from us pushing it too quickly. As Visla Maktan was quite clear about this one's worth, I think we both know which option he will prefer."

It was the emmik's turn to hold his tongue and grudgingly agree, though he was not thrilled by the turn of events. Samara enjoyed his tiny comeuppance, even as her face remained utterly impassive.

"What are you laughing at?" he growled.

"I am not laughing," she replied.

He studied her with a hard stare, noting the slightest hint of amusement behind her cold eyes. "Damn Ghalian," he said, then stormed out of the room.

Things were getting a bit messy, and Samara worried that they could get worse yet. With Visla Ravik dead, the reins were largely released, and that was not good. Ravik, as bad as he may have been, was at least a good buffer for Maktan. *That* one was *truly* power hungry, and she had already seen full well that he was willing to do just about anything in the pursuit of more of it.

For the time being, however, she would simply have to deal with the cards she had been dealt, even if that meant putting up with Ravik's former lackey and his newfound power trip. He was only an emmik, after all, and his reaction to his sudden rise in the ranks was somewhat understandable, though annoying.

"Is the girl back in her cell?" Samara asked.

"Yes. But she'll be out for a while. The process is a bit *draining*," Niallik said, casting a little smile at the blood-sucking killer. "Something I'm sure you can understand."

Samara ignored her. There was simply no point in engaging Maktan's newest henchwoman. So she didn't. Instead, and a bit to Niallik's disappointment, the deadly killer simply walked from the room without another word.

CHAPTER TWENTY-TWO

The lean, pale woman's presence in the smelting and weapons manufacturing facility had put the workers somewhat on edge from the get-go. They had known of her working for the two vislas, of course. Rumors were quick to spread, and they'd known of her for some time.

But when their entire operation on Gravalis was upended and forced to relocate on a moment's notice to a distant planet, seeing the Wampeh walking the halls of their new home had left them all a bit ill at ease.

She was a Wampeh Ghalian, after all. Or, she had been, anyway. Whatever her status with that organization, one thing was perfectly clear. She could end all of them in an instant without batting an eye, and though she was under Maktan's employ, there was still enough of a lingering sense of danger surrounding her that no one on the grounds was truly comfortable with her presence.

"Open the door," she said when she arrived at the holding chamber.

There were only two guests at the moment. Both of them wearing control collars and sealed into their cells. But the emmik had seen to it that there was a guard posted at the door at all times. Given the value of the pair inside, she supposed his paranoia made some sense, though if an intruder made it through the weapons smelting facilities and as far as the cells, he would have far more to worry about than that.

"I'm sorry, but Niallik has instructed me that no one but her and her staff are allowed to enter," the guard said.

Samara stood stock-still, fixing her unblinking eyes upon the man. She had no intention of harming him whatsoever, but she knew full well the unnerving affect her gaze could have and was wielding it to its maximum potential.

The poor man blinked and swallowed hard. She just stood quietly. The guard's gaze flicked to either end of the corridor, hoping someone with more authority might happen along to save him from this uncomfortable situation, but no relief was coming.

Samara simply continued to stare. The poor guard knew what she was and what she could do and was damn near soiling himself under the assassin's probing gaze. Finally, she twitched one eyebrow upward ever so slightly in a questioning arch.

"Um, I don't know," the guard stammered.

Samara added a minute head tilt to her expression.

"Well, I..."

Her arm crossing and sigh served two purposes. One, it showed her annoyance with the delay caused by his indecision. Two, it more clearly revealed the pair of daggers clearly strapped at her waist.

Of course, those, while useful, were only worn as a distraction. Only in the most dire of circumstances would she draw the weapons that were actually visible to others. Samara was a skilled assassin, and the weapon she would end you with, you would never see coming.

In this instance, the little display served its purpose well, and without the need for words expended in the pursuit of convincing the man to step aside.

"Well, you *are* with Visla Maktan," the guard reasoned. "And *he*'s the boss, so..."

He stepped aside.

"Thank you," Samara said, quietly disarming the wards guarding the door and passing through before the guard could even disable them for her.

It was only a minuscule waste of magic, but the effect it would have on the rest of the staff when the man blabbed how easily she passed through the protective spells would only serve to enhance her air of mystery. And in a place like this, having others wonder just what you might be capable of was not a bad thing, if for no other reason than it would make them leave you alone.

Samara resealed the door behind her and cast a muting spell on the threshold as she did so. Privacy was something she valued, especially in this place. And this was a visit she wished to keep to herself.

She padded silently to the cell and gazed down upon the slumbering girl. She could sense the lingering effects of whatever odd magic Niallik had used still keeping her under, but it was clear that it was slowly fading away and the captive's natural power was already restored with no lasting ill effects.

"Fascinating, isn't she?" a man's voice asked from the adjacent cell space.

Samara's keen eyes easily made out his shape in the dim light. Visla Jinnik. The father of the boy she had seen Hozark protecting. The man coerced into doing Ravik and Maktan's bidding. At least, up until recently.

He looked a bit ragged for a visla, and thin to boot, despite being well fed. Clearly, the constant forced draining of his power was taking its toll on the man. And yet, he still carried himself with the air of a man of his stature and power. Even imprisoned.

"Indeed, she is," Samara agreed. "And a strong young woman at that."

"Yes, most definitely," he agreed, not even bothering to attempt to conceal Henni's power.

By this point, they had figured out what was within her and were doing all they could to extract it. Lying and misdirecting would no longer work now that they'd managed to tap into it, even if it was only to a small degree. Samara, however, was not interested in that.

"So, do you think she has the power they believe she possesses?" she asked.

Jinnik paused a moment, as if in thought. "Well, she certainly does have some power to her."

"That is not what I mean. Do you believe she possesses the *unusual* power of which they speak? The power akin to that of the Zomoki?"

Jinnik thought a moment, searching for the right words. "That's hard to say," he replied, doing his best to protect the unconscious girl from further harm.

But he also knew that their captors had tapped into her magic, so there was only so much he could do in the way of misdirection. Bald-faced lies were out of the question, so he had to make do with careful wording as best he could.

Samara looked at the girl. "Hard to say, yet she is obviously a power user."

"She has some sort of power to her, that's for certain. And yes, it is an unusual variety indeed. But the girl is not skilled with it. In fact, before coming to this place, I very much doubt she even realized what was inside of her. So far as I've seen, it appears she has no idea how to even use it."

"I gathered as much. The sudden jump spell she cast would seem to bolster that belief," Samara noted.

This was an unusual turn, and one that caught Jinnik's attention. "You think that was out of her control?"

"It most certainly would seem that way, though the others undoubtedly harbor doubts about what she knows of her true abilities. I cannot help but wonder exactly what she is capable of."

"Well, it seems your friends are having a hard time stealing it from her. At least for the time being."

Samara's face did not shift, but a cool air seemed to form around her all the same.

"They are not my friends."

"Oh?" Jinnik replied. "Then why do you do this? Why serve these masters?"

Samara stood quietly a long moment, as if mulling over the question, though she clearly had no intention of answering.

"I have my reasons," she finally said, then turned for the exit. "Rest, Visla. You will need your strength."

CHAPTER TWENTY-THREE

Demelza's return raised something of a stir within the walls of Master Prombatz's home, though not for bad reasons. She had brought with her a wealth of treats from Master Corann, an update on the feral boy they had rescued, as well as a message only for Ghalian ears.

Happizano and Laskar both dug into the baked goods while the three Wampeh quietly discussed the news in another chamber.

"He is called Jokka now. While he is still quite wild, he does seem to be making at least some progress," Demelza informed them.

"It is all we can ask for," Hozark mused. "But what of this errand she wishes you to embark upon? It seems an unusual thing to ask of a Ghalian."

"I agree," Prombatz said. "Under most circumstances, yes, indeed. But it sounds as if Corann actually thinks she has found trace of the Quommus. Is that true?"

"It is the task I have been given," Demelza replied. "And I do not believe she would send me on it were there not substantial reason to believe in its success."

"I would tend to agree," Hozark said. "However, the Quommus has been sought by adventurers and treasure hunters for centuries. Longer, even. And its location, or even the proof of its existence, has never been held by the Wampeh Ghalian. What has changed in our absence?"

Demelza held out the parchment she had been given. "The last message from Master Orkut," she said. "It is quite cryptic, but Corann believes it shall lead to the resting place of the actual Quommus."

The two Ghalian masters examined the page. It seemed to be in Master Orkut's hand, and he *was* an old and very knowledgeable swordsmith with ties to a great many ancient orders, as those providing unique weapons oft tended to be.

"Imagine it," Prombatz said. "If she could truly obtain the Quommus, what an advantage we would have over our adversaries."

Hozark agreed with his Ghalian brother, but he also knew that relying too much on outside means to complete one's tasks could leave an opening for enemies to escape. Or worse, to counterattack.

But possessing a powered item that could mask their own power signatures could prove most helpful indeed. If Demelza could find it.

"She wishes you to go on this quest alone?"

"Yes, Master Hozark. Corann believes that my extended period working under Orkut gives me an advantage in interpreting his meaning and following the clues to the Quommus, should it in fact exist."

The master assassin nodded. Corann was right, of course. If this truly was the last directive of the reclusive bladesmith, Demelza was best prepared for this task. She had spent a great deal of time with the man, and though he would not admit it to her, it was clear the man held her in high regard.

"Then you shall begin at once," he said. "We shall outfit your ship with additional resources as might be needed for this task. Supplies, bribes, weapons. Whatever may speed you to your goal."

"Thank you, Master Hozark. But before I depart, I do wish to bid my farewell to Happizano. It may be some time before I am able to return, and I would make this as non-traumatic a separation as possible for him."

"Wise," he agreed. "We shall accompany you."

Hap was growing up far faster than a boy his age normally would, but he was still young, and having one of the few stable people in his world suddenly vanish could be a bit of a blow to him regardless of his strides toward manhood. He was still not even a teen, after all.

"You're going away? *Again*?" he griped when she came to tell him of her pending departure.

"Yes, I am," she replied. "And I shall not lie to you, Happizano. This may take some time, and I do not know when I shall return. But before I depart, I would very much like to see what you have been learning while I was gone. Has Aargun helped you with your knife skills?"

"Oh, yeah," Hap said, perking up a bit. "But there's been so much training. All the time, every day!"

Hozark, Prombatz, and Aargun all chuckled from where they sat. It was a feeling any Ghalian was well acquainted with.

"Life is training," Demelza said, repeating the words each of them had drilled into their heads when they first started on the long path toward becoming full-fledged Wampeh Ghalian. "Years of practice for those few seconds that matter most."

"I know, it's just tiring sometimes, is all."

"As it should be. The more you sweat in practice, the less you bleed in combat, Happizano. It is a lesson all Ghalian learn. And for most it holds true, but even then, sometimes no amount of training is enough."

"But you guys make it look so easy."

"Yes, it *looks* easy. But it takes many, many years of hard work, and blood and sweat to achieve this level. Remember, the ease of mastery comes only with the effort of training. And you are still on the early steps of your journey. But in time I believe you may become a great warrior."

"You really think so?"

"I do. Now, you were going to show me what you and Aargun have been practicing. How is your throwing progressing?"

Hap took a few steps from Demelza and turned to face the wooden target. In one motion, he drew his blade from its sheath and threw it. He used an unusual underhand motion that was a favorite among the Ghalian for both its speed and difficulty to detect before it was too late.

The knife flashed through the air, a bit off target, Demelza noted, but Hap's concentration did not break, and with a whispered nudge from his power, he steered it back on course, the tip digging into the wood with a satisfying thunk.

It wasn't the greatest throw ever. It wasn't even a particularly good one. But the boy was putting the pieces together surprisingly fast, and his progress was impressive for a non-Ghalian.

Aargun nodded his approval, his sharp ears registering the knife finding its target. He then threw his own in an unusual backhanded motion, the target not remotely lined up with his body. But, as Happizano had done, Aargun used his magic to steer the blade, curving its path and sending it home to the center of the target.

Demelza glanced at the others with a bit of surprise. Aargun had not uttered a word, yet she could sense his magical grasp on the blade had been strong.

"You are getting much better at silently casting," she complimented the wounded Wampeh.

Aargun smiled and gave a slight nod.

"Great, he can toss a knife," Laskar grumbled. "But all of this waiting around is *boring*. When do we get to do something? When do we take out Maktan once and for all?"

"Patience," Hozark replied. "Sometimes our lives are full of action, but other times we must wait. That, too, is part of the process."

The copilot merely grumbled and sank back into his seat, sipping on his tall drink.

"Indeed, it is," Demelza added. "And now I must take my leave of you all. I hope to see you again sooner than later."

She cut the farewell short, turning and heading to her ship without another word.

"When do you think she's gonna come back?" Hap asked.

"I cannot say for sure," Hozark replied.

"What about Bud? He's been gone a while."

"I know. But each person has their own mission to perform, and their timetables are their own. But, if fortune smiles upon our friends, we shall all be reunited soon."

"And with a new advantage, we hope," Prombatz added.

"What? You think Henni's an advantage?" Laskar joked.

"While she is amusing company, I refer to Demelza's quest," Prombatz replied. "We shall have to wait and see, however, though I hope her errand is not a futile one."

Hozark nodded his agreement. "If Demelza is truly as skilled as I believe her to be, we shall know one way or another soon enough."

CHAPTER TWENTY-FOUR

The fine red dust was choking, the omnipresent, swirling clouds covering nearly the entire terrestrial landscape on the backwater world. It was an utterly miserable rock in an entirely unremarkable system. And something of a shithole. A place the locals had taken to calling Muck.

It wasn't the planet's real name, of course. The name given to the world by its original colonists was Mulannis. But the oppressive heat, combined with the insidious grime that worked its way into every nook and cranny, regardless of clothing or protective spells, led to a sweaty sort of sticky filth that would accumulate across the damper regions of a person's body. It was far from pleasant, to say the least.

Hence the name.

Muck.

If not for the rich veins of ore used in the fashioning of konuses and other magic-retaining devices, the planet would likely have remained uninhabited. But with resources such as those, some semblance of civilization was always bound to follow. Coin, and the opportunity to make more of it, were powerful motivators.

Miners were by their very nature used to rather harsh and unpleasant conditions, but those typically abated once they returned from their day's shift to the surface. On Muck, however, it was just as bad up top, if not worse. At least in the mines the temperatures were a bit more pleasant, though a good haul could lead to a nice bonus, and that meant more cooling spells for the group housing.

It was easy for Demelza to blend in with this group of coin-hungry men and women. There were all sorts of races there, with the notable exception of the amphibians, whose gills and skin simply could not withstand the planet's harsh environment for any significant length of time.

Demelza didn't even have to cast a disguise spell. Not with the layer of red her body soon sported. And she fit right in with the raucous crews immediately. For a sturdily built, hardworking woman, no one much cared what color her skin was so long as she did her job. And she did her job well.

She had stopped off at a half dozen backwater worlds along the way before setting up on Muck. Master Orkut's cryptic message had been written not only in plain text, but also with a combination of minor spells and a smattering of arcane symbols peppered throughout the message. No one who read it would have the slightest idea what it meant. No one but someone who had spent time with the man.

The text, she realized, was a diversion. A false trail designed to send any who might intercept the parchment on a wild Bundabist chase. And she had very nearly fallen into that trap herself when something about the sigils caught her eye. After a moment's careful casting, she realized she had *felt* those curious markings before.

They were power runes. Symbols that channeled magic, but of the most ancient variety. She'd heard that there were secret, underground sects of craftsmen who still utilized that type of antiquated scribbling to communicate, and it seemed the aged swordsmith was one of them. He had written a message for none but those of his hidden clan. No one else would have the slightest idea what to do otherwise.

But Demelza had seen those markings before, and, given the recent nature of the message's drafting, it seemed a certainty he knew if the parchment found its way to her hands, she would recognize them. She had always had an impressive memory, even for a Ghalian.

"The anvil," she realized when one of the ancient sigils suddenly leapt out from the page at her as its familiarity made itself known.

She'd only seen it upside-down, but that was because it had been stamped into the very metal of one of Orkut's anvils. It was smaller than most of them, and tucked away in a corner. It was also very, very old, from what she could tell.

"Used for a very specific type of blade," he had told her with a curious little wink.

At the time, it seemed like it was simply for easier manipulation of some certain variety of hot metal. But now she realized the anvil no doubt possessed a unique magical property. One that was tapped when cooling metal was forged on its surface.

It had taken her a bit of digging to find other instances of that symbol, but at last her searching paid off. It appeared it was occasionally associated with a particular, antiquated religious sect. One still occasionally found in mining communities.

It made sense, actually. An anvil would be a logical item for a metal working and mining order to imprint their sigil on. But it seemed to be far more difficult to track down active temples of this group than anticipated.

She had quickly flown to several more worlds in the search, always coming up empty or mostly empty-handed. Eventually, however, she found the remnants of a few of the order's old temples. And from there, rumors of where the remaining members had been scattered. After that, it was just a matter of a lot of leg work and a liberal use of the Ghalian spy network to find the few temples still standing.

Most had been converted over the centuries, she found. Rather than smithing and metallurgy, the buildings now centered around other forms of commerce, typically agricultural. But some of the ancient carvings still remained in the stone of the temples, and Demelza was managing to piece together a rough translation of the additional symbols.

It wasn't a map, exactly. But it did provide her a means to narrow her search of the potential sites identified by the Ghalian network. And Corann had pulled out the stops for this endeavor, loosing every spare set of eyes and ears to relay what they could without jeopardizing their current assignments.

Possibilities began trickling in, and Demelza was making quick time of those closest to her.

It was this combination of bits and pieces of intel that brought her to Muck. But fortunately, and unfortunately, the temple on that particular world was still somewhat active, and it would take a bit of recon and careful planning to spend enough time inside it to do a thorough search for clues as to the whereabouts of the Quommus.

To start things off, Demelza decided she would do what made the most sense for one in her situation. Namely, she would spread some coin in the tavern, make a few new friends--ideally ones who just happened to frequent that temple--and then weasel her way into the building.

It was a bit more difficult than she had originally anticipated, though. Unlike most commerce worlds, this was a hardworking, but not hard-drinking, place. The heat and difficult labor made water a more sought-after commodity than alcohol, and tongues were quite a bit harder to loosen without that liquid relaxant.

Nevertheless, Demelza's skills at infiltration soon paid off, and she was comfortably nestled in with a small group of filthy but welcoming miners. It struck her as funny how all of the past weeks and months of trials and tribulations had led her to this, of all places. A backwater dust bowl, hanging out with this sweaty lot.

But *this* motley bunch just so happened to also be followers of the particular sect she was interested in. With a little gently placed suggestion, she would be invited to join them, no doubt, but her casual conversation about all things mysterious and mythological had not yielded her any results in the search for the Quommus.

"That thing? Sure, I've heard the stories. My mom told 'em to me when I was a little kid," said an enormous man whom she had trouble imagining ever being little.

"Yeah, some kind of sword, right?" asked a wiry woman with short-cropped burgundy hair that matched her lightly-scaled skin.

"No, it wasn't a sword," an older, heavily scarred miner said. "It's a scroll."

"Don't be stupid. A scroll wouldn't survive out in the world," the large fellow replied. "It's gotta be durable. Smaller. Portable."

"Like what, then?" the woman shot back. "Some kind of trinket? A belt? A freaking hat?" she asked with a laugh.

"Hell if I know. Like I said, I was just a kid when I heard those stories."

The discussion went on like that a short time, then drifted into other topics, including inviting their new friend to join them for the evening's visit to the temple, which Demelza readily accepted. Just as planned.

As for the Quommus, the discussion was quickly forgotten, the topic deemed not really worth spending any more time on. It wasn't surprising, though. The Quommus was one of those things everyone had heard of but never seen, and what it actually was, down to the size, shape, and very nature of the thing, had been lost to time centuries before. Many had tried and failed in the search for it, but finding an object with no idea what it looked like was an impossible task.

Fortunately for Demelza, the Wampeh Ghalian considered the impossible just another day at the office.

CHAPTER TWENTY-FIVE

"Wow, that's quite impressive," Demelza said as she followed her new friends into the imposing stone building looming at the town center.

It seemed a lot of the locals were heading that way for the evening's post-labor sermon.

"Yeah. Not bad for a backwater planet, right?" her extremely large new friend said with a proud grin.

His name, it turned out, was Garoosh, and he had been mining ore on this world for nearly seven cycles. Most got tired of the heat and dirt and gave up after only one or two, but not Garoosh. The man seemed to get a kick out of subjecting himself to extremes, for whatever reason. And his love of proving his worth in harsh conditions actually somewhat endeared him to the assassin.

He was in no way of the mindset required to be one of the elitest killers known, but for a casual, he was admittedly rather notable for his physical endurance and his resistance to pain. Two things you needed in abundance to survive more than a few cycles on Muck.

"Come on, we can get a good seat up front," Garoosh said,

waving to someone he knew who appeared to be holding a place for him.

"Slide over, Oona, we've got a newcomer here to hear the sermon."

"Name's Alanna," Demelza said. "Pleased to meet you."

"Pleasure's mine, Alanna," Oona replied. "You chose a good night to drop by."

"Oh? Why's that?" the disguised Wampeh asked.

"It's the end of the lunar cycle. Big night. You'll see," was all she got in reply.

Demelza looked around at the worn and battered interior of the building. It had survived this harsh environment for centuries upon centuries, but the clime had taken its toll in many ways. Paints on the frescoes had faded where the magic keeping them vibrant had been neglected. Structural members were worn and smooth from years of people passing, rubbing their hips or shoulders along the wall as they passed.

But there, among all of the confusing mix of symbols and artwork were what she had been looking for. Sigils. The runic symbols carved into the stone of the building itself. No matter how many times the structure had been rearranged and repurposed, the bones of the thing remained the same.

"Brothers, sisters, welcome!" a voice rang out.

Demelza turned her attention back to the source of the magically amplified sound. It was a middle-aged man in priest's robes. But unlike most religious folk she'd encountered, this one was rippling with solid muscle beneath the fabric. His forearms and wrists were visible outside the ends of his sleeves, and their thickness spoke to a life of hard work, even for a holy man.

Moments later, Demelza realized why.

The priest held up a large blacksmith's hammer, gleaming in the magical light, and began speaking to the assembled faithful. Here on this planet, it only made sense that one such as he would be leading this flock. Demelza focused her gaze on the side of the hammer when he stopped gesticulating for a moment.

Yes, there it is, she thought as she spied the same sigil as had been on one of Master Orkut's smithing implements.

On the dais with the priest was a large and ornately forged anvil, the sigils of their sect woven into the designs themselves. Where Master Orkut had a simple yet effective version, this was something altogether different. And it seemed to be barely used. An odd thing for what she'd learned about the sect so far.

The priest spoke to the congregation, praising their work and promising the gods would look down upon them with great pride at the quantity of ore they had brought forth for magical endeavors.

The forging of magic-possessing metal was profitable, and their goods would have significant value. It was making more sense why this group might have developed a means to hide their magic signature from others in the past. They'd have been a tempting target otherwise, and protecting themselves from roving thieves could easily be seen to have been a top priority, especially if those thieves were vislas.

And the Quommus would have been just the thing for that job. Whatever the hell the Quommus actually was, that is.

In addition to their approval of the quantities mined, it also seemed that the gods, though rich in sacrificed ore, wanted coin as well, though Demelza always wondered what exactly a non-corporeal deity needed it for. But the congregants dug deep without hesitation.

The assembled quietly tossed coin in the several baskets that were quickly passed through their ranks. Demelza, not wanting to offend, contributed as well, drawing a pleased smile from her new friends. The baskets were then whisked away for the finale of the service.

Demelza had expected some sort of symbolic sacrifice, as was common with so many cults and religions. Perhaps some fruit, or alcohol or bread, laid out for their deity in thanks. But she was mistaken. And she would very soon learn that the anvil was not merely ornamental after all. It was just not used to forge metal.

The beast was unlike any she had seen before. Smallish, perhaps standing a little higher than her waist. It possessed a bony head with thick ridges that ran from its nose all the way down its back, where sturdy haunches carried its mass with ease.

"Is he going to--"

"Shh. You'll see," Oona hissed, her eyes fixed on the beast being led to the anvil.

"In your honor, oh great ones. Grant us prosperity!" the priest said as his assistants pulled the animal's head onto the anvil.

Moments later the hammer swung true, the sheer force of the priest's arms cracking right through the animal's seemingly impenetrable skull and rendering it to mush. It was impressive, the strength the man possessed, but he was apparently not done yet.

The assistants quickly pulled the animal's remains farther onto the anvil, where the process was repeated, though with a much wetter thunk. Over and over this occurred until the entire beast, from tip to tail, had been pulverized.

As sacrifices went, it was one of the strangest, and bloodiest, Demelza had ever seen. She was a brutal killer, and the spectacle hadn't bothered her in the least, but it was no wonder the sect had faded away on more civilized planets.

"What a moving display," she said finally.

"Amazing, isn't it?" Oona said, her eyes shiny with excitement.

Garoosh nodded in agreement. "Next, they'll prepare the lunar feast for the priests with the remains."

"Great, if you like mashed bone in your meal, I suppose," Demelza mused.

Oona looked at her with shock. "Don't blaspheme!"

"I'm sorry, I didn't mean any offense."

Oona's hackles lowered, the apology accepted with a glance, if not words.

"Well, that's it for the service. You want to maybe come back to my place to have a little refreshment and talk about the finer points?" Garoosh asked with a warm smile.

Demelza knew exactly what he *really* meant. "Maybe in a little bit. But first, I'd like to stay a moment to take a look around. It's such an impressive building," she said, actually managing to sound sincere.

"Okay. I'll be at the tavern for a bit. Come meet me there if you find the mood takes you," he replied with a grin, then walked out confidently without waiting for a reply.

She had to give it to him, the guy was surprisingly smooth for a miner, but she had far more pressing things on her mind than pressing bodies with him.

The throng was thinning as she moved along the perimeter of the building. The tall stone columns had tapestries draped over parts of them, but much of the original sigils and carvings were clearly visible above. There seemed to be a pattern to them, but being so unfamiliar with them, it was difficult to make out what it might be.

"I am sorry, but the service is over now," a voice said.

She recognized it at once, though it was unamplified now. Demelza turned to face the holy man. She was a Ghalian, and at this proximity she could sense his power. An emmik, though not a terribly strong one. Still, the man had power of his own. That explained the strength behind his hammer swings.

"Oh, I'm new here," she replied in the most demure voice a literal killer of men had ever used. "Garoosh and Oona invited me to hear you speak. It was a wonderful oration."

"Thank you. I am Emmik Sitza. I am glad a newcomer would find my words moving. Are you considering joining our flock?"

"I'm not sure yet. I've only just arrived, after all. But the service was very moving. You have a strength to you that radiates through your words," she said, feeding his ego. "And I'm sorry if I overstepped," she said, gesturing to the emptying temple. "It's just this is all so new and thrilling, and I wanted to get a better look at this amazing art and architecture. This building must be quite old."

"Indeed, it is. One of the oldest of our temples in fact."

"Oh, really? Wow, that's amazing," she gushed, then pointed to a row of sigils on the nearest column. "I don't know if it's too old for you to know how to read it, but what does that mean?"

The emmik grinned, eager to show off his learning in the more arcane ways of his order. "That means 'blue sun,' and next to it is 'strong hammer.'"

She studied the markings, then turned to another set. "What about those? Do you know what those say too?"

"Of course. That line is a bit more flowery, but it says, 'The light burns bright, the two eyes of Orakis staring down from above.'"

"Wow, you really *do* know a lot."

"It is just the old language of our forbearers," he replied.

Demelza's enthusiasm was contagious, and soon she had the man eating out of her hand, happy to postpone his feast for a few minutes to show her the other art and carvings that graced his temple, translating them for her as he did.

Demelza, for her part, was memorizing every last one of them, her razor-sharp Ghalian mind creating a sort of mental Rosetta Stone of their meanings. In short order, she had compiled a solid list of nearly all of them.

"So does this one mean 'the red jewel?'" she asked.

"It does! You are a very quick study!" the holy man gushed. Clearly this woman could well become a very devout follower if she decided to join the order. "So, what do you think now that you've seen more of our sect? Do our teachings speak to you?"

"You know, they do, actually. I am thinking this might be a good fit after all. I'm so glad to have come tonight."

"Emmik, we are ready to begin the roasting ceremony," a temple assistant said as they quietly approached the duo. The rest of the temple had emptied while they spoke.

"Dear me, I seem to have lost track of time. But please, come back tomorrow, and let us carry on this discussion further."

"Thank you, I would very much like that," she replied. "But I was wondering, I would really love to study this amazing artwork just a little while longer. Might I stay for just a bit?"

He thought on it for just a moment, then smiled broadly. "Of course. Please, enjoy your time here. Ignatz, my assistant, will come around when you are finished and lock up behind you."

"Thank you so much. I really appreciate it," Demelza said with a fervent gleam in her eye as she scanned the walls and columns.

"It is my pleasure," the holy man replied. "And welcome to Mulannis."

CHAPTER TWENTY-SIX

Demelza was several systems away by the time her muscular new friend and the temple's holy man began to wonder where the recent arrival might be. But in the relatively short time she had spent within the structure, she had acquired more than enough of the data she required.

Floating in the darkness of space between systems, Demelza worked at translating the sigils and markings embedded within the scroll Master Orkut had left her.

"Well done, old man," she said with a little smile as his true message slowly became clear. "Clever indeed."

He had given her credit for her intellect when she had trained underneath him. Little did she know that high regard would one day in the not too distant future lead her on a most unexpected quest, and a surprisingly focused one now that she had found the key. With the rough translations she had gathered from the temple walls, Demelza was well on her way to possessing a map of sorts.

A great many of the sigils and runes were filler words, it seemed. But some fit within the framework of Master Orkut's writing. It took her an entire day's study and trial and error until she felt her translated work might steer her true. It was a clever use of arcane symbols intended to guide her to something. But was it the Quommus?

She had a feeling it could not possibly be that easy. And when she finally jumped her ship to the world at the center of the system loosely named in the scroll, she knew that to be the case.

There was but one habitable planet there, and upon it, but one temple of the sort she was seeking. It was a fortunate turn of events that the structure was well known, for searching each of the hundreds of cities and towns across the world would have taken weeks, if not longer, even with the help of the repurposed spy network.

Unlike the temple on Muck, the building here was in extremely good condition, though it was no longer used as a place of worship. Centuries prior, it had been converted to a marketplace when the order fell out of favor with the local government. But she could see what the place had once been. Magnificent. Ornate. Robustly built. And on a world such as this, it had not had to face the harsh conditions of the dirty mining town. More than that, this building, while in far better condition, was clearly older.

"What do you have for me here, Master Orkut?" she quietly asked the dead man as she walked through the tall entryway and into the marketplace contained within.

Magical lighting illuminated the place, and row upon row of tented vendor stalls and tables, butting right against one another, tapestries strung above them as the wares lay stretched out in an organized grid. This was no haphazard place of commerce. This was an established trading ground. But what secrets might it hold for one looking not for commerce, but for something far more difficult to come by?

Demelza walked the perimeter, slowly visiting vendors, acquiring a few goods to help her fit in as a shopper, all while making detailed mental note of the symbols and glyphs on the walls. But most seemed to be near identical to what she'd seen on Muck. The stories were the same, with a few small variations, as one would expect in diverse systems.

She made a complete circuit of the building's walls, but was no closer to an answer. The flooring was simple stone, and though there were signs of markings having been carved into them at one time, they were long since worn by centuries of footfall upon them. The ceiling was decorated, but a series of arches truncated sections and prevented a clear view of the entire place from one location.

It was not until the completion of her careful search grid, all under the guise of shopping, that she arrived at the central-most of the tented stalls. It was an open area of the floor, far from any columns, and there was clearly nothing of use for her. The stones had been worn so flat from all of the foot traffic over the years they may as well have been hewn smooth.

One thing caught her eye, though. A solid, heavy anvil at what appeared to be the dead center of the building. At first, she thought it surprising no one had taken it over the years. The sect it belonged to was long gone, after all. But then she noted the base.

The metal, it seemed, ran through the floor and into the structure of the building itself. And it still possessed a small magical charge to it. Suddenly, it made sense. If any had ripped it free, the ensuing damage to the building might very well have taken the whole thing down with it.

She walked right up to the anvil and bent close, only to be disappointed with what she found. It was like the one she had seen on Muck, and the markings were exactly the same. No new information for her here, it seemed.

Demelza was beginning to wonder if she had misinterpreted the scroll's text somehow when a slight shift in the magical light illuminated the dim ceiling a bit better. Standing at the anvil, there was no tapestry hung over her head, affording her a clear view upward. With all of the tents being covered areas, their lighting had remained contained within, not brightening the building itself.

Demelza quietly cast upward. An illumination spell directed right at the ceiling. Unless the vendors sliced open their tents and looked up, it would likely go entirely unnoticed. But from her lone unobstructed vantage point at the one place no one could set up a stand, she could see what others would miss.

The sigils stood out clearly now that she knew what to look for. Slowly, she spun in place, looking up and taking careful note of the new symbols. It quickly became clear what she was looking at. This was an old temple. A very old one, in fact. And on the ceiling, a form of star chart was laid out, but with ancient, long-forgotten names of planets and systems.

This particular building was not just a temple, but also a hub. A place from which she could backtrack to even older temples of the sect. But there was just one problem. She could navigate through space quite well, but this was far beyond her skills as a Ghalian. There were uncharted systems included, and lines of spell jumps that were utterly unfamiliar to her. She couldn't help but wonder if the others were having as difficult a time as she was, wherever they were, whatever they were doing.

But that was neither here nor there. Her next steps were clear. Demelza, it seemed, had found a map, but one that needed a guide to go with it. She was going to have to seek out a navigator.

CHAPTER TWENTY-SEVEN

"Breach the hull the moment we cast the grappling spells," Bud said as he triple-checked his bandolier of weapons.

The others in the small pirate attack craft were doing the same. A hardy bunch, all of them, and each armed to the teeth and ready for mayhem.

"Yes, Bud, I know," Saramin replied, surprisingly calm for his young age.

He had been rapidly rising in the ranks of Captain Lalaynia's crew, and before entering his twentieth year he was already the official leader of a boarding squad. Of course, in this instance Uzabud had been given his old position back and was leading the charge, but only with Saramin's tacit agreement.

Bud realized he might be stepping on toes just a bit, but he knew Saramin could handle it. The young man had impressed the hell out of him with not only his prowess, but also his calm manner under fire. He'd make a damn fine captain one day. So long as he avoided capture and the gladiator arenas where their kind so often wound up, that is.

This particular assault was not the sort of thing that would land any of them in control collars, though. Not today. For a while now Lalaynia had been helping Bud on his search for Henni, but she also needed to pay her crew. When a Tslavar mercenary supply ship came to their attention, it seemed like the perfect opportunity. Not only to keep the crew happy, but also to resupply her ship without needing to land. And if they could rid the galaxy of a few of those Tslavar bastards in the process, all the better.

The green-skinned Tslavars might not have always been mercenaries for the Council of Twenty, but even before that particular bit of employment they had nevertheless enjoyed a rather violent reputation.

Normally, Bud was loath to paint an entire race with a broad brush. There were good and bad in all cultures, after all. But the Tslavars were so tribal and vicious in their nature, he had never in his many days encountered one he would truly call kind or friendly. At least, not to any non-Tslavar.

"Bud, we'll be on them in under a minute," Saramin called out. "The rest of you, nut up. These are Tslavar mercs, not some casual transport crew, so stay sharp. Never leave an enemy standing behind you. We clear?"

"Clear!" the men replied in unison.

Bud nodded his approval. "You've come a long way, since we first met."

"As have you," the young pirate said with a grin. "Now, get your game face on."

"Isn't that my line, kid?"

"It is if you're quick enough, old-timer."

"Old-timer? Hey, now that's just mean."

Saramin's grin cracked wider. Then he became very serious. "We have contact in twenty seconds," he called out.

The small pirate craft's pilot was skilled, pulling up sharply just before contact so as not to disturb the target ship's hull at all. Saramin cast the docking spell and quickly put the first umbilical spell in place. Others would reinforce the invisible airway linking the ships as they passed through once the vessel's skin had been breached and the first men had made it aboard.

It was pirate rules fighting from there on out. Protect your men, watch your back, leave no one injured and able to attack behind, and above all, do not use magical attacks. Lalaynia's men had been in the game a great many years, and were all well-versed with what could go wrong if that happened.

"You ready?" Bud asked as the spell pried the target ship's hull open.

The stream of men leaping through the forced entryway answered that for him quick enough. He jumped in, Saramin right on his tail. A pair of sentries remained behind just in case the heavy warding spells keeping their enemies from crawling up through their accessway failed.

If all went well, this would be over too fast for that to even be a concern.

More accustomed to straight-up assaults with Hozark, Bud hadn't been in a true pirating situation in some time, and for the first few moments, it felt almost foreign to him, watching his comrades loot as they fought. But muscle memory quickly kicked in, thanks largely to the pair of Tslavar mercenaries who were very actively trying to remove his head from his shoulders. And pirates knew a thing or two about fighting dirty.

Bud dove low, slicing the knees of the nearest attacker then driving his dagger up under the falling man's jaw, putting an end to him quickly and efficiently. He didn't sit around to enjoy his little victory. Bud threw himself forward and rolled aside, bringing up his sword to deflect whatever attack the other assailant might bring.

The second man dropped on top of the first, a nasty hole in his chest where Saramin's sword had done its work.

Bud nodded to the young man and wasted no time, leaping back into the fray with the others. It was almost cathartic getting to release his pent-up aggression without reserve.

He'd been upset at what had happened to Henni but had really been limited to roughing up a handful of potential leads. But now he was finally able to let loose, and he soon had a trail of fallen mercenaries in his wake.

"Command!" Saramin shouted to him, then took off running toward the ship's base of operations.

Bud immediately fell in behind him, the two picking up a few more of their men and women along the way. The command center was well defended when they arrived, several of their comrades having already been chipping away at the Tslavar defenses as best they could.

But it was a tight access point, undoubtedly designed that way for precisely this sort of occurrence. They might eventually force their way in, but it would be at the cost of far too many lives.

"Shit. This is bad," Saramin muttered. "Bud, what do you think? Is there any way to push past them?"

Bud hadn't been a pirate in ages, and the siege and seizure of a ship's bridge was no longer his strong suit. He scanned the area, hoping for an alternative. Fighting had been brutal, the pirates and mercenaries having flung one another into the walls with great force as they fought. He stared at the carnage a long moment in thought when something unusual caught his eye.

This ship was a Tslavar ship, but it was also meant for resupplying their mercenary forces. And before they had gone all-in with the Council of Twenty, they would likely have faced scrutiny at some ports of call. Bud turned and rushed back the way they came.

"Bud? Where the hell are you going?" Saramin called after him. "Shit. Stay here. I'll be right back," he told the others, then followed his friend as quickly as he could.

He found the smuggler at the next corridor over, his back against the wall for cover, just in case, while he studied the walls and floor of the ship.

"What are you doing? We need to––"

"Shh. Gimme a sec, here."

"Bud!"

"Hang on, I think I've almost... yeah, there it is. Got it, you bastards!" He was grinning like a madman as he leaned down and slid his konus onto his wrist.

"You can't cast in here! You know the danger using one in space-based combat. You could kill us all!"

Bud ignored him, and the konus began feeding his quietly spoken spell power. "I'm not fighting, kid. This is something else," he replied with a growing grin. "And I think you're gonna like it."

A faint seam suddenly appeared in the floor's smooth surface about a meter square in size. Bud cast a clamping spell and lifted it free. Saramin was shocked, to say the least.

"Where did that come from? How the hell did you do that?"

"I'm a smuggler now, remember? And this is an older model Tslavar ship. One that might have needed to hide certain cargo at one point in time. And you know what? If I'm not mistaken, this little network of hidey-holes connects to command. So, if you're not too busy," he said, then jumped down into the hole, his weapons ready for a fight.

Saramin quickly rounded up a small group of their best fighters and followed him into the crawlspace. They moved as quickly as possible, right on Bud's heels. He stopped abruptly and put his hand on the smooth panel above him.

"This is it," he whispered. "We're gonna have to move fast and act with decisive brutality. Killing strokes only. Until we're all clear of this bottleneck, we're vulnerable, so the first out have to make it count. Got it?"

The pirates nodded.

Bud held up his hand and began quietly casting the spell to unlock the floor. He knew the mercenaries above them wouldn't be looking down. Not with all the mayhem just outside their door. All of their attention would be focused on that. All he could do was hope none of them happened to be standing atop this particular section.

So far as he could gauge, given the model of the ship, they would be coming up at the end of the command center farthest from the lone entryway. If he was right, that would hopefully put them out of the defenders' line of sight for at least a few moments. And if they moved quickly and quietly enough, they could hopefully take out several before the real fighting began.

"On three," he said, raising his fingers, then silently counted down.

The floor section lifted easily, he was pleased to note, and when he pushed it aside enough to get a peek out, he saw a trio of nearby Tslavar crewmembers, but all with their backs to him. It looked like he was right, and the fighting at the entryway had all of their attention. They simply didn't expect anyone to come at them from a direction with no doorway. It wasn't possible.

Or so they thought.

The first two went down in a gurgling heap as daggers did their close-up work. The third nearest the covert access, however, turned in time to call out an alarm to his comrades before a brutal sword stroke silenced him forever.

The pirates had almost entirely cleared the opening by that point and were already moving on the command center crew with brutal efficiency. The guards protecting the entryway from just outside of command heard the ruckus, but they didn't know what to do. The attackers were pressing on them from down the corridor, but it sounded a hell of a lot like a full-fledged battle going on *inside* the chamber.

Finally, a pair of them came back inside to see what was going on. One managed to turn to call a warning to his comrades outside before being run through with a wicked-looking blade. The other was not so lucky, falling silent at the skilled hands of Saramin almost as soon as he entered the room.

From that point it was a mismatched clean up, and within but a few minutes both the corridor and command were taken.

"The ship is ours!" Saramin transmitted over the boarding team's group skree. "Round up any survivors. Offer them one chance to surrender. Kill any who still fight."

It was a brutal command, but it served two purposes. One, it was simply the way pirates treated Council forces and their lackeys. And two, it had been sent over open skrees, meaning the order could be heard clearly throughout the ship. If any had hopes of survival, this was their one opportunity.

Saramin's team wound up with a half dozen survivors in custody. They'd be sold off as gladiator fodder, no doubt. A fitting end for the Tslavar goons. As for the ship, they now possessed a fairly well-stocked craft to bring back to the rendezvous point. Lalaynia would be pleased.

"Not the best ever, but still, not a bad haul," Saramin said, clapping Bud on the shoulder. "And nice work, that bit with the floor. You saved a lot of lives with that trick."

Bud nodded, but his mind seemed to be elsewhere. "So, I just wanted to reiterate that my share of our haul will help fund the captain's support of my search for Henni, right?"

"That's what she said. So long as the crew is paid and fed, she's at your service."

"And any pillage beyond the regular cargo is still first come, first served, correct?"

"Yep. You can go rifle pockets and crew quarters to your heart's content," Saramin replied.

"What about other things? Not cargo, but perhaps other valuables located aboard?"

"I'm not sure what you mean by that. I would think so, but that's a question for Captain Lalaynia. What did you have in mind?"

"I'll run it by her when we meet up," Bud replied.

An hour later, the pirate craft and its captured prize arrived at the rendezvous point on the far side of a small moon in a rather boring system. The perfect place to avoid prying eyes.

"Nicely done, gentlemen," Lalaynia said as she walked the newly captured craft. "Very nice indeed."

"Captain, Bud had a question for you about his share and rights of plunder."

"Oh?"

"Yeah," Bud said. "Beyond the cargo, whatever we dig up is ours to keep per your rules, correct?"

"Yes."

"And my share of the main cargo prize is going toward expenses for your providing your services while I hunt Henni, yes?"

"You know it is, Bud. What are you getting at?" Lalaynia asked.

"I just wanted to be sure we were on the same page, is all," he replied. "So, I've bought a little bit more time with my share of this haul."

"That you have."

"Well then, how about you tell me how much more *this* will buy me?" he asked, then cast an unusual little spell.

Seams suddenly appeared in the walls and floors all across the ship. A few even revealed themselves in the ceiling directly above them. Lalaynia pulled one open, revealing a small smuggler's cargo hideaway jammed with contraband. Despite working for the Council, it seemed the Tslavars were running a little side venture. She assumed the other compartments were likewise filled.

The pirate captain let out a truly amused laugh. "Oh, Bud. *This* is why I miss having you around. You always did have the best surprises up your sleeve. But why did your search spell work and not ours?"

"A smuggler's specialty," he replied. "Given the nature of this ship's earlier life, I figured it was set up a bit differently than most. Something my particular skill-set helped me suss out."

"Designed to avoid those looking for hiding spots," she said.

"Yep. But it just so happens that hiding stuff is my profession. So, about that additional flight time."

Lalaynia grinned. "You've earned more than your keep today, Bud. Very, *very* well done indeed. This will buy you quite a bit more than just a few more days of my assistance. So, what'll it be? You've seen the intel my people have been able to dig up. We have quite a few options, but nothing really solid. So, tell me. You obviously don't wish to overlap Hozark and his friends' efforts. Where would you like to head next?"

CHAPTER TWENTY-EIGHT

Hozark was very practiced at not revealing his true thoughts and emotions, but after so many recent turns of events even he was feeling the pressure build. Of course, his visage showed none of that concern. To any who may have observed him, he was as calm and steady as ever.

Corann, however, had known him many years and could sense his unease.

"The Council has been shuffling craft around, but the spies are working hard on verifying Maktan's location," she said as they sipped tea on her porch. "And, of course, they are still seeking out Henni as well."

He had left Hap and Laskar in a training facility in a nearby system as soon as he received the message that Corann requested his presence.

"I have also had word sent to the other members of the Five to have their personal connections keep an ear open for any information," she said.

"Thank you, Corann," Hozark said. "I am hopeful we can complete this contract soon. Visla Maktan has caused more than a little trouble for the order, and the sooner he is no longer making waves the better."

"In this we are in agreement," she replied. "The Maktan contract is a top priority for the order. And there has been a new development."

"Oh?"

"One of Dohria's closest associates brought the message. It seems that the party interested in ending Maktan's life has also made this a top priority. The price has nearly doubled if we can achieve our objective within the next two weeks."

Hozark raised a brow. "That seems suspicious," he said. "We are already engaged on this task. Adding coin to the pot does not make us more likely to succeed."

"True. But the Ghalian ways are a mystery to those of the outside, and if they wish to enrich the order further, we shall gladly take their coin."

"I still feel this is suspicious, Corann."

"Yes, as did I when I received word. However, in speaking with Prombatz, he made a valid point about a sense of urgency. With Visla Ravik now dead, there is a power void in the Council. With both the other members, as well as a handful of aspirants jockeying for control of his seat, it makes sense that this would be seen as the opportune moment to eliminate Maktan in all of the chaos."

Hozark thought on it a moment and nodded. "Utilizing the internal strife already in play within the Council to not only spread their normal defenses a bit thin, but also to focus possible blame upon the Council itself."

"Though each member possesses their own personal guard, the Council's general ranks will be overtaxed with the current situation."

"But we know for certain this contract did not come from one of the Twenty," Hozark noted.

"Indeed. And this has been verified by multiple agents across the network. Our people have done a deep search among their contacts within the Council to ensure as much. Despite our goals aligning this once, we would not wish to be doing the Council's dirty work for them, after all."

"Indeed."

"Has there been word from Demelza?" Corann asked.

"None yet," Hozark replied. "It was a very unusual task you sent her on, Corann. We are not normally in the business of treasure hunting."

"No, we are not. But on this occasion and with the intelligence we possess, for this relic, it seemed worth the effort. The Quommus would be an incredibly valuable tool for the order to possess. Especially if it can be obtained before the attempt on Maktan."

"If any could succeed in this effort, I have confidence Demelza is up for the task. I would even say it is readily apparent that in recent months she has proven herself to be an asset far beyond her standing in the order."

"Agreed, and we shall address that disparity in ranking soon. She has more than earned it. For now, however, we have another pressing matter that has been brought to my attention."

Hozark chuckled. "It would seem there is *always* something arising of late. Strange times we are in."

"They are at that, Brother. And this is particularly alarming. There is unrest on Sooval."

"Sooval?" Hozark asked, a bit alarmed. "It is not Maktan, is it? The man is actively seeking any power he can acquire."

"We cannot be certain at this time, but our spies have informed us that word has reached the network that a power user, likely a member of the Twenty, has somehow come across the location of the resettled Ootaki on Sooval."

"There are a great many Ootaki hidden there," Hozark said. "The power contained within the group is enormous. The order has spent many years and a great deal of coin helping hide those recovered slaves on that world, and a great deal keeping them secret as well. How could this have happened?"

"That we do not yet know. And for now, it does not matter. What does is that someone, whether Maktan or another in the Council of Twenty, or even an outsider, has learned of their likely presence."

"Verified it, or they are just investigating a rumor?"

"It seems they are not entirely sure as of yet. But word is they will be coming in force regardless."

"Then we still have a chance," Hozark said. "Hopefully they will not send a full attack fleet until they've verified. And if it is Maktan's forces we are dealing with, we cannot permit him to gain that additional power."

Corann nodded. "Agreed. It cannot be allowed under normal circumstances, but especially not now. Not with our contract on Maktan pending, and certainly not after what he has done to Aargun and Prombatz."

It was a bit strange to discuss. This was not what the Ghalian did, providing protection services for groups of freed slaves. But this case was different. These Ootaki had been rescued in the course of Ghalian contracts over the years, and the order felt they had an obligation to continue to keep them from falling back under another's control.

And if it really was Visla Maktan who had discovered them, it was even more important than ever to keep all of that stored magic out of the power-hungry man's hands. He had already been building a stockpile of magic weaponry, using Happizano's father as a primary source, but if he acquired an enormous group of Ootaki, Visla Jinnik might very well become expendable.

"I shall inform Happizano and Laskar I will be away for a time, then redirect to Sooval immediately," Hozark said, placing his cup on the table and rising to his feet.

"You shall need numbers for this, Hozark."

"Indeed. Numbers would not be in my favor, even if Demelza and Bud were present."

"Agreed. I shall send word for a contingent of our mercenary contacts to take up arms and meet you on Sooval. They will not be informed of the exact details of the assignment beyond that they shall possibly be fighting a numerically superior force. But knowing them, with enough coin, I doubt they would truly care even if they knew it was the Council itself."

"True. For enough coin, some are quite willing to risk it all," Hozark agreed.

Corann rose and bade him farewell, giving him a warm hug as they were in public view. No matter the urgency of the situation, her cover as sweet old Corann had to be maintained.

"Our contact on Sooval shall be awaiting your arrival," she said, releasing the hug. "Good luck, and fly safe."

"What do you mean you're leaving?" Hap griped when Hozark returned from his brief visit with Corann.

"Yeah, what's this about flying away without us?" Laskar asked. "You'll need the power of the mothership for anything important."

"I appreciate the concern, Laskar; however, my own craft is more than adequate for the task I have before me."

"Still, it sounds like you'll be doing something dangerous. And you know I'm good in a pinch."

"Your offer is appreciated, but I shall be fine on my own for this short while. And besides, you have earned a bit of rest time. There are fine establishments here to cater to your needs."

Laskar knew the drinking and carousing facilities Hozark was speaking of. He'd already become quite familiar with them, in fact. But being left behind was not something he enjoyed.

"So, what's the mission? A contract? Are you getting closer to Maktan?"

"Nothing so exciting," Hozark replied. "I am merely running an errand for Corann. One that requires one of the Five, I am afraid, otherwise I would have tasked another. But that is no matter. I shall return quite soon."

Laskar had a feeling the man was lying, but he knew better than to pry. That was all he'd get from the assassin.

"Why can't I come with?" Hap whined.

"Because I have already spoken with Master Turong, and he has agreed to allow you to stay with him for a bit longer while I am away. To take you into his training house and teach you all he can as if you were one of his own students."

"Really?" Hap asked, suddenly less upset than just moments before.

Master Turong ran a non-Ghalian martial arts facility of the highest order, and his pupils often went on to become great warriors in whichever endeavors they decided to pursue. And he had agreed to tutor Happizano for a few days while Hozark paused on his world. He owed more than a few favors to the Wampeh Ghalian, after all, and besides, Hozark was the closest thing to a friend he had within the order.

To the master's great pleasure, Happizano seemed to take to the training quite quickly, picking up both magical and martial skills with an impressive ease. He had mentioned this to Hozark, complimenting him on priming the boy's mind and body for the difficult lessons that come to the older students.

The boy showed initiative and drive, and that was more than he could say for several of his students whose parents had spent enormous sums of coin for their children to learn at his feet.

"Master Turong was very impressed with you, young Jinnik," Hozark said. "So much so that when I mentioned a task out of system, he offered to take you into his training house without hesitation. For the short time I am gone, you will experience the *true* intensity of his instruction."

Hap's disappointment at being left behind was already a

thing of the past. He'd been training at all of the facilities Hozark stopped at for some time now, but Master Turong was something of a legend, even among the other martial arts houses.

"This'll be great!" he said, thoroughly cheered by the turn of events.

Hozark was glad for the change of attitude. He would leave the boy here regardless, but if he was happy about it, the process would be far more pleasant.

"Just remember, young Jinnik, that while you may travel under my protection, while you are here, you shall be under Master Turong's wing and treated just as any other student."

"So I'll really live there full-time?"

"You will. All has been arranged. But know that the path to mastery is a difficult one. This will not be easy."

Hap's jaw set with determination. "I don't want easy."

Hozark grinned. It was music to his ears. The boy had changed so much since he'd first rescued him from Maktan's men. Who knew the difficult young pest would grow on him like this? Hozark was a man who notoriously did not like children, and yet, he was actually becoming rather fond of this youngster. He was becoming someone the assassin was proud of, and that happened very rarely indeed.

"Very well. You shall undoubtedly get your wish. This will be a challenging, but also rewarding, experience. Master Turong has a great deal of wisdom he can impart to you, and I look forward to seeing what you have learned when I return."

"So you're just gonna leave him here? After all we've been through? I guess you'll want me to keep an eye on him while you're gone," Laskar said.

"On the contrary. Happizano shall be within the walls of Master Turong's training grounds. The decades of protective magic layered there, as well as the master and his top disciples' skills, will be more than enough protection should the need arise. The facility is almost as impregnable as a Ghalian stronghold. Rest calm and enjoy your time off, Laskar. Happizano shall be in good hands."

"Good. Then I can *really* enjoy myself," the pilot said with a lazy grin. "See ya, Hozark. Good luck with whatever you're off to do. I'll see ya when you get back."

"Indeed. Enjoy the downtime," he replied, then turned back to Hap. "And as for you, let us get you situated with Master Turong. Then I shall take my leave. I think this will be an experience you shall treasure the rest of your days."

CHAPTER TWENTY-NINE

The flight to Sooval was relatively fast, despite the rather small Drookonus Hozark was using to power his craft. His shimmer ship was simply not large enough to accommodate one of the big and powerful ones that allowed truly long jumps, so he was chaining shorter ones together as best he could.

Time was of the essence, but so too was arriving at the *right* time. If his backup was not there yet, he would be walking into a situation the likes of which even a master assassin could not hope to prevail in.

Even so, the Drookonus was quickly overheating from the magical strain placed upon it. The faint orange glow from its receptacle made it quite clear it would be done for by the time he arrived.

But that was why the order had caches of necessary equipment, and spares of this nature were no different. He would burn this one out, no doubt, but there were multiple backups within the craft. Hozark just hoped there would be no cause to burn those out as well, for if there was, it would be a bad day indeed.

With just a few more jumps until he reached his destination,

Hozark found himself reflecting on the times he'd been to Sooval in the past. Most recently, he had dropped off a small handful of rescued Ootaki, the poor men and women he had unexpectedly saved from slavery in the aftermath of a Council versus pirate battle.

By now they would be well absorbed into the existing colony and blended in with the locals without issue. There was an extremely talented stylist who worked at the most exclusive rejuvenation spas who just so happened to have been saved from a great deal of trouble by the Ghalian in the past. And now she offered her services for others they rescued, as they had done for her, free of charge.

It was that which was one of the main saving graces for the magic-haired people. Their golden hair was a giveaway anywhere in the galaxy, but this woman had managed to develop a spell that made her carefully crafted dyes bond with their magical locks. It was difficult, and nearly all who ever attempted such a thing failed, but in this instance, she had met with great success.

As a result, the Ootaki were able to live normal lives, not constantly looking over their shoulders for fear of someone kidnapping them for their hair. Now they blended in with everyone else, albeit with particularly long hairstyles, as was their custom.

All in all, Sooval had been a peaceful colony for quite some time, out of the way and unnoted by all.

But now either Maktan or one of the other Council members had somehow gotten wind of them, and that was decidedly not good. These were innocents the Ghalian had freed and relocated, and their recapture and return to a life of slavery was not acceptable. Not if the Wampeh Ghalian could help it.

It was a matter of honor.

Many would have been surprised to learn of the codes the Ghalian lived by. There were plenty of killers for hire in the galaxy with no scruples whatsoever. But the Wampeh Ghalian were a different item altogether.

Hozark's shimmer ship popped out of its final jump just as its Drookonus began crackling from the strain. He quickly hot-swapped the spent device with a fresh one, dropping the destroyed one into a sealed vessel to contain the smoke wafting from it.

The brief moment of power loss was insignificant under his skilled flying, and the ship quickly made its way to Sooval's orbit. He could have plunged straight into the atmosphere, making a rapid descent to his destination township, but there were things that needed to be done first. Like making several quick circuits of the planet's orbit to see if any of the attacking ships had arrived yet.

Luckily, it seemed there were none, though Hozark did note several smaller craft that appeared to be benign, but he knew to be cleverly disguised mercenary vessels. Fortunately, these were *his* mercenaries, sent by Corann to bolster his defense. That meant things would be ready for him on the surface.

Quickly engaging his shimmer cloak, Hozark redirected to make a circuit of the area below. There were multiple large gathering places, akin to a town square, but a bit larger, dotting the area. The city itself was comprised of several relatively tall buildings surrounding the more plentiful squat structures that made up the bulk of the township.

Despite what was evident above, apparently, a lot of the construction was subterranean at least a few levels down, utilizing the natural insulation of the soil to protect the inhabitants in the hot summer months. A logical bit of construction that saved on magic expenditures for cooling spells.

He completed his final flyover in no time. All seemed quiet, so he veered off toward the landing area outside the town, then tucked away in a little field not too far distant. Camouflaged as it was, his craft would remain safely hidden, far enough from the pending fighting to be secure, yet near enough for rapid retrieval should he require it.

Hopefully, the inevitable combat would be quick and decisive. But he knew full well that when it came to armed conflict, just about anything could happen no matter how prepared you might think you were.

He strapped his vespus blade to his back, adding to the already impressive number of weapons secreted upon his body, then slid a powerful konus onto his wrist, tucking another into a hidden pocket for later use should the need arise.

His own internal power was still strong, but not nearly as strong as it had been when he drank from Visla Ravik. *That* had topped him off with a heady bit of magic, but he had been forced to tap into it a few times since then, and unlike the visla, he did not regenerate that power. What he took from another was all that he had, and he would have to drink to procure more.

The vespus blade, however, also possessed an impressive amount of magic, having been filled to the brim with the overflow from Ravik's demise. And if it was indeed Maktan whose forces were heading toward the Ootaki enclave, he would need every bit of it.

The jog into town was uneventful, even with Hozark not using his shimmer cloak to mask his arrival. These were people under Ghalian protection, and seeing one of the order in their midst would be of great relief to them, no doubt. Of course, the other citizens would just see a Wampeh and think nothing of it. Why would they? There was no reason to suspect a *Ghalian* would ever bother visiting this small world.

Hozark slowed his progress, making a small circuit on his way to his final destination. In addition to letting the Ootaki see his arrival, it also afforded him a ground-level chance to better survey the area on which he would soon be fighting. Indeed, most buildings did seem to have subterranean areas. Good for hiding the locals when the time came.

The taller buildings were spaced out far enough that they would not hinder any craft from landing, as he was sure the attackers would do, surely choosing to drop right into town instead of the marked landing area not far away. But that was no matter. Their overconfidence would be their demise.

As he strode the streets, dyed-hair Ootaki gave a slight nod to the Ghalian. A sign of thanks and respect. He returned the slightest of nods and carried on his way.

The other citizens in the area were far less interested in his arrival. To them he was just some random man walking into town. But even if any did take note, the unexpected fighting soon to break out would erase any thoughts about it soon enough.

CHAPTER THIRTY

"I assume you're Hozark?" a wiry man with clear gray eyes and shiny silver stubble gracing his face and closely shorn head asked the Ghalian trotting into the center of town.

He was dressed in average civilian clothes with a hooded tunic worn on top of his base attire. It was a very casual and comfortable ensemble. All the better to hide weapons beneath, and easily discarded at a moment's notice.

Hozark looked at the fellow a moment. His skin, normal as it seemed, was clearly of a harder substance than it appeared, and his stubble was not mere hair, but wire-sharp in its composition. Cut to a short length as it was, it made his entire head and face a potential weapon. The man was a Rakanni, and judging by the bits of scarring he could see peeking out of his hooded collar, a mercenary. This was his contact.

"Indeed, I am. And you would be Andorus, if I am not mistaken," Hozark replied.

"You are not mistaken," the mercenary replied with an amused gleam in his eye.

Hozark grinned. He liked the man's demeanor. Casual in the face of hostilities. Competent and confident. This one would be a good ally in battle. "Then it is a pleasure to make your acquaintance," the assassin said. "What are our numbers thus far?"

"We've got seventy-nine men and women spread throughout the township. All armed and ready to go on your command."

"And the locals?"

"It looks like a few of them might be good for a fight, but most seem pretty timid, if you ask me."

"Yes, it is a rather helpless group," Hozark admitted.

"If you don't mind my asking, why these folks? I mean, I'm happy to fight, but there doesn't seem to be much worth protecting here."

"True, it does appear so, but the Ghalian made a pact a long time ago, and our word is our bond."

"Which is partly why so many showed up on such short notice," Andorus said. "The Ghalian have quite a reputation. Everyone here knew whatever your reason, it was a just one. Even if it was for this placid lot."

Little did the mercenary know a good number of the timid folk he was referring to were actually peaceful Ootaki. The value of the magically charged hair in that town would have been enough to make all but the most loyal have second thoughts about which side to back.

But the Ootaki were extremely well disguised, and thus were seen simply as yellowish-skinned locals but nothing more. The other inhabitants were varied in race, but were likewise a mostly gentle group. It had been part of the reason this place was selected for resettling in the first place.

But now it seemed that same peaceful demeanor meant it would be pretty much entirely up to the mercenary forces to keep them safe once their adversary arrived. And from what the Ghalian network had reported, it looked like they would be arriving any time now.

Hozark quickly walked the neighborhood, acting as though

he was no more than passing through. Andorus had been in the game a long time and didn't bother pointing out his people to the assassin. He knew they'd been spotted by his sharp eyes the moment he strode into town. Finally, they arrived at the home of the leader of the hidden Ootaki. A woman named Piri.

"Thank you for your protection, Master Hozark," the woman said as she poured both men tall glasses of chilled water. "You say we are at risk?"

"You are," he replied. "But we have forces here to help protect you and yours. Quietly spread the word. When the intruders arrive, you must have your people hide in the most secure location possible. That is the only way we can be sure you will remain safe while we drive them off."

"And after that? We will have to relocate all over again."

"Yes. But first things first. You cannot relocate if you do not first survive."

She nodded. "Of course. Yes. I'll tell the others. And thank you. Thank you both."

The men nodded and downed their drinks. It would be thirsty work, fighting off Council forces, and every bit of hydration would be welcome.

"So, relocated?" Andorus asked.

"Refugees from Council aggression. The order helped settle them here some time ago," was all Hozark said.

The mercenary nodded. The explanation was good enough for him. "Well then, now we wait."

The wait was not a long one. One of the mercenary scouts casually strode up to his leader just a short time later with news from above. A Council base ship had just jumped into the system a distance from the planet, launched a pair of nondescript landing craft, then immediately jumped away.

"Seems like they're making a sneak attack," Andorus said.

"Yes. And by jumping the base ship away and using

unmarked craft, it will make the attack seem like a band of raiders, not official Council forces," Hozark noted.

Andorus nodded. "Yeah, but they should still be easy enough to pick out, I'd wager. I mean, despite lacking markings, they'll still be wearing the same basic garb as one another most likely."

"They shall, indeed. Now, prepare your people. When the attack begins, we shall have to allow them all off of their ships before we respond. Only then will we best utilize our element of surprise, cutting them off from easy retreat."

The mercenary nodded once and took off at a jog to spread the word. The enemy was coming. Soon it would be time to fight.

Only a few minutes had passed before the pair of ships came in hot through the atmosphere, the bright orange of their heat-displacing spells glowing in the sky as they descended. Both landed right in the middle of town, settling in hard in the open town squares between the taller buildings. Hozark turned slightly to protect his eyes from the small cloud of dust raised by their arrival, but making sure to never lose sight of the enemy.

It was time, and the intruders were not wasting any of it. The instant the ships touched down, their doors opened and many dozens of Council mercenaries streamed out of each of them, all clad in the same uniforms, totally devoid of any markings, as expected. It was a shock-and-awe campaign designed to be brutally fast and efficient. Typical Council tactics.

The invaders rushed forward, ready to dominate the poor, helpless people of this place. People were shoved against walls and to the ground, and none of them lifted a finger. It was all going according to plan. Or so they thought.

Andorus and Hozark watched the ships carefully. Finally, the stream of troops ceased. It was time to fight back, and the Council goons would regret their overconfidence.

Their ships were not Council in appearance, at least not on

the exterior, and the uniforms could have been from any rebel band, but Hozark knew better. And even if there had been some lingering doubt, that would have evaporated in an instant with what he saw next.

A tall, lean woman with pale skin stepped out and surveyed the scene with an air of annoyance. She did not appear happy about their situation one bit, but that would not stop her from doing her job.

"Begin," she commanded.

The Council forces started manhandling the locals, pulling them toward their ships for collaring and imprisonment. Or so they thought, but a shrill whistle rang out through the air. A moment later all hell broke loose.

"Wait. What the hell?" one of the Council goons blurted just before the seemingly benign local shed his cloak and skewered him with a short sword.

In an instant, the roundup became a full-on battle, blades and spells flying with fury. There were more Council forces present, but as the defenders had hoped, the element of surprise had given them a significant advantage.

Fighting, magical and conventional, raged through the streets and town squares as the two forces engaged. Samara stood quietly a moment as it all unfolded, realizing the mistake the fools who had planned this had made. She drew her vespus sword, fully charged and crackling with blue magic, ready to stride into the fray, but she paused.

Samara cocked her head slightly, sensing something familiar. She turned and gazed across the battlefield. It was *him*. Even if not for the vibrant blue sword in his hand, she would know him at a glance.

A little smile tickled the corners of her mouth. "Hello, Hozark."

CHAPTER THIRTY-ONE

The ferocity of the regular mercenary combatants clashing in the streets and courtyards was a thing to witness. That is, if any of the locals had stuck around long enough to see it. But they had wisely fled the moment the two ships dropped down into their home.

The Ootaki had already quietly made their exit from public view well ahead of that, thanks to Hozark's warning, and were safely tucked away deep beneath one of the more secure buildings in the area. It was still possible they might be taken, but it would require quite a bit of effort finding them first.

Meanwhile, the battle raged above, the opposing forces laying into one another with the skill and efficiency one would have expected of seasoned warriors. The Council goons, while paid thugs one and all, were nevertheless talented combatants. The Ghalian-aligned mercenaries, while fewer in number, were also extremely skilled, and were holding their own against the superior forces quite admirably.

Blades, fists, cudgels, and spells were all being wielded with great efficacy and violence as the forces sought to gain advantage over one another. The magic had flown fast and furious at the onset, but the ranks quickly blended into one another in a seething mass of fists and assorted implements of harm, leaving few clear shots for spell casting.

It was for the better that way. Too powerful a spell could easily cause a catastrophe, taking out your own men as well as your enemy's. It wasn't the same degree of risk as combat in space, but the risk was there all the same.

But for all of the masterful violence being meted out on the battlefield, there were two whose clash put the others' skills to shame. In fact, as the assassins' blades rang out against one another, their magical sparks flying from the force, many of the other fighters from both sides even paused as if by a temporary unspoken truce to gawk at the spectacle.

Two Ghalian fighting one another? It was unheard of. Those combatants from each fighting force nearest them quickly learned the error in their hesitation when Hozark and Samara sliced them down with the slightest of effort while their swords flew in a blur of motion.

If they could even the odds for their side in the process, why not? In addition, if any were foolish enough to actually think to attack either of the pair, their fate would be met so laughably fast that their descendants would feel embarrassment from it for generations to come.

So the former lovers were left to it, a wide buffer quickly forming around them as they fought with both blades, bodies, and magic. It was epic combat, the two having trained together their whole lives, and thus countering one another on sheer instinct. It seemed supernatural how fast they were moving, and yet, they still pushed harder.

This was no mere combat. This was a fight to the death between two people with history. A *lot* of history. And despite being cool and collected assassins, the raw emotion flowing through each of them was almost palpable in its intensity. There was so much left unspoken all these years, but even for fighters as skilled as they were, there was simply no opportunity for a breath, let alone conversation.

Samara finally landed a solid kick to Hozark's chest, sending him flying backward into a building. She followed up with a brutal force spell, hoping to slam him into submission. But Hozark was already casting his defense before his body even hit the wall, and Samara's attack was blasted apart, taking down several nearby combatants with its shattered force.

He leapt from a low crouch, casting a series of deceptively small attacks, all requiring Samara to respond, even though they would cause no significant damage. But the point was not to cause harm. It was to set up his next move. The *real* attack. Hozark's vespus blade flashed in front of Samara, barely missing her chest as she contorted herself to her limits to dodge it. But this was precisely as he'd planned.

The worst part for her was she realized exactly what he was doing as it happened, but regardless, there was no other logical choice but to avoid the blade and absorb the kick that followed it.

The spinning kick drove his shin hard into her lead leg, spasming the muscles momentarily and forcing her to retreat. Until her pivot leg regained function, Samara would be on defense. Fortunately for her, she'd trained long and hard to fight through these things, and this was by no means the first time she'd felt this sort of pain. It was not even the first time Hozark had landed that particular blow on her, though previously it had only been in training.

She forced the surrounding muscles to fire hard to take the load off of the cramping ones while they recovered. Many would have moved in immediately for the kill, sensing she was weak and vulnerable.

And it would be the last thing they ever did.

Hozark, on the other hand, knew full well what Samara was capable of and treated her with the respect her formidable skills deserved. He circled her, assessing the situation. The mercenaries defending the township were doing an admirable job of it, it seemed, and the invaders were certainly having a hard time with them. It was looking as if Andorus and his men would come out victorious.

The thought had only just passed through Hozark's mind when a massive magical explosion rocked the street, vaporizing combatants from both sides with its force. Everyone paused and looked up. A Council drop ship was heading right for them, firing off deadly spells one after another. The ground shook from the impacts, and those who had been trying so hard to kill one another just moments before suddenly gave up their fighting and scattered, running for their lives.

Hozark and Samara were no different, the pair ducking into a nearby building as quickly as they could, narrowly avoiding what would have been a fatal blast for the both of them. They looked outside. Everyone was taking cover wherever they could as the descending ship rained down death upon them.

"Why are your people doing this?" Hozark demanded.

"They're not my people," she replied as the tall building next to them suffered a direct hit.

The ground rumbled menacingly as the structure swayed, then began to topple. Right toward their hiding place. Hozark and Samara locked eyes. They both knew there was no time to flee, nor any chance of getting clear of the impact zone. But inside the structure as they were, they might just stand a chance.

Without a moment to lose, they wrapped their arms around each other tightly, casting the strongest defensive spells they could, joining their power in a way few ever could. But they had cast together since childhood, and there was only one spell that would work for this threat. The spell they both cast simultaneously.

Power flowed from their bodies, their konuses, and even their vespus blades, creating a swirling bubble of crackling-strong magic. The building toppled upon their hiding place, which absorbed some of the impact but by no means all of it. The walls crumbled, the support columns buckled, the floor itself collapsed to the lower levels.

But when the rumbling ceased and the dust began to clear, the two remained standing. Safe in their little sphere of power. Safe, but shut in.

"It has stopped, Hozark," Samara said.

"Yes. Of course," he replied, releasing their embrace.

The two had been trying to kill one another just moments before, and their sweaty bodies stuck together awkwardly a moment as they pulled apart.

Hozark shifted his attention and cast a minor illumination spell, allowing them to take in the damage around them. The situation was not good. They had survived the tumbling building, but were now facing a deadly problem of another kind.

"It seems we are trapped down here," Hozark said. "Sealed in by what I would assume to be an impressive quantity of rubble."

"An astute assessment," Samara replied as she scanned the aftermath.

Hozark looked at her a long moment, then slid his blade into its scabbard. "Truce?"

Samara considered it a few seconds, then likewise sheathed her sword. "Truce."

Their murderous antics on hold for the time being, Hozark and Samara then quietly stared at one another in the dim light, each of them wondering what might come next.

CHAPTER THIRTY-TWO

"Come, let me," Hozark said, reaching out with his internal power to heal a small slice Samara had gotten on her arm during their combat.

It was nothing major, her reflexes were far too quick for that to have been a damaging blow, but the fact that he'd landed it at all showed just how seriously he had been taking their fight. It was a battle to the death, and neither had been holding back.

The spell did its work quickly, a slightly itchy burn flaring around the wound while the magic mended the injured flesh. A mere moment later, her arm was as good as new.

"Thank you. And now, allow me," she said, gesturing to the bloody spot on Hozark's tunic. In all of the excitement, he hadn't even noticed it.

Samara made quick work of the healing spell, repairing the damage in no time.

"Much appreciated," he said when she'd finished.

They looked at one another a long moment. With a truce in place, there was now no reason to harbor any hostile feelings or intentions. And as they both knew and trusted one another to the fullest extent, there was simply no way either would violate the agreement.

That meant they were free to apply their efforts to things other than killing one another. Like getting out.

Hozark broke the gaze first, his eyes looking up at the curved dome of rubble imprisoning them. A little smile formed on his lips. They had both cast together, the same spell emanating from each of them at the same time. And unlike so many who had tried and failed to do this sort of thing, their magic joined and amplified the spell perfectly.

A strong dome of magic was surrounding them, very much intact, and from what he could sense of the spell's stability, it would likely remain so long after they suffocated to death.

"The air will not hold out terribly long," he noted, dimming the illumination spell to look for any sign of light seeping in through the rubble. There was none.

"At least we shall not perish from being crushed," she replied with a little grin.

"Then I shall look forward to suffocation, shall I?"

"You know better than that, Hozark."

"Yes, Sam. I do."

It was bad, yes. But the two had survived worse, and despite the years apart, this unlikely reunion left them both quite confident they would get out of this mess.

Somehow.

"If we lower our spells, the rubble atop us may very well shift and come down on our heads," Hozark mused. "And that was a substantial building that toppled over onto our sheltering place."

"Yes, it was. It even drove us partly underground with the impact," Samara noted. "Quite a spectacle, indeed."

The levity, though understated as all Ghalian humor tended to be, was a breath of fresh air for Hozark, even as their oxygen slowly ran thin. If he had to go, he thought, this would not be the worst of ways. But he had no intention of that happening.

He also wished to take this opportunity to get some clarity, now that they were talking rather than fighting.

"So, do you think we will be able to bolster portions of this spell in a manner that would allow us to dig our way to the surface?" he asked.

"Perhaps. Digging is a sound plan," Samara replied. "However, with the destruction lying atop us, it might make more sense to go down, rather than up."

"The old city's ruins?"

"Why not? They were built on top of a long time ago, but the substructures still remain."

"You have done your homework on the history of Sooval's inhabitants," he noted.

"I am not one to enter into a hostile situation unprepared," she replied. "As you well know."

He certainly did. In all of their years together, he had never encountered another with quite the knack for preparation as Samara. She was damn good, and it showed. But even she could not have known the Council would turn their attacks on them all without thought for those on the ground.

"Samara, why would the Council attack their own people like that?" he asked. "They opened fire on everyone on the ground, regardless of affiliation."

Samara sighed. "Ultimately, we are all disposable to them in the pursuit of their goals," she replied. "Yes, some of us may have more value to them than others, but to the Council, only their own have any real worth."

"A rather mercenary attitude," Hozark said as he scanned the rubble at their feet for a possible way down, if the route up was impassible.

"Well, we do know a thing or two about those," Samara replied.

"So often the fodder, as you said. But tell me, Sam, help me understand. If you are expendable to this degree, why do you work for Maktan, then? And Ravik? And the others?"

"Let it go, Hozark. Just let it go."

He could tell by the look in her eye that this particular part of their conversation was over. The truce, it seemed, might become tenuous if he were to push any harder. Realizing this, he shifted tack.

"I am glad to see you are well, Sam," he finally said with an amused little grin.

It was a funny thing to say, given they had been trying to kill one another just minutes before. Now that they weren't fighting, he was finally able to take a good, long look at her. It had been ten years since she had faked her death, but she hadn't seemed to age a bit. At least not to his eyes.

Of course, he did note the finest of lines that had begun to form on the face he knew so well, but they were inconsequential in his mind.

"I am glad you are well too, Hozark," she replied as she also scanned the rubble for possible weak points that might lead to an egress. "That is quite a crew you are flying with these days. How did you wind up with them? And who is the young Ghalian? She is quite talented, and undoubtedly a great asset to the order."

He thought on it a moment then decided to answer. She had seen all of his associates in action already, and more than once at that. Samara would gain no tactical advantage from his reply.

"The Ghalian you speak of is Demelza. She has been something of a surprise, really. An above-average member of the order, no doubt, but one who has blossomed in recent months."

"Quite a skilled swordswoman as well."

"You inspired her," Hozark replied. "She redoubled her training after your first encounter. She trained until she nearly dropped from exhaustion, in fact."

"All to better fight me?"

"Indeed."

"I like her even more now. And the pilot?"

"Uzabud. A good man who has been flying smuggling operations for some time. In recent years he also flies for me on occasion."

"A former pirate, I take it? His fighting style was familiar in that regard."

"Yes, he is. Good eye. You know, you were always quite perceptive."

"Thank you."

"Of course. Now, rounding out the crew are Laskar, our copilot and navigator, and Happizano, the boy you have kidnapped more than once."

"Again, not my design."

"Of course not," he replied unconvincingly. "In any case, Laskar is a minor power user in his own regard but an enormous pain in more than one unspeakable part on a regular basis."

"Stubborn?"

"Like you wouldn't believe. And an ego the size of a small moon."

"I know a few like that. Sounds like a pleasant traveling companion indeed. And what of the boy?" she asked. "I saw you defending him. You even seemed concerned for him. Most unlike you."

Hozark seemed to swell ever so slightly with pride. "Happizano Jinnik. The son of the visla your employer has kidnapped. He is a handful. A little over ten years old and full of fire. But he has come into his own in recent weeks, and with a little direction, he is becoming quite an impressive young man."

"Are you actually growing fond of a child? You always hated them."

"Times change, I suppose."

"That they do," Samara said, a curious little look flashing

across her face. "And what of the little one? The feisty creature? She seems to have quite a bit of potential herself."

"Henni was a stray we happened to pick up while tracing Master Prombatz's assailants. He is better now, by the way, though his student is permanently maimed."

"Yes, I heard. I am truly sorry for that, Hozark. You know I would never be a party to such acts."

"I assumed as much," he replied. "But I will tell you this: I will get Henni back. Her kidnapping will not stand."

Samara smiled. "I know you shall try," she said. "Honestly, I would not be surprised if all the stone and sand and bleached bones in the galaxy couldn't keep you away."

A section of cracked floor suddenly shifted at her feet as she probed for weak points. Samara lifted the piece free, revealing a small, but passable, space that appeared to descend to a large and surprisingly intact cavern below.

"But that is a discussion for another time," she said, casting an illumination spell in the newly revealed chamber. "Come. Let us see where this leads, shall we?"

CHAPTER THIRTY-THREE

The remains of the old city lying beneath the new one was not as sprawling and cavernous an expanse such as one might expect to find on a massively developed world where space was at a premium. In those places, older structures were often left intact below the surface as the new ones stretched skyward.

On Sooval, however, it was a different story. The township was small, the planet rather quiet, and available land plentiful. Excavation was typically kept shallow as the naturally occurring caves that dotted the area were not exactly a friendly habitat for people. The earliest settlers had learned that the hard way. Nowadays, however, the creatures that lived in the caverns kept to themselves.

So long as they remained undisturbed, that is.

As a result, while the older substructures in the center of inhabited areas might have occasionally been built on top of rather than excavated and replaced, most new structures were simply constructed on fresh ground where the depth of their underground chambers could be more precisely gauged.

Fortunately for the trapped Ghalian, the particular building in which they had taken shelter was one that happened to possess a subterranean footprint, though it was quite small. As it had proximity to the newer towers, one of which had tumbled directly atop them, that meant the likelihood of finding a connecting passageway was decent.

The chamber into which they had descended was not particularly spacious to begin with, and with the destruction above, much had collapsed, rendering the entire place a maze of debris and fallen stonework.

"I do not sense a breeze," Hozark commented as he and Samara crawled through the rubble beneath the chamber in which they'd been sheltering. "I believe, while we are in a slightly better situation than prior, we are still cut off from above."

"The air is definitely stagnant," she replied. "I think we shall have some way to travel upward before we might encounter a gap in the rubble large enough to permit airflow." Samara scanned the ruined chamber they found themselves in once more. "I believe of the available openings, this would provide the best opportunity," she said, moving closer to the smaller of the gaps in the rubble.

Most would have immediately headed into the largest and easiest to pass. But Hozark trusted her knack for survival, and if Samara said this was the best chance to get out, it almost certainly was. And besides, just because a passageway was larger did not in any way guarantee it would lead anywhere useful.

Being the leaner of the pair, Samara took point, crawling into the opening first. It was a vulnerable position, being on her hands and knees as she moved ahead, but between the illumination spell traveling ahead of her and the sheer quantity of deadly abilities she possessed, she was about as prepared as any could be.

She pushed aside a bit of debris blocking the way, then exited the passage after ten meters, standing to nearly her full height in what appeared to be an old food storage cellar that had clearly been abandoned some time ago. Hozark crawled out behind her and surveyed the chamber.

Its low ceiling had buckled, but the thick walls and columns had managed to keep it intact. They would have to duck, but the doorway at the far side appeared reachable.

The floor beneath them was another matter altogether. Sections had fallen away into a dark void so deep the illumination spell could not touch bottom. This building had been carefully constructed, the lowest level stopping well above the caverns below. But the sheer force of the destruction above drove the whole structure down, cracking through to the underground caverns.

Samara and Hozark nimbly avoided the gap, levering off of one another for support, using each other's body as a counterweight to safely clear the opening. Feet were anchored against the walls and support columns as the pair slid into their familiar rhythm. It seemed their old ways returned as if it was just yesterday they had parted rather than ten years earlier.

But it *had* been a decade. And Samara had faked her own demise and left Hozark and that life behind without a word of explanation. It had troubled him since the first moment he'd learned she was still alive. But that was not open for discussion. Not now at least.

In any case, for now they had to focus all of their attention on overcoming the obstacle at their feet. Repositioning as needed in unison, their movements were as precise and fluid as a pair of dancers as they made their way safely across to the far doorway. But instead of garnering applause at the end of the performance, this successful ballet above the precipice had allowed them to continue breathing.

"A bit reminiscent of Master Ditzal's obstacle courses, wouldn't you agree?" Hozark joked as they moved on toward the next chamber.

Even in the dim light, a little grin could be seen tugging at the corners of Samara's lips. "Similar, I suppose, but without the magical bombardments he was so fond of," she replied.

"He was always one for making it interesting."

"Yes, he was."

The pair moved through the next chamber with speed, each of them taking a side, surveying the space for exits while also remaining alert to possible threats. They had fully embraced the routine they had once been so familiar with, and the sweep of the area was rapid for it.

The room was mostly intact, apparently shielded from the intensity of the collapse by some fluke of construction its designers had never intended for this purpose. A much finer layer of dust was found, but nothing near so heavy as on other levels. More from disuse than destruction.

"Stairs," Hozark said when he opened a heavy door.

Samara nodded and followed as he stepped through, a pair of small blades in hand as they ascended to the next level above. While it was their own people up above, if they stumbled into a cluster of either of the armed forces, they might very possibly be forced to defend themselves against their own allies until proper identifications could be made.

It would be unfortunate, but the Ghalian had no intention of being on the losing end of any such misunderstanding. Fortunately, the level above was uninhabited. There were some newer items stored there, as well as a pair of doors at the far end.

One seemed to descend to another sub-basement area. Likely long-term storage, or even an abandoned space the likes of which they'd already passed through. The other door linked to a long corridor that connected to what must have been an adjacent building's chambers. If that was the case, then it seemed likely that they were still somewhere in the center region of town, where many prime parcels were controlled by the same families. Hence the connecting of their properties.

It was a way for people to easily move goods or supplies from one building to the other without requiring climbing all the way to the surface to do so. And in case of emergency, it would allow an egress without any being the wiser. It was fair to say, however, that none of those involved in the design had ever envisioned a situation such as this.

"I believe this is our best option," Samara said.

"I concur," Hozark replied.

Without hesitation, the two stepped into the long corridor, venturing farther into the unknown labyrinth of the city's buried past.

CHAPTER THIRTY-FOUR

"This structure appears to have avoided serious damage," Samara noted. "At least on this lower level."

"Indeed. Let us hope the pathways to the upper reaches were likewise spared. Or, if not, that there is at least some form of clear egress remaining. I much prefer fresh air to stale, as I am sure you do as well," Hozark said.

Samara looked back over her shoulder. The smile on her face, though small, was genuine. The little grin curving Hozark's lips was as well. The two had so easily fallen back into that place of casual comfort with one another, it was as if no time had passed at all.

They quietly passed into the adjacent building, walking in silence as they listened to the eerie sounds of debris settling above them. Whatever the condition of the subterranean corridor at the moment, it seemed quite possible it might become compromised at any time.

The pair adjusted their pace accordingly.

They made quick time through the chamber at the far end of the corridor. The doorway formerly sealing it off had been broken and lay on the ground amid tumbled crates and fallen debris. This was a somewhat damaged area, but the structure seemed sound enough for the moment.

As they carefully walked, the pair stole little glances at each other in the dim light. Once in a while, one would catch the other in the act but let it pass. Both were stoic, as was their nature, and would not openly show emotion, especially not in a situation such as this. But the feelings this unlikely partnership brought rushing back were quite mutual. And it felt like coming home.

"Samara," Hozark finally said, breaking the silence, "I must ask you––"

A deafening roar echoed in the chamber, followed by several more. The walls shook slightly from the volume in the enclosed space, and a fine mist of dust and debris rained down from above as the damaged roof settled.

The illumination spell did not reach the darkest, farthest reaches of the chamber, and something, some*things*, were moving there. The Ghalian quickly expanded the spell's range, but they had been utilizing a lower intensity light to help preserve their night vision. Unfortunately, that only made it easier for the beasts that had apparently made their way up from the dark caverns below.

There were five of them. Large, muscular, covered with a wiry, pale hair that had never seen the light of day. The skin beneath was gray and tough, leathery, and likely as strong as many forms of lesser armor. All four legs were on the ground, long claws clattering as they walked. The largest two reared up on their hind legs, enormous fangs exposed and ready to tear and rip and kill.

For their bulk, the creatures were impressively fast. And as Samara and Hozark drew their vespus blades, taking swipes at the beasts to defend themselves, it became clear the attacking creatures were quite nimble as well, despite their size.

Hozark instinctively stepped into the clearest space, Samara doing the same as both positioned themselves back-to-back as defense against the approaching beasts. Neither dared use even the slightest bit of magic while stuck down beneath the ruined buildings as they were. They did not know how stable their surroundings were, and they did not wish to tempt fate by casting to find out.

A set of long talons flashed out as one of the circling creatures abruptly changed course, barely missing Samara's face. Her swinging blade's reply found only empty air.

Hozark's back pressed hers in a way she knew so well, the shift telling her to move to her left while he circled with her for an attack. They moved in unison, Hozark's vespus blade transcribing a deadly arc where one of the beasts had just been. But the creature somehow managed to spin away from the weapon faster than it should have been able to. Nevertheless, Hozark had managed to make contact, albeit slight.

The animal roared once more, the others settling into a series of agitated clicks and grumbling sounds as they moved around their prey. One circled close to the illumination spell's brightest point, and at that moment, Hozark realized what they were up against.

"We need noise," he hissed.

"Noise? It will bring this place down upon our heads."

"And theirs. Trust me, Sam."

She only hesitated a moment. Despite their trying to kill one another not so long ago, she would nevertheless trust him with her life.

"Very well. Say when and I shall cast."

"The loudest spell you can think of," he said. "Then follow close."

She nodded once just as the beasts began moving closer for a group attack.

"Now!" Hozark shouted.

Samara cast a shrill alarm spell so powerful it often made

intruders flee out of sheer panic. Hozark took off running at top speed, which was really saying something, and Samara stuck to him like glue, casting the entire time. The creatures, rather than pursuing, were writhing and bellowing in distress, clawing at their heads while the ceiling above them began to crumble.

Hozark ignored all of that and was casting a protective spell above them both as they ran. It would not be enough to support the weight of the chamber if it caved in, but it would keep them from harm should any large chunks fall in their path, as several had just done.

They had just made it to the doorway at the far end of the chamber when everything rumbled as the ceiling gave way, dropping tons of debris into the space. Hozark powered ahead at full speed, charging up the stairs the door had led them to. It was blind luck, but he had chosen the exit that led upward, and the two of them now bounded toward the surface, taking the steps three at a time.

The stairwell was tall, and unlike the prior one discovered in the adjacent building, this one kept going up. It was a good thing, as the walls were shaking fiercely as a portion of the structure sank down into the shattered level below. Up and up the two ran until a faint light was apparent through the heavy dust.

Hozark shifted his spell and cast a force push directly ahead of them. The broken stone that was partially blocking the exit shattered and flew free as the two assassins burst from the opening, trailing a whirlwind of dust behind them. Moments later the stairwell collapsed, spewing out a cloud of sharp bits of stone.

The two dove to the ground in a heap together, the majority of the flying chunks whizzing by clear over their heads. Those that came lower were deflected by the duo's joined spells, the mixed power once again shielding them from harm. The rumbling slowed, then stopped, and the air began to clear.

"How did you know?" Samara asked.

"Dark dwellers. They had no eyes."

"Ah." She nodded, then the two awkwardly released their hold upon one another and rose to their feet.

They were free. Safely returned to the destruction of the surface. It seemed the Council ships had been quite indiscriminate in their attack, judging by the carnage wrought. Not too far off, however, Hozark saw the dyed hair and familiar face of one of the Ootaki he had helped relocate there.

She was a dusty mess but appeared unharmed. More importantly, when she saw Hozark, she smiled and gave a little nod before running off. Her people were safe, it seemed. At least for the time being.

Samara had also seen the woman but was not privy to what she really was. Just a survivor, so far as she could tell from that distance, though up close, given her own Ghalian skills, she'd have likely noticed the woman's power despite the dyed hair.

Samara and Hozark dusted themselves off, each assessing their bodies for injuries. They were both intact and unharmed. And more importantly, they were no longer bound by their truce.

The two paused, sharing a long look. Then by silent agreement, they relaxed their postures. They would fight again, but it would be some other day. For now, they would let this go. But there were things that needed to be said. Questions that lingered unanswered.

Samara could tell Hozark was mulling over his many questions in his mind, so she did the one thing she could. She simply turned and walked away. And, reluctantly, he let her.

A moment later, she was gone.

CHAPTER THIRTY-FIVE

"Impressive. Well done," Visla Jinnik said as he cast a very minor spell. He was able to do so only because he had found, after a bit of trial and error, that his control collar did not perceive this one as a spell used as an attempt to escape.

Henni had been focusing on her shielding spell. He had taught it to her days prior, but only now was it really starting to click. She pushed back his probing attack with relative ease, though to be fair, it was nowhere near what he'd have been able to do if not constrained by his thick golden collar.

"It's making more sense," she said. "The whole *intent* part of it. I think I'm getting it, finally."

"You most certainly are," the visla said with a sense of pride.

She had been picking up his lessons faster in recent days, and their captors, for whatever reason, seemed to be allowing them more time between draining sessions.

Henni was only minorly reduced in power and strength, though she slept like the dead every time she was brought back to her cell and woke fully restored.

Jinnik, on the other hand, was showing the wear and tear of the constant reduction of his magic. He mused that if not for the extra little bit of recharge time they had both been fortunate enough to enjoy, he might not have been able to last much longer.

Even for a power user with as vast a reservoir of magic as he, eventually the well would run dry if not allowed to replenish. Whether Niallik realized this and ordered more respite for him, or if it was merely a pleasant coincidence, he did not care. What mattered was he was finally starting to slowly climb out of the deep pit of exhaustion that had claimed him for far too long.

He was missing his son terribly, and he would do anything necessary to reunite with him once more. But taking this rowdy young woman under his wing had given him something his confinement had been lacking. A sense of purpose. And in nurturing her blossoming powers, he found his parental instincts kicking in once again.

That this unlikeliest of cellmates had actually been helping protect Happizano was an additional motivation to help her. She had done right by his boy, and he would aid her in turn to the best of his ability.

Jinnik relaxed his grip on his spell, allowing Henni to take a brief respite from her defenses. But rather than pause to catch her proverbial breath, the feisty, violet-haired young woman immediately tried to cast an attack spell. It wasn't anything significant, her collar would not allow that, but had she succeeded, it would have made an impression.

Unfortunately for her, the spell misfired and fizzled out into nothing.

"Damn it! Why won't that work?" she griped. "Every time it's the same thing."

"You excel at defense, and your magic has true potential. But it would seem your talents do not lie in the offensive arts."

"But magic is magic. If the power is there, then it *should* be able to work, right?"

"It should, yes. But, for whatever reason, your powers seem

restrained from offensive casting. I've never felt a magic of your kind before, so I am afraid I cannot be of any more help than that. But with practice, I think you might yet succeed in your attempts."

What he did not tell her was that he sensed more than just her unusual flavor of power. As he trained her and got a feel for her gifts, Visla Jinnik had become more and more of the opinion that her power could possibly be of a magnitude rarely seen, if only she could learn to tap into it.

Controlling her power was the difficult part, however, but for that he had a radical solution. It was possible, he believed, that if they were continued to be allowed longer rest periods to regain their strength, he might be able to break one of their collars. To gain their freedom.

So far, the increased power he had recuperated was minimal. Henni, however, was only ever slightly drained, and she recovered quickly. If he could just get a few more days of this additional rest, he hoped he could show her how to join power with him. To combine their casting.

It would be difficult for a novice such as she was, but given his exceptional skills and her innate strength, it just might work. And if it did, they could force off one of their collars and fight their way to freedom.

Of course, if they could do so, it would make the most sense to free Jinnik as he had no problem whatsoever with offensive spells. But it took him a long time to recover, and if they were discovered too soon after the attempt, he would be too weak to defend them both.

Henni, on the other hand, had a different skill set. She may not have been able to cast terribly well, but if they managed to free her of her restraints and could place something sharp in her hands, there was a very good possibility she could take down enough guards to give them a fighting chance at escaping.

It was something he would continue to ponder as his power

slowly returned. For now, however, it was just a hypothetical. But one he felt could very possibly become a reality.

Later that evening, the guards came into the cellblock to haul one of them off to be drained yet again.

"Be strong, Henni. I shall be back soon," Jinnik said as they entered his cell and muscled him to his feet.

"Oh, you're *both* coming with us," the nearest man said with a menacing laugh. "Niallik wants to try something new."

"Wait, what?" Henni blurted as additional men joined them, pouring into her cell and scooping her up like so much baggage.

"Leave her out of this," Jinnik demanded.

"You're in no position to make orders," the guard said, not intimidated in the slightest. "Now, get moving."

The pair were then marched out of the cellblock and down the corridor. Soon enough they would find out what fresh hell Niallik had in mind for them.

It was two hours later the pair of prisoners were dragged back to their cells, damp, exhausted, and drained.

Jinnik was dumped onto his cot in a heap, falling fast asleep as soon as his weary body hit the thin mattress. Henni, likewise, seemed to pass out immediately.

The guards snickered and sealed the cells, then left the two alone in the dim chamber. Jinnik was out cold. Henni, on the other hand, was still only partially drained, though she had played it up in hopes of perhaps gaining an advantage at some point. Her mind was a bit fuzzy still, and the power they had managed to pull from her was enough that she actually felt it this time. But it hadn't rendered her unconscious for some reason. Maybe it was because Jinnik was involved. Had he somehow helped her fight it off?

She didn't know, and until he woke up, there was no way to find out. Henni glanced over at the slumbering visla. His cheeks were sunken and his skin ashy. He was utterly drained. It would be some time before he roused, so she did the one thing that made sense in that situation.

She took his lead and went to sleep, hoping they would both wake refreshed. She knew it was a long shot, but it was all she had. And after what Niallik had done, she needed to focus on something positive. Anything at all.

With thoughts of escape and revenge swimming in her head, Henni quickly drifted off into a dreamless slumber.

CHAPTER THIRTY-SIX

Niallik was pacing.

The weapons makers were always nervous when she started pacing--more than once they'd faced her wrath when her feet finally stopped moving. But this time it seemed like she was agitated in a good way.

She was utterly fixated on the small, magically sealed vial in her hand, staring at the swirling mixture of power barely contained within it as she moved. So deep in thought was she that, despite their pressing timeline and fear of Visla Maktan's displeasure if they delayed, none of the workers dared interrupt her.

Only after a good twenty minutes of her disconcerting focus did she finally stop moving, looking up from the vial in her hands to the expectant faces of her lackeys. A little smile crept onto her lips.

"I believe I understand how we can utilize this power," she said with clear relish. "Prepare a konus to be charged."

The master smelter and weaponsmith took this as his cue to finally speak. He was a tough fellow, having made implements of death and destruction for many in his day. But this job put him on edge like no other. They were playing with a power none of them fully understood, and the risks were daunting.

"That is excellent news, Niallik," he said, attempting to look strong in front of his lackeys, while also being careful of the woman's dangerously fluctuating mood. "But since my people have more experience bonding magic to metal, perhaps we should let them take a good look before we proceed. The magic you managed to extract from the girl is of a type none of us have ever dealt with before, and I think it would be wise to--"

"You know our timetable," she cut him off, her eyes again fixed on the swirling, magical fluid in the vial. "Prepare the crucible at once."

There was no openness for discussion in her voice. Their task was clear, and that was all there was for it.

"Um, yes, of course. We've got the metal nearly ready to pour. I'll have them bring it to full temperature immediately. We should be ready shortly."

She smiled at him. It was both pleasant, yet unsettling. The painstakingly extracted, and likewise difficult to contain, power in her hand, had seemed an impossible task for Visla Maktan's previous head of staff. But Niallik had a different way of doing things, and her reputation was well known. She *would* get the job done. No matter what.

Unfortunately, no matter what often came with a steep price, and not just in coin.

Yet she had managed to do what no one else could. She had pulled an enormous amount of power from the captive Visla Jinnik without killing the man. And the newcomer, the one with the strange power unlike any had seen before, had finally given up a bit of her power as well.

It was out-of-the-box thinking that led to her breakthrough. Of course, she knew the visla had been helping the girl tap into her power. There was no way she would leave an asset like that unmonitored, unlike her predecessor. And observing how he interacted with her, using his own magic to help her focus hers, and despite his being exhausted no less, led to her breakthrough idea.

She had been struggling uphill when there was an easier way to tap into them both. Their willing merger of power, no matter how slight it may have been, provided her the opening she needed. They could be used against one another, and without even realizing they were doing so. Draining both of them *together* was the key.

The girl would only give up the slightest trace of power when submerged in Niallik's rather specialized tub, but the visla had already succumbed to more conventional methods of extraction. She had continued to use the chair on him, as it worked quite effectively, but when she put him in contact with the liquid while working her magic on Henni as well, the visla's power seemed to flow far easier.

And, to her great delight, with the ease of extraction came a significantly reduced toll on the man. It was almost as if he were suddenly a willing participant, and as such she was able to pull far more magic from him as a result, the additional power flowing out, but without much of a detrimental effect on the man.

He would need additional rest to replenish his potency for the next session, no doubt, but the increased extraction rate of his power from this new process more than made up of the relatively minor delay of his lengthened recovery period.

It had been quite a coup on her part. But in addition to that, she had succeeded in pulling more of the strange girl's power with it. Henni's magic had blended with Jinnik's in the extraction process. Niallik had expected that to some degree and had planned on simply filtering and separating them into their respective containers.

But the magic seemed to resist her efforts, the swirling forces having apparently developed some sort of bond in the process, stymieing her efforts. Visla Maktan could undoubtedly force the two diverse powers apart--he was a man of exceptional strength--but Niallik knew her glory, and thus reward, would be diminished if she had to wait for his assistance to complete her task.

And so it was that she prepared to power up a new batch of magical weaponry with the potent mixture of powers still combined. If she failed, she would simply put additional effort into finding a way to separate the two. But if she succeeded, it would be quite an achievement indeed, and the visla would undoubtedly reward her greatly.

"We're ready," the weaponsmith informed Niallik a very short while later.

They had been keeping the crucible hot and ready to smelt, knowing full well the woman's propensity for bursts of inspiration. It was far better to exert the effort to keep the forges going in anticipation than to face her disappointment.

Niallik followed him to the chamber they had been using as their main experimentation facility. There were other larger spaces available, but this one had thick walls and was far enough from the other goings-on that any magical bleed out would not taint their other work.

The air had an acrid, metallic tang to it from the molten fluid awaiting its power. This was the most delicate and dangerous portion of the entire process. The adding of power to the just-poured metal, bonding the magic to the device being made as it cooled. On a good day it was challenging. With Niallik's requirements, it seemed almost impossible.

But the weaponsmiths were some of the finest coin could buy, and they had provided weapons aplenty to many unsavory causes in their storied careers. And if they could somehow make this connection work, the financial bonuses would be substantial, to say the least.

Niallik handed the man the little vial of condensed power.

She estimated it contained enough raw magic to charge at least a dozen konuses, if not more. But with the mix of Henni's strange power in it as well, she really couldn't be sure. She didn't know what that one's gift might do when put into a receptacle like this.

"Prepare the channeling spells," the man said, carefully positioning himself just beside the konus mold, the vial in one hand, the other outstretched and ready to cast the words that would drive just a little bit of the power he now held out of its magical containment and into the molten konus.

"Ready," the two handling the glowing-hot crucible replied.

"Begin the pour."

The crucible tilted slowly, a fine stream of liquid metal pouring into the magically reinforced mold that would form the new weapon. As the metal flowed, he chanted the words he knew so well, using his own power to direct the volatile magic they were attempting to tame into the nascent konus.

His decades of experience had given him a skill few possessed and the confidence required to wield it. But this magic fought back as he worked, and that was bad.

The difficult thing was all magic beyond the very specific spells to charge the konus had to be kept clear of the workspace lest a catastrophic failure occur. It was a safety protocol that had been used for centuries, and it had been drilled into his head since his first day as an apprentice.

But this magic was different. *Squirmy*. Trying to break free. He struggled to direct it into the konus, forcing it to bond to the hot metal as he'd done so many times before. The magic, however, had other ideas, and was fighting back like none he had ever felt.

Niallik was the first to notice that something was wrong. *Very* wrong. Like the moment of calm on a beach before a tsunami, when the water suddenly pulled out to sea, leaving a silent void, the chamber felt eerily still.

The weaponsmith was struggling with the spell, and it was a

battle he was clearly losing. Without another moment of hesitation, Niallik lunged across the room, making for the doorway as fast as she could. Seeing her flee, the others immediately followed her lead.

All but one. His hold on the unstable magical blend was tenuous, but he was going to keep trying if it was the last thing he did.

It was.

The structure shook from the blast, a fine dusting raining down from the ceiling as the containment spells did their work, slamming into place to contain the event, holding the building together. But only barely. It was clear that if not for the safety precautions Visla Maktan had cast while preparing this facility, they would certainly all have perished in the incident.

Niallik and the others rose to their feet and dusted themselves off. The weaponsmith's associates were in shock at what had just transpired. They were also quite afraid of how Niallik would react. Her entire vial of magic had been lost in the blast, after all, spilled and dispersed when the fraction of it being used took out the room. But, to their dismay, she was actually smiling.

Had the entire amount gone critical, the whole facility would likely be a crater no matter how many containment spells Visla Maktan had left in place. But that had not happened, and she had just learned something incredibly valuable.

Henni's magic, it seemed, was exponentially more powerful than she had thought. It was unstable, just like its source, yet it was remarkable. It was unique. It was also incredibly dangerous, as they'd just learned the hard way. But if she could perfect the extraction process and learn how to properly harness the young woman's magic?

With it, Visla Maktan would be unstoppable, and the troublesome Visla Jinnik would finally no longer be necessary.

And Niallik would become a very wealthy and *very* well-connected woman.

Niallik turned to the master weaponsmith's second-in-command. "Well, that was interesting. It looks like you just got a promotion. Congratulations."

"But I'm only the––"

"You've been promoted," she said again, fixing him with a hard stare. "*Congratulations.*"

The man swallowed hard. "Uh, thank you, Niallik."

"Now, this is your chance to shine. Let's see if you can step up and do what your former associate could not."

"But the power. It was destroyed in the blast."

Niallik seemed utterly unfazed by his words. It was a bit unsettling, given how much effort she'd put into extracting that vial's worth of power. But she simply reached into her pocket and withdrew a tiny little tube no bigger than the tip of her finger. Inside was that same swirling mix of magic.

"You saved some!"

"Of course," she replied. "Do you think I wouldn't be prepared for such an event?"

What she didn't say was that this was her personal stash she had been planning on keeping for herself. It had been a bit of a chore, siphoning it away from the main container, but she'd managed, and if the power could truly do what she hoped it might, her little sample-sized vial would be worth a pretty sum.

But that was far less important than completing a konus with this magic. Maktan would want results, and she simply could not delay. She handed the man the little vial.

"Let's try again, shall we? And this time, do try to not blow up the facility."

They made their way to one of the adjacent chambers. It had a more rudimentary setup in place, but it was still a fully functional smelting operation. In no time the man and his team got the magical fires stoked and the raw ore melting into molten liquid potential.

Having seen what happened to his former superior, the newly minted weaponsmith was far more cautious with his casting, barely trickling the power into the newly forged konus as the metal just began to cool into its shape. He hoped that by waiting just that little bit of time, the magic would not react so violently as it had before.

Even so, he struggled with the spell, fighting the unstable magic the entire time. But this was different. It was a challenge, yes, but it did not feel like a cascading disaster as it had been the prior attempt. Finally, after a great deal of work, the magic bonded to the cooling metal, sealed within and providing it a magical charge.

"It won't be ready for use until it is fully cooled, I would believe," he said. "It shouldn't take more than a few hours.

"You won't dunk it in water?"

"I think it's too unstable when hot," he replied. "I understand you're in a hurry, but given what just happened, I think––"

"Yes, yes. Fine," Niallik interrupted. "We've waited this long, I suppose."

The hours crept by painfully slowly, but finally the device had cooled until it possessed but a tiny bit of warmth.

"It's ready," the man said.

Niallik picked it up and slid it onto her wrist.

"Are you sure you don't want one of the men to test it out first?" he asked.

"Oh, no," she replied, an excited look in her eye. "I'm quite prepared for this risk."

The rush of being the first person ever to wield a konus powered by this utterly unique form of magic was a thrill like no other, and she had no intention of letting anyone else steal her moment of glory.

Carefully, and with only the smallest bit of intent, she cast a basic force spell at the heavy stone work table nearby. It slid across the room with ease, nearly smashing into the far wall.

Niallik's smile grew wider. "Oh, yes. This will do quite nicely," she said, turning back to her new chief weapon maker. "Now, prepare yourself. After the next extraction, you'll need to create more of these."

CHAPTER THIRTY-SEVEN

Demelza was not enjoying her flight to the next system in her quest for the Quommus. It wasn't that the voyage itself was particularly long or daunting, or that her shimmer ship was at all uncomfortable for such a trip. The odor of her undesired, but necessary, companion, however, was something in a class of its own.

The woman was called Itzalla, and she was a Nagalian, with the coarse hair the color of rotting sea grass and folds of rough, yellowish skin that were common to her race.

Most of her kind who ventured out into mixed company were quite aware how pungent the trapped oils and sweat they produced could be to others and washed or used masking spells accordingly. No one held it against them, it was just their own physiology at work.

This one, however, didn't seem to care one lick about other people's sensitivity to her aroma. And given that her diet consisted largely of low-quality foods of the greasiest nature, the effect was only exacerbated.

But, despite that huge drawback, the woman was one hell of a navigator. And more importantly, the only one in three systems Demelza had found who could make any sense of the cryptic star charts she had cobbled together from the temple glyphs, runes, and sigils.

She had originally tried to simply purchase a set of legible charts, consolidated and modernized for her quest. But the navigator, despite her talents, was living on a rather shitty world in an even shittier system. And she had a different price in mind.

"I want off of this stinking rock," she said.

The irony of her complaint was not lost on Demelza, nor her nose. And her resolve, and price, were as readily apparent as her stench.

"You wish to be dropped at another world? Provide me the chart and I shall do so."

"Nah, I don't just wanna go from one dump to some other crap planet. I want to see what's out there. To stretch my legs."

"We shall be in a ship."

"You know what I mean. I've been cooped up too long, and I want some adventure."

Demelza hesitated.

"Or you can just find someone else who happened to have studied ancient system references, planet names, and antique star charts as a hobby growing up. I'm sure they're easy to find."

Obviously, they were not. And given the woman's personality, it was apparent why she had taken up such a solitary pastime in her youth. Like it or not, Itzalla was her best, and only, option.

"You wish to accompany me, then?"

"You betcha," the woman replied. "These chart glyph thingies you found are wild. Never come across anything quite like 'em, and I'm looking forward to seeing exactly where they take us."

The Ghalian paused, weighing her options. There was only one.

"Well, let us gather your possessions. We can then—"

"Got all my stuff packed and ready," Itzalla said. "Gimme five minutes and I'll be aboard and all set to go."

And just like that, Demelza was saddled with an unwanted crewmate. Having an outsider taking up residence aboard her ship, even briefly, was far from ideal. But it seemed there was little choice.

Itzalla quickly made herself at home in the small bunking space aboard the vessel. It was not a craft designed for a large contingent, and it would be a bit cramped. Ghalian worked alone, and this was a shimmer ship designed for silent infiltration and escape.

But the occasional need to house an additional occupant had been taken into consideration in its fabrication, so the malodorous woman at least had her own quarters, however cramped they might be. It certainly beat sharing a room with her.

Demelza began casting odor masking spells as soon as they boarded the ship. It was in no way her strong suit, but if they were to be cooped up together for any length of time, it was not a luxury but a necessity.

"This is the navigation console," the assassin said, showing her guest her place in the command chamber. "You shall work from here."

"Oh yeah, this'll do just fine," Itzalla said, messily spreading her notes, scrolls, and charts all about the surface.

"So, where do the markings guide us?"

"Hold your Malooki. Give me a minute, here," the navigator said as she shuffled things about.

"You said you could guide me to the place named in the runes. The one called the 'Red Jewel.'"

"Well, yeah. But you can't rush an artist."

"You are a navigator."

"And there's an art to navigation. Like the saying goes, 'Rush the navigator and you might fly into a sun.'"

"I have never heard that saying."

"Well, it's a thing. Trust me."

Demelza was beginning to have second thoughts about bringing this one aboard. But they hadn't taken off yet, so it was still possible to rid herself of her passenger if she proved all talk and no skill.

But Itzalla *was* skilled. Just a bit peculiar as well.

"Oh yeah," she said as she rearranged the seemingly chaotic pile in front of her. "Yeah, that's it."

"That is what?"

"The first part of breaking this down into something we can actually use. I mean, all of the stuff you gave me is old. I'm talking *really* old. Names that haven't been used in centuries. Some even longer."

"Yes, I am aware."

"But you had a couple of useful bits in there with all this mess. The 'Red Jewel' has to be a red dwarf star. Whether it's the sun at the center of the system we're looking for or is just a road marker isn't clear yet. But it gives us something to work from. And then there was this other bit. Where did I put it?"

She shuffled through the parchment until she came across the piece she was looking for.

"Yeah, there it is. '*The light burns bright, the two eyes of Orakis staring down from above.*' Kinda cryptic, but those old-timers were big on flowery language, ya know?"

"Yes, I've heard. But can you decipher it?"

"I'm getting to it. See, the two eyes of Orakis almost surely mean a dual sun system."

"How can you be sure it is a system and not mere solar markings on the map?"

"Because of the way it's worded. '*Staring down from above.*' Get it?"

Dizzying as the woman's train of thought might be to follow, Demelza actually did. "Of course. *Above* signifies standing on a planet's surface looking upward."

"Yep."

"So our destination orbits twin suns."

"If they haven't gone and blown up since the time this was all written, then yeah."

"This is excellent work, Itzalla. Set a course and we shall depart at once."

"Hey now, hold on a minute. This all makes *some* sense, but these are ancient names and arcane symbols for planets and systems. It's gonna take me a bit."

"But you can do it, yes?"

"Of course I can. Some of the systems look familiar, and once I backtrack a few and develop a proper key, I should have us a course plotted."

"How long will it take you?"

"What did I say about rushing the navigator?" she snarked. "Tell ya what. Why don't you go and grab us some food and I'll see what I can do?"

Demelza fought down the reflexive urge to smack the sass out of the woman and instead simply smiled and nodded. "Of course. Please, continue with your work. I shall return shortly."

The Ghalian strode from her ship into the fresh air outside and breathed deep. It was almost amusing, Itzalla's penchant for smart talk. *Almost.* Had she known she was mouthing off to a Wampeh Ghalian, she likely would have minded her manners far more. But so far as the troublesome woman knew, Demelza was simply an ordinary Wampeh traveler seeking a navigator.

And so Demelza trekked back into the marketplace to acquire some fresh food for her new guest. She would feed her and take her off of this planet, as promised, but she intended that their tenuous union be as brief as possible. She was a solitary being by nature, and her new navigator was cramping her style. But if all went well, she would reach her destination, and Itzalla would find a happy new home. At least she hoped so.

CHAPTER THIRTY-EIGHT

Itzalla had been good to her word, directing them to what appeared to be the next leg of the search, rather than the final destination. It had taken a fair bit of work on the navigator's part, scouring countless star charts, cross-referencing ancient names of worlds that only kind of sounded like what was written in the sigils and glyphs from the temple markings. But Itzalla had finally done it.

"Two eyes of Orakis. It references a deity who carried a big hammer and defeated all who threatened his realm. Which was a pretty hot and shitty one, legend has it. Just like that planet right there. Yep, that's your system," she announced proudly, kicking her feet up on the console and stuffing her face with bread smeared with warm Giggis cheese.

It was not a snack most would choose, nor one most could stomach. But hers appeared to be of cast iron, as Demelza had learned over the few days in transit with her.

They had stopped at three planets on the way. Each time at the request of Itzalla. She said it was to help her dial in her bearings, but after just the first layover, Demelza realized quite clearly that the woman simply wanted to sightsee under the guise of seeking further information from locals.

What she also noted was that she would come back to the ship with new items after each new world. Nothing huge, nothing too flashy, but certainly things that were beyond her somewhat limited means. Itzalla, it seemed, was a bit of a thief as well.

Demelza would have to keep her eyes on this one. And on her own ship as well. The situation was far from ideal.

Finally they arrived on the hot, dusty planet with twin suns that also happened to line up with the other markings in the chart. It was the first time Itzalla showed no interest in sightseeing.

"I hate the heat," the woman said. "And I hate dust. You go on without me."

It made sense. With her rolls of skin, the heat would be miserable, and dust would gather and chafe. So Demelza made the solitary trek through the city that seemed to have the highest concentration of industrial trades, but not before pocketing her Drookonus and setting a few additional wards in place on her ship before heading out.

It was not the biggest or most exciting city on the planet, but it was the most likely place to find a temple aimed at metalsmiths and ore miners. But as she surveyed the worn structures of the town, Demelza soon realized this inhospitable environment would have destroyed the temple ages ago.

Yet those old orders tended to stick around once established, and there could still be a few residents around who might know something, anything, that would help her to her next destination. To the "Red Jewel."

"Excuse me," she asked a woman selling a cold, tart-smelling beverage. "What is that drink you are selling?"

"Trannis juice? You don't know Trannis juice?" the woman said with barely hidden contempt for the stranger.

"I am not from this system, and this is all new to me."

"I could tell," the woman said with a snort, noting Demelza's pale skin. "Wampeh, right?"

"Yes."

"Don't see many of your kind around here. Too bright. Too hot for you folk. You know, with the twin suns and all."

"The eyes of Orakis, I'm told. A most marvelous story."

The woman's attitude shifted slightly. "You know about Orakis?"

"Only a few stories I heard in the temple many years ago."

"The temple, you say?"

"Yes," Demelza replied, tracing the sigil found on the anvil in the magical frost on the drink container.

The vendor's attitude shifted immediately. "Well, I'm sure you'll find *our* temple to be quite a sight. Most do."

That caught her attention. The temple was apparently still intact, much to her surprise.

"That is why I stopped here. I was hoping to visit it before continuing my journey. But I see the elements have worn the buildings here greatly."

"Oh, our temple isn't subject to that sort of thing. Head to the center of town and look for the markings. You'll see them," the woman said, then poured a glass of the tart beverage and handed it to Demelza.

"Thank you so much. What do I owe you?"

"It's on the house. Welcome, Sister, and enjoy your stay."

Demelza graciously accepted the offering and headed farther into the network of squat buildings and narrow streets. All designed to provide shade from the blistering suns and protection from the sandy wind.

At the center of town she saw what she was looking for, just as the woman had said. But it was not at all what she had expected.

The structure was a single, tiny building with thick, worn

walls. The magical warding on it was slowing its erosion, but not stopping it entirely. The heavy door, however, seemed in excellent condition. It was metal, polished bright by the winds. And upon it was a single marking. A sigil.

Demelza strode to it and tested it for hidden traps or defenses. None were present. The metal was cool under her hand, despite the heat outside. It was an odd dichotomy, to say the least. She pushed the door and stepped into the cold air of the chamber.

Immediately, she saw the reason for the temperature shift. This was not a temple, it was an access shaft to an old mine from which the cold breeze was flowing. She sniffed the air. There was the distinct smell of a subterranean water flow.

Now it made sense. They had built the temple in the one location it would be safe from the elements. Where it would be comfortable to congregate. In a cool underground cavern. And in this inhospitable place, one with flowing water would provide precisely that.

Demelza walked down the stairs hewn into the rock, the treads worn smooth by years of footfall upon them. A calm, magical illumination lit the way down and down. It was not a trek for the infirm or weak, but in this place, she guessed those didn't survive long anyway.

The chamber at the bottom of the stairs was not as large as she had imagined, given the vendor's comments, but it certainly lived up to her description as impressive, though for different reasons.

The cave's domed ceiling was dotted with small spells of varying color and strength, their glow casting light down upon the chamber. It was beautiful and unlike anything she had ever seen before.

In the center there was a brightly polished anvil, as she expected, but around it there were no columns or other decorations at all. At the base, however, was an ornate grill encircling it. The faint sound of water could be heard through it.

Ah, the sacrifices bleed into the water. A way to pay homage to the lifeblood of this place, she realized.

Demelza walked to the perimeter and slowly made a circuit of the cave. There were a fair number of people down there, resting and taking refreshment despite there being no temple services at the moment. As the coolest location in the city, most likely, the temple followers seemed to use it as a general gathering place as well as one of worship.

It was clever, really. By its very nature it was an appealing place to congregate, and what better way to bring newcomers into the flock than by providing them comfortable refuge after a hard day's work?

She cast a small disguise spell, darkening her skin to match the locals' sun-kissed complexion better, and continued her walk unnoted by the others. It was an ideal situation for gathering intelligence but for one thing. All of the markings on the walls were mere repetition of what she already had.

They were ornate, and they were marvelously preserved among the beautiful works of art that had been painted and carved into the stone, but they offered her nothing new.

She began to doubt Itzalla's navigation, but this was exactly what the cryptic runes and sigils had said. Two suns, and locals with knowledge of the ancient deity Orakis, and a temple of the sect? It had to be the place.

Demelza turned her attention again to the carvings in the ceiling. This particular temple had an illumination system of its own, so she did not need to risk drawing attention to herself by casting one above. But as she looked at the markings, it was clear they were essentially the same as the others.

Frustrated, she allowed her mind to drift a moment, her eyes unfocusing slightly as she pondered what to do next. The slight flickering of the lights above was rather relaxing, she thought. Pleasant to stare at, not unlike--

"Stars," she gasped.

Demelza carefully looked around. No one had seemed to notice her reaction. She turned her gaze back to the ceiling and ignored the markings, focusing instead on the lights dotting the dome. It was a star chart. And the twin suns above them were clear as day.

More importantly, though there were many red dwarf stars in the galaxy, this particular chart only had a few marked. And only one of them glowed and flickered with any intensity.

She smiled to herself and took careful note of her findings. She was willing to bet all of the coin in her ship that the red light marked the way to her prize.

Demelza locked the image in her mind as only a trained Ghalian could, then slowly and without drawing any attention to herself, made her way back to the stairway and ascended to the surface. She knew where she was going next. And hopefully it would be her final destination. Just a quick confirmation with Itzalla and they would be good to go.

She stopped at the Trannis juice vendor and purchased a container to take with her, thanking her all the while and telling her that indeed, this temple put the others to shame.

The woman was pleased to hear the words of praise from a sister from another world and bade her safe travels as Demelza walked back toward her ship.

Itzalla was sprawled unconscious on the deck when she stepped inside her climate-controlled vessel. Demelza shook her head, disappointed, but not surprised. She then began removing all of the things her navigator had attempted to pilfer from her ship.

The coin and small weapons were expected, but the woman had also stolen Demelza's small vial of Nasturian she had acquired from an herbalist during the making of the cure for Happizano's poisoning some time ago.

Had Itzalla known what she had picked up, she would likely have put it back immediately, as the intense burn from just a drop of the extract could fell the strongest of men. And the magical properties of the plant only made countering the effect near impossible.

She slid the vial of dangerous fluid into her pocket and continued retrieving her things from the slumbering woman. Once she had put all of her belongings back in their place, she slid the Drookonus into its receptacle and prepped for takeoff. Once that was done, she turned her attention to the woman on the floor.

"Wake up," she said coolly as she cast the rousing spell.

"What? What happened?" Itzalla asked, still slightly dazed. "I must have fallen and hit my head."

Demelza merely stared at her with a disapproving glare. The navigator's hands casually moved to her pockets. It was then she realized the game was up.

"Look, I was only taking a few things to trade for some food."

"There is food in the ship."

"Well, uh, yeah, but I wanted to get you something nice. As a thank you, ya know?"

"By selling my own possessions?"

Itzalla could tell this line of reasoning was going to go nowhere so she shifted tack. "You know, that was really not cool of you. You could have really hurt someone. I mean, what kind of sick fuck puts stun wards inside their own ship?"

Demelza smiled, her fangs slipping into full view. "*This* kind," she said with an icy tone.

Itzalla didn't piss herself, and Demelza had to give her some credit for that. But the sight of those fangs, and the realization she'd just tried to rob a Wampeh Ghalian, turned any backbone she'd developed to putty.

"Look, I'm sorry. Please don't drain me."

"I have no intention of drinking from you," Demelza said, walking closer.

Itzalla instinctively backed up, trying to keep what little distance she could between herself and the deadly killer. Demelza continued forward until the woman had backed all the way to the ship's external door.

Demelza spoke the words and opened it, a little gust of hot air rushing in.

"Out."

"What?"

"*Out*."

Itzalla knew better than to argue and stepped out of the door and into the heat. It was looking like the Ghalian didn't want to dirty her ship when she beat the thief, but Demelza stopped in the doorway and just stared at her. Finally, she spoke.

"You shall live, Itzalla. But let this be a lesson to you."

Itzalla's expression shifted from abject terror to confusion to a different kind of fear. One mixed with the horrible realization of what Demelza meant to do to her. She almost hoped for death. Not really, but sort of.

"You're going to leave me here?" she asked, gesturing to the blistering-hot city and its dusty breeze. "This is worse than where I was before!"

Demelza remained impassive. "Again, let this be a lesson," she said, then turned her back and sealed the door. Itzalla's begging and pleading was entirely muted by the ship's hull. A moment later Demelza lifted off and headed for space, minus a ridealong, her ship once again her own.

CHAPTER THIRTY-NINE

Demelza had made several jumps before arriving in the destination system plotted out on Itzalla's rather messy star chart. The woman may have been talented at the navigation portion of her job, but where she excelled in that, she was profoundly lacking in organization.

As a result, it took Demelza a solid hour to triple-check that she was interpreting the charts correctly before she finally engaged her first jump. She mused the annoying woman's words just before casting the spell.

"Do not rush yourself into a sun, Demelza," she said with a little chuckle, then engaged her Drookonus.

In the gaps between jumps she studied the charts and cryptic words surrounding them as the Drookonus cooled before its next use. Master Orkut had definitely clued her in to the right trail. Or, at least a trail she could follow, but she found herself wishing he had simply told her where to go.

"The eyes of Orakis. Would it not have been just as easy to say, 'Twin sun system'?" she mused. "And now, to the red jewel where the Quommus lays 'beneath azure.' That is not terribly helpful, Orkut. What ever did they mean by that?"

She studied both her own and Itzalla's notes, comparing them for any key or codebreaker to help her decipher the text. But the more she looked, the more apparent it was that nothing so simple would present itself. She would simply have to make her way to the red dwarf solar system and find her next step from there. Somehow.

She had wondered for a while if it could have signified a blue sun from a nearby system, but as there were no such stars burning anywhere near where she was heading, that seemed highly unlikely. And besides, the markers had all aligned, leading her to this particular star in this particular system with its planets orbiting a red sun.

Demelza felt the frustration rising as she went over the sigils and runes she had copied forward and back. It was only when she exited her final jump into that system and began her approach toward its center that the key to the riddle presented itself.

"Of course," she said as soon as her eyes fell upon the main inhabited world in the system.

It was an oceanic planet, with over eighty percent of its mass covered by water. A beautiful, blue orb floating in the dark, circling the red jewel at the system's center. The planet Galaloom.

The connection hadn't registered with her until she put the visual with the name. She had been to that world before many, many years ago, when she had first become a full-fledged Ghalian. It had been a simple job, putting an end to the boss of a particularly nasty mob faction.

She had performed her task and left immediately, not once thinking back on that experience. Not until now. *Now* it all made sense.

Galaloom's surface was sparsely populated. A result of the limited dry land. But it had a thriving culture and robust population elsewhere. Beneath azure, as the clue had said. She was going to the planet's underwater cities.

They were not subaqueous in the truest sense of the meaning. There was no powered dome of magic dividing air space from ocean. But the many large caverns that dotted the undersea realm were close enough and certainly fit the description. And she now recalled from her recon on her assassination there that the world had once been home to a large mining culture before the planet had been stripped of most of its easily accessible riches.

The miners had been rather well off, and it only made sense that they would go to great lengths to protect themselves from detection by those seeking to steal their wealth. And what better way to do so than to create the one thing that could keep their magical protections guarding their riches a secret? They created the Quommus.

Of course, once the wealth ran out and the sect scattered and spread across the stars, there would have been little use for such a thing. But if the temple remained intact, that would be its most likely hiding place.

Whatever the hell it actually was.

Demelza strode down the long path from the surface, the briny breeze of the undersea realm wafting up to her through the long, volcanic tube leading from the tiny spit of land to the sprawling city below.

There had been a great many more cities at one point, before the great glacial thaw, but only those whose terrestrial accessways happened to be higher than the level of the rising sea had ultimately survived. And the main city of Magal had been one of them.

Demelza had not visited this particular city on her prior trip, as her contract had been on a man located in a different, smaller, and far more feudal township a fair distance away. *That* place, under new leadership, also still existed beneath the waves, so far as she knew, though her former target no longer did.

She continued down the long pathway for some time, passing a few others along the way, though it was mostly a solitary walk. Finally, she felt a larger gust of air as she neared an illuminated bend in the path. Rounding it, she saw that she had finally arrived at her destination. And it was magnificent.

The stone dome appeared to have been cooled during some of the planet's earliest volcanic activity, clashing with the sea around it and hardening into a solid shell. On top of that, more had been deposited until this place was created, safe and secure underneath both rock and water.

A large bay lapped gently against the shore where several dozen specialized craft floated. The underwater tunnel providing them access was a long and deep enough one that only ships with some rather specialized casting could manage the trip. Space was one thing, but the pressures of the deep were another entirely. And this city, unlike so many others, was very, very deep.

Demelza stepped off the path and into the magically illuminated streets and walkways, the constant glow given off from the spells anchored to the dome above providing a pleasant, warm light. It was early in the day, and the light was brighter accordingly, shifting to match that of the surface above, though never going completely dark at night.

She had no trouble finding the old temple, for not only were sigils and runes carved into the very stone over her head, but they all converged above one specific point. And that point was one of the more ornate structures in the city.

The temple was apparently still very active here, and the steady stream of parishioners heading into and out of the building made it clear it had a very large following. When she stepped inside, she realized why.

The entire building had been converted from a mere place of

worship into a sort of combination bunkhouse and feasting hall, with hundreds upon hundreds of men and women from all manner of race milling about or resting on their cots.

Normally, providing food and shelter left a place with a different feel than this, though. *This* felt threatening. Dangerous. Like a cornered animal on edge and ready to fight. Looking to the sigil-marked anvil, she saw why.

The gleaming metal was there, as expected, though its topmost surface seemed a bit worn from excessive use. The priests here must have been performing far more sacrifices than the other locations had. Or so she thought, until she saw the pile of bones neatly stacked high against the rearmost wall.

Not animal bones, though. People.

One of the temple workers noticed her staring and walked over, not exactly menacing, but not welcoming either.

"May I help you?" he asked.

"Oh, I was just admiring the temple," Demelza replied, using a soft and non-threatening voice. "The temple back home is not so grand as this."

"Oh, a sister of the order? Where do you call home?" he asked, his tone friendly, but her trained senses told her this was a test.

"You probably haven't heard of it. I come from Mulannis, though most just call it Muck."

The man's posture stiffened rather than relaxed. That was unexpected, so she dove further into her story.

"Emmik Sitza was teaching me the writings of the ancients. When he heard I was heading this way, he said I absolutely had to stop off on Galaloom to see the marvelous temple. And he was right. It truly is a sight."

"Emmik Sitza is indeed wise," the man said, relaxing his guard a bit.

"But tell me, why all of the bones? That is not a normal thing in our temple."

"Ah, yes, those. I can see how they could be a little off-putting," he replied. "You see, Galaloom has been something of a treasure hunter's destination for some time."

"Really? But why?"

"They seek fame, fortune, what have you. All in search of the Quommus."

"But that doesn't really exist. Everyone knows it's just a children's tale."

The man smiled. "Yes, but some persist regardless and foolishly desecrate our temple in their search. Over the centuries those caught have paid the highest price for their blasphemy," he said, gesturing to the anvil where they had undoubtedly met their end.

"As it should be," Demelza said. "To think they would dare!"

The man nodded his approval of her reaction. "Indeed, it is both blasphemous and ignorant. To think that they would find something here. If the Quommus truly did exist, and if it ever was here, it was removed long, long ago."

Demelza nodded her rapt agreement, her eyes looking on the gleaming anvil with the adoration of the truly devout. But it wasn't the anvil she was looking at. It was the structure it was built upon. A raised dais of heavy stone, surrounded by thirteen small, forged anvils, each of them bearing sigils of the sect.

They were not terribly large, and a sufficiently strong person could lift one if they really tried. But they were positioned as an integral part of the altar itself.

But her eyes saw something else, clued in not by Master Orkut's cryptic note, but by a training technique he drilled into her head when her arms were at their weakest after a day's labor.

He would require her to scratch out a particular symbol in the sand with the tip of a sword. Delicately. Slowly. Over and over until her shoulders and arms burned from the detailed movement. She now realized what he had been teaching her.

Doing so in a way that not even a spy observing them would suspect it. But to her it all made sense now, and she saw what all the others before her did not. What not one of the treasure hunters or priests or faithful had noticed in all the centuries.

There, on the fifth anvil, a different sigil was forged in the metal along with the ornate ones they all possessed. The one she knew from so much muscle memory. It was easy to miss, the shape formed by the decorations themselves. But she saw it clear as day.

She had found the Quommus. And it was impossible to retrieve.

CHAPTER FORTY

Dozens of high-strung priests who doubled as guards. Hundreds of devout, and quite possibly fanatical, followers. And a temple that was always open and always packed with people. Stealing the Quommus was looking a lot like a suicide mission, and Demelza was rather fond of breathing.

There was simply no way she could fight them all directly. And even if she were to attempt to steal the unwieldy item in the middle of the night, there would still be many priests and guards awake and pacing the grounds. And on top of that, the entire temple would be full to the brink with slumbering devout.

And adding to the mess that this quest was quickly becoming, it seemed this particular branch of the sect had devolved into something of a fanatical and rather violent cult.

She had witnessed the afternoon sacrifice, playing along and swaying in prayer with the rest of the congregants as the head priest, an unpowered man, so far as she could tell, whipped the group into a frenzy. And they all wanted the same thing.

Blood.

Living on a mostly oceanic planet meant that their sacrifices would logically be from the sea, so when the assistants brought a Bundabist to the altar she was quite surprised. Not only that an animal from above would be used, but because, so far as she had seen while making her initial descent and scout of the world, they simply did not live there.

That meant they were actively bringing in sacrifices from other worlds. It was not entirely unheard of, but extremely unusual. She leaned over and whispered to the rapt woman next to her.

"Sister, this is a truly wondrous sacrifice. Is this a holy day I was unaware of?"

The woman, distracted as she was, turned to the newcomer. "No, Sister. But tonight we dine as one, and Orakis provides!"

She didn't know exactly what to make of that statement at first, but suddenly the large cauldrons made sense. They were going to prepare a single massive meal for all of the congregants. It was no wonder they had garnered such a devout following. Feeding and sheltering those in need could do that, and in no time at all, people could be swayed from convenience seekers to true believers.

The priest said a prayer and raised his ornate hammer, bringing it down upon the Bundabist with a wet snap. The animal went limp immediately, killed by just one stroke. Perhaps the priest possessed some power after all, she mused. And the Quommus might be what was masking it.

That, or he was merely a strong man with a good swing.

In any event, his bloody work was far from over. It seemed that there were more animals, as well as creatures from the sea, all slated for sacrifice. By the time he was done, there would be enough to feed the entire chamber full of people. And it would also instill in them a Pavlovian response and lust for bloodshed.

It was abundantly clear there was simply no way she could steal the Quommus without a fight, let alone approach the altar. She would need something different. She would need a diversion. But what could work on so many?

"Sister, you are new here. Will you be helping in the preparation?" the woman beside her asked when the service ended.

Not one to miss an opportunity, Demelza smiled brightly and declared that she would be honored to assist. Now, if only she knew what exactly she would be preparing. That was made clear soon enough when she followed her new friend to the food preparation area.

Cooking. She was going to be cooking, it seemed. Not exactly her strong suit, but surrounded by others who were skilled in this way, she could follow along and blend in just fine. But first there was a more gruesome job to do.

"The bones all go in here. They are slow cooked for three days to make the broth," the woman told her as they cut and pulled free the shards of shattered bone from the sacrificed animals.

Had they not been slaughtered in such a brutal manner, the task would have been quick and easy. But death by hammer had rendered each and every one of the creatures a mess of pulp and bone fragments. Demelza was not one to shy away from blood, but she put on a little show of hesitation for the others anyway. She was the newcomer, after all, and it would be expected.

It was slow work, and much of the afternoon passed as she and the others in her group worked their way through the sacrifices one by one, until at last they had cleaned them all.

She rose and washed her hands in a nearby cistern then prepared to leave.

"Where are you going?" one of the women asked her. "Are you not preparing with us?"

Demelza was surprised by this glaring weakness in their security. But because she was a woman, they assumed she would be participating in the preparation of the food, not just the cleaning of the meat. It was a backwards way of thinking, and, she realized as she felt the comforting bulge of her vial of Nasturian extract in her pocket, it would be their undoing.

"Of course I am," she said cheerfully. "I was merely going to relieve myself before we began. Could you please direct me?"

"Oh, yes. Through that archway, on the left," the woman replied.

"Thank you. I'll be right back," Demelza said, then hurried off to the restroom.

She didn't have to go. But it was a tried and true means of overcoming suspicion because everyone, no matter their rank or station in life, knew what it was like to have to go.

She returned a short while later and set to work with the others. It was tedious, cleaning and cutting all of the ingredients, but as it would simply be several enormous cauldrons of stew being prepared, it really wasn't terribly complicated work.

Cut, pile, then move on to the next ingredient. Once they were done with that phase, they carried the massive platters to each of the cooking vessels and dumped them into the bubbling broth, prepared from the bones of previous sacrifices.

Demelza was gifted at sleight-of-hand, and her addition of a healthy splash of Nasturian to each cauldron went utterly unnoticed. And as the extract possessed no scent, so long as no one tasted the dish before it was served, this could work.

She was counting on the longstanding tradition that no one ate until the head priest did was also observed here. For if it was, she would disable the entire congregation at once. Nasturian could bring grown men to their knees. She could only imagine what it would do to those less hardy.

As she had hoped, the temple was rearranged come dinnertime, the cots and seats moved, replaced by long tables and benches. Loaves of bread were placed intermittently, and bowls of stew were set at each place setting. The congregants, regardless of whatever hunger they might have been feeling, sat quietly, awaiting their leader's sign.

Demelza smiled on the inside as the priest motioned for all to rise, then said a brief blessing, then sat once more. The others mirrored him and likewise took their seats.

When the priest raised his spoon and dipped it into his stew, the entire dining hall moved as one hungry beast, eagerly digging into their steaming meals.

The thing about Nasturian was it did not act instantly, but rather, it took a few seconds before the heat began. Soon after it would become near unbearable, but if one were hungry enough, and eating quickly, it would be possible to get several spoonfuls down before the pain began.

The shrieks commenced only moments later, quickly growing into a chorus of howls and groans. In less than a minute, the entire congregation, priests and all, were writhing in pain, guzzling water in a desperate attempt to ease the burn.

Of course, that didn't work with Nasturian. Nothing did. Once you ate it, you just had to ride it out. And that could take hours.

Demelza rose and walked to the altar. In their pain, no one even noticed. Or if they did, they simply didn't care. Not at that moment. She reached out with her power, sensing for traps or wards, but there were none. At least, none that she could find. But with the Quommus, she had no idea how one could ever be sure.

But there was no time for indecision. She slid her konus onto her wrist and called up a lifting spell. The small anvil protested at first, having been rooted in place for so many centuries. But finally it shifted and floated into the air.

She quickly draped a bag over it, making it appear as if she was carrying something light, not levitating something heavy. The Ghalian then made straight for the exit, leaving behind the many cries of pain in her wake. The Quommus was exceptionally heavy, and she wasn't sure if the spell would be sufficient for the entire trek to the top of the tunnel to the surface, so she moved fast.

If the Quommus did drain her spell, she would be forced to carry the thing. It was relatively small, no bigger than a small loaf of bread, but it was dense, and incredibly unwieldy. The hike would not be a pleasant one.

Fortunately, she made it to the top without incident, the spell holding strong all the way back to her ship. She secured the little anvil in her storage bay, then immediately made for the safety of space. Once there, she jumped away without hesitation, her escape coordinates already punched in before she had even first headed to the surface.

Demelza leaned back in her seat and smiled. She had done what countless others had sought to accomplish for centuries. It was a heady feeling, to say the least. But her work was far from done. Without any further delay, she engaged her Drookonus and jumped.

And like that, in a flash, she was gone.

CHAPTER FORTY-ONE

He was one of the Five. A Master Ghalian. One of the most dangerous men in the galaxy, capable of improvising and carrying out the most complex and daring of missions on a moment's notice if the situation required it.

And he needed some time to think.

Fortunately, the events that had led him to determine his next destination allowed him precisely that.

After the fighting had ended and the survivors regrouped, Hozark had thanked Andorus for his and his men's efforts in the fight against the Council. He then paid the surviving mercenaries a hefty bonus for their troubles. The sizable quantity of coin was gladly accepted, and Andorus laughingly said he was sure the group would be more than happy to help the next time they were needed.

The mission had been a success, and despite some losses, and just about everyone being injured to one degree or another, the mercenary forces had driven off the Council goons in a resounding defeat.

It was a bit of a coup, the lopsided victory. That is, until the bombardment from above put an abrupt end to the fighting altogether.

It seemed that those firing upon the combined forces were from a different arm of the Council, though they were not sure under whose direction. All that had mattered was they were apparently not fully aware of the bounty of magical beings hiding below, only that another visla was somehow attempting to amass power against them. Once they laid waste to the area, they had simply left.

Samara's forces wanted nothing to do with any more fighting and limped clear of the city to await their base ship, knowing it would return to pick them up when it was safe to do so. In that time, however, the Ghalian had dispatched their waiting transport ship to move the Ootaki while the opportunity was good.

Dohria herself had arranged it, though none had even known the master spy was on Sooval in the first place. But that was her strong suit, and even most in her own order couldn't track her if she didn't want them to.

His duty to the refugees complete, Hozark had departed for the comfort and quiet of space. But he had plans. A destination of sorts. A lead, obtained from a captured survivor from Samara's forces, extracted with a bit of force and a healthy dose of terror. By the time the man spoke, Hozark was quite sure he was telling what he believed to be the truth.

It seemed that while Visla Maktan's true location was a closely guarded secret, there were a handful outside of his personal guard who knew the few locations he was moving between. And one of them just so happened to be coming within jump range in just a few days.

The cargo ship would seem innocuous. Just another craft loading up on supplies for the Council. As such, no one would dare harass it. But the captain of that ship was one of Maktan's personal crew, resupplying his concealed ships as they moved their charge from safe location to safe location.

It was something of a long shot, but if the captain could reduce the likely target to even a dozen possible locations, it would greatly help the Ghalian spies narrow their search as they focused on those specific targets, however benign they might seem.

Hozark was glad for the downtime in the interim. Though he would not say so aloud, his encounter with Samara had left him a bit off-kilter. They had history, and he needed to refocus his mind if he wished to be at his best when he next stepped into combat.

When the cargo ship finally jumped into the system he had been guided to, Hozark had already been lurking in the darkness on a small asteroid floating between worlds for a few days, waiting patiently and saving his magic.

The tactic may have slowed his approach to the ship when it arrived, but this way he would not have the excessive expenditure of magic required to properly shimmer cloak his ship in space.

As soon as the craft exited its jump, though, he immediately engaged his shimmer cloak and launched into a hot pursuit. Or as hot as one could be in the freezing void of space. In any case, the cargo ship would not be moving at a terribly fast clip, and there would be no evasive maneuvering if his shimmer cloak held.

Given the magic he had saved by waiting on the little hunk of rock, he was confident it would.

Hozark nevertheless flew in the ship's blind spot, sensing the protective spells shielding the craft from not only debris, but also sneak attacks. It was a common functionality on Council vessels, given the frequency of transporting high-value cargo. And for an emmik or visla to layer a few extra spells was a well-justified use of power in their minds if it meant no interruptions in their delivery schedule.

But Hozark knew his way around those, and without using any force to bypass them. Instead, he lowered his craft until he was just above the shielding, matching pace perfectly with the vessel below. Then he carefully cast a very specialized spell, parting the protective layer just enough for his much smaller ship to slip through. It was tough work, no doubt, and any mistake would alert them to his presence. But he was a professional, and he made the approach and insertion look like child's play.

Hozark guided his cloaked ship down to the cargo craft's hull and skimmed its surface until he found the section he was looking for, located right above what should be a small and typically unused storage compartment on this type of craft. He settled down and applied his locking spells, binding his invisible ship to the hull.

He took a moment to center himself, then cast the magical umbilical spell that would create a breathable conduit from his ship to theirs. He wasted no time crossing the space, sealing his ship behind him as he did. He then focused his attention on the Council vessel's hull.

With great care, he cast a trio of boarding spells, splitting the ship's skin while also momentarily applying pressure to it to prevent a rapid loss of air that would alert the crew to his presence. The third spell muted all sound within the chamber below, allowing him to drop to the deck silently and reseal the rent in the ship's hull without worrying about being heard.

Inside, he paused and listened. Not a single sound of warning. The insertion was a success, and no one was any the wiser as to his presence aboard. The assassin activated his shimmer cloak and quietly slipped into the corridor, invisible to all. He had one task, and that was to question the captain and get what he needed by any means necessary.

The best place to do that would be the man's personal quarters. Once inside, the crew would not bother him unless there was a real emergency. But before he moved, Hozark hugged the wall and stood perfectly still, listening. Getting a feel for the ship itself.

Something was wrong. Suddenly there were voices, and a fair amount of movement coming his way. He pressed as flat to the wall as he could, his camouflage rendering him unseen by the hurrying men.

That was more than a bit unusual. The additional weaponry he noted the crew carrying as they passed him, oblivious to the assassin's proximity, was vexing. The ship seemed far too heavily guarded for a mere cargo run.

But if there was something else going on, he would pry that from the man as well. For now, he had to make it to his quarters, where he would then wait until he could have some *quality* time with the captain.

Suddenly, the ship lurched and shook, something that was not normal in any way, shape, or form. They were in flight, and with their protective spells, there should be absolutely no turbulence in space. Hozark's sharp ears then picked up another sound far away in the ship's corridors. The sound of shouts and fighting.

Oh hell, he thought as he realized what was going on. It was the worst possible timing. Almost comically so. But there was no mistaking what had just happened. He sighed and shook his head.

The ship was under attack.

And it was being boarded.

CHAPTER FORTY-TWO

The sounds of fighting were clear enough to determine the rough location of the incursion in the ship. Obviously, this was a skilled group making the attack or they would have been either taken out by the ship's defenses or repelled by the magical shielding before ever reaching the hull.

As neither of those things had happened, that left but few options as to who might be boarding the ship, and none of them were conducive to Hozark's plan. With the craft on not just a high alert, but now on a battle footing, there was simply no chance whatsoever the captain would return to his quarters at all.

On top of that, the command center would be locked down, and the already robustly armed crew would strike at anything remotely suspicious. There was simply no time for a carefully crafted disguise and infiltration into the heavily guarded chamber.

Hozark was racking his brain for the fastest, most viable solution to the problem when the fighting abruptly took a turn and flowed his direction at alarming speed. The defenders, it seemed, were being driven back by a rather ferocious onslaught.

But there was no magic being used, so that at least was a positive. And the attackers appeared to be well disciplined. Professionals would at least not accidentally get them all killed with an errant spell. But the battling men and women had now spilled into the corridor that led to the command center, effectively blocking the assassin's path.

It wasn't intentional, of course. It was just incredibly inconvenient. And camouflaged in his shimmer cloak, Hozark could very soon face the possibility of being accidentally injured by the wild attacks of combatants who could not see him.

A decision had to be made, and quickly by the look of it. Without further hesitation, Hozark shed his camouflage and drew his lesser weapons. The vespus blade would remain sheathed for now. The glowing blue sword would only draw more unwanted attention to him in the thick of battle, and in these confined spaces it would be far more difficult to avoid multiple attackers and fend off their blows.

But at least he would not be accidentally hit, so that was something. And if he was to be attacked, it would be far better it be intentionally. It was a funny thing about fighting, that. The attacks of trained fighters were far easier to predict and handle than those of neophytes who were fighting on instinct alone.

Patterns of attacks and defenses were so drilled into the heads of most forces that their movements could almost always be counted on and dealt with by those with a bit more expertise. And Hozark had quite a lot more than just a bit.

The first of the ship's crew rounded the corner to where the Ghalian was standing.

"And so it begins." He sighed, then lunged into the fray.

The Council forces only had a moment to register the new threat laying waste to their ranks before they shifted tactics, now dealing with attackers from both ends. The invading force was efficient in their progress, he had to give them that. That degree of skill was not often seen, and were he not actively slaying crewmembers left and right, he might have enjoyed stepping aside to watch them work.

Judging by the flashes of garb he was able to make out in the churning sea of blades and blood, it was a pirate crew that had attacked the Council ship. Cocky of them. Confident. He admired their pluck as much as their skill. But their actions had jeopardized his plan, and tracking down Visla Maktan was a high priority.

Not wishing to engage the pirates as well as the ship's crew, Hozark began pushing his way through the carnage toward the command center. Men and women fell to his blades, their bodies at his feet slowing his progress more than their feeble defenses had. He was a terror at work, and the crew seemed to be realizing that the lone assailant coming from the wrong direction was far more of a threat than the boarding party.

They shifted a large portion of their forces to meet him, but Hozark drove forward, his arms and legs a blur of motion as he struck with blade and fist, with foot and pommel, until he had reached the intersecting corridor that would take him the final distance to the command center.

But the pirates were there as well, and they were quite active in their combat. Hozark disabled one who had spun and swung at the newcomer to their fight by sheer instinct. The assassin did not kill him, though. He merely rendered him unconscious for the moment. The Council forces, however, did not meet the same end.

He felt a presence lurch toward him and spun, his blades ready to strike, then pulled back at the last instant as Bud's familiar face grinned at him in the middle of this bloody battle.

"Hozark? What are you doing here?" the pirate asked.

He had smears of blood on his cheek and clothes, but it did not appear to be his own. There was also a look of joy in his eyes from the adrenaline coursing through his veins. He hadn't been a pirate for years, but it seemed he missed it more than he realized.

"I am here for the captain," Hozark said, neatly disemboweling a man foolish enough to charge at the pair. "And you? I thought you were seeking Henni."

Bud flinched at the name ever so slightly. "I am. But Lalaynia's people said this ship was one of the special ones. The kind that resupply the Council's dark sites, among other things."

"I heard the same. You are with Lalaynia? That explains the skill of this boarding party."

"Yeah, they're good people. And it seems we're here for a similar reason. Partly, anyway. To take the cargo, that's their main goal. But mine is to find out where Henni has been taken."

"Then let us find this captain together. I am certain the questioning will be most enlightening," Hozark said, turning his full attention to the defenders before them. "Are you ready, Bud?"

"Let's do this," he replied. "This way! To command!" he cried out to his fellow pirates, then he and Hozark charged ahead, laying waste to those either brave or foolish enough to attempt to stop them.

The wave of pirates at their back made the crewmen standing just outside the command center door duck inside as their colleagues did their best against what was looking like an unbeatable foe.

Hozark and Bud had fought together many times, and the duo made quick work of the forces in their path. Limbs were severed, heads lopped from necks, and vital organs riddled with holes as the two tore through their ranks until they were right at the command center door.

Bud reached for it, but Hozark snatched his hand back.

"Wait," he said. "There is something wrong."

Hozark reached out with his power, sensing the door and surrounding portion of the ship's hull. It wasn't a booby trap or scuttling spell he had sensed, however. It was something else entirely. And rather surprising, he had to admit.

He cast a strong sealing spell over the door and turned the other way.

"Wait, what are you doing?" Bud asked. "We just fought through all of that mess to get here."

"Inform Lalaynia the ship is hers," Hozark replied. "The captain has given up the vessel."

"How can you be so sure? We haven't even seen him yet. It's hard to surrender from hiding after all."

"He is not hiding, Bud. Nor did he surrender. Not exactly," Hozark said. "The captain has separated the command center and escaped the ship."

It was something Bud had heard rumor of but had never actually seen. A configuration that allowed the forward most portion of a select group of ships to detach from the main craft as an escape vessel. He'd thought it was only something told to fake out would-be raiders, but apparently it was a real thing.

"Shit. They just bailed like that?"

"They did. But be glad, Bud. In their haste, they were unable to scuttle the ship. The craft is yours."

"Yeah, great. But there's no way Lalaynia can cut loose to pursue him. Not with everyone on board, and not if the command center itself is no longer part of the ship."

Hozark grinned. "Do not worry, my friend. You forget, I have a ship as well, and it is under no such constraints. Now, time is of the essence. They will make for the surface, undoubtedly. We must catch up with them before they have time to disperse into the landscape."

Bud followed Hozark as they ran back through the dwindling fight to where his shimmer ship was docked. Lalaynia was striding through the craft like a conquering Amazon, finishing those who dared raise a weapon toward her with bloody ease.

"Laynia, the command center is gone," Bud called out.

"What?" she replied. "And, Master Hozark, what are you doing here?"

"I am afraid there is no time for a discussion. Suffice to say, Bud and I are going to take my ship in pursuit of the captain," he said.

"How big is your craft?" she asked.

"Small. A Ghalian shimmer ship."

She nodded. Lalaynia was a very sharp woman, and her tactical prowess was strong. Immediately she turned to Saramin, handing him an additional konus.

"You, go with Bud and Hozark. They'll be outnumbered. Provide whatever help they need and keep us informed of your location. We'll finish up here then meet you on the surface as soon as we're able."

Hozark was already in motion when Saramin pulled his sword from the chest of the man he'd just slain. "On it, Captain."

"Great. This way, kid," Bud said, then took off running, the young pirate in tow with his captain's blessing.

It would be one hell of a pursuit, and success was in no way a certainty. But despite the odds, the young pirate felt a warm happiness in his chest as he followed his old friend and his new one. Really, he couldn't ask for better people to be going with. Even if it might be to their end.

CHAPTER FORTY-THREE

It wasn't exactly cramped in Hozark's shimmer ship, but he generally flew solo when utilizing it. Having not one but two passengers as he pursued the escaping Council forces was a tiny bit uncomfortable in the command chamber.

He quickly put that from his mind and focused on the tiny speck far ahead of them. It was slower than they were by a substantial amount, and apparently it lacked jump capability, otherwise the captain would no doubt have left the system immediately.

When he separated from the main body of his craft, the connection with his Drooks was severed, and he had to rely on the small Drookonus powering the escape ship. That not only limited its range, but effectively neutered its jump capability. But they had a lead on their pursuers, and that was a problem.

"Shit, they're entering the atmosphere," Bud said as the dot ahead of them began to glow orange.

"We shall catch up with them," Hozark said. "The size of their vessel will hinder them as they drop into the atmosphere and require a bit of attention in order to land. We, on the other hand, have no such restraints."

"Can we shoot them while they're still aloft?" Saramin asked, always looking for the fastest solution to a problem, even if it was the most violent. "Your ship is armed, I assume."

"It is, but we do not wish to risk catastrophic damage to the craft. We require intelligence from their captain, and the risk of even minor strafing fire is simply too great."

"Good idea, though," Bud said. "Thinking on your feet. I like it."

"I just hope we took out enough of their crew before they detached," the young pirate said. "Because those guys were far better trained than we expected."

"It is an elite force," Hozark commented as they began to buck and shake from the first stage of atmospheric turbulence. "A group assigned to high-value operations."

"So, that, along with the fact they actually have the escape ship we'd heard rumor of, all seems to point to this not just being an ordinary cargo ship for the top tier elite at all," Bud noted. "Good. I'm looking forward to getting some answers from these bastards."

"If we can take them alive," Saramin said.

"Oh, we will, right, Hozark?"

The Ghalian said nothing, focusing all of his intensity on the ship ahead of them. It would land before them, but not by much. That was good. The crew would not have the time to scatter, as had been his main concern. Hunting down all of them to find the one he wanted would have been a trying experience to say the least.

The planet they were taking refuge on was inhospitable at best, but the atmosphere, while uncomfortable to breathe, would not cause any lasting damage in the short term. More than enough time for them to either capture their man or slay every last one of the Council goons. Possibly both.

The Council forces streamed out of their downed ship and raced toward the nearby rocks as soon as it hit the ground. They had landed in a rough bit of terrain. A dry landscape with craggy valleys and rocky outcroppings as well as fields of massive boulders, tumbled from above during rock slides in the past.

In short, there was a lot of cover for them, and a lot of places to hide. But, as Hozark and his associates learned as they came in to land, this lot was not one for hiding.

"Shit! Spells incoming!" Bud called out as the first wave of magical bombardments from the surface buffeted the shimmer ship's defensive spell array.

"Those are strong," Saramin noted. "They're a bit too well armed for just a transport cargo ship, wouldn't you say?"

"That they are," Bud replied, then cocked his head slightly as the next wave of attacks bounced from their shielding.

"And this magic is off," Saramin said. "It feels strange."

Hozark and Uzabud both knew why the power that was trying to knock them from the sky felt like that. It was a new flavor of magic. Something novel. Something Saramin had never encountered before. But they had. They knew it the moment the first spell hit.

"That's Henni's power," Bud said. "I'd bet my life on it."

"Don't say things like that," Saramin said. "At least not until we're on the ground."

Hozark spun and dove quickly, avoiding a barrage of spells as he did, landing his ship behind a large group of boulders and engaging its shimmer cloak immediately. It would use a fair bit of power after what they'd just been through, but he didn't want anyone targeting it while they were fighting on foot.

He leapt from his seat and made for the door. "Come. We must meet this opponent head-on."

The others didn't hesitate, quickly falling in behind the Ghalian as he raced from the camouflaged ship toward the waiting opponent. Freed from the confines of the ship above, the

Council forces were unleashing the full force of their magical weaponry, and it was impressive.

"They've drained Henni," Bud said, returning fire then ducking behind a boulder. "Bastards drained her."

"But the magic is combined with that of Visla Jinnik, can you sense it?" Hozark said. "And that means they are both likely still alive. And more than that, we now know where she is being held. If we find Jinnik, we find Henni."

"Yeah, but we're not only outnumbered pretty significantly, we're also outpowered," Bud said.

"Just keep them at bay. Buy me some time," Hozark said, then vanished into his shimmer cloak.

Saramin watched with a bit of awe, though not shock. He was young, but he'd seen enough in his short years to have had plenty of dealings with shimmer cloaks. But never one wielded by a Wampeh Ghalian.

"So, what do you think?" he asked. "Wait here, or advance on them before they can flank us?"

Bud leaned out and peppered the advancing Council forces with a cluster of stun spells, conserving his magic for when they got closer and the fight *really* heated up.

"I count two dozen of 'em. There must have been an additional troop contingent stationed in that escape module," Bud grumbled. "We're seriously outnumbered here."

Saramin popped out and felled one of the advancing men with a carefully placed killing spell. "Yeah, but that doesn't mean we have to go out like cowering children," he shot back.

Bud's hackles raised, and he fired off a trio of killing spells despite the distance and drain on his resources. He was pleased to note that one of them actually managed to land.

"Are you calling me a cowering child?"

Saramin grinned. "No, I just wanted to get you riled up a little. We're gonna need all you've got to get through this."

Bud couldn't help but smile. Saramin was going to be a great pirate one day. The kid had leadership written all over him. But if he hoped to see that day come, they first had to survive this battle.

They'd pursued expecting a much smaller force to deal with. Instead, they had nearly double the number, and far more heavily armed to boot. It was a damn suicide mission, but they hadn't realized that when they signed up for it. And it would be some time before Lalaynia could send backup.

But it was too late to do anything about that now.

"They're getting close," Bud said. "That gives us a tiny bit of an advantage."

"The overpowering numbers are closing in, but that's to our advantage?" Saramin asked.

"They're trying to flank us. Their people are scattered among the boulders taking cover while they advance. That means that all but the absolute front-most of them have to be extremely careful of their spells lest they hit their own people."

Saramin smiled as the significance became clear. "And we have no such restrictions."

"Precisely. We can fire away at will until we get right up to them. At that point it's gonna be down to hand-to-hand anyway, and it's gonna get rough. But at least there will be no spellcasting involved. And we're pirates, godsdamn it. And no one is better at close-quarters fighting than we are, right?"

"You're damn right," the youth agreed.

"Okay, then. You ready, kid?"

"Ready as ever, old man."

"You really gonna keep calling me that?"

"Tell you what. If we survive, I'll reconsider."

"Good enough for me. And if not? Well, today's a pretty good day to die," Bud said.

"I was thinking more along the lines of kicking ass with such style and intensity that they sing epic songs about us."

Bud chuckled. "That'd be nice too." He then rushed from behind his boulder, spraying every deadly spell he could muster.

Saramin did the same, and for a few moments the sheer magnitude of the display they put on had the advancing attackers on their heels. Multiple spells landed, cutting the odds a tiny bit more in their favor. If they could just get in close enough, the bladework and lack of casting would even the odds still further.

Their tactic seemed to have worked, at least for the moment, allowing them to move in close and fight with their swords and daggers. The Council crew may have been skilled with konuses, but the pirates definitely outclassed them with blades. But the numbers were still not in their favor, and it was only a matter of time before they would be overcome.

Regardless, the two fought with an intensity and skill that would have made Lalaynia proud. But they knew the numbers, and each had made peace with the fact this might be their last battle.

All around them the madness of battle spun and churned. But something seemed a bit odd. The enemy ranks seemed to be thinning out faster than the two pirates were capable of. In fact, a good number of Council forces dropped dead in their tracks without them even touching them.

They didn't pause to mull it over though, but instead ramped up their efforts, the battle swinging in their favor. More and more of the enemy fell until suddenly, it stopped.

Bud and Saramin stood in the middle of the killing field, surrounded by nearly two dozen corpses, each of them gasping for breath from the prolonged effort.

From behind a boulder, an unconscious man in captain's garb slid toward them, one foot up in the air. For a moment it didn't register in Saramin's mind what was going on. Bud, however, smiled wide.

"Took you long enough," he said to the air.

Hozark unshimmered, revealing himself to the duo. "Yes, well, I was slightly hindered by your spells," he replied. "I did not wish to fall to friendly fire, after all."

Saramin and Bud laughed like only those who just narrowly escaped death could. They might sing songs of them one day, but the two of them would be alive to hear them with their own ears.

Hozark dropped the captain's leg and stared down at the unconscious man. "So, I think it is time to return to Lalaynia's ship and see what our friend here can tell us."

CHAPTER FORTY-FOUR

Uzabud had to give the Council ship's captain some credit. Tied to the wall in one of Lalaynia's ship's cells and facing a Wampeh Ghalian, the man had withstood his interrogation admirably, and for considerably longer than most. He had even managed to not soil himself in the process, which, given Hozark's expertise in evoking fear, was truly saying something.

In the end, however, it had been good old-fashioned self-preservation that had won the day. Not the save-your-own-life kind, but rather, a far more visceral variety.

While Hozark was very intent on finding the whereabouts of Visla Maktan, the captain had insisted repeatedly that he was making deliveries to multiple locations and simply did not know and thus could not provide the answer he was seeking. The thing was, Hozark believed him.

"Mind if I give something a try?" Bud asked his friend.

"Be my guest," Hozark replied.

The pirate walked over to the bound man slowly, then stood in front of him a long while, staring at him. Not threatening him, not beating him, just staring. Finally, he drew his small, enchanted dagger from its hidden sheath and began slicing the man's clothes off.

"What are you doing?" the captain asked, more out of curiosity than fear.

It was clear the Wampeh was not going to kill him. And if this one did, it was still better than what would befall him if he betrayed Visla Maktan's trust. If it came down to it, he would hold his tongue until the end. It was something he felt sure he could do.

Bud ignored the man as he worked the razor-sharp blade along first his sleeves, then the torso of his tunic. He pulled the pieces free and tossed them aside. Next, he did the same with the man's boots and trousers, leaving him stark naked and tied to the wall.

He then took a step back and simply let him stand there, nude. After a few minutes, the man couldn't help himself.

"I have told you, I don't know where Visla Maktan is. And even if I did, I would not tell you."

"Oh, I believe you," Bud said with a slightly dangerous look in his eyes. "To be honest, I doubt you'd tell us even if you did know. And I respect that."

The man's body relaxed a fraction.

"But," Bud continued, "there is something else I want from you. And you *will* tell me."

The captain was ready to meet his end. At least he would die honorably. But what happened next was a bit of a surprise.

The pirate dropped to one knee right in front of his groin and looked up at him. There was no evil monologuing or exaggerated threat. Just one, simple question.

"Where is Henni?" Bud asked.

"I don't know what you're talking about."

"Allow me to clarify. Where is the girl whose power charged your konuses? I want a location."

"I assure you, I don't know what you're––"

Bud pressed the blade against the man's most tender bits until it drew blood. The enchanted blade was more than merely sharp, and it took a moment for the pain to even register.

"I'm going to make this *real* easy for you," Bud said. "I'm not going to do the usual routine and start with fingers or ears. I'm going to take what means the most to you first. We are not going to build up to the worst. We're starting with it. So, I'm not asking where Maktan is. Hell, I'm not even asking anything about the man. All I want to know is where your konuses came from. Tell me that, and you live. Intact."

The captain hesitated. The fact that it wasn't technically betraying the visla flashed through his mind. A bit of rationalization in the face of emasculation. He was weighing his options when there was a little tug at his groin, followed by a warmth along his leg.

Bud stood and showed the man his testicle, sliced away clean by the little knife.

"Answer quickly enough, and you might just be able to have this reattached and healed. But know that my patience ran out long ago."

Hozark was watching with great interest. He'd seen his friend angry before, but never on quite such a personal level. Henni being snatched from his protection seemed to have hit Bud far more than he had let on. And as he hadn't even tried to hide how upset he was, that was really saying something. If the man didn't answer, and quickly, he'd be a eunuch in seconds.

The captain came to the same realization and started blabbering, spewing out everything he knew about the konuses. They came from another ship and were distributed to the ranks. But that ship usually made runs to and from only a few planets. There were a dozen total, and he named them all. It would take time for the Ghalian spies to do their work, but it was somewhere to start.

Bud popped the testicle in his mouth and chewed with a grin.

"But I told you what you wanted to know!"

"Yeah, you did," Bud said. "But can I let you in on a little secret?"

"What?"

"It's amazing how much a peeled Kortza berry looks like a certain body part," he said with a grin. "Tastes better, though, I imagine."

The captain looked down, scrutinizing himself as best he could from that angle, and realized that the warm liquid was not his own blood. It was heated juice.

Bud winked at him and walked out of the room. "Thanks for your assistance."

"Nicely done," Hozark said as they walked into the large pirate ship's command center.

"Thanks. I'm sorry we couldn't find out where Maktan was though."

"It is of no worry. We shall track him down eventually. But for now, we at least have a lead on Henni's whereabouts."

"Yeah, a *dozen* leads. It's gonna take forever to figure out where she is, and she could be drained dry by then."

"Breathe, Bud. Relax. We shall do all in our power to find her. But first we must retrieve young Happizano from Master Turong's care."

"Turong?" Lalaynia said. "Sorry, couldn't help but hear, seeing as you're standing on my bridge and all."

"Sorry, Captain," Bud said. "Got a bit carried away."

"You do at times. But it's understandable. They kidnapped your friend. Part of your crew. I get it. Now listen, we had quite a nice couple of hauls thanks to you, Bud. And I know the crew feels the same way I do about all of this. I like Henni. She's got spunk. Violent spunk, but spunk nonetheless."

"What are you getting at, Laynia?"

"What I'm saying is, I am offering my help. If you want it, that is."

Bud locked eyes with his friend. "Are you serious?"

"Totally serious."

"Well then, I gladly accept," he replied.

"But first, there is the retrieval of the boy," Hozark reminded him.

"Ah, yeah. We need to pick up Hap from the training house. And get my ship while we're at it. I think we'll need all the firepower we can get."

Lalaynia grinned. "Then it's settled. We go visit Master Turong, then we find Henni."

Hozark stepped a little closer. "How is it you know Master Turong?" he asked quietly. "His training is exceptionally hard to come by, and quite costly at that."

Lalaynia's eyes sparkled. "Let's just say I wasn't always a pirate and leave it at that, shall we?"

Hozark's lips curved slightly. So, Lalaynia had once been a trainee under the great Master Turong. Suddenly her fighting prowess made sense. But she had adapted it for piracy over the years, creating her own style in the process.

It was not unlike what Ghalian aspirants did in their own training. And Hozark heartily approved.

The pirate captain turned to her command crew. "Okay, boys. You heard the course. Plot it and let's go."

A long series of jumps later, they finally emerged in orbit above Master Turong's world. Lalaynia declined to join them on the surface, though, leading Hozark to wonder if perhaps her former master was not entirely pleased with her choice of career.

It didn't matter. He was to retrieve Happizano and Laskar. Once that was accomplished, they would continue on their task.

"He's quite talented, Hozark," Turong said while Hap gathered his belongings. "A marvelous power within him. Once he is grown, he will be a force to be reckoned with."

"And did he behave?"

"Admirably. He did not complain once, though I gave him no quarter and pushed him just as hard as the other students."

Hozark's brow raised slightly.

"Okay, perhaps I pushed him a little harder," Master Turong admitted. "But the boy took it in stride. If you ever wish to bring him back for further training, I would consider it an honor to continue his studies."

For Master Turong to make such an offer was indication of just how much potential he really thought Happizano had. He was not in the habit of taking on students lightly, and especially not for free.

"Thank you. Perhaps one day he may take you up on that offer. But for now, we have pressing matters at hand."

"Ah, yes. Then fly safe, Hozark. And send my regards to Corann."

Hozark nodded but suppressed his grin. There had been a *connection* between Corann and Turong many years ago. Whether it had stemmed from training to near death or not was unknown, but the two had something of an interesting history, though none would speak of it aloud in either of their presence.

"Hozark!" Hap said, rushing out to greet the Ghalian. "It was so cool! I learned how to break boards without touching them! And then there was the casting! And then—"

"Yes, I am looking forward to hearing all about it, young Jinnik," Hozark said with a pleased grin. "But we are on something of a schedule. Come, we must retrieve Laskar and join the others." He turned to Turong. "Thank you again,

Turong," he said, then stepped out of the training house, Happizano in tow.

He had noticed the fair number of bruises Hap was sporting the moment he saw him. It was par for the course in this sort of training. Hozark knew firsthand, having had more than his share back in the day. But the boy's attitude and lack of griping was what really struck him. It seemed he was coming into his own.

Laskar was where he expected to find him. Namely, hanging out in the tavern of the local house of questionable repute. Bud had already found him and was enjoying a drink and catching him up on all the adventures he'd missed.

"Hey, there they are," Bud said as Hozark and the boy approached.

"It's about time. Man, I was beginning to wonder if he was even on the planet," Laskar said. "I didn't see him once."

"Because he was training with one of the finest," Hozark replied. "I hope your downtime was satisfactory."

"Yeah. But it wasn't exactly all downtime."

"Oh?"

"I was getting bored, so I reached out to some of my old buddies, just to see if they'd heard anything in the rumor mill, and one of them said they have what looks like a solid lead on Maktan's actual location."

Hozark was a bit surprised by the revelation, but he was not one to look a gift Malooki in the mouth.

"What is the planet?"

"A place called Essakia," Laskar replied.

"Essakia is the planet to investigate," Hozark repeated in a slightly louder voice. "We shall reconvene with Corann immediately to resupply. Word has been given for the Ghalian network to confirm your intel at once."

Laskar swiveled on his seat. "You mean there are spies *here*?"

"Of course. And one is already on their way to carry out this task."

"Wait, already? They were that close to us? I had no idea."

"Those Ghalian are sure sneaky, aren't they?" Bud joked.

"It is how we survive," Hozark noted. "Now, come. We must see Corann."

CHAPTER FORTY-FIVE

Two ships jumped into the skies above Corann's adopted homeworld, but only one was small enough to descend and land. Lalaynia's massive pirate craft would wait in orbit while she accompanied the others. There were tactical discussions to be had, and she and her crew were going to be an integral part of this plan.

Once they had an actual destination, and plan, that is.

"Feel weird flying in someone else's ship?" Laskar asked the pirate captain as they descended into the atmosphere.

"Not at all," Lalaynia replied calmly. "Though usually when I'm in another ship, it's because I'm about to take it," she added.

Bud swiveled in his seat. "Hey, now. No stealing my ship, Laynia. Not cool."

"Bud, *darling*. Would I ever do that to you?"

"I sure as hell hope not. Taking a fella's ship like that? That's just cold."

"I assure you, my blood is anything but," she replied with a chuckle. "Now, tell me about this Corann we're going to meet."

She knew that Corann was a Ghalian, and as such was a dangerous woman if she chose to be. But Lalaynia had often been described in much the same way, so that didn't really faze her much. She also knew that the Ghalian were very secretive about whom they allowed into their confidence, and to be brought into the fold like this was something of an honor for the pirate captain.

This was one alliance she would do her utmost to nurture. Allied with the Wampeh Ghalian? Why, ships would surrender at the mere mention of her name if they ever knew that. If they allowed her to speak of it, that is. All of which was a moot point until they reached the surface and had their little confab.

Bud brought his ship in slowly, making a casual landing as if he had all the time in the world. The locals knew his craft by now, and when Hozark and his friends stepped out, they were greeted with friendly waves from those nearby.

It seemed that sweet, kindly Corann's relative was back to visit again, and he had brought friends once more. Lalaynia enjoyed the warmth of the greeting that was afforded her as part of that group. Normally, the imposing woman inspired a bit of fear from those she met. Of course, that was a good thing in the pirating game. But here, in this place, it felt nice to not have people running for the hills at the sight of her for a change.

"Hozark! So glad you could make it, my dear," a kindly, older woman with a broad grin and warm, smiling eyes said as she embraced the killer.

Hozark's demeanor had notably shifted, Lalaynia noted, taking on the air of a relaxed and altogether unthreatening fellow visiting family. The way the Ghalian slipped in and out of character was something she'd always admired, and this was no exception.

Corann greeted the others as well, then paused in front of the new arrival.

Hozark made a polite introduction. "Corann, this is Lalaynia."

"Such a tall woman," Corann said with a cheerful grin. "It's my pleasure to meet you."

"The honor is all mine," the pirate replied, offering her empty hand.

"Oh, don't be silly. We're huggers around here!" Corann said, pulling her in close for a warm embrace.

It was not what Lalaynia expected, but the feeling of the rock-solid muscle beneath the woman's softer exterior confirmed what she had already assumed. This woman could kill her before she even drew her weapon if she really wanted to. A most interesting new ally, indeed.

Corann, for her part, was likewise impressed with the new visitor's physical prowess, as well as her air of competence. She took a liking to her immediately. And that meant one thing.

"Come on back to the kitchen. I've just baked up some fresh sweets for the occasion, and after your flight, I bet you'd love a cup of tea."

The pirate captain caught Bud's amused grin as he watched the exchange. Apparently, he was well accustomed to the assassin's motherly antics.

"That sounds lovely," Lalaynia replied.

The group followed Corann back to her home, chatting merrily as they walked, all of them well accustomed to the role she played in public by this point. Once back in the safely muted walls of her home, they could discuss more pressing matters.

With tea and pastry in hand, of course.

"The spies have passed along the information you noted, Hozark, and are attempting to ascertain whether Visla Maktan is truly at that location. It is a bit tricky, however, as that is a location we are not embedded in. I fear it may take a little bit of time."

"We have time," he replied. "Henni's location has been narrowed down to a dozen worlds. I have tasked the network with seeking her out, though if she is being held in a dungeon facility, it may very well take some time as well."

Laskar seemed agitated. "So, we just wait now? I'm telling you, the lead on Maktan is a good one."

"Our people are the best, and if your intel was accurate, we shall know soon enough," Corann replied. "But given what we are up against, caution and planning are the order of the day."

Hozark nodded his agreement, but the others seemed a bit more anxious to get moving sooner than later.

"Can we at least prep the ship?" Bud asked. "We might as well load up and get ready so we're set to go as soon as we hear back."

"A sound suggestion," Hozark replied.

The adults went to work assembling what might be of use from Corann's stockpile while Happizano gleefully showed their host his new tricks learned at the hand of Master Turong. She had been delighted to hear he had sent his regards, and had even commented that perhaps it was time for her to pay her old friend a visit, once this business had been dealt with.

But for now, they had a task at hand, and it needed to be seen to completion.

Evening had fallen when a knock at the door interrupted their dinner. Corann rose and answered it, her exclamations of happiness making it clear this was friend, not foe. Moments later, she closed her door and led their visitor in to join them.

"Demelza!" Hap exclaimed.

"Hello, Happizano," she replied. "Good evening to you all."

"Welcome back, Sister," Hozark said, moving chairs and making space for her to join them.

Corann was already getting another plate of food for the new arrival. That one part of her act had now become so ingrained that it was doubtful she could *not* feed a guest even if she tried.

"Where the hell have you been?" Laskar asked through a full mouth.

Bud sighed. "Classy, man."

"It's all right, Bud. I do not mind," Demelza said. She looked at Corann, who gave her a little nod. "I was on an errand for the order," she continued. "A quest, if you like."

"A quest? Like for the Balamar Waters?" Laskar joked.

Hozark said nothing but thought of the small vial of the priceless liquid stashed in his possessions, taken from the man who had slain his pupil. Such incredible healing power for others, yet so utterly deadly for Wampeh.

"No, not quite like that," Demelza replied. "A bit more mythic, actually."

"More than Balamar?"

"Actually, yes. I was seeking the Quommus."

The table went silent, then Laskar, of course, burst into laughter.

"The Quommus? Oh, that's priceless. People have been on futile hunts for that for centuries. It's just some stupid legend, is all."

"So we thought," she replied. Something in her demeanor said there was much more to this story, and indeed there was. "But the interesting truth of it is, the Quommus actually *does* exist."

Laskar paled at her words. "You're kidding, right? A device capable of masking all magic? It's impossible."

"And yet, I found it," she replied, barely containing her smile.

The table was abuzz at the news.

"You have done a great service to the order," Hozark commended her.

"You're saying it blocks your spells? Makes you invisible?" Lalaynia asked. "I only barely remember the story from when I was a kid."

"If legends are correct, then it blocks nearly all detection of magical use, so yes, I suppose you could say it makes you invisible, in a way. Even the most powerful of target would have to be on their highest guard to stand a chance of overcoming its masking power. But there is still much to learn about it. It is, after all, an extremely ancient and arcane tool."

"I can't believe it. You actually found it," Laskar said, amazed. "Can we see it?"

"Later. Perhaps after we return from our next task. We must retrieve our friend and slay Maktan."

"It could help with that," the copilot continued.

Corann interrupted. "Perhaps, yes. But we do not understand how it works as of yet. For now, it is in a safe place to be studied."

"So what are we waiting for? Let's find the girl and take out Maktan once and for all," Laskar said.

Hozark shook his head. "Soon, Laskar. Soon. But for the time being, we must wait. There are a dozen worlds on which our friend might be, and as for Maktan, we shall only have one shot at him, so we must be certain of his location. A failed attempt would almost certainly render him untouchable. So, for now, we dine, we rest, and we eat. And soon, with luck, we shall rescue our friend."

CHAPTER FORTY-SIX

It was late, and Hap had gone to bed and Lalaynia had returned to her ship. Though Corann had offered her a comfortable place to sleep, the pirate had graciously declined. Her ship was her home, and given her druthers, she'd rather sleep in her own bed.

Corann understood. Especially for ones in so dangerous a profession as theirs. There was a security of familiar surroundings, as well as the countless weapons undoubtedly stashed within arm's reach.

Sitting quietly in the cozy warmth of Corann's dining room, Hozark and his friends drank the relaxingly sweet, and mildly alcoholic concoction their host had whipped up for them. They had discussed many things as the hour grew late, and after a while, it was Laskar who broached a somewhat delicate subject.

"So, you're saying when you went on that little Ghalian errand, it was actually a rescue mission? And for a town full of Ootaki, no less? I'm telling you, you should have told me. I'm great in a fight."

"As you so often remind us," Demelza noted.

"But why didn't you just have me back you up instead of

leaving me and Hap on our own like that? I mean, I get it with the kid, you don't want to go dragging him into a fight, but--"

"I asked him not to," Corann interjected. "The protection of rescued Ootaki is a very sensitive matter among the Ghalian, and where they are relocated is a matter of the greatest secrecy."

"But you're talking about it now."

"Yes, we are. But that is because, I am sad to say, Sooval is no longer their home. It is a shame. They had established a comfortable life there."

"So, where did you send them?" the copilot asked.

Corann smiled warmly. "As I said. It is a secret."

Laskar knew better than to push that point, no matter how his curiosity might be piqued. Instead, his curiosity turned to another tender point.

"Hozark, you said you ran into Samara again while you were there. What happened?"

"She tried to kill me, of course," he replied.

It was his typical stoic answer to that sort of thing, but it was clear something about the encounter was bothering him, and this time it was Demelza who felt the need to pry, though out of concern for her friend's well-being.

"Master Hozark, you have a long history with Samara. She was a Ghalian, and for many, many years. As such, she would share our beliefs about enslaving innocents. Why would she lead an assault on a peaceful Ootaki hideout?"

"I do not know," he replied. "There is so much about her I do not understand. I attempted to ascertain why she would do such a thing, but that discussion went nowhere."

"You talked while you fought?" Bud asked.

Hozark hesitated a moment. "We were trapped together beneath the collapsed city."

"Hang on, you two were stuck together? For how long?"

"For some time," he replied. "And in that span, she was

unwilling to discuss any of her Council duties, or why she was working with them at all."

The frustration just below the surface was almost palpable. He had tried to get answers but had failed. There was obviously something at play with their former comrade, but none of them knew what it could possibly be. And that was dangerous.

Laskar, however, seemed amped up by the idea of the two Ghalian opponents trapped together. "Oh man, you were stuck down there with your ex? Did you two fight?"

"No, Laskar, we did not fight," Hozark replied with a sigh. "Instead of doing something so counterproductive, given the circumstances, we pooled our power and skills to survive the situation."

"So, it was a truce of sorts?"

"Precisely."

"And is there still a truce?"

"Sadly, that ended as soon as we reached the surface," he said. "It is just so unlike her. To turn against us. To lead an attack on peaceful Ootaki. What could have convinced her to do this?"

"A very good question," Demelza said. "Regardless of her reasoning, she has tried to kill you. And me as well. More than once, I might add."

A faint hint of a smile tickled Hozark's lips. "Yes. But as our adversary, would you respect her if she had done anything less?"

"A valid point," Demelza admitted.

"But I cannot help but feel she was disapproving of elements of her tasks. Such as the taking of Henni. Her demeanor when I spoke of Henni's capture... she appeared displeased with the whole affair."

"Perhaps. But perhaps you are reading into the situation what you wish to see in it."

"I am afraid Demelza is correct in her line of thinking on this matter," Corann agreed. "We cannot know anything about her with any degree of certainty. Even if she did disapprove of

Henni's kidnapping, she still allowed it to happen under her watch."

Hozark deflated ever so slightly. "Of course. I wanted to think well of our old friend. To give her the benefit of the doubt. But you are right. I was reading into nothing. Everything she did, everything she said..." He abruptly trailed off into silence.

Bud was a little unsettled by his friend's odd reaction. "What is it, Hozark?"

"Wait. I must recall it."

"Recall what?" Laskar asked.

"Shh, let him think," Bud hushed the copilot.

Hozark furrowed his brow a moment, calling up the exact details from the vault of his mind. After a long pause, a smile spread across his lips.

"She *did* disapprove," he said. "And while she could not overtly aide me in the recovery of our friend, she was able to provide a little road map."

Laskar seemed confused. "What do you mean? You said she didn't tell you anything."

"So it seemed. But we now possess a list of the twelve places Henni might be held. And Samara narrowed the search for us."

"I'm still not following you."

"When we were trapped, I told her I would stop at nothing to recover our friend. She seemed to commiserate, and said, '*I would not be surprised if all the stone and sand and bleached bones in the galaxy couldn't keep you away.*'"

"And?" Laskar asked.

"Don't you see? It is spelled out for us. Hidden in plain sight."

"Of course," Corann said. "It's clever, I'll give her that."

Poor Laskar was nearly beside himself. "What is?"

"She told me where Henni is. And it's so obvious. We've been there before."

"We have?"

"'*All the stone and sand and bleached bones.'* Look on the list of worlds where Henni might be. Only one fits that description."

Bud's eyes widened. "Holy shit, he's right," he exclaimed. "But damn, that's a ballsy move, hiding her *there*."

"*Where*?" Laskar exclaimed.

"Where we would not expect it. Where we have already fought and defeated Maktan's lackeys. A world littered with the bones of those betrayed and slain by one of the Council's most wicked of vislas. Where Visla Trixzal revealed his true treachery." Hozark turned to his pilot. "Contact Lalaynia, Bud. We are going to Actaris, and we leave at once."

CHAPTER FORTY-SEVEN

"Good. Now, again. Focus on your power. Feel it. Own it. Be confident knowing this is yours to control."

Visla Jinnik was kind but firm in his instruction, but he had come to know Henni quite well in their relatively short time together, and he was confident she could handle it. In fact, she was doing more than just that.

While the key element of the lessons and practice were focusing her powers, harnessing them to do her bidding, there had been an unexpected second aspect that had proven to be quite enlightening. Henni, it seemed, was finally getting in touch with herself.

It was something she had never done in her relatively few years. A tough life in slavery, followed by an equally, albeit different, existence on the streets had made her hyper-alert. Always on guard. She had learned from an early age that you simply do not Zen out and turn your attention inward. If you did that, you could get beaten, or robbed. Or worse.

But here, locked deep within this structure, barricaded inside a magically secured cell, she was finally somewhere safe. At least from everything but the guards who would periodically drag her away to be drained. But aside from that, her cell, for meditation purposes at least, was probably the safest place on the planet.

Niallik had figured out a way to pull her power from her by force, after much effort and toil. Apparently, the mix of her and Jinnik's powers being combined had a somewhat symbiotic effect on her draining apparatus. Jinnik felt it far more than she did, however, and it seemed his power took longer to recover.

Whether that was simply a result of his having his power pulled from him for so much longer than her or not was anyone's guess. But whatever the reason, he was initially becoming weaker after every session. That forced Niallik to adjust her methods a bit, allowing them both longer rest periods to regain their strength.

It was in those times, when he finally felt well enough to sit up and focus, that he would continue to tutor his young apprentice. It wasn't an official apprenticeship by any means, but he had taken a liking to the young woman and was finding her training to be the high point in his incarceration.

Henni, for her part, was likewise enjoying their endeavor, and as her senses grew stronger and her connection to her power more defined, she actually began believing him when he told her just how much she could do, if only she had control.

They had made a pact a few days prior. Jinnik would pretend to be even more drained than he was, hoping Niallik would allow him an even longer recovery period. And that she did. It wasn't a lot, but it was enough to allow him to begin to gain in strength.

"I can feel your power," Henni said, sitting cross-legged with her eyes closed.

"Good. And your own power, let it reach out and mingle with my own," he replied.

He shuddered slightly when her magic touched his. It was just the faintest of sensations, but the impossible girl was actually doing it. He had suspected that her abilities as a reader might indicate an ability beyond what she normally used them for. But until this moment it had all been conjecture.

"Now, can you sense the control collar around my neck?" he asked.

"Yes. I feel it resisting us."

"It is designed to restrain me. To keep me from casting with any real power."

"Why don't I feel that from here? Is it the force spell between our cells?"

"No, Henni. This is as I had hoped. A flaw in our captor's methods. You see, because of our levels of power, these collars were specially cast to bind each of us. Normal people all get a standard one, but these were fine-tuned to keep us in check."

She began to see where he was going with this. "So my magic can totally cross over into your collar without triggering it?"

"Precisely. And if we combine our efforts, it is possible that, together, we just might be able to break free."

Henni felt her pulse speed up at the thought. Her grasp on her magic faltered.

"Concentrate, Henni. You can control your power even while your body reacts to other things. In time, you will learn this skill. But for now, breathe slowly and focus."

She did as he asked, concentrating on the forces churning within her. They'd been there her whole life, but she had never truly felt them for more than a fleeting instant, and even then, it was entirely out of her control, usually in a highly traumatic moment.

But now, with the sensation under her own direction, she was beginning to feel something new. She was starting to feel an actual grasp on a degree of power she had until recently not even known she possessed.

Jinnik felt her reconnect with his power, and far stronger than before.

"Good. Now, let's try a little experiment. Focus your attention on the feel of the magic in my collar. Have you got it?"

"I can sense it."

"Excellent. You're doing very well, Henni. Can you sense how it binds together, keeping the collar intact? It will feel like a tugging together. That is the magic forming a secure loop."

She strained her senses, slight creases forming on her brow as she reached out to the unfamiliar sensations. Then, suddenly, she felt it. Something that was like what he had described. A small smile spread across her lips.

"I feel it," she declared.

"Wonderful. Now, this is the difficult part, so I want you to take your time. Recite the spell I taught you. The one to break magical bonds. It is not specifically meant for control collars, but with your power it should at least begin to work. And if you can weaken the bond enough, I might be able to force it the rest of the way."

"Won't that be incredibly painful for you?"

"Oh, there is no doubt about that," he replied. "Now, are you ready to try?"

Henni very much did not want to hurt her new friend and mentor, but she realized that he was right. This could be their one chance at escape.

"I'm ready."

"Good. Do not worry about success at this point. This is more to get you accustomed to the spell and how it should work. When we've had a few more rest cycles, I should have enough power to truly assist you."

"I understand."

"Then, let us begin."

Henni began to cast, quietly speaking the words of the spell he had taught her. The power inside her snaked out through their invisible connection, wrapping itself around Jinnik's collar. Henni pushed on, not even realizing she had stopped uttering the words and was now casting entirely silently.

Jinnik watched her with awe. The sheer potential this petite young woman possessed was awe-inspiring. In fact, much to his surprise, he felt the bond of his powerful collar begin to weaken under her assault. It seemed that he had been correct about the spells binding him. While the collar resisted as one would expect, it did not flare out in the manner it would if he were casting.

"I am going to try something," he said. "Do not be alarmed. Just keep casting."

Jinnik drew upon his reserves of power and carefully probed the weakest part of the collar, where Henni's magic had pulled it thin.

It just might work, he realized. Without a second thought, he cast as forcefully as he could, driving his magic into that weak spot, forcing his collar to begin to separate.

The shocking pain that flooded his body was intense, nearly driving him to the floor, but he continued to cast. The collar was so close to succumbing, he could feel it within his grasp. But he was just too weak. Too drained.

He abruptly released his spell and flopped back onto his cot. Henni stopped casting at once, a deeply concerned look in her eye.

"Are you all right? Did I hurt you?"

Breathing hard, Jinnik let out a little chuckle. "No, my little friend, you did not. You were magnificent."

Henni felt the breath she didn't know she had been holding release from her lungs.

"It would seem I am not quite ready for that," Jinnik said with a pained chuckle, gathering himself and sitting upright. "But you, your control of your power is at its strongest yet. Well done, Henni. Extremely well done."

Henni beamed at the praise. Sure, she was good at stuff, but this was something not just anyone could do. This made her special.

The sound of heavy boots rang out in the corridor outside their cell block. Henni and Jinnik both arranged themselves as if nothing was going on at all. The guards didn't seem to care and walked straight to Jinnik's cell.

"Come on," the larger of the two said, dragging him out of his cell.

"Wait, you're not taking me too?" Henni asked, surprised.

The guard flashed a nasty little grin. "Your time will come soon enough," he said, then pushed the exhausted visla out into the corridor.

Henni waited hours for her friend's return, anxious to hear what new misery Niallik had in store for him this time, and likely for her as well when she was finished with him.

But Visla Jinnik never returned.

CHAPTER FORTY-EIGHT

It was ballsy. Surprising. Arrogant.

That Visla Maktan had chosen the lifeless planet of Actaris of all places to take their friend and set up a new weapons smelting operation was an act of utter hubris. He had outmaneuvered them once again, his cautious and unassuming persona leading the Ghalian to never even consider he would have reoccupied the fallen facility.

They had killed his lower-ranking Council underlings there, after all. Visla Torund had fallen that day, and Visla Ravik had been forced to flee. The men had been an important part of Maktan's work, and the Ghalian had struck the first of several blows to his plans.

Adding to the brazenness of Maktan's move was that Actaris was surprisingly close to Corann's home on Inskip. In just a few jumps they would be there. But Lalaynia's massive pirate craft needed a short moment to collect the men she had sent to the surface to resupply and take a bit of shore leave before they set off for battle.

It had appeared they would have some time waiting for the Ghalian spy network to infiltrate the dozen worlds in question and determine which one was holding Henni. It was only natural, and wise on her part, that her crew should be released to refresh themselves beforehand. Hozark's revelation, however, had just abruptly put an end to that.

"Found her already? That's great news. We'll be right behind you," she said as her men fanned out to recall the rest of the crew. "Give me an hour and we'll be on our way. Half an hour if I can round them up faster."

"I shall assist you," Corann said. "Go on, Hozark. Happizano shall be safe here with me. You need to hurry and take a position above Actaris and make sure no one leaves. Your support forces will join you shortly."

Hozark did not hesitate, rushing to Bud's waiting mothership and sealing the hatch behind him.

"We leave at once," he said, sliding into his seat in command.

"But what about the others?" Laskar asked. "Lalaynia is on the ground, and so are a bunch of her--"

"Corann is assisting her. There is no time to waste. We launch now."

"Okay. But maybe I should skree over to her ship and--"

"You heard the man," Bud said as the ship shot upward. "Hang on to your bootstraps. We're gonna fly!"

Normally, Bud would have launched at a slower pace. His rapid departure would likely draw a bit of attention, and he would have to apologize to Corann for that later. But they had Henni's location, and he was damned if they would move her before they got there. It had already happened once with Jinnik, and it was sure as hell not happening again.

As soon as they cleared the atmosphere he punched it, pushing their coordinates farther than the optimal distance as they jumped to the first of their jump targets. Bud had already pulled a spare Drookonus from his hidden cache and had it ready. If he had to burn this one out he would. Time was of the essence.

The jumps were few enough that the device managed to survive the trip without catastrophic failure; though, given the strain he'd subjected it to, he would have to spend a fair bit of coin repairing and recharging it. But he didn't care. What mattered was they reached Actaris in record time.

"Why don't we use the Quommus?" Laskar asked as they exited their second jump, immediately prepping for the next one. "You've got it with you, right?"

"Because we do not fully understand it yet," Demelza replied. "It is far too risky to utilize new and unfamiliar devices when rushing into battle."

"But it can keep them from detecting--"

"Demelza is right," Hozark interrupted. "Now is not the time to experiment with an arcane device such as the Quommus, much as it could be to our advantage."

Demelza nodded her agreement. "And besides, Corann has already sent it to our finest scholars for study. If any can unravel its mysteries, they can. For now, we shall leave it at that."

Bud licked his finger and touched the Drookonus in its cradle. His finger didn't make that worrisome sizzling sound, which was a good sign.

"We're ready to go," he said, preparing to jump. He turned to his copilot. "Don't worry, we've done this sort of thing plenty of times. If we create the right diversion, we won't even need the Quommus. And it's not like we've ever had anything like that at our disposal in the past."

"Bud is correct," Hozark said. "Visla Maktan is not at this location, only his underlings. Perhaps we may encounter an emmik, but the likelihood of any more powerful than that being present is slim. They have already fought on Actaris, and as they believe they are undiscovered, they are likely to be overconfident in their security preparations."

Much as he wanted to see the Quommus in action, Laskar

had to admit they made good points. "Okay, then. So, what's the plan?"

"We get there as fast as we can," Bud replied. "And we get Henni back."

"That's the plan?" Laskar asked incredulously.

"That's the plan. Hang on, we're jumping."

With that, he engaged the spell once again, sending them hurtling closer to their destination.

When Uzabud's mothership appeared in low orbit above Actaris a short while later, Hozark and Demelza launched their shimmer ships immediately, engaging their camouflage before they even disconnected.

Bud, despite his desire to be first on the ground with them, hung back for the moment, watching from above to make sure no craft departed from their target location. As soon as Lalaynia jumped in, he would take his own away craft and head down as fast as he could, leaving Laskar on his own to work with the pirates and guard from above while blocking any attempts to flee.

The Ghalians' entry into the atmosphere was slow by necessity––a pair of orange-hot streaks in the sky would alert their enemy of their arrival despite the ships themselves being invisible. But once they were through the entry phase, they barreled toward the surface as fast as they could.

It hadn't been the plan initially. They were going to sit in orbit until Lalaynia arrived. But the Ghalian had an additional advantage on their side. They had shimmer ships, and that meant they could begin their infiltration before the reinforcements arrived.

The terrain was as rocky and barren as the last time they'd been there, and the stronghold stood just as they remembered it. Multiple internal courtyards sat empty, the facility itself seeming barely occupied. But they knew better. A few larger craft rested in the landing field beside the structure, and despite the lack of markings, they knew whose forces they belonged to.

Across the landscape, bleached bones still jutted out of the surrounding soil, shining white in the hot sunlight. An ever-present reminder of what Visla Trixzal had done there. Of the thousands he had slaughtered under pretext of Council business.

But today was different. It would be Council forces whose blood would spill and whose bones would be added to that macabre collection.

The two assassins touched down just outside the stronghold, not risking landing within the courtyards despite their emptiness. They would make their way inside under cover of shimmer cloak.

By the time Bud and the others made their attack, dropping into those courtyards, they would already be inside the facility. And if all went according to plan, Maktan's people would not know what hit them.

CHAPTER FORTY-NINE

"Bud, follow us in," Lalaynia skreed to her friend from her small attack ship. There were eight of them, hers being the foremost. "Geist drop-in maneuver. You remember that one?"

"Shadow behind and hit the deck when you peel off. How could I forget it?"

"It's been a while. You might have let that cushy smuggling life get to you."

"Your confidence is overwhelming, Laynia. Just get me close enough to land, and I'll do the rest."

"You've got it. We'll be right behind you once my people establish an air perimeter and engage them from above. Can't have anyone slipping in."

"Or out," Bud added.

"You'll get her back," Lalaynia said. "Trust me, we've got this."

Her massive pirate ship was lurking above in low orbit, ready to fight either incoming or outgoing Council ships. A very respectable contingent of pirates were ready to launch their smaller fighters stored in the craft's hangars as well.

The captain, however, had departed to lead the charge to the surface. It was one of the reasons her crew were so fiercely loyal. Captain Lalaynia never asked them to do anything she wouldn't do herself. She led in the most literal way possible with just two words: "Follow me."

She had arrived far ahead of schedule, much to Bud's pleasant surprise. Waiting while Hozark and Demelza infiltrated the facility was making him climb the walls with impatience. But apparently Corann called upon the neighborhood children who adored her so much to go and run and see if they might find the gregarious men and women on shore leave for her friend.

For anyone else it might have raised a few eyebrows, but Corann had such goodwill among the locals and had helped all of them on one occasion or another that for her to help a stranger, even one as imposing as the tall pirate woman, was right in character.

Bud had launched as soon as Lalaynia's ship jumped into orbit, leaving Laskar to follow him into the atmosphere and provide a mid-range support while the pirates were engaging above and below.

Lalaynia dove right for the stronghold, leading her ships straight toward the facility. It seemed quiet enough. Almost deserted, even. But when she got within spell range, a sudden barrage of defensive chaff was hurled her way.

"Evasives," she called out as she dodged the magical bombardment.

In the rear, Bud was focused on his goal. The small courtyard just uphill of the semi-destroyed area of the structures. It would take a fair bit of piloting to avoid the stone spires of Actaris's landscape, but if anyone could do it, he could.

"In five," Lalaynia called out, prepping for a quick dogfight before leaving the sparse aerial defenses that had launched to her men while she and the small crew aboard her ship landed to storm the gates. "Three. Two. One."

She pulled up hard, banking sharply while deploying a fairly impressive magical assault on the area the defenses were coming from. They were flashy and bright, but were also more for show than anything else. All she had to do was distract them from the lone ship that had not followed the others as they peeled off.

Bud spun hard and dove straight down. It would be one hell of a hard landing--if he survived it, that is. But if he did, the rapid drop would almost certainly keep him from being spotted.

"Come on. Come on!" he growled at the ship as he cast a series of buffering spells to cushion his impact as best he could.

The ship shuddered as the magic did its best to keep it from smashing into the ground, grabbing it firmly and dispersing the force of impact as best it could. It was still a hard hit, though, and there would definitely need to be some repairs made when this was all through.

Bud didn't care. He barreled out of the ship without another thought, armed to the teeth with both blades and konuses. He even carried a more powerful slaap, though he was admittedly out of practice with the weapon.

He ran toward the gaping entrance to the tunnel network connecting the different parts of the fortress, scanning the ground while keeping an eye out for Council goons.

"There you are," he said as he spotted what seemed just like a random little mark on the bottom most stone at the tunnel entrance and went charging in. "Thanks, Hozark."

The Ghalian had left him a secret sign. A basic directional marker that would steer him toward the most likely area to find Henni based on the assassin's initial survey. The place was quite expansive, and without their scouting it could take a very, very long time to just locate the portion of the supposedly abandoned structure that was inhabited.

Still, it would be a lot of ground to cover even knowing roughly where to look. But Bud was *extremely* motivated. And once Lalaynia and her team finished tearing into the parked ships beside the stronghold, they would be able to help narrow the search.

She had been quite excited when they popped into orbit and scanned the target below. The ships on the ground weren't marked, but she knew right away what they were. More importantly, she knew what they were worth, and if they could leverage the element of surprise, she could not only help her friend, but also land an extremely nice haul for themselves in the process.

That is, if they could overcome the Council forces without destroying the ships in the process.

Fortunately, only a few smaller craft managed to make it into the air before her pirate raiders charged the startled guards at the other ships' entrances. They had seen the craft above, but to imagine anyone foolish, or crazy, enough to attack on foot was simply not in the realm of possibility.

But Lalaynia was the sort of woman who did the impossible regularly, either because no one had bothered to tell her it couldn't be done, or because she simply didn't care. She'd garnered quite a reputation for it over the years, along with a lot of respect, as well as quite a few bounties on her head.

"Lalaynia, I'm going in. Call when you're moving, and I'll direct you to me," he called over his skree.

"Sorry, what was that, Bud?"

The reply came through with sounds of screaming in the background. Obviously Council forces. The pirates were a disciplined bunch and never screamed. This was a good sign.

"I said I'm going in. Reach out when you're on the way."

"Will do. Good luck in there."

Bud didn't wait a moment longer, plunging headlong into

the dimly lit tunnel system and connecting corridors. With a short sword in one hand and a dagger in the other--better for confined fighting such as hallways--along with a powerful konus on his wrist, he was ready to take on anyone who stood in his way.

And he was looking forward to a little payback.

Hozark and Demelza were also armed to the teeth, though they were far more calculating in their movements. As they'd gotten a head start on their friend, they were already deep into the fortress grounds.

The pair had split up, each taking a different level as they hunted down their target. Once they'd penetrated to the innermost chambers, the fighting started. The bodies piling up at their feet were clearly mercenaries working for the Council, but their uniforms bore no identifying markings. Maktan's secret army, it seemed.

Interestingly, this must have been a *very* off-book site, because they did not encounter any actual Council troops at all. Maktan was keeping this place secret. The new weapons he was churning out were going to be reserved for himself alone.

Hozark engaged a half dozen well-armed and well-trained guards as he descended a flight of stairs to the next level. They were tougher than the ones he'd fought before, though they fell before him just the same. But this piqued his interest. A moment later he found what they were guarding.

The chamber was full of newly charged konuses. And a great many of them contained traces of Henni's power. Yes, she was definitely here. Or she should be, if they weren't too late.

Hozark increased his pace, slaughtering the men and women foolish enough to engage him with the false confidence of greater numbers. He quickly showed them the folly of their ways with a flash of his glowing blue blade.

The death and mayhem was confined to only the areas the

intruders had charged into so far. Otherwise, all of the attention was focused on the fighting going on *outside*. The element of surprise was still on their side. But he knew that would only last so long and moved even faster, hiding fallen bodies when he could, but mostly killing everyone who might discover them and raise an alarm.

It was brutal, but deadly efficient.

It was also taking too long.

Hozark clashed with another group, but these seemed to have a different look to them. They weren't just troops in the stronghold. These had the air of men with position.

He slowed his assault and toyed with them a moment as he ascertained which was likely the highest ranking of the lot. Judging by the clothing, as well as the way the others looked to him, the stout fellow nearest on his right was the likeliest one.

Hozark dropped him with a quick blow to the midriff, driving the air from the man's lungs. He then spun to the others, removing heads and limbs from their bodies before their leader had even dropped to the ground, gasping for breath.

By the time he regained it, the corridor was silent. And a Wampeh Ghalian was towering over him, blood dripping from his sword, as well as his fangs.

Hozark did not actually drink from the fallen men. They had no power of their own, and to do so would have been not only time consuming and disgusting, but pointless as well. But he had dipped his fangs in the blood that had accumulated on his hands in battle. All the better to terrify his new captive.

It was an old trick. But old tricks worked for a reason. The visceral fear of being in the grip of an alpha predator made most people's brains short-circuit to a degree, and that could be used to his advantage. Scared people talked far more freely.

Hozark lifted the man to his feet, summoning a little spell with his konus to aid him in doing so with just one hand. The effect gave the impression he was so strong he could lift the burly guard as if he were but a child.

The poor man pissed himself immediately.

"You have but one chance to live," the Wampeh hissed. "Tell me where the prisoner is kept. If you lie to me, you die. And horribly."

The guard had already made up his mind that no prisoner was more important than his life. And if Maktan decided to kill him later? So be it. For today, at least, he wanted to draw as many more breaths as he could.

"D-down the hallway. Turn right and then left. There's an archway. Go through and cross the chamber. The left-hand corridor will take you there."

Hozark lowered the man to his feet.

"If you have lied to me, I will return for you," he said, then hit him with a stun spell.

The guard crumbled to the stone. He would be out for at least a half hour, and that was far more time than Hozark needed to confirm whether he'd told the truth.

The uniforms of the men he slayed as he drew nearer his goal were clearly those of a different set of guards. Specialized. Better armed. And he had killed a pair of the green-and-black-skinned weaponsmiths he had seen previously when back in the hidden facility on Gravalis some time ago.

He was on the right path, he was certain of it.

Up ahead he saw a reinforced door. Strong wards were layered upon it, more to keep whoever was inside from getting out than the other way around. This had to be it. A strong cage to hold a strong prisoner.

Hozark focused and pulled from his arcane learnings, carefully disarming the wards one by one. Finally, the last of the defensive spells fell. With a sense of completion, he swung the door open. What he saw was not what he expected.

"Oh, hello," the tired-looking man chained in his cell said. "It is so very good to see you."

This was not Henni. Not by a long shot. But it was another he had been seeking.

"Hello, Visla Jinnik," Hozark said. "What do you say we get you out of that cell?"

CHAPTER FIFTY

The wards holding Visla Jinnik within his cell had been a slight challenge for Hozark at first. It seemed whoever had set them in place had looped them into the containment spells in the man's control collar. He had to admit, it was a rather novel use of those spells. The person who had come up with the method definitely thought outside the box.

But outside the box was precisely what he needed right now. More specifically, to get Visla Jinnik outside of his magical box. Rather than fiddle with it, wasting valuable time, Hozark ran back to the unconscious guard and hefted him over his shoulder, then raced back to Jinnik's cell, dumping the man in a heap on the stone floor.

"Dead, eh? Couldn't have happened to a more deserving--"

"He is not dead," Hozark said, slapping the slumbering man with an awakening spell.

"What? Where am--" the man abruptly fell silent as the fog lifted and he remembered what had happened to him. Then he noted he had been moved.

"You are to open this cell. Drop the containment spells,"

Hozark demanded. "I do not need to remind you the price for noncompliance."

It was a statement, not a question.

At this point, the guard, once cruel and haughty in his perceived power over his prisoners, was reduced to a groveling mess at the feet of a far more apex predator than he.

"Of course. B-but I need a konus. I'm unpowered."

Hozark pulled one of the konuses he'd taken from the guards he had killed on his bloody path to this place. Never leave weapons that might be used against you behind, if you can. At least, not if they are relatively powerful. So he took them.

These konuses were fairly weak, but they contained traces of Henni's power. Likely the first iterations as they experimented with her unusual magic. He handed it to the guard, the blood of his comrades still wet on the metal. The man fought down his bile and slid it onto his wrist, then cast the unlocking spells.

"Now the collar."

"I can't do the collar. Only the bosses can undo it."

Hozark stared at the man a moment. It was clear he was in no mindset to lie. "Very well," he said, pulling the konus from the man's arm and sliding it back into his pocket.

Visla Jinnik, though restrained by his control collar, at least had the strength to stand. Soon, though Hozark did not know precisely when, it would likely engage, trying to keep him from fleeing. But he would deal with that when they came to that point.

"Can I borrow that?" Jinnik asked, pointing to the dagger on Hozark's left hip.

"Of course."

He handed the blade to the visla, having a pretty good idea what was about to happen. He was not mistaken.

It was a bit of a disappearing trick. Namely, the length of the blade disappeared into the guard's chest, piercing his heart, dropping him stone dead. Jinnik hadn't struck Hozark as the vengeful, killing type when he had engaged him and Demelza to find Hap. But imprisonment and torture can change a man.

The visla pulled the blade free and wiped it on the dead guard's clothes, then handed it back to the assassin. "Thank you," he said, and left it at that.

Hozark saw the wobble in his step and moved close, catching him before he fell. Apparently the visla had been drained more than he had thought when he first laid eyes upon the imprisoned man.

"We must get you out of here," Hozark said, walking Jinnik to the door, the exhausted man's arm draped around his shoulder.

He hurried him along, back through the route he'd just passed. This wasn't what he had planned, but the likelihood of finding Jinnik had been a possibility. He would have to leave the recovery of Henni to the others for the time being, until the visla was safely tucked away on his shimmer ship.

Hozark's vespus blade leapt to his hand as he neared a corner in the corridor. The sound of rapidly approaching footsteps was clearly echoing off the stone walls.

"Holy shit!" Bud exclaimed as he nearly barreled into his friend.

Hozark stayed his sword, carefully resheathing it. Fortunately for Bud, Ghalian training had honed his reflexes so finely that the odds of accidentally striking an ally were slim to none. Still, in this particular setting, charging headlong into a deadly assassin could still have some pretty negative consequences despite all that training.

But not today.

Bud looked at the man and saw the control collar on his neck. Another slave, it seemed. But that wasn't his concern. "Did you find Henni?"

"No. Demelza is still searching another section of the grounds, but they are vast."

"I've been checking everywhere but no luck. I saw you've been here, though. Nice trail of bodies you left back there."

"I was in a bit of a rush myself," Hozark said.

"I know where Henni is," the man draped over the assassin's shoulder said.

That got Bud's attention. "You do?"

"Yes. Or, at least where she is most likely to be. Our old cell. I watched when they moved me. If you follow this corridor and go down two levels then turn left, there will be a large banquet hall. Cross through it and take the right-hand exit. Go down one more level and you can't miss it. The cells are right there."

"How do you know all of this? Who are you?"

"I am Visla Dinarius Jinnik."

"Hap's father? So, you're a visla, then."

"Yes, but weakened and restrained, I am afraid," he said, touching the collar on his neck. "Now, hurry. Henni is learning to harness her magic, but she is vulnerable and still needs assistance."

Bud and Hozark shared a look. If Henni was truly learning to control her power, she could be a very dangerous woman, indeed. Hozark tightened his grip on the weak man's arm.

"Find her, Bud. I shall take care of the visla."

Bud nodded once and took off at a run, his blades ready for anyone foolish enough to get in his way. The visla, however, slipped to the ground, exhausted and in pain. Hozark bent to examine the man, hoping his friend would be successful in his rescue attempt on his own.

Bud followed the visla's directions in a flash of speed and metal, the guards he came across dead and falling to his sword and dagger before they even realized he had been running at them. It was the epitome of a blitz.

A lesser fighter might have missed the vital points of their opponents, but Bud had been a pirate a long time, and had been traveling with a Wampeh Ghalian for quite a while as well. His blades flew true, leaving death in his wake. Eventually, he would tire and have to fight more conventionally, but for the moment his adrenaline was high, and damn near nothing would stop him.

CHAPTER FIFTY-ONE

In her cell, Henni could *feel* the conflict brewing within the stronghold. She didn't know how, or who was fighting, but her newly heightened senses were screaming out that there was death all around.

Despite her recent training, she felt a bit of panic build within her. The control collar around her neck responded, shocking her, which only served to ramp up her emotions even higher. The collar reacted in kind, increasing its shock spell until it was excruciatingly painful.

Henni writhed in pain on her cot, pulling at the collar with rage. She had been a slave once before, and she had escaped. There was no reason she could not do so again. And this time, she *knew* she had the power.

She turned her attention inside of herself, doing her best to ignore the pain and focus on her power. She latched on to it, holding it tight and building its strength. Then, with a mighty push, she unleashed it through her hands and into her control collar.

The metal turned orange hot, but somehow her skin only blistered slightly, her magic protecting her as she melted and contorted the golden band around her neck. She pulled with all of her might, her muscles straining from the effort. The collar thinned at one point, its magical bond failing. Henni could feel it. She knew her freedom was within reach.

With a shriek, she pulled even harder, the tendons in her hands and arms standing at attention from the incredible force. A shockwave blasted out within her cell, shattering the magical cell wards and knocking the chamber's door off its hinges.

Henni looked at the remnants of the control collar cooling in her hands in a bit of shock.

"I did it," she whispered. "I actually did it."

The violet-haired young woman rose and strode to the doorway. There it was. The way out just down the hall. The stairs they had dragged her up more than once. She was still unarmed, but despite that, she felt confident, somehow. Free. And she was *angry*.

She took off running, barreling up the staircase two at a time. She swung her fist hard out of pure instinct as she smacked right into a man's chest, punching him hard in the jaw.

"Ow! Dammit, Henni!" Bud said, rubbing his face. "Where did you learn to hit so hard? And where the hell did you come from?"

Henni's eyes went wide. "Me? Where did *you* come from?"

"I came to rescue you, dumbass," Bud groused, his eyes filled with joy.

Henni hesitated just a second, then wrapped her arms tight around him. Bud returned the embrace, holding her snugly in his arms.

Finally, they released their grasp, their eyes a bit moist, and not from any smoke in the air. Bud pulled a bundle from his small hip pack. A roll of leather straps and their accompanying shiny bits held out in his hands.

"My knives!" Henni exclaimed, eagerly taking them from him and securing them to her body.

Now she felt at ease. Whole. And ready for anything.

Footsteps rang out in the corridors, and from the sound of it, there were a lot of them.

"You ready for this?" Bud asked.

"Ready? I'm *looking forward* to it."

Ten guards exited the staircase, Niallik following close behind. She had thought to make a run for it with her prize pet, but it seemed someone had let the little woman out of her cage. No matter, her men would take care of the interloper while she reeled in the young woman herself.

Niallik cast her shocking spell.

Henni stood tall, unaffected.

Niallik had a moment of confusion before her eyes realized what she had missed at first glance. Henni was not wearing her collar. Somehow, she had forced it off. And that should not have been possible. The girl was dangerously powerful. But worse yet, it seemed she was now armed.

A quick shift in tactics was called for.

"Kill them both!" she bellowed, her guards reacting immediately, charging into the fray.

Bud and Henni, however, were in their element, and the two played off one another like two parts of the same beast, slashing and slicing, advancing and retreating, each striking down attackers with a blinding flurry of blows.

Niallik pulled up her magic. It was frowned upon, using it while her own people were still in its path, but sometimes friendly fire happened, and stopping the girl was far more important than a few guards.

She spoke the words of her spell, casting with all the force she could muster. If this didn't stop them, nothing would.

The spell blasted down the corridor, slamming her guards to the ground with its force. But somehow, Henni and Bud remained standing, totally unaffected. Bud looked around, confused. The woman down the hall had just cast a killing spell, and at close range, even though her own people were in its path. Yet he had survived. But how?

"Henni, what just happened?"

The young woman's eyes sparkled with her power. "Jinnik said it. I may not be great at offense, but I've got a knack for defense," she said. "Now step aside, I've got something to do."

She didn't hesitate a moment longer, racing down the corridor, daggers flying along with spells. Niallik desperately tried to defend against the multi-pronged attack, but she was unaccustomed to this sort of fighting. Others did the grunt work for her while she cast from a safe distance.

There was no safety. Not now. And there was no distance, as her former captive was upon her in a flash. Henni's daggers lashed out in a frenzy, a blur of silver quickly changing color in the mist of blood they unleashed. This was not merely removing an obstacle or opponent from their path. This was far more visceral than that. Cathartic.

Henni's pinwheeling arms slowed, then finally stopped. The woman had been dead for a while, but Bud was not about to get in the way of his young friend's revenge.

Henni ripped free a relatively clean piece of Niallik's clothing and wiped the blood from her face. Next, she cleaned her weapons and returned them to their sheaths. Slowly, she stood, staring down at the *very* deceased woman at her feet. She turned to Bud, the rage that had been burning within her tempered quite a bit.

"So, about that rescue," she said. "We gonna get out of here, or what?"

CHAPTER FIFTY-TWO

Given the immense power that typically flowed through Visla Jinnik's body, seeing him twitching on the hard stone of the stronghold's passageway floor was disquieting, to say the least. A fine gleam of sweat had even broken out on his brow from the exertion.

This wasn't him simply being a tired man pushed to move quickly for his escape. This was a man whose control collar had activated but who was either too proud or too stubborn to admit it. Either way, it was clear he would not be able to go much farther under his own power.

"Visla, your collar," Hozark finally said as the man tried, and failed, to rise from the ground.

Jinnik looked up at him, the pain in his eyes clear in spite of his best efforts.

Hozark simply nodded and reached into a small, hidden pocket within his tunic. As a Ghalian assassin, he had countless items hidden on his person at most times, and this was no exception. In fact, given where they were going and what they were about to attempt, he had even packed a particularly rare item for this occasion.

The flash of soft gold caught Jinnik's eye as Hozark pulled a slender ribbon of the brightest, most iridescent material he'd ever seen. Tired as he was, he knew at once what it was. And what Hozark intended to do.

"Hold still. I shall have this resolved momentarily," Hozark said, carefully working the end of the ribbon under the visla's collar, then wrapping it around and around until the entire circle was covered.

He gently tied it off and stepped back to assess his handiwork.

"Better?"

Visla Jinnik rolled his neck and took a slow, deep breath, forcing his muscles to unknot now that the pain was gone.

"Yes, much," he replied, gingerly rising to his feet. His fingers lightly touched the material around his collar. "Ootaki hair ribbon. And powerfully charged at that," he said appreciatively.

"Kept for emergencies."

"Such as this?"

"Indeed. I thought it might be of use. I am pleased to see that it was."

Ootaki hair was a rare enough item as it was. To possess even a few long strands of the golden, power-storing locks was considered a fortune. But the truly wealthy, on rare occasion, had it woven into fabric. Some in the order even wove it into their clothing, providing additional power in dire circumstances.

Hozark had more in his personal, hidden storage facility, but the length of ribbon was all he had with him when they learned of Henni's location. There was simply no time to travel to retrieve the rest.

But the hair did what it was intended to do, effectively cutting off the control collar's spells for a time, though it had been something of a roll of the dice given how strong the collar was. Of course, it was restraining a massively powerful visla. It was only natural the collar should be equally strong.

The hair, Hozark noted, was already growing warm from its clash with the collar's magic. That could prove problematic if it continued at that pace.

"It would be best to be far from this place should the Ootaki hair fail," Hozark said. "I know you are tired, but we must get moving immediately."

"No. There is more to do."

"Bud is rescuing Henni, do not fear."

"No, not that," the visla said. "They've been draining me for some time. Putting my power into weapons to use against innocents. And now they've figured out how to pull power from Henni as well."

"We have encountered these konuses," Hozark noted. "An unusual amalgam of magic."

"Then you understand we cannot allow those to be sent out to Maktan's forces. They must be destroyed."

Hozark paused in thought a moment. "How many are there?"

"I can't say for sure. Hundreds, no doubt. Perhaps more. The time has all begun to blur together here."

Hozark put the visla's arm around his shoulder and began walking again. "I will contact our allies to see if they have any weaponry aboard their ship that might be capable of destroying them."

"Wait. There's another way. And it's already here," Jinnik said. "When Niallik first pulled Henni and my magic together, it combined into a highly unstable mix. Just a tiny mistake and her lead weaponsmaker was killed, his smelting lab destroyed in the process."

Hozark could see where this was going. "Do you know how much of this power has been stored?"

"Not a precise amount, but unless they've already managed to force it into konuses, there should be more than enough for our purposes."

It made sense. The smelting and forging of each konus took time, and the bonding of its initial magical charge with the cooling metal was a very tricky and very time-consuming task. There was simply no way to rush the process. And that meant that while some of the stolen power had been used, most of it was likely sitting idly by, barely contained and ready to burst out.

It was perfect.

"The bulk would not be stored anywhere near the smelting facilities," Hozark mused. "Too volatile a location to keep that sort of power."

"It will almost certainly be in Niallik's chambers," Jinnik replied. "Knowing her and her distrustful tendencies, she would have only kept it close."

Hozark had a decision to make. The Ghalian disliked ever using skrees for communication simply because they were privy to the fact that the devices were not as secure from eavesdropping as people believed. But in this instance, the risk was worth it.

"Bud, Demelza, anyone. Have you found Henni?" he sent out to all of their people.

There was a long silence. Finally, one voice replied.

"I've got her, Hozark. We're almost to my ship," Bud said, obviously winded from running.

"Good. Then we are leaving. Everyone evacuate to your ships and leave this place immediately."

"No time for any more pillage?" Lalaynia asked over the skree.

"Only what you can haul off with you at once."

She knew better than to question the man, and his tone only reinforced that. "Okay. Everyone, back to the ships. Take what you can and get out."

The ground team had actually managed to overcome the crew of one of the disguised Council ships outside the fortress walls and quickly launched it into the sky, taking their booty up into space where it could be properly sorted through at their leisure.

"You need me to come get you?" Laskar asked. "I can be there in three minutes."

"No. Stay clear. We shall come to you in orbit. Exit the atmosphere and meet us there."

Laskar had no idea what was going on down there. From the sound of it, Hozark and the others were being forced into a hasty retreat. Perhaps the ground forces were tougher than they'd expected. In any case, he followed his instructions and pulled higher, popping through the atmosphere into the vacuum of space.

"Do you know where this woman's chambers would be?" Hozark asked the visla.

"No. I was always kept in the cells. But it would be something regal. She had that attitude about her. She wouldn't stay in just any quarters."

Hozark knew the type all too well. A little too full of themselves for his taste. But that cockiness made finding her rooms easy. He simply moved upward until he was clear of normal staff chambers, then looked for the most ornate decorations.

With the visla slowing his pace, it took far longer than he wanted. There was little time before possible reinforcements might arrive. But Jinnik was right, the weapons had to be destroyed.

"There!" Jinnik pointed down a hallway.

It was a tapestry worth more than many people's cities. They were in the right place. Hozark put the visla in a chair and quickly raced through the connected rooms until he came upon a very well-hidden vault. He retrieved the visla, not about to leave him on his own, then began working on the warding spells.

It was tricky, but this was not a visla or even an emmik who had secured it, and opening the spells would not take too long. But it would require quite a bit of power. Hozark drew his vespus blade and pulled magic from it, shattering the spell, though at the cost of a quantity of his carefully saved reserves. The situation, however, warranted it.

"That's a magnificent weapon," Jinnik said. "And obviously a worthy owner."

Hozark nodded once and set to work, opening the vault and sifting through its contents.

The stored magic was readily apparent. A swirling mix of glowing power, barely contained within a robust magical flask. Hozark couldn't know for sure, but it felt like there was enough stored magic to power a thousand konuses.

But he felt something else as well. The sheer danger of the unstable mix. Jinnik had been right. The perfect weapon to destroy this place was in his hands. Now he just had to get it to the armory without accidentally triggering all of their demise.

"The weapons are stored near the lower-level smelting facility," Jinnik said. "We go down there and it will be apparent. I saw them when they would take me to and from my cell."

"Thank you," Hozark said, then carefully carried the deadly flask in one hand while assisting the visla with his other.

Again, it was slower going than he would have preferred, but there was simply no other way. And now he had two things to worry about, and in each hand, no less.

But they did not encounter another soul as they descended. It seemed the fighting outside had drawn most of the guards, and those tasked with protecting the inner sanctum had been slain by the Ghalian and his friends.

Hozark took the flask and set it deep within the weapons chamber, setting a booby trap to agitate and detonate the vessel when a fake tripwire spell was disarmed. It was a rather inspired bit of trickery he had used on occasion, setting multiple tripwires tied to a series of dangerous, but small spells. They were concealed, naturally, but not too well.

They would be detected and disarmed, one after another, until those doing the disarming grew confident in their abilities. *Over*confident. And when that one particular tripwire was severed, *that* would trigger the spell. But there were more than enough of the spells to disarm before the final one to ensure they would be able to reach his ship and fly free before anyone could clear them enough to reach their weapons stockpile.

"Can you run?" Hozark asked when he had completed his work.

"I'll try," Jinnik replied.

The two moved at a fast but loping pace. Even with Hozark's assistance, the visla was fading fast. He simply had no energy left after his ordeal. In fact, Hozark realized, it was a miracle he'd managed to keep up so well to this point.

A trio of blades sliced through the air where the assassin and his weary prize had just been. His senses were sharp, but with the additional burden he had only barely gotten them both clear.

Hozark dumped the visla unceremoniously as he dove into a roll, springing to his feet back in the direction of their attackers as his vespus blade flashed from its scabbard. Two of the men mounted a brief defense after seeing their comrade sliced neatly in half.

A moment later, however, they joined him.

"There is no time," Hozark said as he sheathed the blade once more. "My apologies, Visla. This may be unpleasant."

He threw the man over his shoulder like a sack of grain and started running, his konus ready to blast out death upon any who stood in his way. Only one guard happened to be so unfortunate, and Hozark made it back to his ship just a few minutes later, a bit winded, but no worse for wear.

He dropped Jinnik into a seat and slid into his command

chair, casting the launch spells in an instant. The ship blasted upward into the sky and out into orbit.

"Are we all here?" Hozark skreed his comrades.

"Present," Demelza's voice replied over the skree.

"Here," Bud said.

"Yeah, I'm here too," Laskar added.

"We're all clear," Lalaynia said.

"Then jump at once to our first rendezvous point."

"But why are we in such a--" Laskar began to say when the fortress far below exploded into a massive eruption of magical fire, destroying the facility entirely. But there had been stored weapons there as well, and the compounding force of that magical destruction was sending shockwaves toward the outer edges of the atmosphere. And there was no telling if it would stop there.

"Jump now!" Hozark commanded the others, then jumped away.

Laskar was stunned, almost frozen in his seat, but his self-preservation instinct kicked in and he jumped. Moments later the others followed close behind, leaving behind charred fragments of the continent on which the fortress had once stood.

CHAPTER FIFTY-THREE

The small group of ships exited their jump several systems away at a rally point distant enough from Actaris to allow them to breathe easy and lick their wounds. It had been a tough fight, and Lalaynia had suffered a few losses from her crew.

She had also scored a rather significant pillage. It was a costly trade off, but it was the pirate life her people had signed up for. And they wouldn't have it any other way. The freedom of the skies was well worth that price.

Her captured Council ship was now flying with them as part of their little flotilla. It would take a bit of work to empty it of all valuables and convert it into a warship, but she had high hopes it would prove a useful asset in future raids and conflicts. After all, seeing a Council ship enter an engagement was enough to make most enemies think twice. And this one was all hers.

Hozark, Uzabud, and Demelza flew back to dock with Bud's mothership now that they were in the clear. The larger craft would be a far more comfortable means of travel back to Inskip than their much smaller attack ships.

But as he docked, Hozark felt a renewed sense of concern. Visla Jinnik was weak. The constant fight with the collar fastened around his neck had taken a lot out of him. Now, even with the Ootaki ribbon shielding it, he could still feel the magical restraint struggling to regain its hold over him.

Hozark was both frustrated yet impressed. It was a most powerful collar, indeed. And if the Ootaki hair gave out mid-flight back to Corann's home on Inskip, there would be little he could do for the man. He had to try something.

"There is a change of plans. Set a course to Master Prombatz's home," Hozark instructed the pilot as soon as he had set Jinnik up with a bed and made his way to command.

Bud and Demelza were both there already, having docked before him. Bud looked up from his seat.

"Why the new course?"

"Visla Jinnik is in a precarious way, and Prombatz is several jumps closer than Corann. I am hopeful his assistance might prevent the man's control collar from regaining a grasp over him."

"Oh, shit. We'd better get there fast, then," Bud replied. "Laskar, plot it out and get us moving. I'll skrec over to Lalaynia and let her know what's going on. We can meet up with her a little later than planned. We're making a slight detour."

"You got it," Laskar said, beginning the calculations. "So, is the guy gonna be all right?"

"I cannot say. He is quite weak," Hozark replied.

"I've gotta let Henni know," Bud said, rising from his seat. "The visla took good care of her while they were in there. She'll want to know."

"Where is that little troublemaker, anyway?" Laskar asked. "I thought it seemed a bit too quiet in here."

Bud flashed him a grim little smile. "She's washing off the blood from all of the people she just killed," he said.

Laskar's grin faltered. "Oh."

"Yeah. *Oh*. Anyway, I'll let her know. He in the chambers next to yours, Hozark?"

"He is."

"Great. Thanks."

Bud strode out of the command chamber with purpose and walked straight to the showers.

"Henni, you need to hurry up in there."

"Leave me alone, creeper," the young woman replied, but something had changed. This time, her tone was one of amusement rather than reproach.

"We're making a detour to Prombatz's place. Hozark is hopeful he can help Jinnik."

"Help with what?"

"Jinnik is in a bad way. I'm not sure exactly what the deal is, but Hozark seemed concerned. And Prombatz is much closer than Corann, so he was hoping we could get there fast enough to help. That's why you need to finish up in there. I thought you would want to check in on--"

Henni burst from the showers, soaking wet and half clothed, pulling on the rest of the blood-free attire she'd laid out as she ran. She didn't care one bit that Bud had seen her that way. Jinnik was in trouble.

Henni raced straight to the quarters he was in. Bud hadn't told her where the visla was, but her powers were flowing strong, and she picked out his familiar magical scent in an instant, following it like a tracking animal on its quarry's trail.

She burst into his room. The exhausted man turned his head painfully but did not rise from his cot.

"Ah, hello, Henni. I'm sorry I left you all alone down in that cell, but they relocated me to another part of the facility. Apparently, Niallik caught on to my helping you train."

"She's dead," Henni said with cold certainty.

Jinnik saw the look in her eye and nodded. He didn't need any more confirmation than that.

He winced as the collar's power flared, his movement having shifted the Ootaki hair slightly, stirring the device's powerful protections once more. The magical ribbon was slowly losing strength, and it was only a matter of time before it failed entirely.

"No," Henni growled, walking to her friend and grabbing the collar firmly in her fists.

Hozark and Bud arrived at the chambers at the same time, both crowding in at once.

"What are you doing, Henni? That is the only thing keeping him protected. Stand back," Hozark said.

"No. I've got this," she replied with an unusual confidence in her voice. She turned to her friends. "You may want to step outside. I don't know what this will do."

She then focused her power on the collar with a furious intensity. Hozark sensed it immediately, and even Bud, less sensitive to those things as he was, felt the flare in magic and conflicting powers.

"Uh, I think we better do what she said."

Hozark was already halfway out the door. "I agree."

Henni ignored everything around her, focusing on her power as Jinnik had taught her, reaching out and grasping control of it and shaping it to her will. She drove the magic through her arms, down to her hands, and into the collar at the receiving end.

The Ootaki hair began to glow as she unintentionally fed some of her magic into the ribbon instead of the collar. Henni adjusted her power and refocused, sending the entirety of it into the golden band fastened around her friend's neck.

It warmed and began to bend under her hands as the energy surged through her. Hers was not remotely the same magic as his, and though the band instinctively defended itself, it was simply not geared for this kind of fight with a novel form of power.

Bud peeked in the door.

"Holy shit. She's stretching the metal," he gasped.

Hozark pulled him back into the corridor and applied a strong containment spell to the doorway. "We do not know what will happen next, Bud."

"Oh, yeah," the pirate replied. "But how the hell is she doing that?"

Hozark hesitated a moment. "I cannot say for certain, but it would appear our friend has learned to control her power, though to what degree is unclear."

A loud snap emanated from Jinnik's quarters, accompanied by a bright flash of light and a crackling of dissipating power. The light quickly returned to normal, and all traces of magical conflict faded.

"It's safe to come in now," Henni called out.

Hozark and Bud stepped inside, amazed at what they were seeing.

Henni's eyes were blazing with energy, though it was slowly calming to her normal sparkle. On the ground lay Visla Jinnik's shattered control collar, broken to pieces by her odd magic. And in her hands was the Ootaki hair ribbon, glowing with warm golden energy.

Henni, it seemed, had pumped quite a bit into the strip of material in the process of freeing her friend.

"This is yours, Hozark," she said, handing him the ribbon.

"Thank you, Henni," he replied, carefully rolling it up and tucking it into his pocket.

Visla Jinnik was still too weak to sit upright, but he smiled up at his pupil. "You have come a long way, Henni," he said, reaching out for her hand and squeezing it with pride.

Hozark stepped forward when the moment seemed right. "Visla, we have taken a bit of a detour on our return to your son. I believed you would require the assistance of another of my order to overcome your control collar and heal from the effort. Obviously, I was mistaken,"

"A pleasant surprise, indeed," Jinnik said.

"I shall have the ship change course at once."

"Wait," the visla said. "You mentioned healing. Is this friend of yours a rehabilitator? A healer?"

"Not exactly, but he has those under his employ who have such gifts. Why do you ask?"

Jinnik tried to sit up, but his strength failed him. Henni wrapped her arms around him and helped until he was finally in a seated position. Jinnik took a deep breath, composing himself as best he could.

"I would like to spend a day or two with this friend of yours before completing our journey, if that is possible."

"Of course, Visla."

"But don't you want to get back?" Bud asked.

The look in Jinnik's eye spoke volumes. "More than anything," he replied. "But not like this. When I see my son, I intend to walk to him tall and strong on my own two feet."

Bud realized he was right. Visla Jinnik was an immensely powerful man, and to be reduced to a shell of himself like this was difficult for him. As an adult, he could deal with that, but for his young son, that was another story entirely, and he had no intention of subjecting the boy to seeing his father in this state.

"I'll get us there fast," Bud said. "The sooner you rest up, the sooner you see your boy."

Jinnik smiled and lay back down on his cot. "Thank you," he said just before drifting off to sleep. "Thank you all."

CHAPTER FIFTY-FOUR

By the time Bud's mothership had set down in the landing zone nearest Master Prombatz's home, Visla Jinnik had managed to rouse himself from his drained stupor and eat something. Henni had gone all out in the galley, focusing her efforts on replenishing the man's energy the only way she knew how.

Uzabud had stepped away from command and left the flying to Laskar for a while so he could help her however she might need. Whether that was assistance slicing and dicing, or just being an ear to listen, he was there for her.

The others left them to do their thing. They had some issues to deal with, both of them, be it Henni's guilt over what had been done to Visla Jinnik because he had helped her, or Bud's for letting her be captured under his watch.

What they talked about, no one knew, but when the two emerged carrying a pair of trays of easily digested food, it seemed both were at least in decent headspace.

Jinnik was slow to eat at first, sticking with Arambis juice supplemented with a bit of powdered Zoramin powder for additional nutrients. The sugars hit his system first, flooding his bloodstream with that initial spark of vitality he was so desperately in need of. After that, his recovery accelerated as he slowly worked his way to solid foods, gratefully sampling each of the dishes the pair had made for him.

"You say you made this? It is delicious," Jinnik asked between mouthfuls.

"Yeah. Bud helped, though."

"Hey, I was just lending a hand. This is all Henni," Bud said, not wanting an ounce of Henni's spotlight.

"Well, I must thank both of you. I'm finally starting to feel at least a little like myself," the visla said, gingerly rising to his feet.

He swayed a moment, then sat back down, but far more in control of his body than he had been just a few hours prior. If he continued to improve like this, his stay with Prombatz would be a short one indeed.

"So, tell me a bit more of this place we are going to."

Master Prombatz was a killer of rare skill, but also one who had quite a healing setup within his spacious residence. It was not at all normal for a Ghalian master to do so, but prior to arrival Visla Jinnik had been informed that in his particular case he had been caring for one of his pupils gravely wounded in battle with the Council of Twenty.

"They ambushed a Ghalian?" Jinnik asked when they landed, astonished that even someone from the Council of Twenty would be so brazen.

"Yes. We later learned that Visla Maktan was behind the plot, working to capture a Ghalian master to attempt to harvest our unique abilities," Hozark informed him as they stepped from the ship. "They failed, but others of our kind were not so lucky. Not Ghalian, but Wampeh with our gift, captured and drained."

"It's horrifying," Jinnik said. "I've heard of people attempting to enhance their power with another's—abhorrent experiments performed on children, most often--but never something like this."

"The guy deserves what's coming for him," Laskar said. "Hey, here comes Prombatz."

The Ghalian approached on a floating conveyance large enough to carry them all. Normally they would simply have walked the relatively short distance to his residence, but as his esteemed guest was mending, that simply would not do.

"Visla, it is a pleasure to make your acquaintance. Please, take a seat, and we shall ferry you to my home."

"Thank you, Master Prombatz. Your hospitality is greatly appreciated," Jinnik replied.

The group loaded onto the conveyance and were quickly whisked away to Prombatz's spacious but unassuming abode. Little would any looking at it dream of the myriad deadly defenses and countless layered protective spells guarding the place. Even Visla Jinnik could not sense them all, though he could make out a good many of them.

This was as safe a place as any to convalesce. He was hoping, however, his stay would be a brief one. Already his legs were recovering more of their strength, and as he walked into the building his body felt even more like his own once more. His power was coming back as well, and faster than his physical body, in fact. This was good. It meant he was not defenseless should they fall under attack. It also meant--

He paused. A strange magic tickled his senses. There was unusual casting going on here. Not like Henni's but equally unique.

"I'm sorry to impose after only now entering your home, but I feel the presence of an unusual sort of magic. And not that belonging to our violet-haired friend here."

Master Prombatz smiled. "Very impressive, Visla. Impressive indeed. Come, I shall introduce you to the source of that power.

A former pupil of mine, Aargun. And yes, his power is unusual, indeed."

They walked up a level and through the building toward the large training room at the far end. With every step, Jinnik felt more and more certain he was close to something special.

"I should warn you," Prombatz said, "Aargun suffered great disfigurement at the hands of Maktan's people. They took his eyes from him, as well as his tongue."

"I see. But if they took his tongue, who is it I sense casting?"

"As you said, *most* unusual," Prombatz replied as they stepped into the chamber. "Aargun, we have guests. And look who is back."

Henni ran across the room, wrapping her arms around the blind, mute assassin. "Aargun!"

He smiled and returned the hug. For a stoic Ghalian aspirant, the display was rather unusual, but his and Henni's connection was as well.

"What? No, Hap's not with us. But we found his father!" Henni said, pointing to Jinnik.

Aargun cocked his head, and for just a moment Jinnik could feel a mild probing spell tickle his senses.

"Don't worry," Henni said. "He's a good man. You can trust me on that. He's the only reason I survived Maktan's goons."

Jinnik stepped forward, his legs feeling sturdy beneath him. "No, Henni, your strength is the reason you survived. I merely helped guide you as best as I could given our circumstances."

Aargun felt comfortable with the reply, nodding once to the visla. He had no eyes, but nevertheless, to Jinnik it felt like he was looking right at him.

"I felt something just now. Henni, that wasn't you, was it?"

"Nope."

"Then, Aargun, you can cast silently? But you are a Wampeh. It's not something your kind, or any kind for that matter, can do. Besides Zomoki, Henni is the only person I've ever seen do it."

"Yeah, well, whatever they did to him when they were experimenting on him kinda changed all of that," Henni said. "What? Oh, yeah. He says he regrets the losses from what happened, but this would almost make up for it if he could get the hang of it."

Visla Jinnik crossed over to the young man and sized him up with an appraising gaze. Barely out of his teens, yet possessing that self-assured confidence of the Wampeh Ghalian. And it seemed as though his senses had sharpened to such a degree that he could function as well as if he still had his eyes.

He made a decision then and there.

"I am still recovering my strength, but having worked with Henni to help her get in touch with her power, I wonder, when I am whole again, may I be of assistance to you in learning to control yours?"

Aargun's eyebrows raised.

"Really?" Henni said, and it was clear her words were for her friend.

"Yes. It would be my great honor to at least partly repay all that your friends have done for me in this way. Once I have my boy safe by my side, I would very much like to help you, if I may."

Aargun's smile matched Henni's. "Oh, he knows Hap," she said. "He was teaching him how to throw knives."

"To throw knives?"

Aargun's arm was a flash of motion, no more than a blur, and a dagger suddenly appeared in the target across the room, dead-center. The young man hadn't even turned his attention that direction.

Jinnik laughed with amusement. "Oh, that's marvelous. And Happizano actually showed enough patience to try it himself?"

"He's actually getting pretty good," Bud interjected. "Kid's learning to push the blades with his power and everything. Rather impressive for his age."

Visla Jinnik's spirits seemed to be returning to him at an even faster rate. "This is wonderful. Most wonderful. I look forward to helping you while you in turn continue to tutor him," he said to Aargun. "If you wish, of course."

Aargun nodded.

"He says he'd be glad for the opportunity," Henni said.

"Yeah, I think we could all get that without your translating," Laskar said.

Prombatz looked over at his Ghalian comrades. All seemed quite glad with the way that had gone. Having a powerful visla working to help Aargun was something of a coup for them.

"Then it is settled," Prombatz said. "But now, let us dine and relax. You have all come a long way, and I am sure you are hungry."

"Damn right I am!" Henni chirped.

"You're always hungry," Bud chuckled.

Prombatz turned for the door. "Then come. Let us share food and companionship. I wish to hear all about your victory at Actaris."

CHAPTER FIFTY-FIVE

The two nights spent at Master Prombatz's home were a wonderful time of bonding and levity for both Henni and Visla Jinnik. The smell of free air and the taste of good food just seemed that much better after their recent enslavement.

Being under the care of not one but two Wampeh Ghalian masters had also put them both at great ease as Jinnik regained his strength. But now the visla was back to his old self. Not one hundred percent. Not even close. But more than enough to be the image of a strong father his son needed.

"I am ready," he informed Hozark on that second morning after enjoying a hearty breakfast with his new friends.

"Then we depart as soon as the ship is loaded," Hozark replied. "I shall inform the others at once."

It was a novel feeling for the visla. He had *hired* this man and his associates to find and protect his son, but somehow along the way he wound up requiring their assistance as well. That, along with the bond he and Henni had formed as he helped her realize her true potential, had imparted him with something he had not expected from that initial arrangement.

New friends.

They had transcended the employer-employee relationship and were now something else. And he was glad for it.

The flight to Corann's home was a relatively quick one. In just a few jumps they arrived at the quiet little world of Inskip. Corann had been aware of their coming, of course. Hozark had seen to it that the network informed her of their detour and subsequent movements the moment any change in plans had been made.

Happizano stood beside a kindly looking older woman, waiting patiently as his father stepped off of Bud's ship. Jinnik beamed at the sight of his son, a comforting wave of relief washing over him as the two were finally reunited.

Hap was smiling as well, but patiently waiting for his father. Not too long ago, the boy would have simply rushed to him and wrapped him in a hug, but the child had seen much and endured many hardships since he'd been taken from their home. He'd been forced to grow a bit, but this was something else. This was maturity.

Training with a variety of masters in the short time he'd been with Hozark and his friends had tempered his enthusiasm and taught him restraint. But even those lessons flew out the window when his father finally drew close.

Hap ran forward those few steps and hugged him hard. Visla Jinnik wrapped his arms around his son, tears of joy running down his face. Once, he would have proudly held them back, but he was a changed man now, and for the better.

"Look at you," he said, releasing his embrace. "You look like you've grown since I saw you last. And is that muscle you've put on?" he asked, squeezing the boy's shoulders. "It seems you'll be a man sooner than I'd expected."

"I got to train with a bunch of really great teachers," the boy said, his characteristic excitable nature bubbling back to the surface. "I even got to spend some time with Master Turong!"

Even Jinnik had heard of the legendary master. He'd trained

a great number of men and women who went on to do amazing things. He had even taken on some young gladiators once as a favor, though he swore never to do so again. But those fighters became some of the finest the arenas had ever seen. He turned to face the Ghalian where they had gathered.

"Thank you. Thank you for all you have done."

"It was our pleasure," Hozark said.

Henni strode out of the ship, a big smile on her face at the sight of the boy and his father together again.

"Henni!" Hap called out.

She hurried over and gave him a hug. "Heya, Hap!"

"You're back!"

"Yep, I am. You good while I was gone?"

"Yeah. And I got to learn all kinds of cool new stuff."

"Really? You'll have to show me."

Jinnik watched the exchange with amusement. It seemed his boy had formed some true friendships during this whole ordeal.

"You have gone far beyond merely retrieving my son. I owe the Ghalian a debt. If you ever need my help, you have but to ask."

Corann nodded but said nothing. The offer, however, was cataloged in her mind, though she hoped such a favor would never need to be called in.

"Happizano has proven to be a most pleasant young man," she said. "And he has shown great promise in both the magical and martial arts. But I prattle on. I'm sure Happizano has much he wants to show you."

"Yeah, come on! Henni, you wanna come?"

"Will there be knives?"

"Of course."

"Then sure, sounds like fun."

"Great!" Hap tugged at his father's tunic. "Come on, the training room's this way. And there's a target there. I can throw knives now! Did you know that?"

"That's wonderful, son. I can't wait to see." He gave Corann an apologetic but thankful smile.

She fully understood. There was a time for discussion, and a time for bonding. It was clear which was more important at the moment.

"Go on, you two. We can talk further after dinner."

Jinnik followed his excited son, his heart full and his spirits restored.

Late that evening, long after the others had finished their meals, chatted over some tea, and finally gone to bed, Visla Jinnik sat alone in front of the dwindling magical light of the small fire in Corann's sitting room, deep in thought. He was so focused that he did not even hear the footsteps of the woman approaching.

Of course, she was a Wampeh Ghalian. He likely wouldn't have heard them even if he'd been trying.

"Would you like a little company?" a warm voice asked.

He turned to see the matron of the household standing in the doorway.

"Of course, Corann. I was just thinking, I will depart in the morning and take Happizano home. To try to restore his life to some sort of normalcy."

"The boy deserves no less. But do keep up his training. He has not only an aptitude, but also an enjoyment for it. Do not waste the opportunity."

"You're right, of course," he said with a little smile. "And thank you again for your hospitality. For me as well as my son. Especially him."

"It has been my pleasure. Happizano is a good lad."

"He can be a handful at times."

"What boy his age isn't? And considering the trauma he has gone through, I would say he has emerged from it all in surprisingly good condition, all things considered."

"You are wise in your council, and your words are appreciated. You know, he seems to almost be unaffected by what has happened, though I still sense the change in him when he lets his guard down."

"Children are like that," she replied. "But he is strong in his power. Like his father."

"I noticed that. His powers are far more developed than when I last saw him. And he can actually propel and guide a blade now? Oh, how my boy has grown in such a short time."

"Yes, he has. But I was not referring to his powers. I was referring to the strength of his character, just like you."

A shadow fell across Visla Jinnik's countenance. "I fear I am not worthy of that opinion any longer." He paused, searching for the right words to express what had been troubling him for so long. "I have done terrible things, Corann. Horrible crimes."

"Done in order to protect your son. It is understandable, and most would do the same."

"But most are not me. They don't have my power and the responsibility that comes with it." He paused, a look of true despair peeking out from behind his mask of calm. "I have killed, Corann. I know for the Ghalian that is a normal occurrence, but I am not a violent man."

"So I have heard."

"But because of my actions, *thousands* have suffered enslavement or even death. I have done the bidding of my Council masters like a good pet, and it haunts me every moment I breathe free air and they do not."

Corann appreciated his candor just as much as his view on slavery. He aligned well with her own personal beliefs on that topic, which was one more reason she found herself liking the man. Despite his enormous power, and possibly rather entitled existence, this whole fiasco had broken him out of that shell and revealed who he really was. And he was a good man.

"It is true, horrible things have happened, and you were a

part of that. But you were a tool being used, not the hand wielding it. While I know this will haunt you, at least know it was not entirely your doing. Not your fault."

A faint crackle rippled across his skin. It seemed his powers were returning, and with them, the tell-tale sign of his agitation. A visible reminder of just how dangerous he could be.

"I want to make amends, Corann. To do whatever that would entail. But I cannot take on the Council of Twenty."

"No, you cannot. But you can return home and be the best father, and best *ruler* your people have ever known. They are under your care, *Visla*, do not squander that opportunity."

His mood seemed to lighten a moment, but only just. "But how, Corann? How can I rule now? The Jinnik name is pariah. The very mention will bring anger and sadness whenever it is spoken."

"Then change it," she said, simply.

"But I..." He struggled with the concept.

It was so simple, yet such an alien thought to a man whose whole identity had always been as Visla Dinarius Jinnik. Corann watched him struggle with the idea. It was only natural he would be reticent.

"If not for you, then for your son," she said.

More than his own needs, those of his boy were paramount. And if something as difficult, yet also simple, as a name change would spare his boy a life burdened by his father's actions, then he would do it.

"You are wise, Corann. Far beyond your years."

"Oh, I am not so young these days."

"I would beg to differ," he replied. "You are as lovely as any I've encountered."

Corann smiled and accepted his kind words, as a tactful woman would, then changed the subject back. "So, what name will you choose?"

The man soon to no longer be Jinnik cocked his head a bit in thought, but the answer came to him almost immediately.

"Happizano should bear a name he can be proud of. The name of a great person. The kindest one I ever knew, and whom I loved with all of my being," he said. "His mother's family name would do him well. Henceforth, we shall go by Palmarian."

Corann nodded her approval. "Well, Visla *Palmarian*, I wish you the best of luck."

CHAPTER FIFTY-SIX

It was a bittersweet farewell.

Hap, despite his bumpy start, had become close with his unlikely guardians, and they had, much to all of their surprise, grown to feel the same way. Even the master Ghalian had developed an affection for the boy, despite his prior, and well-known, dislike for children.

Henni razzed him like a big sister would, and he gave as good as he got, while also making her promise to come visit. She readily agreed, of course. Free food and board in a visla's estate on Slafara? It would be *epic*.

"Palmarian, eh?" she said. "I kinda like the sound of it."

"It's gonna be weird, though."

"Only at first. You'll get used to it. Hell, you got used to all of us, right?" she said with a bright laugh.

"Good point," the boy replied.

He had already said his farewells to Corann and the others over the course of the morning, and more than a few tears had been shed. This was likely the single greatest experience of his young life, and now it was coming to an end. But he would be home with his father, safe and secure.

And after watching his son excel at so many spells and fighting moves learned in their separation, the visla was very much looking forward to not only teaching his boy to control his magic, but perhaps accompanying him to learn the more physical arts from one of the great masters. A novel bonding experience they could share as father and son.

And so, the pair left their new friends, bound for a home soon to be renamed. A fresh beginning for them both.

"Will I see you again?" Hap asked Hozark as he and his father boarded the ship Corann had arranged for them.

The Ghalian master rested his hands on the boy's shoulders. "Young *Palmarian*, I would enjoy nothing more. You may count on it."

Hap's smile warmed his heart, and watching the door seal behind him and the ship quickly shrink into a dot in the sky, Hozark was surprised to realize he would actually miss the boy.

"Well, that's what I call a happy ending. At least for Hap. If only we were so lucky, right?" Bud joked. "I mean, we've still got one really, *really* big task on our agenda. Once we figure out where Maktan has actually gone off to, that is."

"Indeed. And when we do, we shall make an end of the troublesome man once and for all," Demelza said.

Corann cleared her throat. "I did not wish to interrupt the happy family's departure, but about that location."

"You have received word?" Hozark asked.

"Only just before the Palmarians began saying their farewells."

"But there wasn't anyone here," Laskar said. "Just the porter carrying the--hang on, that man was one of your spies?"

"*She* was."

"*She*?"

"You should know by now, Dohria is exceptionally gifted, even among our kind."

"But it was a man."

"Your point being?"

Laskar seemed a bit flummoxed at the woman's talents. The others, however, found the rest of the matter of more interest.

"We have a location, then?" Bud asked. "Just give me a name and I'll reach out to Lalaynia for backup."

"Thank you, Uzabud. It is appreciated. And gratefully accepted," Corann replied. "In fact, I shall also be calling in the aid of a particular group of mercenaries as well for this contract."

Hozark raised a brow. "Andorus and his crew? Highly unusual, Corann. What prompts this? A massive diversion, while a favorite trick, might seem a bit obvious given our recent tactics in retrieving the others."

"This is not merely a deception, Hozark. Maktan has been confirmed to be on Rimpalla, as Laskar's sources suggested," Corann said.

Laskar beamed with satisfaction. "See? I told ya."

"But he is not alone."

"Well, of course he has guards."

"Far more than guards, I am afraid," Corann replied.

"Hang on a sec. What?"

"Visla Maktan is in the company of several powerful Council representatives. Power users, most of them, though not on the Council itself. And it would seem another of the Twenty is there as well. Visla Egrit has joined him at the Council estate on Rimpalla."

"Egrit?" Laskar asked. "He's partnered up with Egrit?"

"It would appear that way, though we cannot be certain."

"But Egrit's far less powerful than he is."

"But possesses many connections in systems Maktan does not," she replied.

Bud seemed more than a little concerned. "This means there will be *two* Council members there. And both vislas. Oh man, this is not good."

"Do not forget their high-ranking underlings," Corann reminded him.

Bud shook his head. "Oh, we are so screwed."

Hozark shook his head. "We are not screwed. We must simply adapt our strategy appropriately."

"But why would he do this now? He doesn't usually engage with the other members of the Twenty. I mean, except Ravik, that is. But that guy's fucking dead, so..."

"I would posit that perhaps he finds himself forced to attempt to consolidate power in a different way now that his secret weapons cache has been destroyed. Even though some had been deployed, it was an enormous blow to his plans when we not only rescued the visla and Henni, but also stumbled upon that stockpile."

"Shit, I hadn't thought of that. I mean, I guess it makes sense. The guy just lost what? Months of work? More? And not only are those weapons gone, but even if he gets a new smelting operation up and running."

"Which he undoubtedly will," Demelza interjected.

"Yeah, no question on that. But when he does, he's still gotta find a new way to charge all of them now that we've got Henni back and Jinnik is gone."

"*Palmarian*," Corann corrected. "But you are correct. His plans have been set back significantly."

"So this is the time to strike!" Laskar said.

"Indeed, it is," Hozark agreed. "It shall be a challenge, but I believe it is an objective we can achieve." He turned to Demelza. "You and I shall make an approach under cover of our shimmer ships while the others prepare their diversion."

"Like we just did?" Bud asked. "Don't you think they'll be expecting that?"

"We shall land far enough away that they do not note our arrival. Once on the ground, Demelza and I shall then apply our strongest disguise spells and make our entrance into the facility on foot."

"You're going to use the Quommus?" Laskar asked.

"No, there is still some study required to learn its secrets, and Corann will be hard at work attempting to ready it for use. But even so, until an actual threat is perceived, Maktan will not be expecting the Ghalian, and thus his guard will almost certainly be down against magical disguises."

"So, we just have a bunch of mercenaries and pirates bum rush the compound to try to kill the guy? It's going to be a madhouse with that many people going after him," Laskar said.

Corann shook her head. "No, the others shall not know of the Maktan contract, nor shall they be directed to the area where he is determined to be. They will be paid well, and there will be ample pillage and plunder should they succeed. But all they shall be informed is that there is a resetting of the balance of power against the Council's forces. That is all they need to know. And given their dislike of the Council, I think that shall be more than enough incentive."

"It'll be quite a blow to the Council, that's for sure," Bud said. "I mean, losing not one but two members in such short order? Three, if we wind up taking out Visla Egrit in the process. Damn, that would really put those power-hungry bastards back in their place."

"It will lessen their aspirations for conquest. At least for a little while," Hozark agreed. "But they will still possess enormous power."

"Seems like it'll knock them down a peg or two, though," Laskar said. "At least until they straighten out their leadership in the restructuring. So, when do we do this?"

"Arrangements are already being made and payments forwarded," Corann replied. "You shall depart at sunset. By then things should be well in motion."

Henni looked at the others, a bit shell-shocked at how

quickly things just ramped up from some relaxing downtime after rescue to an all-out assault on one of the most dangerous power users in the galaxy. But that seemed to be how life was with this lot, and she was glad to call them her friends.

"So, if that's the case, we'd better start eating now," she said, drawing amused stares from the others. "What? Who knows when we'll get to eat again?"

"Admittedly, she has a point," Demelza noted.

"Yes, she does," Corann agreed. "Come, let us have a proper meal to ready your bodies as well as your spirits."

"A good idea," Hozark agreed. "And then we shall put an end to this troublesome visla once and for all."

CHAPTER FIFTY-SEVEN

The approach to Rimpalla was a tricky one. The assassins, pirates, and mercenaries were more than up to the challenge, of course, but with not one but two members of the Council of Twenty present, there was sure to be additional protection even beyond what they had been told of.

They didn't know what, though. Perhaps scout ships disguised as civilian vessels, surveying the outer edges of the system. Or extra ground forces disguised as locals or traders. One really couldn't be sure.

Normally, those sorts of tricks weren't used by the Council at all. They simply relied on their overwhelming power to protect their leadership. But now, operating in a covert manner as they were while Maktan was amassing power and the Council was in turmoil after Ravik's death, no one really knew exactly what to expect.

The two Ghalian shimmer ships jumped to the dark space just outside the system in preparation for their approach. Rather than arriving with Bud's mothership and detaching, they placed themselves as close as they could without being seen. Then they waited.

The others in the assault group would be coming shortly, but when *they* arrived it would be a far less subtle occurrence. Until then, the two stealth ships engaged their shimmer spells and made a rapid but cautious approach to the Council estate on Rimpalla.

The amount of magic needed to keep the ships invisible to the degree required was substantial. Shimmer cloaking was notoriously difficult to utilize in space. But the Wampeh Ghalian were experts in the temperamental spells required, and with the additional konuses Hozark and Demelza had brought for this purpose, they made it all the way to the planet's surface without raising a single alarm.

Of course, they had to land a significant distance from the actual target location. Vislas as powerful as Maktan and Egrit would be able to sense their ships if they were actively alerted to the possibility of an attack. They shouldn't have been expecting anyone, but it was far better to play it safe than be sorry.

The approach through the outskirts and eventually the city itself was straightforward enough. Hozark and Demelza were each using minimal disguise spells so they could more quickly shift to a new look as soon as they disabled and then replaced one of the staff or guards with access into the inner reaches of the estate.

It wasn't a fortress or impenetrable stronghold they were infiltrating, just a fairly opulent property that happened to have what appeared to be a few visitors at the moment. Little did the locals know, it was a pair of vislas, members of the Twenty, no less, who were meeting in secret a mere stone's throw from their homes.

Demelza was the first to find a suitable identity to assume. A member of the cleaning staff who just so happened to be in the wrong place at the wrong time. Wrong for her, that is. For Demelza it had worked out wonderfully.

The woman was only stunned, though, her slumbering body

tucked safely away where no one would stumble upon her while the impostor worked her way deeper into the estate. Had she been a Council guard, Demelza might not have been so kind, but mere support staff had nothing to do with the dealings of those who employed them. To kill one served no purpose.

She quickly made her way through the corridors, getting the lay of the land without encountering any pushback. The benefit of the woman's job was that no one tended to look too closely at support workers. They were the lowest ranked and therefore not worth the effort or attention. And that afforded them an unexpected bit of freedom.

Demelza, wearing this new appearance, continued moving deeper into the grounds, cataloging everything in preparation for the distraction from above.

Hozark's entry took a little longer. It was just a fluke of luck that none of those cleared to enter the perimeter in his general area were traveling alone. Always in groups of three or more, and infrequently at that. And farther in the city, the unmarked goons he knew all too well at this point were congregating in far larger groups than that. This was going to require a shift in strategy.

Of course, he had known it would be a trying day no matter the circumstances.

"You know she'll be there, right?" Bud had asked him before they boarded their ships for the final departure.

"Yes, Bud. I am aware."

"So, you know she's gonna be fighting with those unidentified Council mercenaries again."

"Yes. His off-book goons."

"What are you going to do, then? I mean, you two had a bit of a truce there."

Hozark imperceptibly sighed. "It was short-lived," he replied. "And this shall end today. One way or another."

The tiny bulge hidden within a secret pocket on the inside of his tunic well ensconced in layer upon layer of protective magic was a heavy weight for him to carry. But what he said was true. One way or another it would end today, even if he had to break out the weapon of last resort he never hoped to use.

The vial of water seemed normal enough, but to nearly all of the species in the galaxy, just a few drops of the Balamar waters would provide great healing benefits, even increasing their magical powers and recovery abilities.

It was utterly priceless, and this vial had been captured from Emmik Rostall when he had been slain. And it was on that day the waters were used for their other purpose. To kill Wampeh.

Enok had been his name. An aspirant out for his final test. A difficult assassination, but one he should have been able to complete. But the target, a lower-ranked emmik by the name of Rostall, had surprised them with the one trick no one expected up his sleeve. Balamar waters.

Just a drop had reduced Enok into a pile of ashes. A quirk of the magical water that what healed so many more was the deadliest thing known to the Wampeh. It would be a dangerous but valuable addition to the order's collection.

But Hozark had kept the vial rather than place it safely away in the Ghalian vaults. For on that same day he had learned that Samara was alive. And he knew then that the day may come that he might need to go so far as to sacrifice *both* of their lives to end her.

If it came to that, it was a price he was willing to pay.

Hozark had been lurking around the two entry points to the facility closest to where he had landed for some time when a decision had to be made. The others would be jumping into orbit soon, and he would either be inside, or be forced to fight his way in with the others. Reluctantly he donned his shimmer cloak, hoping beyond hope that its magical camouflage would not be detected given the extremely unusual circumstances.

At long last an opportunity presented itself. A large

contingent of guards were shifting out, the doorway open for their passage. It would be a tight squeeze, and a lot of moving bodies to avoid in hopes of not being noticed by an errant step or stray arm brushing against the invisible man.

Hozark tucked as close to the wall as he could as he shadowed the group. A bit of inspiration hit him, and he quietly cast a novelty spell. Not the usual fare for deadly assassins. But in this case, it just might work.

The guards sniffed the air, the rank stench of someone's gaseous bowels wafting from closest the wall. None would claim the offending flatulence, and all instinctively shied away from its origin.

It wasn't elegant by any stretch of the imagination, but it got Hozark inside, and that was all that mattered.

He dropped to a crouch as a large platter was carried through the space he had just occupied. The metal barely cleared his head as those carrying it hurried along. Food for a feast, it appeared. More likely than not, the troops were being fed the excess from the visla's personal meal for himself and the other Council representatives below him.

One thing the Twenty did well was entertain, and given all of the wealth they had amassed over the years, cost was not an issue. And if they were feasting, perhaps their guard was down more than he'd expected.

He stood once more when the coast was clear and rushed deeper into the estate. He had intended to take another's identity, but that was obviously not an option that was going to present itself. So Hozark stepped into a small storage chamber and assumed a generic guard's look.

He just hoped no one would stop and ask who he was. That this could be done quickly and quietly without additional casualties. Though highly unlikely, ideally, the killing would begin and end with Maktan. But he knew the situation was anything but ideal.

CHAPTER FIFTY-EIGHT

Bud's mothership jumped into low orbit above Rimpalla just before Lalaynia and the mercenary band led by Andorus arrived. The pirates and mercenaries were right behind, but the immediate reaction from the seemingly benign ships in orbit was already both violent and intense.

"Definitely disguised Council ships," Bud growled as he spun into a quick dive to evade the blistering barrage of both spells and magically lobbed projectiles.

If the ship hadn't possessed the additional shielding provided by Corann's clever overlapping of the defensive spells of the smaller craft on its hull joining with the larger vessel's, they would almost certainly have been blown from the sky. As it was, the impacts were enough to shake loose a few less robustly secured bits, including one of the smaller shuttle craft.

The little ship was destroyed as soon as it had pulled free of the conjoined defensive shielding. The Council forces were not playing around, and their response had been to throw everything they had at the intruders.

"Where the hell are the others?" Bud wondered as he and Laskar unleashed their countermeasures against the swarming ships. "Get here, Lalaynia! We can't handle all of these on our own!"

As if she had heard his plea, the massive pirate ship flashed out of jump nearby, spewing out its contingent of fighter craft the instant it arrived. The pirates were here, and they were more than ready for a fight.

Hot on their tail, the cluster of heavily armed mercenary ships jumped in as well. Suddenly, what had seemed like a very lopsided fight had become a massive space battle between two very potent forces.

Bud's ship dove toward the surface while the others took on the space-bound craft. The plan was to draw the surface ships up to meet them, leaving the ground forces with less craft to provide any sort of air support. It was a risky move, and Bud's ship would take a beating, but it was fast and the most heavily shielded of their rag-tag fleet.

"You got this?" Bud asked his copilot.

"Yeah. Just get it done," Laskar said, taking over the controls and firing off a spray of deadly defensive spells, powered by the many konuses linked within the ship.

"See you on the other side of this mess," Bud said. "Henni, let's go!"

He took off down the corridor, headed straight for the fastest ship mounted on the hull, his violent little friend close on his heels, armed to the teeth and ready to fight.

Outside, the first wave of pirate and mercenary ships heading for the surface also began their descent. In just a few moments the duo boarded and strapped in, then immediately detached from his mothership and peeled away, quickly, joining them in the dive for the surface.

"Nice shielding system you've got there, Bud," Lalaynia transmitted over skree. "You'll have to show me how you did that when this is all done."

"Let's just survive first," Bud replied.

He was straining his piloting skills to the max as he and the others dove through the magical chaff and defensive spells, heading for the surface and the battle that awaited them there. But he nevertheless felt a tiny rush of calm at Lalaynia's voice. Knowing she had his back was a comfort in such a massive engagement.

On the surface, the Council forces were taking up positions, prepared to defend the compound against these surprisingly organized attackers. None had expected any to be so bold as to attack a pair of Council members, and as a result, their response was a bit slow at first. It was just so unlikely.

But then again, most would not even know the Council members were there. One of the downsides to being so secretive. For all they knew, the attackers were oblivious to what they were really stirring up.

Regardless, once the initial surprise wore off and the fighting began in earnest, the well-trained Council guards quickly split off into their battle stations, ready for the inevitable clash on the ground.

What they didn't know was that the *truly* dangerous invaders had already infiltrated and were behind their defensive lines.

Hozark and Demelza rushed through the grounds with the others in the somewhat chaotic call to arms, fitting in just as they had hoped. Demelza had shed her servant's disguise and was now sporting the appearance of one of Visla Egrit's guards. Hozark had also upgraded, having been able to separate one of Maktan's men from the others in all of the chaos, ending him and taking his persona.

Inside the facility, word was spreading that the two vislas were aggravated that their meeting had been interrupted by some so brazen and foolish as to attack the facility. Of course, their presence was a secret, so it appeared to simply be a very unfortuitous bit of timing for a band of pirates and mercenaries to go on a raid.

But the two power users had something up their sleeve. *Power*, to be exact. And they were both actually looking forward to seeing the looks of surprise on the attackers' faces when the two of them stepped out onto the battlefield and revealed who the fools were *really* engaged with. Oh, what a surprise it would be. Or so they thought.

"Where's Visla Maktan?" Hozark asked one of the guards rushing past him. "We need to protect him!"

"Haven't you been told? He's heading to the front gates with Visla Egrit. They're going to take on the pirates!" the guard said, positively giddy at the prospect of two Council members showing what they could really do.

"Is that wise? I mean, there are so many?"

"You know how powerful they are. A little band of pirates is no match for two of the Twenty!"

"You're right," Hozark said, matching the man's enthusiasm. "Let's go. I don't want to miss this!"

Caught up in the moment, the guard didn't even question Hozark's legitimacy, instead leading the assassin directly toward his target. If Maktan truly did intend to step outside onto the battlefield, he would be on a high level of alert.

It would be best if Hozark could take him out before he did so, while he still felt safe within the walls. It would save a lot of innocent lives, as well as provide him a much cleaner way to carry out his contract.

But when they arrived, it looked like he was already too late. The gates were open, and the sounds of fighting were thick in the air. Maktan and Egrit were both standing there, calm as could be, a nice, safe wall of magic in front of them, blocking all of the attackers' pathetic attempts to reach them.

Hozark noted the guards coming and going from behind the defenses, peeling off to the sides then rushing out into the fight. The two vislas were foolishly overconfident in their security and had only cast in front of themselves, not all the way around.

Standing in the doorway with their stronghold at their backs, they didn't see how anyone could possibly slip past to attack from the rear.

In one regard, they had a point. There was quite a healthy contingent of modestly powered men and women standing around them. The underlings and assistants, each powerful to some degree, though a few did seem to rely on konuses as well.

Hozark scanned the area. It was looking like this might be a bit more difficult than he'd originally thought, and he hadn't expected it to be easy. But with Lalaynia's pirates in the mix, the neat and orderly fighting was sure to become very asymmetrical very soon.

Andorus's mercenaries would then use that to their advantage, the two very diverse fighting forces playing off of each other as they swept forward through the skilled but outmatched defenders.

Hozark stopped and pulled back, stepping into the shadows behind a cluster of guards awaiting their opportunity to rush into battle to prove themselves to their visla. Something seemed odd on the battlefield.

Someone else was there, leading a group of Council soldiers with no insignias on their uniforms into the fight. And she carried a glowing blue sword.

Samara.

But the forces under her command seemed to be fighting all they encountered, pirate, mercenary, and even the occasional Council guard who got in the way. Something was going on.

Hozark looked closer. The fallen guards were Visla Egrit's, a group of them having been closest to Samara's point of incursion. A double-cross? It was beginning to look as though Maktan might have lured the other visla here with something other than an alliance in mind.

Whatever it was, he would worry about that afterward. For

now, he had one task on his mind. And that was ending Visla Maktan once and for all.

CHAPTER FIFTY-NINE

For all the talk about how Visla Maktan was the least threatening of the Twenty, personality-wise, the man still possessed an enormous amount of power. Far more than most of the others on the Council. But he typically avoided conflicts, choosing to hang back and let the other, more overtly power-hungry members get involved.

But despite his supposedly calm and restrained demeanor, seeing him in the thick of a major engagement proved one thing. The man was still a member of the Twenty, and you didn't maintain a place among that lot by being sweet and lovable.

The two vislas had continued to hold back, allowing their underlings to flex their power a bit, rushing out into the fray and casting some rather impressive spells, showing their vislas what they could really do.

The attacking forces countered them, though, overlapping their defensive spells to better diffuse the bombardment while still allowing others within their ranks to cast offensive replies.

It was a brutal push and pull, and it seemed likely the two sides would carry on this way for some time if allowed to. Of course, the pirates and mercenaries were using charged weapons while the Council lackeys were powered individuals.

Everyone knew they would not replenish their internal power fast enough for that element to be a real threat in battle. Both sides would slowly use up their magic until they were down to their blades.

And then there would be no stopping the vislas.

Really, there wouldn't be anyway, most likely, even if the attackers were fully charged. The Maktan bloodline had a long history of possessing significant power, and Egrit was no slouch either. But they were being cocky. Underestimating the threat. And that left an opening Hozark and Demelza could exploit.

The assassin scanned the guards not engaged in the fighting, hoping to see Demelza's familiar shape. She would not have used too much magic in her disguise lest the feel of it put the vislas on guard. But a modest amount would allow her to assume the look of a Tslavar guard, permitting her to edge closer without being seen.

Of course, Samara would also notice any substantial disguise magic. She was a Ghalian, after all, and would be particularly sensitive to that sort of thing, even while engaged in heated combat.

Hozark watched her mowing down her attackers. It was a mixed feeling observing her fight. On the one hand, she was slaying his backup, pirates and mercenaries falling to her blade. On the other, a small feeling of pride welled up within him watching her move with such expert precision. She was good. Damn good.

More importantly, she was preoccupied. This was as good a chance as he would have to move against Visla Maktan. His guard was down against attacks from all directions but one, but there were too many people around him to cast a killing spell from any distance. Likewise, a thrown blade could too easily be intercepted by an unintentional target stepping in the way.

Hozark would have to do this up close and personal.

A bit of commotion caught Samara's attention, and thus Hozark's as well. It seemed a violet-haired dervish had entered the fray and was eagerly stabbing anything in her path. Hozark was pleased to note Bud close at her side, powered up with both konus and blades.

The two were working in tandem, laying waste to those in their path. And Henni seemed to be defending herself with some pretty decently cast spells as well. Apparently, Jinnik's lessons had made a difference. One that she and Bud could now enjoy the fruits of.

Across the way, just outside the door, a familiar fighting style caught Hozark's eye. Sword and dagger used in tandem, not fighting the opponent, but rather the opponent's blades. Demelza had made it to within striking distance of the visla as well, but had become embroiled in the fight with Samara's men. And by the look of it, her hands were quite full.

It seemed that the task of finishing Maktan rested entirely on Hozark's shoulders. And he was ready.

Hozark watched as another wave of guards rushed out from behind Maktan and Egrit's shield spells and into the fray. Their entrance into the battle, combined with the Council casters already engaged, brought the balance of power on the field squarely in the defenders' favor.

But pirates were not ones to quit, and the mercenary forces had not only been well paid, but they had also been offered a hefty share of whatever pillage might remain should they be victorious. It was quite an incentive, and they fought with the strength of several times their number for it.

Hozark joined the line of guards edging toward the shield perimeter, slowly marching forward to do battle. It was a fairly sound tactic, feeding them out from within the estate's walls in a stream with protection rather than multiple unguarded exit points. It allowed them to avoid the enemy's longer distance spells and also quickly rush them once clear of their protections, moving in too close for magic to be used.

Hozark drew closer to the visla, and as he did, he felt a tickle brush against his disguise magic. Nothing major, but it was there. Quickly, he released most of his disguise spell, letting it dissipate smoothly to avoid further detection. In the rush toward the fight, he just hoped those all around him wouldn't notice the man beside them slowly shifting into a pale-skinned assassin.

He realized that with the proximity of the two vislas, it would be near impossible to strike Maktan down and avoid the wrath of Egrit. But his order had been attacked by Maktan, his people tortured and experimented on. This contract had to be completed, and if he fell in the process, so be it.

But an inspiration hit him as he drew his non-magical dagger from its sheath. Perhaps there was a way to survive. Or, at least, he hoped so. It was risky as hell, and he would likely be gravely injured in the process, but he might just survive.

He was about to pass the visla, not quite within striking distance, but so very close. It was now or never.

Hozark let his fangs slide into place. If he could drain even a portion of the visla's magic, he would be able to heal the injuries he was about to receive. If not, his internal store of magic could rapidly be drained to empty.

"Another ship is descending!" he shouted, pointing to the sky.

All eyes shifted upward, even those of the vislas, as all scanned for the new threat. Hozark had but a fraction of a second to act, and he did.

With two powerful strides, he doubled back and dove at Maktan, casting a disabling spell as he did. The visla sensed the magical attack and extended his defensive magic accordingly. Hozark's spell shattered at once, leaving the visla safe from the pathetic attempt.

But what he hadn't noticed was the utterly unmagical blade

driving toward him. A moment later he did, though. When it plunged into his chest.

"Assassin!" someone shouted, dozens of hands pulling at Hozark, keeping his fangs from finding the dying visla's neck.

Visla Egrit turned, and for just an instant, caught sight of the fanged killer so close by. Then he realized what had happened as Visla Maktan fell to his knees, clutching his chest. He blanched at the sight. It was so unlikely, so utterly impossible that any could lay hands on either of them. Not like this. But it was clear the pale man had done just that.

Hozark's blade had struck true, piercing the man's heart, and no healing spell would be able to fix *that* hurt. His deadly efficiency also meant that with the people striking him, pulling him back, Hozark would not be able to reach the visla's neck to take his power before the man's life was fully extinguished.

So, rather than fight futilely against the pull in a hopeless attempt at power that would be gone by the time he got there, Hozark instead pushed off and back into the crowd, surprising the troops and knocking many over in the process.

He quickly slapped on the most basic of camouflage spells, darkening his skin so as to not stand out quite so much. Even a second of confusion could give him the time he needed to escape. Egrit would detect him soon enough, but if there were enough of his own men around him, there was the possibility he would not cast and kill them all along with the assassin.

It was a risky move, but it was all Hozark had.

Demelza saw what had happened and immediately dropped her disguise, casting a killing spell directly at Visla Egrit. The unexpectedly deadly spell shattering on the visla's defenses had precisely the distracting effect she had hoped for.

"Ghalian!" the visla exclaimed. "*Two* Ghalian assassins!"

Apparently, Egrit was not nearly so confident as he'd seemed when working with another more powerful visla. Now that Maktan had actually been slain, he realized that he was very much in jeopardy. They always worked alone, everyone knew that, but he felt his adrenaline surge. His eyes flitted about, worried there could be more Ghalian at any turn.

Egrit scanned the battle and saw another pale shape, swinging a glowing blue blade, no less. A vespus blade. A weapon of the Ghalian. That meant there were *three* of them here. A decision was quickly made, and it was for self-preservation. Egrit immediately wrapped a protective bubble around himself and retreated into the building.

"Bring the body!" he shouted to his men.

Those nearest Maktan's corpse tried to grab the deceased visla, but they were stymied by a barrage of magic. The few who remained unscathed hurried after their master. Visla Egrit had seen it. They *all* had. Visla Maktan killed by a Ghalian. It would set the Council on the highest of alerts.

While those of Egrit's forces close to the visla began to retreat, Maktan's troops seemed to be enraged, fighting even harder after what had just happened. And the remains of Egrit's joined the surge.

The fighting grew more intense, and bodies from all sides began to pile up. Hozark felt the injuries adding up, but he was still able to mend most of them, though at the cost of his internal power. How much longer he could keep it up, however, was anyone's guess.

CHAPTER SIXTY

Demelza, her disguise shed, found her hands full, fighting attackers from both of the vislas' forces as well as Samara's. But this was what she had trained so diligently for. To mete out death.

She moved through her opponents in a blur, a dervish of gleaming metal, her blades ringing out as they clashed with the swarming attackers.

Bud and Henni were also powering through the foot soldiers, but having a bit more trouble with the sheer numbers of them, despite the help from their pirate comrades. It was the Council power users creating problems. They were holding back a bit at a distance, providing cover for their forces while picking off those who happened to be in the clear of their own people.

Maktan was dead, and Visla Egrit was already in retreat. But fleeing to regroup was not an option. Samara's forces were in the thick of the fighting, and none could avoid their attacks. It seemed that the insignia-lacking attackers confused the Council guards, even more so when they engaged them as well as the pirates and mercenaries.

The fighting grew in intensity, and Hozark was beating back

wave after wave of attackers, his own internal magic nearly spent. He hadn't been able to drink from Visla Maktan, and that power was gone forever. But the Council casters who remained behind would do quite nicely, if he could just get to them. And it was looking like that would be very, very difficult.

Hozark felt the tiny vial tucked away in its protected pocket. Given his injuries, it was looking like the weapon of last resort might just have to be used after all, he mused as he watched the slender woman with her own vespus blade approach.

Samara slashed her way over to her former lover, leaving a trail of the dead or dying in her wake, her glowing blue blade dripping with the blood of her enemies. She paused, the two of them enjoying a brief lull in the fighting immediately around them.

"Hozark."

"Samara."

Niceties completed, the two assassins launched into combat, their swords clashing in sparks of bright magic as the two killers put on a display of magnificent swordsmanship.

Hozark was slowed a bit by his injuries, but the adrenaline surge of facing Samara more than made up for it. For the time being at least. But he knew his strength would only hold out for so long.

Bud and Henni both stole glances at the pair. Watching Hozark move with the speed and grace they'd rarely seen him unleash was awe-inspiring. But against a fellow Ghalian with no holds barred, he had let it all out. But so had Samara.

Round and round the two went, slashing and slicing, dropping any who happened to get too close as they battled to the death. It should have been an epic duel, but the grim reality of fighting on a crowded battlefield put the kibosh on their combat, just as Hozark felt his strength begin to flag.

Respite came in the form of a wave of fighting, a surging mass of men and women from all of the varied factions, a chaotic mix that washed right into them, separating the two Ghalian, forcing them to fight not each other, but the dozens of others who now wanted a piece of them.

Hozark and Samara shared a glance. A look of almost amusement that their final battle had been interrupted in this way. No matter how hard they tried to kill one another, history was thicker than blood, and that was something they had a lot of.

"Hozark! Over there!" Bud called out, gesturing to a pair of Visla Egrit's casters who had been separated from the other magic users in their group. They were holding their own quite well, but without the support of the others, they were just what Hozark needed. Namely, fresh magical blood to replenish his internal power and heal his injuries.

Hozark shifted his attentions, pushing through the sea of fighters toward the two casters. They didn't see him coming, or, they didn't realize he was a direct threat as they were busy stopping all comers foolish enough to attack them head-on.

Samara saw what he was doing but knew she couldn't reach him in time. And if he topped off on power, it would be she at the disadvantage when their blades next clashed.

Bud and Henni watched Lalaynia and her pirates adjust their ranks, communicating with Andorus and his mercenary troops so as to rearrange their forces in a more effective manner.

"Look out!" Bud shouted, throwing his dagger over Henni's head.

The Council goon dropped in a gurgling heap at the young woman's feet. She nodded her thanks, but her gaze suddenly shifted, her face one of surprise. Bud turned to see what had caught her eye.

Laskar was there, walking through the battlefield right toward them. How he had managed to land the ship with all the fighting going on was anyone's guess. Bud sincerely hoped his copilot hadn't crashed the damn thing.

"Laskar! What the hell are you doing here?" Bud called out, but it seemed his friend couldn't hear him over the din of fighting. That, and he seemed focused on something else.

Bud shifted his gaze to follow Laskar's. It seemed Hozark had closed the gap on the two Council casters and was only steps away from taking them down. Bud felt a tiny wave of relief at the realization. Hozark at full power would be a very good thing for their side.

Hozark cast a pair of rapid stun spells, using the final dregs of his power and draining his konuses as well. It was his all-or-nothing last-chance attempt, and his magic flew true.

The two casters stumbled as those around them fell to the ground. He would cross the gap in mere moments and drink deep. His power would be restored. *Then* the fight would get interesting.

"*Azkokta*!" Laskar barked, sending his spell barreling across the battlefield.

The two casters crumpled in a heap, quite dead.

Hozark felt the raw power of the spell and turned to see where this new threat came from. Bud stared, wide-eyed, at what he'd just seen. Laskar? Casting a killing spell? It made no sense.

"Laskar, what the hell? How did you do that?" Bud asked.

His copilot ignored him and kept walking, the combatants on the field all giving this new, and clearly *very* powerful, man a wide berth. Samara alone stood in his path.

"*You* are Laskar?" she asked. "Uzabud's copilot? The one who has flown all this time with Hozark?"

The man smiled. It was not in any way a warm expression.

"Step aside, Samara."

She hesitated a moment, a sad look in her eye as she glanced at Hozark, realizing just how badly he and his friends had been played. Then she did as she was told, falling in beside the surprising new player to enter the deadly game.

"What's going on?" Bud demanded, the fighting only now beginning to slightly ramp back up, although well clear of the man and his Wampeh companion.

Laskar turned and uttered a spell, blasting a wave of stun magic at his captain. Bud drained his konus to its capacity defending himself, but without Henni's assistance, he'd have fallen. The spell dissipated, though, and he still stood.

"What the hell, Laskar?"

His copilot laughed. "Oh, you can stop calling me that now. The name isn't actually Laskar." He turned toward Hozark, wanting to see the look on the man's face. "My name is Tozorro. Tozorro *Maktan*, but you may call me *visla*."

It was impossible, but Bud realized it had to be true. There had always been a little something off about his copilot, but he could never quite put his finger on it. Now it all made sense. The man he had known as Laskar had been playing the long con.

"Curse your sudden but inevitable betrayal!" Bud growled.

"Oh, really, Bud. Don't blame yourself. I've worked long and hard to make my plan come to fruition. And now it finally has."

"I don't get it."

Hozark did. It was abundantly clear. "Familial ascendancy," he informed his friend. "This has all been no more than a Council power grab."

Tozorro Maktan laughed brightly. "Well, you certainly catch on fast, although a bit late."

Hozark felt a rage rising within him, but without power to latch on to, he was horribly outclassed. There was simply nothing he could do to the man he'd known as Laskar. Not now that he could sense his long-hidden power. And not with Samara at his side.

"He needed his father slain by someone else," Hozark explained. "Seen by all so he would be free of suspicion."

"Precisely. And now I can take my father's seat on the

Council with none the wiser. And with that power in my hands, I will show them what a true Maktan can do."

"But they heard you admit it," Bud said triumphantly.

"Afraid not," Maktan said, gesturing around them. "Muting spell. One of your friend here's favorite tricks, in fact. This has been just between us old friends."

"Why couldn't I sense him?" Henni asked, still stunned.

"Oh, sweet, ignorant child. Because I knew of your talent and blocked it every damn moment we were together, which is quite annoying, I'll have you know. But since you all saw fit to deliver those Ootaki to Visla Sunar when you believed you were rescuing me, I'll let it slide."

Bud's face grew red. "You weren't a captive at all, were you?"

"Nope. The visla is a good friend of mine. And, in fact, Sunar was acquiring Ootaki for *me*. Quite the irony, wouldn't you agree? My plan was sheer elegance in its simplicity."

All around them the fighting had begun raging once more, and was spilling into the little bubble of calm that Maktan's show of force had provided. It finally burst through around Bud and Henni first, forcing them to shift their attention back to the *other* dangers on the battlefield.

Maktan took the opportunity to cast a little stun spell. Nothing huge, just enough to cause Bud to falter. It was all it took. Blades found their way home, several piercing his body as he struggled against the magic.

"No!" Henni shrieked, her magic sparking and flaring around her. She was exhausted, but that didn't stop her from casting as best she knew how, trying to control her power to slay those around her as she dove at them with her blades.

Many fell to her hands as she defended Bud's prone body, but soon she too succumbed to the sheer number of blows her weakened body received, falling to the ground on top of Bud, her blood mingling with his as it slowly trickled from their bodies onto the soil.

Samara watched with conflict in her eyes as the events all unfolded, digesting the realization of just how badly she, too, had been used.

Demelza saw what was unfolding but was too far away to have stopped the attacks, but nevertheless she slashed her way through the combatants, leaving a trail of carnage as she raced to her friends. Hozark began running toward them as well, hoping he could at least save his friends if not himself.

Laskar, the *new* Visla Maktan, let him. There was no escape, and seeing his friends fade before his eyes would make Hozark's defeat that much more painful. Precisely what he wanted.

Hozark slid to his knees beside the bleeding pair, digging inside of his tunic with great urgency. Visla Tozorro Maktan just watched with amusement at Hozark's futile efforts.

"Well, I suppose that's enough of that," he said. "It's been fun, but the fun's over."

He began to cast a killing spell at Hozark when a cold prick on his neck startled him. But his strength was massive, and he could withstand the initial attack. Laskar violently flung away the Wampeh who had dared bite him.

Samara flashed her bloody fangs at him, but she had only taken a tiny portion of his power. He looked at her as one would an ill-behaved pet, then shifted his gaze back to Hozark. The Wampeh was barely paying attention to him, all of his focus on his dying friends.

"Goodbye, Hozark," he said, then cast his killing spell.

The magic flew true. Hozark, powerless as he was, was as good as dead. But as the last syllable of the spell left his lips, Samara lunged in front of him, blocking the spell with her body. Maktan's magic struck her, fighting his own stolen power now flowing within Samara, then tossing her aside.

She hit the ground in a limp pile.

"Samara!" Hozark bellowed, the grief in his voice plain to hear.

Maktan grinned. He was enjoying this more than he expected, even if it did mean the loss of one of his favorite servants. But then his smile faltered.

Uzabud, his clothing still soaked in blood, slowly rose to his feet, not only unharmed, but positively buzzing with energy. But that wasn't what alarmed him. It was the *other* one.

Henni *floated* up into the air, her eyes ablaze with power, her magic crackling all around her in a focused rage. This was very much *not* the uncontrolled young woman he knew and ridiculed. And for a moment, he actually felt scared.

Sensing a shift in the tide of battle, others turned their attention to the lone visla on the battlefield. Maktan might have been able to take them all, but with Henni's newfound power, he knew he was at far too great a disadvantage to risk all he'd just achieved.

So he ran.

Henni raced after him, actually floating over the ground. She had no idea how she was doing it; her instincts had simply taken over. Maktan threw powerful spell after spell behind him, slowing her as best he could as he raced to the parked mothership. He began casting the jump spell the moment he was inside its doors, risking an in-atmosphere jump despite all of the reasons you never did so.

For one, jumps from atmosphere were hardly accurate. You could jump into a sun if you weren't careful. For another, debris oftentimes got carried along, damaging the craft catastrophically upon exiting its jump. But the former copilot didn't care, trusting both his piloting skills and his power to see him through the day.

Henni felt his power surge, and her own flared to match it. She jumped, flashing out of existence and reappearing where the mothership had just been seconds earlier.

She had missed him. Laskar, aka Visla Tozorro Maktan, had escaped.

CHAPTER SIXTY-ONE

Henni was no longer flying when she made her way back to the battlefield. It seemed that her display of truly frightening magic had sent everyone scattering. The Council forces had fled, once they realized their support was gone and one of their vislas was dead. There was simply no reason to keep fighting, so they retreated with great haste and abandoned the Council estate.

The pirates and their mercenary compatriots let out a huge victory cry, then set about pillaging the grounds of anything of value. The Council would be back to retake the property in a show of force, and they had no intention of being anywhere near when they did.

Bud, Demelza, and Henni looked across the field of carnage at their friend but did not approach. It didn't require magical skills to know he needed space.

Hozark sat quietly on the bloody soil, cradling the broken shape of his former lover in his arms. The power she had taken from Maktan had lessened the killing spell, but her breaths were ragged and labored, and it was clear she had but moments left.

Despite the many times they had tried to kill one another, Hozark felt his heart shattering into a million pieces as he felt her weaken, sliding closer to oblivion. Samara surprised him one last time, though, her eyes unexpectedly flickering open with a surprising clarity.

She focused on his face and smiled. Then a look of urgency flashed in her eyes. She tried to speak, but her voice was but a whisper. Hozark leaned in close, feeling her last breath warm on his ear as she spoke her final words.

Hozark's body went rigid, then heaved but once. To any watching it might have been nothing more than a muscle tic or a stifled sneeze. But his friends knew better.

He slowly rose to his feet with Samara's body in his arms, her vespus blade tucked under her hands like a fallen warrior queen. Weak, injured, and exhausted as he was, he carried her to his shimmer ship, his face a block of stone. The others didn't say a word as he passed.

He would be gone for a while. There was no telling how long it would take. But he was Hozark. Eventually, he would show up at Corann's to debrief. He may have been hurting, but he was a Wampeh Ghalian through and through.

"Uh, Demelza? What exactly just happened?" Bud asked, his fingers examining the myriad bloody holes in his clothing, as well as the mended flesh within.

She pointed to an empty vial lying on the ground, a single drop of water clinging to its lip.

"Master Hozark has given you a priceless gift," she replied, eyeing the water warily.

Henni crouched down and dipped her finger on the lone droplet. Her magic flared brightly, and her eyes began to glow even brighter than before.

"Whoa! What the hell is that stuff?"

"That was a vial of the Balamar Waters," Demelza replied.

Bud paled at her words, knowing full well what that meant. "The vial he took when he killed Emmik Rostall?"

"The same."

Bud was silent a long while, his emotions churning within.

"What's that all about? And who was Emmik Rostall?" Henni asked.

Demelza stepped in for the shocked pilot. "Rostall was the man who killed Hozark's pupil. Reduced him to ash with his vial of Balamar waters, the very one you now hold."

Henni looked confused. "But they just healed me. Healed Bud. And they made my magic so much stronger."

"Yes, they have that effect on nearly every species in the galaxy. Applied topically, even a drop can cure a great many ailments. In quantity, they can heal even severe wounds, such as you both received."

Bud's eyes glistened.

Henni looked at him. "I don't get it. What's wrong with you? You're being all emotional. Quit it, it's weird."

Bud wiped his eyes and turned to his violet-haired companion. For once, there was no snark in his tone.

"He risked his life for us, Henni."

"Well, yeah. We were all fighting for our--"

"No," Bud interrupted. "You don't understand. He used the Balamar waters on us. And if just a single drop had gotten on him in the process, he'd have died in burning agony."

The implication struck the young woman.

"He kept the vial, that I knew," Bud continued. "It was supposed to be locked safely in the Ghalian vault after Enok was killed."

"But it wasn't?" Henni asked.

"No, it wasn't," Bud said.

Demelza sighed. "It is true. Master Hozark kept it with him in case he could not defeat Samara. As his fail-safe weapon."

Henni seemed confused. "But if he splashed her, it would almost certainly have gotten on him too."

"Indeed," Demelza replied.

"But..." she trailed off as the implication set in. "But he

risked his life to save us, and before Samara had even been hurt."

"And poured out a fortune doing so," Bud added.

"What do you mean?"

"A few drops of that stuff is priceless. And that whole vial? You could buy a small city. Or a moon, even," he replied. "But now it's in us. And I suspect we're going to have some lasting effects from it, if I'm not mistaken. Right, Demelza?"

"It is true, you shall both be more or less impervious to injury for a short while. How long is unclear. But in the long term, you will undoubtedly see a great extension of your lives, as well as some other more *unusual* side effects in Henni's case."

"Does that mean my magic will *stay* this strong?"

"There is simply no way of knowing," Demelza replied. "You are unique, Henni. And if your magic is truly akin to that of the Old Ones, then it is quite possible this change may be permanent. Or at least very long lasting."

Henni was floored by the implications. She might have power. *Real* power. But if she did, it would require some serious training to learn to control it. But with Visla Palmarian at her side, the idea was suddenly far less daunting than she expected.

"So, Demelza. Uh, I need to check in with Lalaynia, but after that, could you give us a ride back to Corann's? It seems my treacherous *former* copilot has stolen my ship."

Demelza allowed herself the tiniest hint of a smile. "Of course, Uzabud. It would be my pleasure."

Henni hesitated. "But what about Hozark? Will he be okay?"

Demelza knew he would be, in time. But what he had just endured was enough to challenge even the most resolute of Ghalian.

"He is Hozark," she finally said. "Of course he will."

Outside the compound grounds, Hozark walked silently into his shimmer ship's small cargo bay. In it, he removed a long cloak he had worn for many years. It had been a gift from someone very dear to him a long time ago. And now he wrapped her body in it, returning it to its giver all these years later.

He gently secured her, then stepped into his command center, setting a course for an uninhabited system he had not visited in a very long time. He lifted his ship up into the air and made his way to the vacuum of space. Then he jumped.

The planets of the system were nothing spectacular. Just a few small, uninhabitable worlds and a handful of utterly average moons. But the sun itself was something altogether different.

The black sun radiated its invisible spectrum of light and power with a steady thrum. Even through the hull of his shielded ship, Hozark could feel the healing power of the dark star. It was an uncharted system that he and Samara had discovered together not long before her supposed death a decade earlier.

They had stumbled upon it quite by accident, a slight mishap with their Drookonus having put them a bit off course. But it had been something of a happy accident, and the pair wound up spending a few days orbiting that sun, enjoying its rays as well as each other.

The memory cut deep as Hozark gazed upon the lifeless form of his childhood pal. His lifelong friend. His lover. Quietly, he cast a protective spell around himself and opened the cargo door. The rays of the sun were even stronger now, and he could feel his minor injuries itching as they began the long process of mending.

Hozark gently pushed Samara's weightless body out into the void, set adrift toward the dark blaze of the sun she would become a part of. Maybe, he thought, one day he would come back to visit her. One day.

He closed the cargo door and repressurized the

compartment. Then he slid to the deck and cried. Cried for the first time in over a decade. Since the last time Samara had died. But this time it was for real. Final. And just as before, he would mourn her in private.

Hozark spent several days silently orbiting that sun as Samara drifted closer and closer to the system's center. Then, finally, he cleaned himself, put on fresh clothing, and settled into his pilot's seat.

He had things to do. Important things. For Samara's final words had driven into his heart as surely as the point of any blade ever could.

CHAPTER SIXTY-TWO

Several months had passed since Visla Zinna Maktan had fallen at the hands of a Wampeh Ghalian. Many had seen it, including Visla Egrit, and the entire Council had gone on a defensive footing ever since. To have two of their vislas slain in short succession meant great additional precautions for the remaining members.

Of course, there was the matter of filling the two vacant Council seats. While Visla Ravik's brother was weak by comparison and thus challenged for his position, Visla Maktan's son, Tozorro, was as strong, if not stronger than his father. And while he had steered clear of the Council for his entire life, he seemed ready to take up his father's mantle and represent the Maktan line when the situation was brought to his attention.

It was touching. The man had seemed quite distraught at the news of his father's demise at the hands of an assassin, but he soon pulled himself together, vowing to make his father proud and help lead the Council to new glory.

After that, it was just a matter of time before he began slowly swaying other Council members over to his side. Being the neophyte, always glad to ask questions and learn from his elders, it was easy to get them to commit to supporting him, each hoping to hold sway over the powerful newcomer. In but a few short weeks he had already formed alliances with several of the most powerful men and women on the Council.

Of course, the manipulation was entirely on his part, and when the time came to truly seize power, he would eliminate the weaker ones while drawing the others closer to him. The destruction of his weapons cache and smelting operation had been something of a setback to those ends, though. But he would rebuild, and this time aboveboard and with Council funds instead of his own.

Tozorro Maktan moved to one of his father's estates on a quaint little world. It was scenic and lush, though the landscape needed quite a bit of work. Fortunately, he acquired a groundskeeper who, despite his rather reclusive personality, had somehow acquired a lovely young new wife, also one of his servants. She was an Alatsav, with their kind's fair green skin and almond eyes.

"Hertzall," he said to his new servant.

"Yes, Visla?"

"I wish you to plant a grove of fruit trees over there," he said, gesturing across his overgrown lands.

"Of course, Visla."

"And a flower garden there. And then clear the brush on the far end of the grounds for animal pens. My son is eager to have some new playthings."

"Immediately, Visla," Hertzall replied.

He was a hard worker, and Maktan was confident the man would have the grounds in top shape in no time. And all for the best. He had been away for ages. His wife and teenage son had been without the man of the house for far too long. He just hoped the offering of exotic beasts would appease his boy.

The grounds themselves had been extensively reinforced the moment he had decided to reside there. The far wall was rebuilt, and the powerful wards on it were increased even more than their original, and rather impressive, levels. The entire perimeter was one giant tripwire, waiting for the slightest tickle to spring its traps on any would-be intruders.

Now that he was no longer hiding his power, Visla Maktan let it surge from him in waves. He began every day by casting his detection spells as a matter of habit, and had personally vetted all of his staff from day one.

Nevertheless, he was a cautious man. Cautious, yet cocky at the same time. He had bested the Ghalian, and he had assumed a great deal of power in the process. And now, knowing the order intimately, as he had spent so much time embedded with them, he felt confident in his safeguards for himself and his family.

A month after he had given Hertzall his orders, the grounds were finished. The man was a miracle worker when it came to vegetation, eager to beautify the property as much for his wife's pleasure as the visla's.

It was just a lucky fluke that she had been bought from a recent shipment of slaves. How she and so unlikely a mate had connected was anyone's guess, but their love seemed as strong as any, and if it kept them happy to work, he didn't mind his slaves bonding. Besides, it gave him one more bit of control should one get out of line.

Maktan toured the grounds with an appreciative eye. Hertzall had done excellent work. But the visla smelled something in the air. Was it magic? He heightened his awareness, probing for any magic in his vicinity. Something tickled his senses in the small grove of trees. He cast a powerful spell, shattering one of the trees into thousands of tiny pieces.

No one moved. No one flinched. There were no shimmer-cloaked assassins in hiding after all. No magically camouflaged killers lurking in the thicket.

Detecting magical disguises and shimmer cloaks was one of

the skills he had honed after witnessing how effective the Ghalian were with them. He also had double the guard the Council had provided with additional men of his own. Better safe than sorry, he reasoned.

Maktan looked at the ruins of the tree and chuckled. It was no worry. Hertzall would have it cleaned up and replaced by morning.

The visla walked into his estate and crossed to the small patio outside his offices. It was his favorite place to sit and think, a tiny patch of vines and shrubbery nestled against the warmth of the building's stone. He did all of his best thinking there. As well as his plotting.

Magda, the youngest daughter of the serving matron, timidly knocked on his door. "Visla?"

"Come," he called out through the room.

The round-faced girl quietly crossed through and out to the patch of sun where he was sitting. "Your lunch, Visla."

"Good girl. Leave it there," he said, gesturing to the small table.

She did as directed, then gave a small bow and left.

Maktan rose and stepped over to the plate of delicacies. So many delightful things to choose from, he marveled. It was good being the head of the household. It was even better being on the Council of Twenty. Everything was coming together as planned. The pieces were lining up for his ultimate power grab, and once he positioned himself just right to seize control--

The blade that pierced his body was so fine he almost didn't feel it enter from behind. It slid in so effortlessly, yet he could tell at once it was not enchanted. Merely honed to a razor's edge.

But it had not been plunged in with reckless abandon. The tip had stopped mere millimeters from his heart. He knew then it could only be one person.

"But I didn't sense you," Maktan said, strangely resigned to his fate. "I was prepared. I cast every detection spell imaginable.

Not even the Quommus could have shielded you from my power."

Behind him Hozark smiled a cold grin, his teeth showing white while the rest of him was a patchwork of green leaves and brown branches. A man-shaped dent was visible in the climbing vines on the wall where he had been standing. Judging by the slight discoloration of the plants, he must have been in position for days before making his move.

Of course he had.

"You may have observed our ways," he said quietly, "but you failed to learn the lessons behind them."

"I learned them well. Deceive the eye and walk right up to your target. I've seen you do it."

Hozark chuckled. "And now you prove my point. The lesson was not the deception. It was the *distraction*. Here you are, so busy protecting yourself from any magically camouflaged attackers that you failed to notice the man simply standing mere feet from you."

"Of course. The Quommus."

"No. It is far too large and unwieldy for one to carry."

"But it was made out to be the ultimate magical protection."

"And it is. For a building, perhaps. One day the order will find a use for it."

"So, no magic?"

"Not a drop."

Visla Tozorro Maktan couldn't help but chuckle, even knowing he was about to die. "Well done, Hozark. You know, I––"

Hozark shifted the blade into his heart, ending him on the spot, denying him the satisfaction of a dying speech. He did not even drink from him, instead letting all of that power drain out onto the stone floor.

This was not a matter of Ghalian business. This was personal.

Hozark heard a voice in the next room coming from its open window. A young boy, no older than perhaps sixteen or so. Maktan's son. The assassin froze in place, utterly silent until the voice faded.

Yes, he could end the Maktan line here if he so chose, but the boy was but a mere teenager, not yet a man. There would be no honor in killing him, no matter what power he might contain. And who knew? Perhaps the boy would not follow in his father's footsteps. Perhaps young Yoral Maktan would grow to be a good man.

Silently, Hozark slipped out of the grounds to his waiting shimmer ship. He flew it over the visla's collection of fancy vessels, then carefully docked it atop the dusty, unused craft that had been abandoned at the far end of the landing area. He descended into his friend's mothership with a sense of homecoming. Bud would be glad to have it back, though it had taken a bit longer than expected.

Hozark then fired up the Drookonus and lifted off, leaving the Maktan estate, never to return.

CHAPTER SIXTY-THREE

Uzabud and Henni had taken up residence with Corann for a while after the final battle with their traitorous crewmate. Days, or even weeks, were normally allowed, but, a stay of this length by a non-Ghalian would have normally been unheard of.

However, as Demelza was with them, and given the remarkable powers Henni was manifesting, allowances were made. This pair had more than earned the trust of the Ghalian.

Master Prombatz and Aargun had been regular visitors, coming to Corann's home every few weeks. Normally it would not have been thought of, having two of the Five in the same place with any regularity. But as Bud was in a bit of a funk at the loss of his mothership, borrowing Corann's little craft just didn't feel the same.

Lalaynia even offered him his old spot on her crew again, which he politely turned down. "I'm just gonna sit and *be* for a minute," he told her.

"You sure you're gonna be okay, Bud?"

"Yeah. I'm fine. Don't worry about me," he'd replied.

But Lalaynia was worried about him. Bud had been moments from death, and that sort of thing can change a man.

Shift his priorities. It was only natural he would need some time for introspection.

"You keep an eye on him," she said to Henni as she prepared to head back up to her ship. "His head's not on quite right."

"Is it ever?" Henni replied.

Lalaynia wrapped the girl in a fierce hug. "Be good, kiddo."

"Never," she replied.

Lalaynia departed, knowing that Henni, for all of her sass and spunk, would not let any harm fall upon her friend's head.

As for Henni, Corann had been fascinated by her new powers and was doing all she could to help guide her in their use. Visla Palmarian even came for a visit, along with an almost unrecognizable Happizano. Cleaned up and in his finery, he looked every bit a visla's son.

Then he opened his mouth, streaming out an excited update on all the things he'd learned since he had gone home. Same old Hap, they were all glad to see. Visla Palmarian spent a few days helping Henni focus her power while the Ghalian trained his son in the finer aspects of knife work and martial skills. When they finally departed, it was only after extracting the promise that Henni would come visit them on Slafara.

"Soon," she said, nodding toward Bud.

Visla Palmarian got the hint.

It was unknown when the former pirate would feel up to venturing out, but when that day came, they would take the visla up on his offer. For now, however, they were content to enjoy the warmth of Corann's hospitality.

Bud was lounging on a reclining seat while Henni practiced launching spells and knives at a target in Corann's training room when he suddenly leapt to his feet.

"What's up?" Henni called after him as he ran from the room. She scooped up her knives and followed in a hurry.

Bud raced the short distance to the landing field nearby, tears welling up in his eyes. There she was. His ship, settling down gently, looking a bit dirty from neglect, but still beautiful to his eyes.

Hozark strode from the ship, tall and at ease, a great weight clearly lifted from his shoulders.

"Hozark, you should have told me. I would have helped!"

The Ghalian smiled. "I like surprise endings, Bud."

"Of course you do. You're an assassin. Your entire life is pretty much the epitome of a surprise ending."

The two laughed, Hozark's relaxed goodwill spreading to his friend. Bud had his ship back. At long last, all was right in the world. Henni arrived a moment later, leaping up onto Hozark with a giant hug.

"You're okay!"

"Yes, Henni, I am okay."

She stared at him, her eyes sparkling. "No, I mean it," she said, looking not at him, but into him. "You're *okay*."

He grinned at the violet-haired imp. "Yes, Henni, I truly am."

"Sweet! Come on, then, the others will be glad you're back."

Hozark nodded and began the short walk to Corann's. Bud, however, hung back.

"What's on your mind, Bud?" Henni asked as he stood silently staring at his ship.

"I was just thinking," he said, turning to her with a gleam in his eye. "I kinda lost my last navigator."

"Yeah, but he was an asshole anyway."

"True that," he replied, hesitating a moment. "But I was thinking, you're actually pretty good with those charts."

"He finally admits."

"Yeah, well, you've been a good impromptu navigator in the past. So, I was just thinking. I mean, if you'd consider it..."

Henni took a half step back, looking at him with shocked

eyes. "Are you asking?" she asked, her breath catching in her throat.

Bud's cheeks flushed slightly. "I am."

The smile on her face spread from ear to ear as Henni jumped on him, squeezing tight. "I accept!" she said, her eyes welling up with tears of joy, along with happy sparkles of power. The day had taken a most unexpected turn, and for the better.

As the two walked back to join the others, their fingers touched, and soon slid together, as naturally as breathing. Walking hand in hand, the locals they had come to know so well nodded greetings to them with satisfied smiles. They had long wondered when the two would finally admit it and get on with it. It had been obvious to everyone else, after all.

Hozark found Demelza training with Corann in the home's underground sparring room. It was subterranean to provide additional shielding from not only the magic occasionally used, but also the noises of combat. Why expend magic on muting spells when you could just dig a deep hole, after all?

"Master Hozark," Demelza said, greeting her friend with a slight bow.

"Good to see you back in good health," Corann noted, putting her sword down.

Demelza also put her weapon back on the rack, wiping the sweat from her brow as she did. It had apparently been a rather intense training session, but then, Master Corann was not one to do things by half measures.

The two masters shared a glance. Corann nodded almost imperceptibly. The smile on Hozark's lips was the only outward sign anything had been communicated at all.

"I am confused," Demelza said. "Am I missing something?"

Hozark's smile spread. "Only on your belt, sister," he replied, holding out a carefully wrapped parcel to her.

It was long, and the bindings around it were not ordinary. This was Ghalian ceremonial ribbon. And not for a mere assassin; this bore the marking of a teacher of the order.

Demelza's eyes went wide. "But the Five have not gathered."

"They did not need to," Corann replied. "Hozark, Prombatz, and I have all spoken for your outstanding martial skills, your performance under the most difficult of situations, and most importantly, your knack for imparting knowledge to others."

"I-I do not know what to say," Demelza replied.

"Then say nothing and open your gift," Hozark replied. "And congratulations, *Teacher* Demelza."

It was unheard of, being promoted the way she had been. Despite her training, Demelza felt almost overcome by emotions. Even more so when she unwrapped the parcel.

Within it was a scabbard, well-worn and in no way decorative. A functional blade, not a ceremonial one, then. She nodded, appreciating the utility of the item. Hozark and Corann looked at one another as Demelza put her hand on the grip, knowing what would come next.

"No! It can't be!" Demelza blurted as her skin made contact.

"It is," Hozark replied.

"But Master Orkut is dead," she said, pulling the glowing blue vespus blade from its sheath and admiring the powerful weapon.

"Yes, he is. But a great teacher, a great Ghalian, should have an equally impressive weapon," Hozark said.

It only took Demelza a moment before the familiar feel of the magical blade connected with her. She knew this power. Knew it quite well, in fact. This sword had very nearly taken her life on more than one occasion.

"Samara's vespus blade," she gasped.

"*Your* vespus blade," Hozark said. "She was quite impressed with you, you know. She told me as much. And I am sure it is you she would want to have it."

Demelza spun the sword, feeling the perfect balance of its metal as well as the magical power thrumming within it. With but a few moves, it already felt as if it had been made for her hand. A part of herself. A smile spread across her lips as she looked at her friend and brother with cheer in her eyes.

"Master Hozark, would you be up for a bit of practice?"

Hozark grinned and drew his own vespus with a flourish. "I thought you'd never ask."

EPILOGUE

Hozark had left explicit instructions when he had departed for whatever mysterious task he had in mind. And now that he had returned, the master Ghalian was glad to learn that his orders had been carried out as planned.

While he was away, a young boy had been brought to the training house. A potentially powerful new Ghalian recruit. He was just a boy, no more than ten years old. A mere child. But they all were when they first began the long journey to becoming a Ghalian.

Hozark walked to the utilitarian bunk where the boy had been told to sleep. He had been there for just a few days, but the initial stress was already beginning to show. The transition to life in the training house could be quite difficult at first. Hozark remembered his own arrival as a boy very vividly. It had been rough, to say the least.

He stared at the boy, assessing the new recruit. He was a thin one. Tall, but wiry. His leanness, however, did not seem to be from any mistreatment. He was just naturally slender. Genetics were funny like that.

The orphanage he had been taken from had fed him more

than adequately, and had educated him as well. It was a good life, for an orphan. Apparently, when the Wampeh had been brought there as but a newborn ten years prior, a healthy endowment had accompanied him for his ongoing support.

He was a Wampeh, yes. And he possessed the gift, no doubt. But there was something in his eyes. A flash of a churning tide. He was emotional. Perhaps *too* emotional for a Wampeh who was to be forged into a deadly assassin. But Hozark had been much the same at that age and had become one of the Five. Time would tell.

"Come with me, boy," Hozark said, then turned and walked.

The boy fell in behind him, following quietly.

Hozark took him to one of the smaller training chambers and instructed the boy to stand tall and still. He did as he was told, though his eyes showed great uncertainty.

"You shall be training with the others from now on, and it shall not be easy," Hozark said. "If you are to succeed in this endeavor, remember these words. Your mind is your greatest weapon. And it is yours alone to wield. Learn to control it, and you shall do well. Fail to do so and you will not survive." He paused, a slight hint of a smile tickling the corners of his mouth. "But between you and me, I think you have it in you. Do not prove me wrong."

The words were familiar to Hozark. They were the first, and only, words of kindness he had heard from Master Fahbahl when he had first arrived in a training house when he was a boy. And now he was repeating them to this newcomer. This soon-to-be aspirant Ghalian.

"I shall be here from time to time in this training house," he continued, "and I shall help you practice and grow, as best I can. Should you try your hardest, I am confident you can achieve great things."

"You really think I can make it?" the boy said, coming out of his shell ever so slightly.

"I am certain of it," Hozark replied. "Now, I believe you have a lesson to attend in the next training room. Run along, Bawb. Do not give up. Be strong, and I assure you, great adventures will await you."

The boy looked back once as he walked away and gave the Master Assassin a little smile, then hurried off to his lesson.

Hozark couldn't help but feel a twinge in his chest. But the pain he felt was not from any old injury. Not of the physical variety, at least.

He felt that way because he was flush with both sadness and pride.

Samara was gone, having done all she could to protect the boy, blackmailed into Maktan's service when his existence was discovered. She'd ultimately given up everything for him, and now she was gone. But in a way, she still lived on. For while young Bawb possessed the same temperament as his father at that age, as any who had known Hozark in his youth would attest, the boy also had his mother's eyes.

THANK YOU FOR READING

I sincerely hope you enjoyed reading this series as much as I enjoyed writing it. To help keep those fires of writerly creativity burning bright, if you could, please consider leave a rating/review on Amazon or Goodreads. Just a few moments of your time could really help this indie author.

Thanks for reading!

ALSO BY SCOTT BARON

Standalone Novels

Living the Good Death

The Clockwork Chimera Series

Daisy's Run

Pushing Daisy

Daisy's Gambit

Chasing Daisy

Daisy's War

The Dragon Mage Series

Bad Luck Charlie

Space Pirate Charlie

Dragon King Charlie

Magic Man Charlie

Star Fighter Charlie

Portal Thief Charlie

Rebel Mage Charlie

Warp Speed Charlie

Checkmate Charlie

The Space Assassins Series

The Interstellar Slayer

The Vespus Blade

The Ghalian Code

Death From the Shadows

Hozark's Revenge

The Warp Riders Series

Deep Space Boogie

Belly of the Beast

Odd and Unusual Short Stories:

The Best Laid Plans of Mice: An Anthology

Snow White's Walk of Shame

The Tin Foil Hat Club

Lawyers vs. Demons

The Queen of the Nutters

Lost & Found

ABOUT THE AUTHOR

A native Californian, Scott Baron was born in Hollywood, which he claims may be the reason for his rather off-kilter sense of humor.

Before taking up residence in Venice Beach, Scott first spent a few years abroad in Florence, Italy before returning home to Los Angeles and settling into the film and television industry, where he has worked as an on-set medic for many years.

Aside from mending boo-boos and owies, and penning books and screenplays, Scott is also involved in indie film and theater scene both in the U.S. and abroad.